"Every woman dreams of loving a man who would die for her."

She blinked, and the tears fell to her cheeks. "I'm very thankful to God that you're alive. There's no shame in this, for it is no imperfection. If anything, it only makes you more beautiful." She lowered her mouth to the purple streaks, kissing them gently, tears mingling there with her kisses.

Behringer grasped Rebecca's shoulders, pulling her close to him. "Where the hell are you from?"

"It doesn't matter!" Words of desperation.

"It matters," he said. "You're every fantasy I've ever had."

Behringer lowered his mouth to hers in a harsh tenderness. His hands cradled her face, his roughened fingertips cherishing her. She wasn't close enough to him, not nearly enough. His fingers slid into the shimmering thickness of her hair, pressing her even closer. He wanted to hold her so near to him that she became as much a part of him as her memory was.

He wanted everything that she was . . . .

Love's Timeless Hope

Anne Meredith

SMP

ST. MARTIN'S PAPERBACKS

LOVE'S TIMELESS HOPE

Copyright © 1994 by Bureeda A. Bruner.

ISBN: 0-312-95273-2

Printed in the United States of America

St. Martin's Paperbacks edition/August 1994

10 9 8 7 6 5 4 3 2 1

For Leigh Teel

For Pat Conroy—
in the immortal words
of Peter Pan,
"Thank you for believing."

For my mother
(look inside the cover, Mom)

and
as always . . .
with love . . .
for Joshua

❧ One ❧

"Passion."

Rebecca's voice caught on the word. The power of that single word slammed unexpectedly through her, leaving in its wake the memory of what passion had once meant to her. Her soul ached with it.

The grand ballroom in the Dallas Anatole had been darkened for this formal affair. Over a thousand writers stared expectantly at their keynote speaker. Hazel eyes, now softened to glistening amber, roved over the crowd. Small, white-knuckled fingers gripped the edge of the lectern, and her throat was tight. Only a few more words, she told herself.

"Passion," she repeated softly, forcing her fingers to uncurl. "That's why we're all here this week. Forget the sell-through, and forget the print runs. Remember this. Tomorrow morning when you sit down at your typewriter or your computer, remember one thing.

"Remember that first *I love you*. That charged glance across a crowded room. Remember the one thing in life that so consumed you that living and dying paled by comparison. Because that's what living and dying is all about."

Tears welled in Rebecca's eyes—my God, how long since she'd cried? How long since she'd even considered the true meaning of passion? How many women were out there, hanging on her every word? And believing her?

"You see, you and I aren't in the business of romance writing. What we do is provoke passion. We live in a world that dismisses it, in a time that's forgotten it. And if for one moment, you can help an overworked, disillusioned single mother remember that passion still lives within us all . . . if you can remind a tired housewife that passion needs only a gentle kindling to burst into a blaze once more, then no award your peers can bestow on you, no slot on the bestseller list, will surpass that rich satisfaction."

Thunderous applause met Rebecca as she finished speaking, and she stepped down from the dais. Claudia Zachary, president of American Romance Writers, shook Rebecca's hand vigorously, then took her place to open the Seventeenth Annual Romance Writers Conference.

Linda Matthews met Rebecca with a tissue as she slipped behind the curtains. "Obviously Janelle MacDonald speaking, and not Rebecca Reynolds."

Rebecca accepted the tissue from her best friend, dabbing at her smeared mascara. "I hate makeup," she groused.

"What happened to you out there?"

"I don't know," Rebecca said, pushing a strand of long, dark hair away from her face. "Too many sappy plot lines, I guess."

"Pull yourself together. An old friend of ours is here. Remember Katharine Blake?"

Rebecca rolled her eyes at the name. "Good Lord, I haven't seen Kathy since we were at UT."

"She's Dr. Katharine Blake now. She's lecturing at a symposium at SMU. And for God's sake, don't call her Kathy."

"Does she still talk with that fake Hepburn accent?"

"Shush," Linda whispered. "There she is. Don't let her get under your skin. You know she was always jealous of you."

Rebecca draped a smile across her mouth as Katharine arrived. A dozen years had passed since Katharine went on to graduate school and Rebecca went on to monopolize bestseller lists as romance writer Janelle MacDonald.

"Rebecca," Katharine said, smiling as she approached. "I

just bought my very first romance novel. Will you autograph it for me?"

Rebecca accepted the book with a good-natured grin, glancing up at Katharine. At just a few inches under six feet, she towered over Rebecca. Then again, all women towered over Rebecca. Katharine still looked as serious and condescending as ever.

"How have you been, Katharine?"

"Fine. I was in town and I saw your name in the paper, and I had to track you down." Her eyebrows knit in confusion. "I heard a few years back that you were getting married. I see you kept your maiden name. Very radical of you."

"We called it off," Rebecca explained curtly, ignoring Katharine's taunt, irritated at the reminder of Rick Daniels, the man Rebecca had almost married.

Rebecca signed the book and returned it to Katharine, sparing her the details. Katharine didn't need to know the wedding had been canceled because Rebecca had found her fiancé in a spare bedroom with his best man's sister the night before their wedding.

"*Rapture's Fury*," Katharine read thoughtfully. "What does that mean?"

Rebecca smiled thinly. "It's passion, Katharine. Perhaps you've heard of it?"

Katharine turned the book over, reading aloud. " 'Beautiful, willful Rheanna Devereaux is looking for a man—the man who killed her father, a blockade runner for the Confederacy. When her uncle sends her to Captain Rafe Jared for help, he has no idea he's sending her into the arms of her father's killer . . .' "

The name Rafe Jared diverted Rebecca's attention. A perfect hero—strong, silent, expert in sexual matters. But one detail had always distracted her. He wouldn't have been named Rafe—he would've been named Hiram. No headstone in any historic cemetery she'd ever visited bore the name Rafe. Perhaps because, as any faithful romance reader knows, *heroes don't die.*

Katharine looked up in bemusement. "Certainly relevant to the needs of contemporary women."

"Katharine," Rebecca said impatiently, "women today need exactly what women needed a century ago. I think the success of this industry proves that."

"You put a spin on the word *heroine*, Rebecca. It seems romance has become the opiate of the masses. Don't you ever feel a twinge of conscience? Women need self-reliance, not fairy tales."

"I don't see that self-reliance and love are mutually exclusive," Rebecca retorted.

Katharine smiled indulgently. "Surely you don't really believe any of it."

"You heard her speech," Linda said.

Katharine nodded. "That's the real mystery, Rebecca. For a minute it sounded almost like the old you talking—but badly in need of deprogramming. I remember the stuff you used to write. You could make a twig think twice. What happened?"

And suddenly there was no longer the petty rivalry between old friends. In its stead lay the real and terrifying reminder of the writer Rebecca had once intended to be. The provocative knowledge that passion was indeed what had driven Rebecca since she was old enough to care. That single craving to make even one person care about something that mattered. The benchmark of a serious writer. No one in their right mind would call Janelle MacDonald a serious writer.

Katharine wasn't saying anything that Rebecca hadn't told herself a hundred times over the last four years. Since Rick Daniels had reminded her in the cruelest way that she lived in a time when men and women no longer loved each other the way they once had. Why, she wondered, did she continue to perpetuate the fable of forever-after love when she no longer believed in it herself?

"Keep the faith, Katharine," Rebecca said quietly. "I'll write that thought-provoking something-or-other yet."

"Don't be too quick to write her off as softheaded," Linda

said. "Rebecca's become quite the man-hater since she started writing romance."

"It isn't that I hate them," Rebecca said with a smile, grateful for Linda. "Just that their fictional counterparts are so far superior to reality."

The three women laughed.

Katharine hesitated. "I'm sorry, Rebecca. You're a raging success, and I come in here playing shrewish rival. What are you working on now?"

"As a matter of fact, I'm leaving for Jefferson in the morning to research my next book."

"That little town over in east Texas? My grandfather lives in Marshall. He used to blather all the time about how Jefferson could've been what Dallas is if they'd let some guy have his way with the train."

"Good old Jay Gould. The heartless New York financier who cursed Jefferson for turning him down," Rebecca said with a smile. " 'Grass will grow in her streets and bats will dwell in her church belfries.' I'll have a hard time separating fact from folklore."

Blessedly, Katharine made her farewells. Rebecca looked at her watch, shaking her head. "I guess I've been stood up."

"The antique book guy?" Linda asked. "Your editor set up a meeting with him this evening, didn't she?"

Rebecca nodded. "Too bad. He's on his own."

Linda's eyes went wide. "But isn't he doing a story for *Time?*"

"Jackie said he'd be here before the banquet," Rebecca said. "I'm not going to wait all night for him. She'll get over it."

Rebecca and Linda collected their things and walked to the end of the curtain partition near the door. Rebecca stepped unobtrusively from behind the curtain, and on her way out the door she stopped short. She hesitated, strangely reluctant to leave. As she listened to Claudia Zachary's closing remarks, that distinctive sensation of being watched stole over her, and she turned her head.

The man stood alone. Arms crossed lazily in front of him, he leaned against the wall. Dark hair was silhouetted against a smattering of light from an open door several feet away, but his face was in shadow. Rebecca felt his direct stare. And she couldn't look away.

She blinked, vaguely wishing he would turn his head so she could glimpse his face, vaguely annoyed that he wasn't in the least disturbed to be caught staring. He remained unmoved, gazing at her. An irrational warmth, an inexplicable comfort, an undeniable yearning, filled Rebecca.

Unnerved by the confusion within her heart, she turned away from it all and slipped into the lobby of the hotel. She didn't mention the man to Linda, and they stopped at the front desk to check for messages.

The clerk returned after a minute, bearing a profusion of stunning scarlet roses arranged in a vase. In its midst was the most perfect yellow rose Rebecca had ever seen.

"No phone messages, Miss Reynolds, but these are for you." The girl placed the arrangement on the counter.

"My Lord," Linda murmured in good-natured jealousy. "Someone knows what you like."

"Even a yellow one," Rebecca said with a smile, lifting her hand to trace one flawless petal.

"Well, go on! See who they're from."

"Claudia, I'm sure," Rebecca murmured, reaching for the small note tucked within the arrangement. She opened the envelope, withdrawing the sheet.

> *Forgive me for missing our appointment. I understand you have a passion for yellow roses. This single perfect bloom, rare next to its more commonplace sisters, reminds me of your passion, which shines through in your writing.*
>
> *Your editor tells me you're leaving shortly for Jefferson. I once had very dear ties there, a long time ago. You'll appreciate the place as I do, and perhaps it's best that you experience its adventures before we meet. By then you*

*may see things differently. Jackie will know how to find
me when you're ready for me. I'm anxious to see you,
but of no mind to rush you. Time is on our side.*

"What time did these arrive?" Rebecca asked with deceptive calm.

The clerk frowned. "About four, Miss Reynolds."

Rebecca's mouth dropped. She gave a squeal of impatient,
frustrated rage. "What a smarmy, arrogant, condescending
jerk," she muttered, thrusting the sheet into Linda's hand.
"He never intended to show up. Didn't even bother to sign
his name. What does he know about my passion? And who
the hell does he think he is?"

"A guy who has a contract with *Time*," Linda answered
reasonably, smiling broadly as she scanned the page.

"So he thinks he can renege on an appointment and brush
it off with *roses?*" Rebecca raved.

Linda shrugged. "He said he was sorry."

"Men," Rebecca muttered, hoisting the vase in her arms
and stomping away.

Linda grinned as Rebecca stubbornly claimed the roses
she'd scorned.

Rebecca calmed down as they reached her red Mercedes
convertible. "Why you put up with me and my moods I'll
never know." She sighed.

"Forget it. Tell me more about Jefferson," Linda prompted
her, taking the vase and carefully placing the arrangement
on the floor beside her feet.

"I've always wanted to write about it," Rebecca admitted.
"I just never got around to it. I figure it's now or never."

"Now or never?"

"This is it, Linda. The last one. And this time, I'm not
going to gloss over the truth. From now on I'm going to write
about something besides ranchers who taste minty after a
week on the trail. I might just have my hero die of pneumo-
nia."

Linda grinned. "Where are you staying? You always find the most unique hotels."

"Oh, it's a bed and breakfast called the Behringer Inn. Built in 1840 by a German immigrant. They even have a legend. They say if you stay overnight in Garitson's Room, you'll be in love by morning."

"Guaranteed romance! You can't go wrong."

A gleam of anticipation twinkled in Rebecca's eyes. "I'm going to get it in writing. Maybe a guy comes with the room."

❧ Two ❧

Just after three the next afternoon, Rebecca approached Jefferson. It looked like any other rural Texas town, with teenage boys in pickup trucks rumbling down the main boulevard. At the next corner, an aged sign directed her to the "Historic Route," and she turned down the smaller thoroughfare.

Less than a minute into town, it happened.

There was no logical explanation for it, nor could she specifically name what it was. She couldn't compare it to other times she'd known the feeling, for she never had. Premonition was an insignificant dismissal of the complex, conflicting emotions which filled her: joy, childlike excitement, and indescribable sadness.

She couldn't shake it, and she shivered as it filled and encompassed her. It was impossible. She'd never set foot in this town. And yet, she felt vaguely as if she were returning to a cherished childhood home. The sensation overwhelmed her until she could scarcely breathe.

Rebecca slowed the car, her pulse beating rapidly, unexplainably. And then she pulled the car over onto the shoulder, fumbling for the emergency blinkers. She couldn't go on.

For several moments, she breathed deeply, closing her eyes, unnerved at the inexplicable emotion filling her. Desperately, she shoved open the car door and unsteadily climbed out. Her throat was tight as her chin was compelled upward, as if lifted by an invisible fingertip.

On a spacious spread of lawn stood an imposing white mansion. It waited there, as it had for over a hundred years. Never would she have expected to find a bed and breakfast in such a structure. She'd visited grander mansions than this, yet this was the most hypnotically alluring home she'd ever seen. Home. She didn't need an explanation somehow, but the metal sign at the corner of the yard captured her eye.

THE BEHRINGER INN, 1840.

Her heart seemed to stop for a moment.

Overcome by the unnatural sensation creeping over her, she forced herself to examine the house with her researcher's eye. Greek Revival architecture popular in the antebellum South, its white columns gracefully guarding the face of the house, twin verandahs surrounding both the upper and lower levels. Standing shaded from the merciless August sun in a circle of huge, ancient live oaks, it gave mute testimony of a more gracious age, a golden era that had long ago faded into the mists of yesterday.

Hands trembling, Rebecca retrieved her camera from the front seat and walked into the middle of the empty street, then began snapping black-and-white photos.

With the intrusion of her twentieth-century technology, the overpowering presence left her. Surprised by a jolt of emptiness, she covered her camera lens and returned to the car. For a moment, she scorned her imagination; in the same moment, she knew she had not imagined the oppressive loneliness which had overtaken her.

Thankful for her revived sanity, Rebecca drove across the street and up the gravel path leading behind the house. Gathering her laptop computer and purse in her arms, Rebecca savored her anticipation. She rushed up the stone path around the side of the house.

In her years of research, Rebecca had spent countless hours in structures that had been restored. The Behringer, she had read, had been lovingly maintained, its style not modified since long before the turn of the century. By the family who had built it.

She knew enough about history to know that spending even a single night in this home would be a rare treasure. Surprised at the tightness in her throat, she inspected the stained glass of the door.

Perhaps love had ironically turned up its capricious nose at her, but she'd invested a third of her life in historical romance. Since this novel was to be her last, she determined it would also be her greatest.

She found an envelope tucked between the door and the doorjamb. She read the note on the front of the envelope, written in an elderly scrawl.

> *Miss Reynolds,*
>   *Welcome to the Behringer. Here's your key. You'll find Garitson's Room at the top of the stairs. I hope it's to your liking. I will return shortly and show you the house. Please don't investigate on your own.*
>
> —*Myra Abigail*

Rebecca shook her head in grim amusement; a stranger given the key to a 150-year-old mansion full of antiques. Only in Jefferson.

The heavy door creaked as she opened it, and she lugged her laptop into the hallway, relishing the echo the grand entryway inspired. She locked the front door behind her and ventured upstairs, where she found a door standing open.

The legendary Garitson's Room was large, and a wide bed crafted from tiger mahogany invited her exhausted body. A ceiling fan whirred overhead, and the quiet masculinity of the room was an instant balm to her frazzled nerves. In the corner to her immediate right, a fireplace stood. Before that, a more modern white rug. The room was an antique collector's dream.

Rebecca crossed the room to the verandah and stepped

outside, inhaling the pale, sweet aroma of antique yellow roses rambling profusely over the rail. The rose was similar to those she'd planted alongside her Victorian home in Dallas.

An oak completely shaded the verandah, as well as the nine-foot windows of the room. Reaching above her head, she removed the pins from her long, dark hair and let it fall about her shoulders, then returned to the room. Each window was bordered by antique stained glass. Handfuls of dried scented flowers were tucked into the sashes of the burgundy drapery.

A chest of drawers stood to her right, and she moved forward to open a drawer. She found a quilt folded inside, obviously very old, and very cherished. And as she held the quilt, that overwhelming sense of someone watching her—someone with her—filled her once more. She turned, unable to do otherwise, half expecting to find someone staring at her. What stood there, however, was a simple object, and it drew her forward with the impelling force of a whisper. The quilt dropped from her fingers to the foot of the bed.

Removing the cloth draped over it, Rebecca gazed in wonder at a genuine early Remington. Over a century old. The irony of this piece of machinery standing in her room caused her throat to constrict, and she nervously touched a key. The typewriter was well cared for, practically unused.

An idea stole into her mind. Perhaps her hostess could be persuaded to let her use the typewriter while she was here.

She smiled at her romantic tendencies. The machine was over a hundred years old. Even its keyboard dated it. Even if it was in working condition, where on earth would she get new ribbon?

Arranging her laptop on the desk, she plugged it in and turned it on. The blank charcoal screen taunted her, as it had for two months. She loathed the prospect of typing even one more gooey adverb.

Do you even believe?

She composed pedantic sentences, her initial impression

of the inn. She hesitated then put into words the most un-nerving fact gained thus far.

"*There is a presence in the house, an undefinable something, peculiar and singularly disturbing, and yet soothing. Consoling. It is as if someone is over my shoulder, watching me type. . . .*"

❦ Three ❦

Rebecca spent an hour inside the museum in Jefferson, inspecting various artifacts from the town's influential families. Jefferson's chief claim to fame, however, was the story of an outsider—a Yankee named Jay Gould.

Once a proud, vital river port city known as the "Queen of the Cypress," the town was condemned to an early, unexpected death in the 1880s when her forefathers thumbed their collective nose at the wealthy railroad financier. They didn't need railroad, he was told. Didn't he know he was talking to the second largest city in all of Texas? When Jefferson unceremoniously sent the New Yorker packing, he swore she would see a day when grass grew in her streets.

Jefferson never recognized her precarious fate when Gould offered an alternative, and she paid for her arrogance with oblivion. Now, nothing was left except tourism. History buffs flocked from all over the South to visit the still regal queen, no doubt lining her pockets with the same silver they spent on historical romances.

Deciding a guided tour would be in order, Rebecca walked down Austin Street. She glanced at the red brick beneath her feet, amused at what she saw there. A mischievous sprig of greenery peeked out at her.

Quick, Mayor, get the weed killer!

Near the corner where the horse-drawn trolley awaited, a

curious shop caught her attention. The windows looked as if they hadn't seen a dust cloth in decades, but beyond those windows, she spotted the faint gleam of polished antique glass figurines, jars, and mirrors, and her eyes lit up in anticipation. Asking Rebecca Reynolds to pass up such a well-disguised antique shop was a waste of oxygen.

A cowbell over the door announced her arrival. Her nose twitched at the aroma of the deserted shop. Wood oil and vinegar. Beyond that, the even more enticing odors of leather and paper and resin. She slowly took in the impressive collection of crystal.

An old man, no taller than Rebecca, emerged from the back of the shop, and Rebecca wandered past the arrangements of antique glass, heading in a discreet beeline toward several shelves of old books at the back of the store.

"Afternoon, ma'am," he said.

"Hello," she said, taking a second glance at the man who lingered near the books.

He wore a peculiar shirt and trousers, reminiscent of Victorian times. In Jefferson, such a sight was average. Most of these people still looked on rail as just a fad. His hair was snowy white, and there was an abundance of the stuff, like whipped cream about his head. His blue eyes held merry wrinkles at the corners, and she noticed a jagged scar at his left eye. It looked like the memory of a childhood fall.

"You looking for something particular, ma'am?" His voice was the most distinctive sound she'd ever heard; like the trill of a quaint bird.

"Oh, no. I'm just browsing."

Rebecca quickly discovered she'd arrived in heaven. The shelves were stocked with old books from throughout the country, all of them in varying degrees of preservation, so old she dared not believe she'd stumbled into such a treasure chest by pure accident. The oldest book she could find dated back to 1792. The youngest had been published in 1889. A Mark Twain novel.

"This your first time here?"

Rebecca nodded. "Yes. I'm staying at the Behringer home."

The man's eyes lit up in recognition, and he fumbled in his shirt pocket for a pair of wire-rimmed glasses. He carefully placed the glasses on his face, peering at the shelves of books. "I have something that might interest you. I was looking at it just yesterday. A book about the Behringers. Now where is it?"

"The Behringers? That would be wonderful."

He carefully inspected the books, frowning. "What about that," he murmured unhappily. "I don't think I loaned it out. But it's gone."

Rebecca's spirits fell. "What a shame. What would you take for your entire inventory?"

"My what?"

"All your books. I'd like to purchase them all."

The man was startled, perhaps even offended, at this offer. "Well, I don't know about that. They aren't for sale. You can borrow one if you like, but you'll have to take good care of it."

Rebecca smiled. "Aren't for sale? That's an excellent marketing gimmick."

"Gimmick?" He puzzled over that, then shook his head. "Ma'am, they surely aren't for sale. I suppose I could let you have one. Here. Take this one."

The man gave it to her, and she opened it. It was a cookbook.

"Now I remember. I did give it away, yesterday. Mr. Behringer came in, looking around."

"Mr. Behringer?" Rebecca repeated in surprise. "Then there are Behringer descendants alive?"

The man chuckled, and his glasses slipped down his nose. "Why to be sure. Jacob has two or three side-wheelers that still travel from here down to Shreveport. Course they're talking about getting rid of the raft down on the Red River, and that'll hurt Jefferson. They don't seem worried about it none." He shook his head dolefully at this rumor.

A cold shudder went over Rebecca. She'd never known such an eerie shiver, but she'd never been face-to-face with a certifiable wacko before. Though it occurred to her to throw the cookbook in the air and run screaming from the shop, she nonchalantly placed the book on the counter.

The man noticed her discomfort. "Well now, I hardly took a second glance at you. We're dealing with a right modern lady, aren't we? Twentieth century, I'd say."

Rebecca nodded slowly as he acknowledged the obvious.

"Looks like I've moved about again."

Rebecca pushed the book toward him, increasingly eager to be out of the shop and back on the ground. "I think this'll be all today, but you have to let me buy it from you."

"All righty." She looked at the man as he tallied her purchase. "That'll be thirty-five cents."

She frowned. "It's worth thirty-five dollars."

He gave her a wink. "Now you must be looking to find you a husband. I expect those recipes'll do the trick."

He would accept no more than the quoted price, and Rebecca handed over her coins in confusion. She wandered numbly out of the shop, feeling guilty for taking advantage of the quite insane old man. An obscure wooden nameplate hung over the sidewalk: HENDERSON INTERESTS, MALCOLM HENDERSON, PROPRIETOR.

The group within the surrey was ready to leave, and she sat just behind the tour guide. He sported a well-worn, sweat-stained straw cowboy hat, and he lifted it to wipe sweat from his browned, weather-beaten face as he set the surrey in motion.

Rebecca listened as he described architecture and pointed out landmarks.

"Now over here's Jay Gould's private, bullet-proof car. That man had himself a whole bunch of enemies. You've all heard of the curse he put on Jefferson when she wouldn't let his railroad come through. Historians say Gould's signature in the Excelsior is a fake, that railroad went through Jefferson long before Gould signed that register. They say if the Wizard of Wall Street ever came through Jefferson in the first place, he would've stayed in his railcar, not the Excelsior. Beats me how he'da been able to get a railcar into town in the first place if he was persuadin' them to build rail. All I know is, town nearly did evaporate soon as rail come through."

A curious sense of missing details niggled at Rebecca. Without rail, Jefferson was supposed to dry up and blow away. But even when the railroad went through, the town floundered.

"Jefferson herself's kind of an oddity, some say. She was the largest inland port of the southwest. A huge natural raft down below the bayou in the Red River, 'bout eighty miles long, kept the water deep enough for steamboats to travel. A lot of landowners kept complaining because the backwater ruined their land. So they got Congress involved, and you know what happens when Congress gets involved. They got a whole mess of nitroglycerin and blew the raft to kingdom come. All that water that had been keeping so many steamers paddling their way back and forth to Shreveport spilled right down to the Gulf. Fact is, Jefferson was having hard times long before Jay Gould came along and pushed her over the edge."

From there they traveled out of town about a mile, to the Oakwood Cemetery. They went directly to the oldest part of the grounds.

They stopped before a plot fenced with black ornamental iron, a stenciled sign hanging on its side. DIAMOND BESSIE, it said simply, in block letters. Rebecca grew curious as the trolley disembarked. For her, this was a new piece of the Jefferson puzzle.

"Who was she?" she asked the tour guide.

He shook his head and spat tobacco at the iron gate. "Diamond Bessie Moore. Sad story. Some say she was an actress, some say she was a prostitute. Married to a guy named Abe Rothschild. Wasn't even twenty-five, I don't guess, when her husband killed her. Least they think he was her husband.

Rothschild was a rich boy from up north. Cincinnati. Daddy ran a jewelry outfit. Bessie always wore these gorgeous diamonds, and I guess Rothschild wanted 'em for his own."

"If his father ran a jewelry business, why would he need more diamonds? Wouldn't her husband, the son of a jeweler, likely have given them to her in the first place?" Rebecca asked, losing her patience with Jefferson's sloppy legends.

"Guess you can't ever have too many diamonds," the man chuckled, then went on with his story. "While they were in Jefferson, they stayed at the Brooks House—course, it ain't around no more. That was late January 1877. Anyhow, he took her off over the footbridge for a picnic. Rothschild came back alone, sayin' Bessie was visiting friends in the country. They found her body two weeks later in the snow," he said morosely. "Coroner said she looked beautiful as an angel. Been shot in the head, and her diamonds stolen." He raised his eyebrows in a pointed I-told-you-so.

"Snow?"

"Yes, ma'am."

"But they had gone for a picnic outdoors?"

"Well, the snow had only started a day or so before she was found, you see." He chuckled. "You know Texas weather. Well, they convicted Rothschild in Marshall, sentenced the son of a bitch to hang. But his daddy had this whole set of hotshot lawyers working for him, so o' course they appealed the case. It'd taken 'em years to even get the guy back to Texas from Cincinnati. He nearly shot off his own head before he got here. Took to drinkin' heavy after he killed her, even said some guy was following him around. Went stark raving mad."

"So they hanged him?"

"Hell, no," he muttered. "When the trial came up again, this time in Jefferson, a mighty curious thing happened. He slipped twelve thousand dollars into the room where the jury was deliberatin'—a thousand for each juror—and then every last juror found him not guilty. And he was out of town on the next train. A danged Jefferson jury let that man go scot-free."

Rebecca moved apart from the crowd, troubled by the story.

"Few years later, this strange man showed up. Asked if he could see Bessie Moore's grave, and then stood cryin' like a baby the whole afternoon."

"Was it Rothschild?" someone else asked.

"Don't know the answer to that, mister. I reckon not, seein' how his face was as famous as Robert E. Lee's around these parts back in those days. And Rothschild had blinded himself, ruined his face, when he shot himself. I can't say anyone knows who the visitor was. I figure it couldn'ta been Rothschild, 'cause his heart had to be blacker than the eye patch he wore. He wouldn'ta wasted no tears on Bessie." He paused, then gazed in the direction of the train that rumbled past.

"They say every winter, around the time Bessie was murdered, a train stops here in the dead of night. The man gets off the train, cries over Bessie's grave, leaves flowers for her, then gets back on the train and goes on his way."

"Train coming from Cincinnati?" another tourist asked, eliciting a chuckle from the group.

He cast a glance toward the track near the graveyard's edge, scratching his head. "The way they say it happens, I'd expect the train'd have to be comin' from the west. Dallas."

How like romantics, Rebecca mused bitterly, to tell a story with just enough fact to set idling imaginations in gear. The story of Jay Gould, at least, had a punch line and a point to it. The Yankee millionaire made a great scapegoat for the town's lack of vision.

This was merely an unsolved murder about which the townspeople speculated, and it seemed that in the past hundred years, people had assembled irrelevant bits of lore until it was fragmented nonsense. The girl had lain dead for two weeks, yet they remembered her corpse to be "beautiful as an angel." As far as Rebecca Reynolds was concerned, there was nothing worse than gratuitous legend.

Bitter sympathy arose in her for the young girl; abused, killed by her husband, then manipulated for the next century to turn a steady profit for a town in which she'd only visited and undoubtedly would never have been accepted while she was alive.

"The headstone gives the date of her death as December 31, 1876," Rebecca said, glancing at the leaflet in her hand, "but this says she died January 21, 1877."

"That headstone's a mystery in itself," the guide said. "Turned up in the middle of the night, and flowers there, too, for the very first time. January 21 was the day she went with Rothschild for the picnic. Don't know what happened on the New Year's Eve before. Musta meant something to somebody."

A choking unhappiness began to rise up within Rebecca. Men had progressed only marginally in the past century.

"They say she was expectin' a baby." The old man's gravelly voice intruded upon Rebecca's ruminating.

Her heart grew heavy with the senseless tragedy. What kind of freak would murder his wife and unborn child?

"And some say she wasn't married to Rothschild at all, and she was trying to force him to marry her."

A frustrated hopelessness she didn't understand overcame her, and with it came the soul-wrenching heaviness she was coming to recognize. Even welcome. Rebecca found herself inexplicably in tears for the brutally murdered mother and babe.

Rebecca gently trailed her fingertips along the cold, black iron in silent farewell and walked away from Bessie Moore.

"Now over here you'll see Mrs. Kate Wood, the feisty German lady who owned the Excelsior. That lady never gave two hoots what anybody thought of her. Those two little monuments beside her are the bulldogs she used to let run wild in the hotel."

As the group listened to lighter anecdotes about the cemetery and its colorful past, Rebecca methodically found her way around the well-tended graves of Jefferson's founders and unnamed children as well.

Her gaze lingered on the grave of a family named Frank. A husband, a wife, and eight tiny graves. Unless a child had escaped Jefferson, this couple had lived through burying all eight of their children.

This bleak reality, common to the families of Jefferson, affluent and penniless alike, reminded her of her purpose. Women outlived men, and parents often outlived children. The unnatural law of the frontier jolted Rebecca. Telling about it would not be a pleasurable task.

When the tour was over, she stopped off at the Excelsior and peeked at the glass case displaying numerous famous signatures. Presidents Hayes and Grant, John Jacob Astor, Oscar Wilde, John and Drew Barrymore. Rebecca grimaced at the knowledge that only a romance writer would ignore the historical signatures, searching eagerly for the fraud.

When the clerk complied with her request, she found only a tiny line sketch of a bird, followed by "Gould." It was dated January 2, 1882.

"Some say the jaybird was Gould's calling card," the clerk explained. "Others say he never used a bird, and that it isn't his signature."

Wonderful. She'd lived nearly twenty years of her life thinking Jay Gould had doomed Jefferson, and now she learned his signature was a fake.

Thoughtfully driving back to the inn, Rebecca hoped Mrs. Abigail had returned by now. Exhausted and drained, she was ready to relax.

In the kitchen, she found a tiny old woman at the counter, slicing lemons. She turned, wiping her hands on her apron. "Rebecca, I've been looking forward to meeting you," the woman said. "I've read so much about you."

Rebecca smiled. A fan. "You've read my books?"

"Oh, that's right. You're a writer. Have you seen the town?"

Rebecca nodded, wondering about the woman's words. "Briefly. I spent a while at the cemetery," she confessed.

The woman looked at her and nodded. "Yes. Did you see the Behringers?"

Rebecca shivered at the peculiar phrasing, then shook her head. Mrs. Abigail smiled gently. "I'll show you the house now. Afterward, we'll have some lemonade on the porch, if you care to."

Rebecca swallowed, unable to speak. Unable to do anything other than follow the innkeeper.

The sensation was back. Someone was with her. And it was someone who loved her very much.

Four

Myra Abigail led Rebecca through the hallway, richly paneled in walnut, to the front parlor. She stepped inside and clasped her hands as she spoke.

"The Behringer, as you may or may not know, is complete in its original furnishings." Mrs. Abigail spoke quietly, her voice sweetly flavored with a Southern drawl. She paused to allow the import of her statement to settle in Rebecca's imagination.

"Everything is original?" Rebecca whispered, glancing around at the furnishings of the room, sumptuously decorated in red.

"Yes." She smiled serenely, pleased. "The Behringers were a German family who valued heritage, and they raised their children to respect their past. Each of the families who lived in the home painstakingly preserved the furnishings. Everything in the home is protected by both the state and federal historical authorities, and we're rather discriminating about our guests."

Rebecca stepped into the parlor, her shoes echoing softly on the polished honey pine floor.

Mrs. Abigail crossed the room to stand by a stained glass window, smiling speculatively at Rebecca. "Your staying at the Behringer will make your visit in Jefferson one of extreme comfort. The Behringer's role of status symbol in Jefferson holds some irony. The exclusive ladies' garden club is very fond of the home. The Behringers, however, disliked the snobbishness of the town's society. This speaks volumes of the Behringers themselves.

"Jacob Behringer settled in Jefferson over twenty years before the Civil War, when the town was merely a rough frontier. He came from Germany as a young man, and he loved the wild, spirited ways of the young country." Suddenly, Mrs. Abigail paused, looking at Rebecca questioningly. "But I'm sure you're not interested in all these boring details of a man long dead."

Rebecca's eyes widened. "I'd love to hear his story."

"Jacob was one of the first men to employ a line of steamboats that traveled the Big Cypress Bayou between here and Shreveport. He came from an affluent family in Germany, and his wealth only flourished through his ventures in Jefferson. He had traveled throughout the South in his youth, until he met a young German girl who worked in a tavern in New Orleans."

Her voice lowered to a whisper. "It's said he saved her from 'a fate worse than death' in a barroom fight, and they fell in love that night. The couple married and settled near the Bayou, and just a few years later their children were born in the house they built, not a mile from the area where he launched his first steamboat, the *Maria Elyse*, named after his beautiful bride. The Behringers became a successful, standoffish family in the Jefferson community."

Rebecca stopped her. "When did the last Behringer die?"

Myra Abigail walked to the fireplace. "There are probably Behringers living today who know nothing of their heritage. A son left on the train one day and never came back. He'd had a falling-out with his father sometime before," Mrs. Abigail said, a bit sadly.

"Jacob Behringer loved his son more than his own life. A brilliant businessman, Garitson struck sparks with his father by urging him to close his shipping business and concentrate his efforts on any number of worthwhile alternative endeavors. Jacob refused. They say Garitson left because he wanted nothing to do with a family so steeped in the past that it couldn't accept the future.

"Garitson's preoccupation with the future bordered on obsession, and Jacob was happy with things the way they were. It's said that Garitson was one of the men in Jefferson in alliance with Jay Gould, attempting to persuade the people of Jefferson that rail was necessary for the future of the town. Of course," Mrs. Abigail smiled, "Gould was unsuccessful, and his curse nearly came true. I assume you've heard of it."

"I've also heard it's a myth," Rebecca said with quiet mischief.

Mrs. Abigail smiled vaguely. "Much of America's finest history can't be verified."

Rebecca returned the woman's smile, then turned toward the imposing double doors across the hall, which sealed the room from her prying eyes. "Is this another parlor?"

"That's the ballroom," Mrs. Abigail explained. "The most splendid room in the house."

Rebecca followed her innkeeper as she unlocked the doors and moved into the large, long room. She noticed a sheet draped oddly around a large object which hung from the far wall, marring the room's ornate beauty. As her gaze traveled around the room, she saw a similarly veiled piece hung directly opposite it.

"This was the most elegant of all ballrooms in Jefferson in its day," she began. Rebecca absorbed the grandeur of the room. A massive chandelier of blue and white Sevres porcelain hung from the twelve-foot tiled ceiling, directly over a stunning German table of walnut. Rebecca guessed the table to be close to 150 years old.

"It's said President Grant attended a party here during the time he stayed at the Excelsior House. As you can see, the room is large, to accommodate a grand soiree. Mr. Behringer hired the premier architect of the day to design the home. He loved parties, and he wanted his guests to be comfortable. He was truly a Southern gentleman."

Rebecca smiled, guessing he was more accurately a boisterous German. Her gaze returned to the dismally draped object hovering above the gleaming, polished piano at the end of the room. As Mrs. Abigail went on about Jacob Behringer, Rebecca walked toward the wall, hypnotized. She reached out to lift a corner of the sheet.

"No!" Mrs. Abigail's sudden shriek shattered the soothing atmosphere, and Rebecca turned, shocked.

Mrs. Abigail's face paled, and she touched her temple. "Forgive me," she whispered. "But the sheet is there for a reason. I'm afraid you can't see it. It's expressly forbidden."

Rebecca frowned, suspecting there was more than a little of the eccentric in her innkeeper. "Forbidden? What is it?"

"It is a mirror. As is the one on the opposite wall."

"What could it hurt to look at it?"

"Mr. Behringer called it a vision of hell," Mrs. Abigail said bluntly.

"Well," Rebecca smiled, trying to lighten the oppressive mood, "I never bother with makeup when I'm doing research, but I wouldn't exactly call it a vision of hell. Let's have a look."

"I beg of you," Mrs. Abigail whispered urgently, stopping Rebecca more effectively than if she'd grabbed her. The old woman glanced nervously at the wall opposite the mirror, then walked forward to Rebecca. "Gracious, I've never seen a guest more curious about that mirror."

Mrs. Abigail touched the corner of the sheet, then said somberly, "I will show you each mirror individually. The sheets stay in place, as they have for the past century. Do you understand?"

Rebecca nodded. She peeked under the sheet which Mrs. Abigail drew back, revealing a large rectangular girandole mirror.

"It seems rather . . . neglected," Rebecca murmured.

"It hasn't been touched in over a hundred years." Mrs. Abigail smoothed the sheet back into place and turned toward the other wall. Rebecca followed and was treated to a second private unveiling. This mirror, even older than the other one, hung above the fireplace.

"It dates back to the late eighteenth century," the innkeeper said. "It's another of the many German pieces in the house. Mr. Behringer bought it for Maria on the day of their wedding from a trader in the territory. They say the mirror is magical, or else it never would have survived in the wild bayou country in the early eighteen hundreds."

Rebecca nodded, inspecting the mirror from her awkward vantage point. Oval in shape, the mirror was surrounded by an ornately carved giltwood wreath.

"It's an amazing piece." She looked toward the other wall. "What about the other one?"

"No one knows much about it; it's typical of the period when Jefferson was thriving." Mrs. Abigail replaced the sheet and considered Rebecca pensively, and Rebecca knew that another piece of wild folklore was about to be perpetrated. "It's said that a young woman disappeared in this room one night. She's remembered—perhaps unfairly, some say—as an evil woman who set out to destroy Garitson Behringer the day she met him."

Mrs. Abigail straightened the screen in front of the fireplace before continuing. "Everyone was shocked that night when she appeared at the home dressed in a gown she couldn't afford. Even this caused talk, because no one could imagine where she'd gotten such a glorious gown. It's said she earned it," Mrs. Abigail said, a confidential tone touching her voice, "in a night's work, if you understand my meaning. Some said she was a friend of the family, but she certainly wasn't one of the Behringers' kind.

"At any rate, they say Mr. Behringer was in the process of having the woman thrown out of the house when Garitson took her into this room, with the intention of telling her he could never see her again. At that moment, the woman stepped in front of this mirror, tears streaming down her face, murmured something only he could hear, and vowed she would love him throughout eternity. And then, she looked into the mirror, at the vision of herself in the mirror behind her, looking forward into this same mirror. That night, she vanished from the house."

The innkeeper fell silent, shaken, staring at Rebecca, daring her to believe this latest piece of drivel. "So where did she go?"

Mrs. Abigail gazed bleakly at the fireplace. "She was never seen again. Some say she conjured a spell to vanish, to destroy the Behringers. It's rumored she was from New Orleans, and you know how the black magic was down there back then. But Maria believes the angels looked down and were so touched by the girl's plight that they took her away to heaven in that moment. The very next morning, Jacob had the room sealed off.

"When I was a small child, Maria told me the story; she said she kept it inside her for thirty years, and she constantly begs me not to ever tell anyone." She paused and Rebecca was startled to see tears glistening in the old woman's eyes. "And you must promise the same thing. But I know she wants me to tell you."

Rebecca comfortingly circled the woman's shoulders with her arm, noticing her erratic use of tense, knowing that somewhere between this room and the last, her innkeeper had crossed the line of lucid thought. Maria Behringer, a young woman in the 1840s, could never have lived into the lifetime of this woman.

"Of course," Rebecca whispered. "It's a tragic story, and I would never think of betraying you. Would you like some lemonade?" she offered, cast into the role of caretaker rather than guest.

"That would be lovely, dear."

As they walked through the gallery toward the kitchen, Rebecca asked, "How have you kept guests out of the room all this time?"

"For years, the ballroom was boarded up. If you look at the wood around the doors, you can still see the marks of the nails. The room was opened around the turn of the century, but the mirrors remained covered. Now I think it best to leave them so. The ballroom is kept locked at all times."

"How did the house come into your possession?" Rebecca asked.

"The last daughter of the family was a spinster. Some say Matilda took after her grandmother, Katerina. A wild girl, that one. Mattie died ten years ago and left the house to me, and I felt it was only right to share it. I know Mrs. Behringer would have wanted it that way."

Rebecca poured the lemonade into crystal glasses. Mrs. Abigail accepted her glass, murmuring, "If you don't mind, I'm rather tired. I think I'm going to take mine on out to my house and lie down awhile. I have a little dependency back there."

"Of course. I apologize for tiring you."

"My dear, it's been a delight sharing it with you. I think it's the most fascinating story. If I told everyone, however, I fear I'd be locked away." The woman's pale gray eyes took on a lively note of youth. "Make yourself at home. There's wine in the icebox if you'd like a glass before bed. The house is all yours tonight." She smiled mysteriously.

Rebecca raised an eyebrow. "All mine?"

"You're the only guest. You have the entire home to yourself."

The old woman's words sent a tingle along Rebecca's arms. Rebecca walked her halfway down the path to the cottage behind the main house.

"You're a rather level-headed girl, aren't you?" Mrs. Abigail smiled.

"Definitely."

"That's good. I wouldn't leave the fanciful sort of woman here alone. It's the kind of place that can make an imagination run wild. They say sometimes at night, you can hear a woman weeping in the ballroom."

❦ Five ❦

Rebecca settled into the soft cushion on the porch swing, noticing the anachronism of her sports car parked under the ancient oak tree. As she watched the sun sinking into the western sky, she was regretful to see the day, with all its tall tales, end. Everything she'd heard during the course of the last five hours was far more fantastic than anything she'd dreamed up in the last ten years. And that was saying something. With a sigh, she rose from the swing and walked into the house, locking the door behind her.

As she ventured into the shadows of the house, the closed double doors of the ballroom beckoned to her. For a moment, she touched a doorknob, then turned away. *Give it a rest. It's a fun little story, that's all.*

But where did she go?

Ignoring the pointless question, she went to the kitchen instead, looking forward to a glass of wine before bed. She filled an antique glass with the wine, then took the entire bottle along with her as she made her way into the parlor.

What a romantic fantasy! Rebecca sipped the wine with a smile. *If only I could master the art of materialization,* she mused, inspired. Take two broad shoulders, chiseled cheekbones a requirement, not an option, add one pair of sapphire eyes, mix well in dissolution, stir in equal parts of jealousy and chivalry, throw in a liberal dose of sexual talent, along with a great handful of fidelity, and give it all a name with three or four hard consonants. What woman could ask for anything more?

Where did she go?

Refilling her glass, she touched a flame to the candles on the cherrywood table before the settee, then closed her eyes, considering all the foolishness she'd been fed today. Wonderful, entertaining nonsense, the sort of stuff that would charm Mark Twain. A woman fond of diamonds murdered by a man who was later unfairly acquitted, justice mocked by affluence, a railroad tycoon whose curse turned a thriving city into a ghost town, a man who'd carved an empire out of the wilds of east Texas in the 1830s, and a woman who disappeared.

Where the hell did she go?

Holding the candelabra before her, Rebecca rose from the settee and climbed the stairs to her room, filling the claw-footed tub with steaming water. She set out her scented soap on the porcelain dish by the tub, then returned to the parlor for her wine.

Simply put, she couldn't get that bizarre story out of her wine-fuddled brain. She finished the rest of her glass and once more refilled it. As she swallowed one last sip, she stopped.

Suddenly, Rebecca Reynolds was furious with the entire town of Jefferson. For in her own bathroom at home, full-length twin mirrors lined the walls. And when she looked into one, she could see only the mirror flush behind her, along with the details of the wall around it. Unless mirrors had changed a whole lot in a hundred years, the story was not only a lie, it was a badly contrived one! To view her back, she must glance over her shoulder. It was impossible to see even her face in the other mirror, much less a vision of hell.

Setting the wineglass beside the bottle with a thump, Rebecca rose with surprisingly resolute determination, considering her physical state. She marched across the hall to the ballroom and tested the doorknob.

"Kept locked at all times, huh?" she muttered, pushing back the doors.

Now then, she thought, flipping the light switch that powered the chandelier. *I'm going to have a look at these mirrors, and to hell with the wild stories inspired by a romantic old woman's senility.*

She slowly approached the oval mirror, the wedding gift of a wealthy man to his bride. Stepping on a footstool, she carefully slipped the sheet away. She gasped at the loveliness of the mirror, at the eerie knowledge that hers was the first face to have been reflected there in over a century. She inspected the tooling around the mirror, finding nothing remarkable about it beyond its obvious value as an antique, then crossed the room and purposefully unveiled the other mirror.

Standing three feet away from the mirror, wondering what the woman had seen a hundred years ago as she gazed into the mirror, Rebecca slowly raised her face.

"Now, I don't hear any weeping. Do you?"

Rebecca posed the question to her own reflection, realizing she looked past the image before her and into her reflection in the delicate oval antique on the opposite wall. Hypnotically, she stared into her face on the many mirrors superimposed on each other, each retreating further and further into an eternity behind her. Peering closely at the mirror, she saw that it hung at a slight list to the left. That simple answer made it possible.

She reached forward and straightened the mirror. "There. No more disappearing women."

For a moment, she swayed slightly, then giggled. *That's what you get for getting drunk in an empty old house.* Then, she turned away from the mirror.

The electric lights flickered briefly, but that was it. There were no answers to the many puzzles she'd accumulated during the day, this one foremost among them. She sighed. There was no way she'd ever determine how the mystery woman disappeared, if indeed that had happened. Then she realized with miserable embarrassment that for several hours, she had believed in the preposterous yarn.

"Oh, God. Jefferson's taken my brain hostage."

Shuffling to the entryway of the ballroom, she turned off the chandelier and scrutinized the wood around the door. As Mrs. Abigail had said, the scars of the nails that had been plucked out stood as testimony that the room had been closed up by boards. Rebecca peered closely at the marks, surprised at their freshness. It looked as though they had been made yesterday instead of more than eighty years ago.

She blinked, and when she looked again, the scars weren't there. Only fresh, gleaming cypress wood, still more proof that the whole thing was a joke, and that she was quite drunk, dying to believe it. So much so that she'd actually imagined seeing the scarred wood. She sighed and walked into the parlor to find her empty wineglass. She could've sworn she'd left the bottle there with it, but it was gone.

Climbing the stairs to her bedroom, she placed the antique wineglass on the stand next to the tub, then shed her clothing. She dropped it in a pile by the bed and stepped into the steaming water.

Rebecca relaxed in the warmth of the water's soothing, silken caress, feeling the cares of ten years ebb from the depths of her mind and disappear in the whisper of the ceiling fan. Linda was right; beyond research, the trip was a badly needed escape. Rebecca felt as if she were a young girl again. Closing her eyes, she leaned back against the smooth porcelain of the claw-footed tub and lost herself in another age.

The chant of the cicadas sounded faintly above the whine of the train's horn. She focused on the sound until slowly, the whistle faded to silence. Rebecca sighed.

Slowly, she became aware of the chill of the water, and she reached for the soap. It was gone.

"I left it right here," she muttered, searching for it under the water. She craned her neck to look on the dressing table, then slowly rose.

At that moment the door to her room crashed open.

Grabbing for the towel that wasn't there, Rebecca tried to shield herself. Unable to, she sank into the cool water with a splash that was decidedly lacking in grace. The man who stood there, eyes as dark as the heart of a madman, glared at her in dismay.

"What are you doing in here?" he demanded in a low, smooth voice that sent tingles up Rebecca's spine. A voice as rich as coffee laced with the finest whiskey.

The wine still echoed in her brain. Why had she allowed herself that last glass? Here she was, confronted by an intruder who had managed to get through the locked door, and she couldn't even compose a clear thought.

"What are *you* doing in here?" she retorted, her anger roused at the stranger's nerve. She was shocked to find herself inspecting the unusual clothing he wore with more than clinical interest.

Possibly involved in a period tour, he was dressed in the clothing of another age. He certainly gave the costume an allure no doubt lacking a hundred years ago, emphasized by his aggressive stance; his feet were planted firmly apart, hips thrust slightly forward. Standing but a few feet from her, his strong, lean hands resting negligently on his hips, the man expected answers.

She noticed the sun's bronze glow on his face, cloaked in the most perfect beard she'd ever seen, and her gaze swept every powerful line of his body. The simple black breeches outlined long, muscular thighs. The fine linen of his shirt stretched tautly across his shoulders, and the open collar displayed an inviting sprinkle of black hair against his dark throat. She wanted to rest her fingertips against the pulse beating there, that warm proof of his vitality.

The silence spanned the gulf between them with an intensity that jarred her. Suddenly, the strange man closed the door quietly behind him and crossed to the bed, as though reconsidering her presence. He draped himself across the foot of her bed, propping a shiny black boot on the white lace counterpane. If she'd thought of it, she would have seen that the lovely "grandmother's flower garden" quilt she'd dropped there earlier was gone.

No protest from Rebecca. She only met his eyes with an equally curious gaze. Her eyes glittered as he stared, and suddenly, not knowing why, she was no longer afraid of the stranger. And that knowledge terrified her.

"How'd you get inside?" he asked, a long finger idly stroking a pattern on the counterpane. "Are you a witch? The house is secure. Impenetrable."

"I have a key," she stammered. "I have reservations!"

"I have a few myself, though I'm tempted." The man's face suddenly screwed up in disbelief and understanding. "Oh, no. The mystery wears thin. When will that girl ever grow up?" He chuckled, shaking his head.

"Get off my bed," she commanded quietly. "And get out of my room. I don't know who you are, or where you got that foolish getup, but in five more seconds I'm going to scream."

Rebecca was infuriated when he merely laughed, lights sparkling readily in the depths of those remorseless eyes. Her mouth dropped open as his mirth overwhelmed him. An unruly shock of dark hair fell over his forehead, enhancing his effortless allure.

"The facts are stacked against you, I'm afraid. You're in my room, and you're trespassing. I'm fully dressed. And you're quite naked."

He paused, bringing his feet to the floor with a thump as he straightened his long, lithe frame. He moved with the steady, predatory grace of some sleek animal. He thrust out his legs in front of him, then leaned forward and placed his elbows on his spread knees. Rebecca found herself unable to look away from the magnificent beauty of that body, and she thought, a little wildly, that period costumes weren't supposed to fit quite so snugly.

"You don't look like any witch I've ever seen," he mused with thoughtful consideration. "That wild hair is intriguing, though. Maybe. Are you a good witch?"

Rebecca's eyes threw sparks.

"Ah. A *very* good witch, I'll bet," he murmured, his dark gaze skirting the edge of the tub for a better view. The mischief in that gaze quietened.

"Now tell me why she's put you up to it. I thought Katy had finally accepted Vivian. It took her almost as long as it took me."

Rebecca stared into the water. "I don't know what you're talking about."

He chuckled shortly, then spoke in a deep, patronizing tone. "Of course you don't. That's part of the game. Fine, I'll go along with your fun for now," he began, rising.

That body of his just goes on and on, Rebecca mused. From black boots, to strong, hard thighs, a flat, trim waist, and the singularly most touchable chest she'd ever seen, wide and unyielding. The wine definitely had been spiked with something . . . dangerous.

"I'm Garitson Behringer, as if you don't already know." He crossed the space between them in one stride, and he extended his hand in a civilized fashion. "So delighted to meet you."

She felt his heat from two feet away, and it burned. He seemed suddenly aware of her nakedness, and an answering heat suffused her. As disturbed as he, she made no effort to take his offered hand.

She returned his charming smile with a derisive twist of her lips. "And I, Mr. Behringer, am Diamond Bessie Moore. I'm very tired, very cold, and I want to get a good night's sleep before I go out and have my head blown off. I'd like to be left alone."

He matched her acerbic tone. "I'm very sorry, Miss who-ever-the-hell-you-are. But somehow you've been put in my room. As though," he emphasized, "I don't know who put you here."

The man's exaggerated innocence irritated Rebecca. Beneath his facade of courtesy lurked a powerful sense of humor, and an equally compelling sense of himself. Rebecca knew that standing not two feet from her was a womanizer of the worst variety. An intelligent one. An impossibly charming one. His voice hypnotized her. He spoke with a perfect blend of Eastern Queen's English and Southern honey.

"An oversight, I'm sure. And to show you what a good sport I am, I'll be happy to show you to one of our guest rooms down the hall. Although I'm real tempted to take advantage of Katy's providence." His dark eyes traveled over her like the dance of an errant finger of lightning.

Slowly, Rebecca recognized the authentic cut of his clothes, and she knew this was no costume. These clothes were his normal attire, and they were nearly new.

Rebecca's eyes widened as she sketched a careful inventory of the room. The soft lighting of the electric table lamp was gone, as was the decorative ceiling fan. The room was illuminated only by the candelabra she'd left on the dresser. She gazed at the flickering candles' flames for a moment before she noticed the exquisitely tooled rug on the floor where only minutes before the thick white rug had lain.

Then, the insanity began.

❦ Six ❦

Rebecca's gaze returned to the man's face, a tingle slowly sliding up the back of her neck. "What's the date?"

"The what?"

"The date. What's today's date?"

"August 25." Dark, well-shaped eyebrows drew together.

"The year," she urged.

"Eighteen seventy-six," he answered, smiling quizzically. "At around eight-twenty in the evening."

"I have to get out of here." Rebecca shivered. She'd certainly chosen a vintage bottle this time.

His gaze touched the water, and Rebecca knew she was poorly disguised. "Fine idea," he agreed. "Are you as good at vanishing as you are at materializing?"

"Do you mind?" she demanded, her eyes flashing.

He opened a chest of drawers. "Leave it to Katy to pick out a modest witch."

The man threw her a towel, then turned to face the bed.

Watching him distrustfully, Rebecca rose in the tub, hastily wrapping the towel about her. It was at that moment that the sharp tap of heels sounded in the hallway, followed by a woman's voice.

"Garitson, darling. Are you in there? I can't seem to find any servants."

"Holy mother of God," he muttered.

Appalled, Rebecca gaped at the man. *Garitson Behringer?!*

Behringer quickly glanced over his shoulder before he turned. "I'm in the bath, Vivian," he called, rushing to the armoire, shoving clothes aside. "Wait in the parlor."

"Garitson," the voice said, a petulant utterance.

"The parlor, Vivian," he roared.

The woman sighed impatiently and muttered. Her footsteps faded.

"She's got the patience of a five year old," he grumbled, returning to Rebecca, holding out his hand. He grinned wryly at her. "Are you going to get out, or do you prefer to have your eyes scratched out prior to having your head blown off?"

Glaring at him, Rebecca placed her hand in his, startled at the warmth there. As she stepped from the tub, her head tilted up to meet his gaze. He was very tall.

"This is what you get for being a party to my little sister's schemes," he said, laughter in his eyes, still grasping her hand in his own. The humor mingled there with something else Rebecca had never known before. "What's your name, witch?"

"Rebecca," she said, surprised to find her voice had fallen to a whisper. The candle's flame played about the sharp planes of his face, and she noticed a sprinkling of gray in the inky blackness of his beard. She marveled at its exquisite perfection; she'd never thought of a beard as something beautiful until this moment. Lifting her hand impulsively to touch the beard, she was surprised to find it soft. His frank sexuality was something Rebecca had written a lot about, but had never known firsthand. She was spellbound.

His face grew grim as he watched her. Shocking even herself and unable to do otherwise, Rebecca leaned toward him, brushing her lips against the corner of his mouth, feeling the tickle of his beard against her face. Behringer turned and captured her mouth with his, and a low murmur of surprise rumbled in his throat at her kiss. She trembled at the hesitant, hungry taste of him. His tongue dipped into her open mouth with impulsive playfulness, and she sighed. His head snapped up suddenly, and she blinked at the anger glittering in the dark depths of his eyes.

"She made sure you were sufficiently soaked in the grape before she left," he muttered. "She's gone too far this time, I'm afraid."

Rebecca was unaware the towel had drooped low until she felt Behringer's hands, tightening it closely around her once more. His expression was shuttered, his movements quick as he tucked the corner of the towel between her breasts, his fingertip lingering for a fleeting moment, then trailing away with irritated reluctance. They both heard the footsteps on the stairs.

"Into the closet with you. It'll only be a few moments." His hand grazed her waist as he helped her inside the armoire.

The pungent aroma of cedar surrounded Rebecca as she waited silently in the darkness. Her breath was shallow as she heard the bedroom door open, the rustle of the woman's clothing as she hurried into the room.

"Did you see Katy off on the train?" the woman asked.

Mischief was laced into Behringer's voice, and Rebecca scowled, reading his mind. "Yes, the little jokester." Then, his tone became brittle. "What are you doing here? You know what your father would say if he knew you were here unescorted. And in my bedchamber?"

"Don't be a ninny, darling. We're going to be married in only a few months. What has Katy done this time?"

"Oh, the usual sort of prank. She loves nothing more than to giggle behind her fan while I make an ass of myself."

Rebecca listened to the impatient swish of the woman's skirts. "Well, that divine school in Richmond should solve that."

"I expect her back within the month, trailing broken hearts along behind her. Richmond isn't brave enough to tame that scamp."

"Oh, certainly Katy is ready to behave like an adult by now." The woman sounded bored with the topic. Rebecca knew that as certainly as Behringer doted on his sister, this woman detested her.

"How dreary. I'm rather fond of her 'anything for a laugh' philosophy."

Abruptly, Vivian changed the subject. "Garitson, I've been giving the party a lot of thought. I'm wondering what you'll be wearing."

A quiet overcame his deep, mellow voice. "What difference does it make?"

A girlish giggle reverberated in the room. "Why, my dearest. We shall be the most handsome couple there, of course. Don't you know the whole town will be curious to see which way we're leading them?"

"I don't know if I'm even coming, Vivian."

An abrupt silence shattered the noise of the girl's nervous movement, and Rebecca brought her ear closer to the door. She thought she heard sniffling, and she rolled her eyes.

"Garitson, is there something wrong?"

"Nothing's wrong," Behringer said tightly. "Please stop that. It makes my head ache."

"But," she whimpered, "you care so little for me, while I worship you."

"Oh, for Christ's sake! You know all about the meeting your father's scheduled that night. Of all people, you should know how important it is that I go."

A petulant sigh escaped the girl. "A silly meeting. I did not know about it. This will be the most important party of the summer. You, of all people, should know that."

Rebecca heard a cabinet open, and the clink of glass against glass. "Of course. How could I have put business ahead of your social calendar? You'll have to send my regrets, Vivian. I can't make it."

First, an inarticulate sound of frustration, then, the stamp of her foot, and then, "I'll have Father cancel the meeting. It can't be all that important, and he knows how much the party means to me."

There was a pause, then the glass thumped against the table. "Damn, you're a brat. Fine. I'll go to the blasted dance. But I'm not missing the whole meeting for the distinct pleasure of sipping lemonade with a bunch of maiden aunts."

Placated, the six-year-old child of a moment ago evaporated, replaced by a flagrant flirt. "You're such a dear, Garitson. How shall I repay you?"

"I'm an imbecile." Again, the glass touched glass, and Rebecca heard a small splash, no doubt a suitably stiff spirit.

"Well, it seems we're back to our original dilemma. What do you plan to wear?"

"I don't give a damn if I go in deerhide. Choose something to complement your sunny personality."

A shock ran up Rebecca's spine as he spoke the words, and she prayed the girl had his wardrobe committed to memory. She squirmed in the closet as she heard once more the swish of skirts, headed straight to her hiding place.

The next few moments were only brief glimpses of reality in Rebecca's mind. The doors were drawn back dramatically. Rebecca was treated to a brief glimpse of a heartbreakingly beautiful face just before shock overcame it. That was a terrifying thing. Then, as the girl's gaze took in Rebecca's attire, she collapsed in a faint.

"Oh, for crying out loud," Rebecca said, peeved at the sight of the blonde crumpled helplessly on the floor.

Behringer swore viciously as the doors were opened, and now he crossed the room in a single stride. "Damn. I'd forgotten all about you," he muttered. "Now see what you've done." He grasped her elbow in a fierce grip, yanking her out of the armoire.

Abruptly, he released her. She stumbled, furious at him and at her own fear. "You idiot! Why didn't you just say, 'Look in the closet, dearest, there's a naked woman there.'?"

"You've gotta get out of here. Where are you from? Shreveport?"

He lifted the delicate blonde in his arms and placed her on the couch near the fireplace. He spoke over his shoulder. "Get dressed," he hissed.

She glanced around, unsurprised to find her clothes gone. "I don't know where my clothes are. Katy . . . hid them somewhere."

"Damn it, she's outdone herself this time. Get in her room."

And where might that be? she wondered. "I . . . I . . ."

Behringer looked at her, then frowned. "Oh, hell, is there no end to this mess?"

He grabbed a dressing gown from the wardrobe and shoved it in her shaking hands. "Come on," he muttered, striding out of the room, leaving her to pull the robe around her as she stepped into the hall.

Two doors down, he paused and opened a door. "Don't come out." The anger had darkened his eyes to black, his brows enhancing the threat there. "This little game may end up costing me my future."

Without further comment, he left the room and closed the door silently behind him.

❧ Seven ❧

Unbelievable!

Swiftly tugging Behringer's robe tightly about her, Rebecca collapsed against the door, staring blankly at the room.

Katy's room was furnished in comfortably feminine items. A white, four-poster canopy bed stood against the opposite wall, covered in an ivory silk spread. A writing desk faced the wall nearest her, and a lamp stood on the table in the corner.

Rebecca numbly sank into a rocking chair. It was impossible, far more inconceivable than any ludicrous legend she'd heard today. If she hadn't been as knowledgeable about antiques, she could've believed she'd woven a fantastic dream. The shining, unblemished furniture of Katy's room taunted her with its newness. Terror gripped her heart at the staggering reality. Rebecca Reynolds, the woman who'd lived over a decade of her life in the romantic haze of a nonexistent past, had been vaulted into history. Real history, that place she believed any of her readers would shrink in horror from, should they ever be truly presented with its harsh face. How? *How?!*

She tried to persuade herself that it was only the wine, that she'd probably passed out when she first went upstairs, and that at this moment she was having the wildest dream of her life. It was impossible to reconcile any of it with the reality of Garitson Behringer.

His brief kiss had shaken her. The memory of it sent a pulsing warmth through her that she hadn't felt since her first kiss; it was as though she'd never known a man's touch. The wild impulsiveness Behringer inspired in her frightened Rebecca to the core.

The beautiful features of Behringer's fiancée flashed tauntingly before Rebecca's eyes, and her fingers tightened on the armrests of the rocker. She had to get out of here. Now. Surely once she had some fresh air, this wild fantasy would disintegrate, she reasoned with herself, as though it made perfect sense. It had to be this bizarre old house. The Legend of Garitson's Room. The ballroom. The mirrors.

Rebecca ran to the wardrobe, tugging open the doors. Gowns of gorgeous color filled the closet, but she settled on an inconspicuous gray. She found undergarments in a chest of drawers and quickly slipped into them, then slid the dress over her head, quickly buttoning it to her neck. She briefly offered a prayer of thanks when the clothing fit. The shoes were roomy, but better than bare feet.

Rebecca listened for noises down the hall. Pulling aside the gauzy drapery to scan the verandah, she noticed the oak and snatched a deep breath. Despite her own staid reassurances that she'd checked into a haunted hotel, its rich reality was hardly spectral. She shuddered to think of what she might have faced in the Belle of the Bayou during her heyday.

Without lingering over consequence, she quietly opened the carved jewelry box on the dresser. On the burgundy velvet lay a brooch which, even in the dim light, looked to be of great value. Tucking it inside the pocket of her gown, she tiptoed out on the verandah.

Yanking the muslin skirts up to her thighs, Rebecca scrambled over the rail and into the branches of the oak tree. Once on the ground, she slowly crept around the side of the house to the edge of the yard. A buggy stood outside the picket fence. Her gaze followed the street, and she dismally realized that what once had been a busy thoroughfare full of automobiles was now only a secluded, red clay country road overshadowed by immense trees.

She glanced at the porch, knowing there was no time to plan a discreet getaway. Gathering her billowing skirts in one hand, she ran as fast as she could, straight toward town. At least she'd had time this afternoon to familiarize herself with the streets.

Her heart pounded as she raced down the deserted road to town. It wasn't until she stood at the corner of Vale and Austin Streets, gasping, pressing her hand to the stitch in her side, that the sinking realization hit her. Looking down the main street of Jefferson, she knew that little was different, yet nothing was remotely the same.

She collapsed against a tree, blinking in disbelief, wishing she'd paid closer attention to the wrinkled old tour guide. She'd been so preoccupied by the abundance of antique shops she'd neglected to remember the original purposes of these buildings. It was irrelevant; many buildings before her now had not existed during her tour.

The old red brick museum was gone. The lovingly restored restaurant across the street from the Excelsior was only a private home. To her left, the staunchly reassuring familiarity of the Excelsior stood. Along Austin Street, where cars had been parked just a few hours ago, horses nickered restlessly. On the sidewalk, a tattered poster advertised Jefferson's centennial celebration.

No, she realized with overwhelming queasiness. The country's centennial. She wanted to scream, and for a moment considered actually doing it.

In the distance, the horn of a steamboat wailed as it approached the ferry. Women in brilliant satin gowns strolled arm in arm with men. Raucous laughter rang out from the corner saloon, blending with the discordant jangle of the piano. And there she stood, wearing another woman's clothes, the dust of the street clinging to her skirts and to her face in the sticky heat, with nothing to help her gain shelter for the night except a stolen brooch.

Rebecca quickly snaked her way into the crowd of people milling about the Excelsior. As she walked, she desperately mined her richest resource for help. Involved in her scheming, Rebecca nearly stepped on a honey colored bulldog before she ever saw him, and she stopped short. The dog tilted his head curiously at her, then resumed his nap. With unnerving certainty, she knew she was looking at one of Kate Wood's famous dogs.

Rebecca sensed she was being watched, and she noticed a tall, fair-haired man staring openly at her. Repulsed by the gleam in his green eyes, she quickly turned away. Still she felt his gaze upon her.

By the time she arrived at the registration desk, part of a story had been woven. A man stood there, regarding her disdainfully.

"I need your help," she whispered, the hysteria in her voice authentic. "I was on the boat from New Orleans, and I managed to get separated from my party when we stopped a few miles from here. I must have some shelter for the night, and all I have is this brooch." She lay the brooch on the counter beside his hand.

Leaving the piece untouched, he tapped his pencil on the desk. For several moments, he looked at the brooch, then at her, then he cleared his throat. "I see. And your name, miss?"

"Rebecca Reynolds. Would it be possible to arrange it?"

The clerk tilted his head. "I'm sure you know the brooch is worth far more than several months' stay at the Excelsior."

She blushed, embarrassed at her blunder. "I have no money," she stammered. "I have no choice."

Again, he nodded. "Of course. Where did you get such an exquisite piece of jewelry?"

She responded in character, arching an eyebrow. "My father purchased it, sir."

"Ah." That word said it all. Spoken with a patronizing

twist of his delicately waxed mustache, it had attracted the attention of several people nearby.

"Mr. Atkins." The words, spoken in a distinctly German accent, shattered the chill composure of the desk clerk.

Rebecca followed the stricken clerk's stare. A dark-haired woman just past middle age stood there, dressed primly in black from neck to toe, a large pitcher of beer clutched in her hand.

"Mrs. Wood," he murmured, clearing his throat. "This young lady—"

"The young lady would like a room for the evening, and you are making it terribly difficult for her. Show her up to the suite, as she can obviously afford to rent the entire hotel for the evening. When you return, see me in the office immediately. And bring the brooch with you." With a regal sweep of her skirts, she passed him and walked farther back into the hotel.

Silence surrounded Rebecca as men and women nearby observed her with curiosity and hostility. Rebecca stared after the woman, for a moment truly feeling like the woman from New Orleans who'd never had an ounce of respect in her life, being defended by this paradoxical community matron.

Atkins accepted the brooch and led Rebecca up the stairs and down the hall, deferentially opening doors here, warning her to watch her step there. She grinned to herself. If only the woman knew.

Once inside the suite, she collapsed in an armchair near the window. For the first time, she was able to catalogue the injuries she'd sustained as she shinnied down the tree. Various cuts and scrapes of which she'd been only vaguely aware covered her legs, and her hands were filthy. Her hair tumbled in tangles down her back. No wonder the desk clerk had looked upon her with such disdain.

Crossing the room, she emptied the ceramic pitcher into a basin and quickly scrubbed her body free of the evidence of her flight. Her head began to throb, aching with the persistent hammering of unanswered questions. How, and now, niggling at the recesses of her tired brain, why?

She found a silver-handled hairbrush on the dresser and brushed the tangles from her damp hair. Spotting a mirror hanging above the dresser, inspiration struck her. Staring fully into the mirror, she prayed it would work. She stared stubbornly, unblinking, somehow knowing she wasn't going anywhere. It had to be that mysterious mirror in the Behringer house. Then, she peered at her face, touching the corners of her eyes. It was impossible.

The fine lines that expensive department stores' creams couldn't erase were gone. It was as though the last half of her life had never been inflicted upon her face, and she was gazing into the eyes of herself as an eighteen-year-old girl. Before Janelle MacDonald. Before the countless varieties of Rick Daniels who'd destroyed her trust.

Suddenly sapped of strength, she collapsed in the chair. Maybe a glass of water would help her headache. Setting the brush aside, she ventured into the hall, hoping to find a fresh pitcher of water nearby.

As she stepped into the corridor, she noticed the next door down was ajar. A woman in the room sang a sweet, lilting ballad, and without realizing her curiosity had overcome her, Rebecca peered inside the room.

A young woman sat before a dainty French dressing table, combing her hair. She noticed Rebecca and turned. Black hair billowed around her face, and down the back of her delicate lace dressing gown. Eyes the color of melting snow registered alarm. This woman reminded her of someone.

"I'm sorry," Rebecca quickly apologized, embarrassed at her inadvertent eavesdropping. "I heard you singing. You have a beautiful voice."

A face equally lovely smiled suddenly, a tinge of sadness still coloring her eyes. "Thank you," she said softly. "But I beg of you, don't tell anyone you saw me."

Rebecca was confused. "I . . . I'm not from around

here," she explained. "I must confess, I don't even know who you are."

The woman laughed, and even this was musical. "Oh." Then she rose and walked to Rebecca, extending her hand in the friendly fashion no respectable woman would use in the 1800s. "Then I'm . . . Elizabeth. And you?"

"I'm Rebecca Reynolds," she returned.

"Would you care to come in and share some tea with me?" the woman invited.

Rebecca sighed, thankful for a respite from the emotion of the evening. "Thank you."

The woman led her into the room, then closed the door behind her. "I didn't realize people were still awake upstairs. Benjamin's downstairs." She walked to the silver tea service and poured two cups of tea.

"Benjamin?" Rebecca asked, accepting the cup of tea.

Elizabeth nodded. "My . . . companion. We prefer not to be recognized before we leave for New Orleans."

Nodding, Rebecca understood. "You're an entertainer," she said.

The woman crossed the room and closed the drapes, then nodded. "Yes. Benjamin hates it, but this will be my last trip. He's purchasing a ranch around Dallas, and we're going to settle there, as soon as . . ." At this, her voice trailed away.

Rebecca watched her, and before she knew it, the woman was in tears. Rebecca impulsively rose, putting a hand on her shoulder. "Is there something I can do for you?" She groped to comfort her. "Would you like to talk about it?"

The woman sniffed, then laughed softly. "Talk certainly never helps."

Suddenly the door opened, and a young, pleasant looking man walked into the room with a bouquet of gardenias. Nonplussed to see Rebecca, he paused. Elizabeth crossed the room and slipped her arms around the man's neck.

"Are you all right, my dear?" His voice was soft as he considered Rebecca.

Elizabeth laughed, delightedly raising the white blooms to her nose. "How sweet of you to remember my favorite!"

"And I always will remember, my love."

Remembering her guest, the woman turned. "Benjamin, this is Rebecca Reynolds, a new friend of mine."

His light brown eyes scrutinized Rebecca distrustfully, but he bowed over her hand. "Benjamin Jackson," he murmured. "I'm glad Bessie's made a friend in Jefferson. I do a lot of business through here."

Any other time, Rebecca would have dismissed the common nickname. Now, it was too fresh in her mind. She stared disbelievingly at the face of the young woman who smiled mistily at her. "Not . . . Bessie Moore?"

"So you have heard of me," Bessie said solemnly, placing the flowers in a crystal vase. "I'm sure not all you've heard is true."

A chill stole over Rebecca. She searched for the words to warn Bessie about this man, but the woman was already suspicious of strangers.

Benjamin Jackson? That wasn't the name Jefferson's history had recorded. She struggled to remember. It was an odd one. Perhaps the other man had been innocent after all. She considered the twin threats the woman faced.

"Could you join me in my room for a few moments, Bessie?" Rebecca asked.

"I'm sorry, but Benjamin and I must get some sleep. I've enjoyed meeting you, Rebecca." Bessie tucked Rebecca's arm in hers and led her to the door. "I shall consider you my friend. As Benjamin says, I have no lady friends. I can't afford to trust many people."

Rebecca turned to the woman before she opened the door and hugged her. "Please beware," she whispered. "He will harm you if you give him the chance."

Bessie's face was shadowed with sadness once more. "So you know my husband as well. So do I, my dear," she said quietly. "I am always on my guard. Thank you for the warning, nevertheless. Good night."

Rebecca left Bessie Moore, more confused than ever. Numbly mulling over the chaos beating at her temples, she was unaware of the man in the hall until she opened her door. The next few moments seemed interminable as his steely fingers clamped over her mouth and he shoved her inside the room.

❧ Eight ❧

"Don't make no racket, and I won't hurt you."

Buying time, Rebecca forced herself to relax in his grasp. Assured of her compliance, the man released her. She turned and recognized the blond from the lobby, a strutting peacock of a man who wore flashy riverboat attire.

"Who are you?" she asked calmly.

"J. D. Cullen," he said. "Pleased to make your acquaintance, miss."

She crossed the room and sat in a carved chair. "I don't recall inviting you to my room," she answered coolly.

"You walk into the Excelsior House looking like you been pulled through a weasel hole backwards, toting an expensive fistful of jewelry, then have the nerve to tell me you haven't done this before? Everyone knows how you earned that piece, Missy." He reached inside his coat pocket and withdrew a small sack, tossing it on the dresser. "I'd have to be the world's first fool not to know who you are. Your husband don't ever have no problem with it. Just think of me as a drop-in customer."

Incensed at the man's assumption, Rebecca came to her feet in a flurry of skirts. "You jerk! Get out of this room right now."

"Jerk. That's a queer one," he murmured, smoothly crossing the room to her.

"I know a woman in New Orleans who'd make you the top girl in her house," he boasted. "Heck, you might already know her. Her girls would hate your guts. You're the prettiest little thing I've ever laid eyes on."

"You smell like a distillery," she returned.

"And you're dressed like a damn alley cat. But none of that'll matter once we're in that bed," he spat. Suddenly out of patience, he gathered her kicking form in his arms and tossed her on the wide bed, joining her half a moment later.

"What the hell do you think you're doing?" she gasped, her breath leaving her as he landed on her. She struggled against him, scrambling for the edge of the bed, but the soft feather mattress offered no leverage. Cullen threw his bony frame over hers and crushed her lips with a hard mouth.

Rebecca's nails scraped deep lines across his face, enraging him. With one fist, he split the demure neckline of her dress to the waist. Rebecca recoiled as he suddenly lapsed into a backwoods twang.

"Goddangit, I'm tired of this nonsense. Quit playin' out this faintin' maiden routine. You prob'ly been doin' it since you were old enough to have a body to tell of. I know I ain't been the first, honey, but before we're through, I swear you'll wish I was the last."

"I hardly think so." The voice at the door was quiet, mellow, and surprisingly, amused.

Rebecca collapsed as the weight of the man suddenly left her. Lifting her head, too stunned to do more, she looked at the two men. Oh, boy.

With a mixture of relief and dread, she flinched as Garitson Behringer smashed his fist into the stunned man's face, then jerked him from the floor. "Get the hell out of here."

Cullen glared at Rebecca, but had the presence of mind to collect his money from the dresser before he left the room.

Behringer closed the door behind the man, then took several deep breaths, his hands on his hips. Finally, he turned without looking at Rebecca and walked to the window. Sitting in the chair, he crossed his booted feet casually and rested them on the window ledge.

"Nice room," he murmured conversationally.

"How did you find me?" she whispered, sitting up in the bed.

"How much did it cost you?"

Unable to answer, Rebecca rummaged for a solution. Behringer broke the silence. "How many men did you entertain to pay for it?"

"How many *what?*"

Rising, he turned to her, that same steady calm evident in the depths of his dark eyes. "One? Two? Three?" He chuckled mirthlessly, moving toward the bed with maddening, steady slowness. Just short of the bed, he glanced at his pocket watch, puzzling it over.

"A rather short time for even one memorable ride," he murmured. "Then again, with you I can't imagine it being otherwise."

"It wasn't like that at all," she snapped, her patience reaching its limit. She looked down at her dress, then murmured, bemused, "Can you believe it? The clown ripped . . . my . . . bodice." She shook her head and sighed. "He thought I was someone else."

"Oh?" His dark eyebrow quirked sharply as he moved closer to the bed, leaning against a post.

"Then perhaps you had gold tucked behind your ears before," he theorized. "When you left my room, you took nothing but my robe, wrapped around that deliciously wet body." His eyes touched on her hands, where she clutched the torn fabric together.

"It wasn't—" Rebecca began once more.

Behringer sat on the edge of the bed, nonchalantly bending a knee toward her. "I think it was probably exactly like that," he murmured, trailing his forefinger along her chin. "You wouldn't have had much trouble finding a willing customer."

With gentle fingers, he turned her face this way and that,

inspecting. "A young girl, not even twenty, in a town like this. Eyes like a kitten, and the nature to match. Skin soft as a child's. Mouth pleading to be kissed." Behringer's face hovered over hers, so closely that she tasted the faint sweetness of pipe tobacco. Entranced by the subtle flavor of his seduction, Rebecca was transfixed.

His glance slowly moved down. "And a body God made for only one man. A man smart enough to recognize its incredible beauty." He paused, and his dark eyes were troubled.

Rebecca was moved at the intensity of his statement, terrified by the madness of everything that had happened tonight. The tears slipped down her cheeks before she could stop them, and her own emotional reaction irritated her.

Behringer made an inarticulate sound of exasperation, then drew her into his warmth. "Why'd you do it, little witch?"

"Stop calling me that!"

"On the contrary, it's an appropriate name. You vanish as mysteriously as you appear. You rent expensive hotel rooms without money. You bewitch unsuspecting fools."

"I didn't invite him in here," she defended herself, irritated at the nickname he gave her, disturbed by his nearness. He was so disarmingly male, so alarmingly alive.

"I wasn't talking about that particular fool," he murmured.

"He just came in behind me when I walked in the room."

Behringer laughed softly. "I meant the brooch. That's a priceless heirloom from my father's family in Germany. Everyone within a hundred miles has heard of the Behringer brooch, and half of Jefferson has it committed to memory. You might as well have worn a sign saying 'I've robbed the town's finest family.' "

Rebecca's mouth fell open. "How did you find out?"

He drew a thick strand of hair away from her face. "As soon as Kate Wood saw it, she sent someone over to the house. She's an old friend of my mother's. She won't open her mouth about it, but you can bet Atkins will." He placed the strand of hair behind her ear, and it immediately fell forward once more. "Just tell me why."

"I'm sorry . . . Mr. Behringer. I didn't have an alternative. I don't know anyone here, and I'm stranded without any cash. And I can't go home."

Behringer released her abruptly, as though she'd slapped him, and leaned once more against the post. He folded his arms and gazed at her wryly. "Mr. Behringer, huh?" He touched his beard thoughtfully. "Maybe I could adopt you."

Glowering at him, she struggled to straighten her clothes. "You bet, you doddering old geezer. I saw that child you call your fiancée."

"Ah. The lovely Vivian. A face to launch a thousand ships, and a temper to send them in the other direction."

Shaking his head, Behringer murmured, "That Katy. Her mind has as many twists and turns as the old bayou out there. How'd you meet her?"

She shrugged, knowing this misunderstanding was her only assurance of respectability. "Does it matter?"

"I suppose not. You must love a good joke as much as the rest of us."

Rebecca's lips twisted. "I value a sense of humor, but I prefer not to be the punch line."

A hint of confusion skittered through his eyes. "Punch line?"

Rebecca shook her head. "Never mind."

His eyes sparkled, and for a long moment, their gazes locked. Then, he casually inspected the room. "Well, we have the room for the night. A delightfully appointed one, I must admit. All the comforts of home," he said, his eyes finally resting on her. "And yet . . . so many more convenient luxuries."

"Oh, give me a break," Rebecca said, scrambling once more to get out of the bed, disturbed by the inevitable heat of him. She inched away from him. "I can work in your house to reimburse you—"

"I can imagine nothing more pleasant," he agreed, advancing upon her as she slowly backed away until the wall pressed against her back.

Behringer moved closer still. He calmly placed a hand on either side of her head, ruthlessly, deliberately branding her with his nearness, his size, his intensity. His sheer, unruffled composure. A hot, abrupt sizzle of awareness swept her.

She met his eyes evenly, noticing the glint of amusement lurking there. Desperately she fought the desire that held her in its grip, threatening to overpower her. This man was a deadly mix of everything she loved most in a man. It was terrifying.

"Are you quite certain you're from Shreveport? You don't sound like a young lady from that region."

Rebecca hesitated, wondering what idiom she might blurt next. "Where do I sound like I'm from?" she asked at last, with the slightest edge of challenge.

"Another planet, maybe," he remarked dryly. "Though it's English you're speaking, it's a smoother-flowing form, less concerned with a sentence's details. And from time to time, strange expressions creep in." His gaze raked her torn bodice.

His attention required elsewhere, Behringer abandoned his curiosity, lingering instead over the pale, smooth mounds of flesh promised with Rebecca's next breath.

Forcing an affected and, with any luck, slightly Victorian boredom into her tone, Rebecca said, "I see that regardless of the cut of one's clothes, in Jefferson you're all a bunch of . . . ill-mannered ruffians."

He chuckled out loud, enjoying her prim rebuff. "And you were doing so well with the gentleman from Shreveport, after all. I shouldn't have intruded."

"What's the difference?" she asked, glancing at the flex of muscle in his forearms less than a whisper away from her cheek. A faint sheen of the evening's warmth gleamed there, and for a wild moment, she yearned to taste that sheer male strength. Somehow she managed to find her elusive wits. "Force is force. Men who have so little control over their urges that they can't understand it when a woman says no."

Behringer sobered, tracing the surface of her chin, the tip of his thumb not quite grazing her face. "You don't seem to realize I'm inexperienced when it comes to force," he said, his voice silky.

Behringer's thumb followed the willowy column of her throat, a shadow of a caress that sent a sultry tingle throbbing through her veins in the wake of his touch. He brushed his thumbnail over the delicate valley at the base of her throat.

"If I wanted you now," he murmured, kissing her temple, "you'd be in that bed, and most willingly." A strong, tanned finger delicately traced the torn line of her bodice. Dynamic sparks followed the fleeting trail of his finger, and she found herself yearning for him to part the fabric.

"If I were so inclined, Rebecca," he said, "you'd beg me to love you in ways that would shock you to the tips of your dainty toes."

She didn't doubt him.

Tantalizingly skillful fingertips slipped downward between the ragged edges of Rebecca's torn bodice as if it weren't there, then rested just below the swell of her breasts. Her eyes fluttered shut in frustration. A Victorian woman would not respond the way she was responding, she forced herself to remember. Not a nice one, anyhow. A woman of her generation should've been too offended by his cockiness. Rebecca, on the other hand, was entranced.

She arched toward him, her body begging for his bold stroke, unashamed to admit that he was right, wanting nothing but to feel his abandoned touch, his freely given lovemaking. *She didn't know him!*

"And if I loved you," he said, his whisper as mystical and reverent as the moonlight that poured in the window, "the only force between us, darlin', would be that same one you're feeling right now."

His dark gaze met hers, then dipped to rest on her mouth. He drew a slow, deep breath, and she watched as his tongue slipped over his lower lip. He closed his eyes.

When he opened them once more, that rakish sparkle of mischievousness stirred within the smoky depths of his eyes as he raised his head and carefully tucked her bodice together. "But rest assured," he said pleasantly, "I will never force you." And with that, he returned to the window.

Released from Behringer's firm grasp, Rebecca slid at least four inches before she caught herself. Glaring at him in disbelief, she wrestled with the rage that rippled through her veins, its raw power mingling with the heady arousal there.

"Get in the bed, Rebecca."

She turned back the covers, slipped off her shoes, then climbed into the bed. "Where are you—"

"Go to sleep." Behringer's voice was tight. "Now."

A narcotic tingle suffused her skin, the effect of Behringer's near-touch, and she forced herself to lie still, torn between conflicting desires. She turned over in the bed, slammed her fist into the pillow, and tried to sleep. Fear, virtually alien to Rebecca, stole through her. Not of the man by the window, remaining here for the sole reason of protecting her, but the strange reality into which she'd projected herself, through her journalist's curiosity and some unexplainable, supernatural force.

Rebecca Reynolds, a thirty-four-year-old, widely traveled professional woman of the twentieth century had looked into a mirror of the 1870s and been transported back to that time. How?

Why?!

And she'd thought the magenta-washed steamy sunsets of her stories were hard to buy into. She thought of Behringer, sprawled in a chair by the window, standing guard while she slept. His protection offered comfort, but history's harsh realities frightened her. If she was up on her historical trivia, the phone had only been invented last year, this time zone. Joseph Lister's antiseptic surgery was still revolutionary. What if she got one of her migraines? She smirked at the thought, which reeked of the twentieth century. Better instead, she told herself, to hope she didn't get polio.

Sighing, she turned once more in bed, facing the opposite wall. The wall Behringer had pressed her against as he ruthlessly tempted her. Memories of those brief, endless moments taunted her as mercilessly as the man had. Behringer apparently presented far more lethal a threat than any disease without cure.

A desolate ache went through her, and she wanted to share the story with him; certainly he would believe her, would know the solution to this baffling mess, would devise a way to send her back to the place where he was only a dim shadow in a past she was never meant to know. She raised her head off the warmth of the pillows to watch him in the moonlight that shone in the window, glinting in his black hair. A betraying warmth for the enigmatic charmer stole over her, softening the harsh reality of this brutal niche in time.

❧ Nine ❧

Clanging, clanging, and more clanging. Reaching toward the nightstand, Rebecca groped for the alarm clock. It wasn't there. Opening drowsy eyes, Rebecca peeked out from beneath the sheet and raised her chin from the lilac-fragrant down pillow. As she struggled to blink away the remnants of sleep, the events of the day before came rushing back. Slowly, those sounds ricocheting in her abused mind gathered into focus until she groaned and buried her face once more in the pillow.

The ringing went on in the street below, along with other nameless noises of a bustling Saturday morning in Jefferson in 1876. The clop of horses' hooves beat an erratic rhythm along the red brick streets, and a boy was selling hot pastries just below her window.

She threw her legs over the side of the bed, then jumped at the sudden tap on the door. "Who's there?"

"Behringer."

"Come in."

The carved wooden door opened and Behringer entered the room. By candlelight he was tantalizing; in the bold honesty of sunlight, his stark virility was arresting.

A crisp white shirt, gray slacks and coat, and a wine-colored vest comprised his morning dress. His black hair curled softly away from his face, and a sprinkle of gray that wasn't readily visible the night before heightened his sensuality. He crossed the room with an armful of packages, depositing them on the table.

"Do you normally sleep until dinnertime?"

"Only when I'm up all night writing." She compressed her lips as the words slipped out.

Too late. "Are you a writer, then?"

Waving her hand vaguely, she laughed as she stood. "Oh, all ladies keep journals, don't they?"

He removed his coat and tossed it on the foot of the bed. "Not the ones I know. Katy would rather have her ears pulled off than spend five minutes engaged in either reading or writing. As well you should know. I think the toughest reading Vivian does is that fashion book. Godfrey's Ladywear, or whatever. What do you enjoy reading?"

Casually, Behringer sat in a chair before the fireplace, crossing his feet before him, waiting for her answer.

"Oh, anything I can get my hands on." She joined him in the sitting area.

"We have a very current library at home. Feel free to use it whenever you like while you're with us."

She nodded. "That's generous of you. But . . ."

Behringer waited patiently, and the uncanny, incomprehensible truth stood poised on the end of her tongue. How could she tell him when she didn't understand herself?

His hard gaze probed into her defenses, seeking answers. When he spoke, however, his voice was soft. "Care to tell me about it?"

She laughed. A cheerless sound. "I can't."

"I see." He continued to focus that searching look on her. Folding his hands across his lap, he ran one long finger absently across the back of the other hand. Rebecca watched his actions, fascinated at the sensuous stroke of his fingertip, noticing the immaculate grooming of those squarely shaped fingers. And yet, she remembered the slightly rough texture of the fingertips as they'd brushed across her body. The hands of a gentleman who didn't turn up his nose at the prospect of hard work.

Almost immediately she saw the scars snaking from the backs of his hands toward his fingertips, a dull mauve that blended so well with the dark tan she hadn't noticed it the night before. Then she realized his motion was an unconscious effort of habit employed to disguise the scars, one which only served to draw one's attention there. She was roused from her inspection when one of those hands gestured toward the table.

"I've purchased a few things for you. Ready-made, but like I always say, better a ready-made bodice than a ripped one."

Rebecca smiled at his gesture. "That's kind of you."

A dark eyebrow raised in disinterest. "Kindness is a virtue I lack. Katy put you in a damn compromising position. Now," he said matter-of-factly, "what am I to do with you?"

Rebecca's contentment melted away. "That's quite a question."

Behringer leaned forward silently, his elbows resting on his knees, and turned his face to consider her seriously. "How old are you?" he asked in sudden dismay.

Rebecca noticed amber lights in his dark eyes as he scrutinized her face. "A year older than Katy," she said, her face warming at the lie.

"Jesus," he said softly. "You're only eighteen years old?"

Disturbed, Behringer rose and walked to the fireplace, then rested an elbow on the mantel. "I thought . . . I knew you were young, but . . . in the lamplight, you looked . . . you acted . . . my God."

Rebecca sat silently trying to figure out what he was thinking in his Victorian male mind.

Behringer spoke without looking at her. "We'll get you on the first boat headed back to Shreveport."

"No!" Rebecca said. "I can't."

Behringer's expression was distant. "Why not?"

She looked at her hands. "There are very good reasons, but I can't tell you. My parents would never accept me."

At this, Behringer chortled without amusement. "If you think to trap me into marriage—"

Rebecca could've groaned, but decided against it. "I do not," she said. "I merely cannot go to Shreveport. Nor am I asking you for a solution to my predicament."

Behringer paced casually before the fireplace, staring at the floor. "Nevertheless, I spent the night wondering what kind of mental ailment my sister suffers to put you in this predicament. If you can't return home, I fear we're back to the original plan."

"Plan?"

"You would make a suitable companion for my mother. Katy and my mother are very close. They were constantly in one another's company before Katy left for school. She's the easiest woman in the world to get along with, but she has few friends outside the family.

"Papa is an influential man, yet Mama has no use for the women of Jefferson. I think it goes clear back to New Orleans." Behringer frowned.

"What about Vivian?"

"What about her?" His face was expressionless.

The clumsy words were impossible to retrieve. Now, she stuttered, vainly wishing this man's thoughts were more easily revealed. "I . . . would think Vivian and your mother would be very close."

He resumed his pacing, his hands clasped behind his back, his tone bored. "That's because you don't know Vivian. Vivian has no interest in any of the things my mother holds dear. Her mission in life is to discover the finest bonnet known to mankind." Then he stopped and stared pointedly at Rebecca. "I'm asking you to take Katy's place in my mother's life while she's gone."

Rebecca hesitated. *I'd love to take the post, dear Mr. Behringer, but I don't know when I'll be popping back to the twentieth century again. . . .*

"Look," she began. "I don't want to sound ungrateful, but you don't know me from Adam. Why on earth would you take me into your house? And what makes you think your mother is open to the idea?"

"Mama's always out for an adventure," he went on. "I think you're just what she needs."

She sighed. For the time being, she had little alternative. If she'd learned anything in her life, it was that young women in the 1800s weren't safe on the frontier. Last night had confirmed ten years of academic research. Sophisticated though Jefferson believed herself to be, it was still the frontier, only a decade after the end of the War Between the States.

"Your mother sounds like a fascinating woman. I hope I don't bore her."

Behringer raised an eyebrow. "I hardly think she'll be bored. Now, unless you plan to wear a pinned-together gown all day, I suggest you dress. I'm starving."

He left the room, and Rebecca untied the packages he'd left, examining their contents: a soft rose gown with cream-colored lace at the sleeves and neckline and maroon ribbon trim at the waist; a pair of slippers; and, finally, lacy underthings which seemed to have been fashioned from the morning mist. Stripping off the ruined gray gown, she quickly splashed her face with water, then dressed. As she finished, there was a brief, quiet tap at the door.

It was Behringer. They walked downstairs to the front desk, and as he paid her bill, Rebecca waited by the front door. Before she realized what was happening, strong, hard fingers were encircling her forearm, dragging her outside.

A person can't stand still in this town, she thought.

"You're going to regret the day you left me, Bessie."

Turning to face her abductor, Rebecca gasped. His brown eyes registered surprise instantly. "God in heaven," he murmured. "I'm so sorry, I thought—"

"Abe Rothschild," she whispered, remembering the Yankee face that would, in another hundred years, grace the walls of more rooms in Jefferson than any citizen of the

Southern town. Ironic, she thought, that Jefferson's most no-
torious historical figures had never lived in the town.

History had, of course, been correct. Bessie Moore's husband was Abe Rothschild, not the soft-spoken Benjamin
she'd met. A cold anguish crept over her for the unprepared
Bessie.

"You know me?" he asked, surprised.

"Oh, I've heard of you."

"Then you must know my wife."

"I just met her . . . a few days ago," Rebecca said, in-
venting as she went. "She was distraught when I saw her.
Her companion, it seems, deserted her. When I spoke with
her, she was on her way to Cincinnati to find you. To somehow reconcile with you."

Rebecca hoped to give Bessie a few days to elude Rothschild, and she was amazed when tears filled his eyes.

"I . . . I can hardly believe it." He cleared his throat,
steadying his voice. "God knows I don't deserve it. She has
every right to hate me, but I swear I've changed. My father
and I have recently reconciled, and I . . . I would like for
us to have a family," he confessed. Then he laughed. "I can't
believe I'm telling you all this."

Neither could she. The sensitivity of his face didn't match
that of a cold-blooded killer.

"Rebecca?"

The quiet voice behind her startled her from her incomprehensible conversation. Behringer stood on the wooden
sidewalk in front of the Excelsior, staring blandly at her.

"Are you ready?" Behringer asked coolly.

Rothschild laughed. "I must explain, sir, that I mistook
your wife for my wife."

Behringer laughed tonelessly. "Today's just your day for
mistakes. Shall we go, Rebecca?"

Helplessly confused, Rebecca watched as Rothschild
pressed her hand. "Thank you so much, miss. I apologize
again for disturbing you."

As the attractive man stepped into his carriage, Rebecca

remembered standing at the Oakwood Cemetery, weeping over Bessie's grave. And she had the chilling solution to her impossible riddle.

Rebecca was here to accomplish one purpose—to prevent Bessie Moore's savage, pointless death, at the hands of yet another savage, selfish man. She still didn't know how it had happened, and it no longer mattered, but somehow the intensity of her sorrow over Bessie's death had touched a softhearted romantic fate and enabled Rebecca to make a difference in this merciless past she'd rewritten so haphazardly and evaded for so long. This time, she thought with an overwhelming sense of purpose, she would rewrite the past so that she affected a life with more permanence than mere afternoon entertainment.

❧ Ten ❧

Behringer led Rebecca into a restaurant across the street, and if rude stares counted for anything, she might've had a spare head growing on her shoulder. The seductive aromas of the restaurant awakened her slumbering appetite. When their plates arrived, she completely forgot her companion as she began devouring the food.

"Why, if it isn't the little lady from New Orleans whose daddy gave her a piece of jewelry identical to the Behringer brooch!"

The vividly familiar feminine drawl dripped just over Rebecca's shoulder as she stuffed a forkful of baked ham into her mouth. Glumly wondering if she was destined to always see this woman at her worst, Rebecca began chewing like a squirrel worrying an acorn, refusing to acknowledge her.

Behringer rose, laying his napkin alongside his plate. Swiftly, he steered Vivian away from the table to a discreet corner nearby.

Vivian Fairchild had to be the most beautiful piece of fluff that was ever set on the planet, Rebecca observed absently as she chewed the ham. She stopped chewing as the woman's voice grew louder, carrying to every restaurant patron within ten feet of her.

"Companion for your mother? What kind of a ninny do

you take me for? I'll not have you making a fool of me right underneath my own roof!"

Rebecca swallowed at long last. The girl would make him a wonderful jealous wife.

Behringer led Vivian outside, gripping her arm firmly. Knowing that her gawking was only prolonging the ordeal, Rebecca continued her meal. What a little twit.

After a few minutes Behringer returned to the table, and she risked a glance at him. His expression was hard, and she knew that the simplest question would invite unwarranted fury. The meal passed in silence.

When they stepped out into the afternoon sunshine, the frown on Behringer's forehead seemed to relax. She waited in front of the restaurant for someone else to snatch her as he fetched the buggy. As he helped her in, she glanced into his eyes. "Are you all right?"

He grinned wryly. "I'm dandy, honey. You're a blithering idiot, though."

Rebecca turned pointedly away from Behringer, heat flooding her as his taut thigh met hers full length. The aroma of leather and horses and the red clay road mingled with his clean, masculine scent, concocting a potent, earthy perfume. She smoothed her skirts as he clicked the horses into motion. "And what, I wonder, have I done now?"

"Darlin'," he said wryly. "Why didn't you just stay in Katy's room, like I asked you to?"

Rebecca fidgeted at the directness of his question. *Because,* she silently answered him, *I was terrified; have I mentioned to you that I won't be born for another eighty years?*

"You had other problems."

"Isn't that noble of you." His face once more grew hard as the buggy went down Austin Street. "You don't have the slightest idea what the hell's going on, do you?"

She shook her head irritably, searching his inscrutable face for clues.

"Half the damn town knows we spent last night together. The other half knows you're wearing clothes—underwear, for

God's sake!—that I picked out for you. Vivian has friends who live in both halves. Need I say it more plainly?"

In a bizarre aberration of logic that fit well these days, Rebecca found herself pleased beyond imagination at the idea of this dark, brooding man choosing dainty unmentionables for her.

"We didn't do anything," she mumbled.

Behringer's eyes blazed as he looked down at her. "I can't decide whether you're the most passionate woman alive, or a goddamned virgin. You must've grown up in the damn swamp not to be able to add it all up."

She bristled. "Everything I add up points to the undisputable fact that you're acting like a six-year-old brat."

"You ought to be a hell of a lot more worried about it than I am," he chuckled.

"I don't have a jealous fiancée ready to rip out my beard," she retorted.

Turning the horses away from town, Behringer shook his head. "I repeat, you're a blithering idiot. Shall I paint a picture for you?"

Irritated to be pegged as a slow-witted child, Rebecca muttered sullenly, "Paint away, Leonardo."

"A young lady alone in a town where lonely young ladies don't survive, given an alternative to an existence of pure hell. And she doesn't give one bloody damn about what people think. Do you want to be known as my mistress?" He looked down at her, his eyes black in their fury.

"If that's the case, I'm going to stop worrying about it. I'll spend my time in more worthwhile endeavors, like laying a firm foundation for their rumors. But once my mother hears such rumors, I can't guarantee what her reaction's going to be. Who am I kidding? Mother'd whittle a hickory switch to use on me," he murmured, shaking his head at his sudden lack of control over his life. "And once those rumors take root, going back to your gentle life in Shreveport won't be an option."

Rebecca's anger burned and fused with shame. "Excuse me

if I'm not preoccupied with choosing matching party outfits. Survival seemed more important to me last night," she said, tilting her head, peering up at him as if she couldn't determine his species. "And just for the record, I wasn't the one who decided to stay the whole night in someone else's room, despite the fact that I was engaged to a jealous featherbrain."

"No, you were the one who decided to stay in the Excelsior House all by yourself, after stealing the most famous brooch in the region and then presenting it as payment for a room less than a mile away. There's some intuitive reasoning, straight from the mouth of Aristotle."

Rebecca fumed silently, her face fast approaching purple. He was right, damn him, and she hated that worse than she hated him.

"Well?"

"Well what?" She shouted the words, her face burning.

"Well, what shall it be? My mother's companion or my mistress? Miss Fairchild assumes the worst, so it makes no difference to me."

"How considerate of you."

"I don't give a damn what she thinks."

"Yes, I can see that the theme here is how little her opinion means." A sudden tightness at the back of her throat appalled Rebecca.

Behringer drew the horses to an abrupt halt in the deserted road. "Pay attention," he enunciated, his eyes rich with rage. "I don't care in the least what Vivian thinks. I do, however, care a great deal what people think about my sister's friends. How you could let the little idiot put you in such a goddamned moronic spot is beyond me."

Behringer raised the straps and slapped the horses' flanks. The animals cantered down the road, and suddenly, Rebecca didn't know why she was angry. Unless . . .

Unless, she thought in misery, it was because she knew she would never have the right to even kiss this impossible man, could never hold him close to her, and should certainly never foster the sort of dreams he had resurrected within her.

And what the hell was she doing entertaining all these childish romantic fantasies in the first place? Yes, she had plenty to be angry about.

Damn him. Why was he marrying a woman with whom he shared no common interests, whom obviously he could hardly tolerate? It was something she would never ask him. She didn't want to hear the logic that made such a situation not only possible, but the only acceptable one. While she was on the topic of blaming him, why did he have to be 120 years older than she was?

"Mr. Behringer," she said, lightly adopting a ladylike Victorian drawl, "I shall be the most proper young woman you've ever known, and this Vivian of yours and I shall become great friends. She shall cease to be jealous of me at all, I'm afraid."

Behringer turned, watching her as though she'd turned into a cotton boll. "Is that so."

"As a matter of fact. And you swear entirely too much. A world of adjectives awaits you, sir."

"How the hell are you planning to accomplish this miracle? The first minute I leave you alone with her, you'll be reduced to a pile of shredded satin."

"I'm sure Miss Fairchild is not the sort of lady to resort to such measures. On the contrary, we shall be friends."

"I see. And do you plan on using a pistol to keep her from ripping out that gorgeous head of hair?"

Rebecca waved a hand at him. "How can you speak of your fiancée in such a disparaging fashion?"

Suddenly Behringer burst out in laughter. "I can see she's going to have a hard time of it, rattling that cool of yours. I get your point. Just watch it with that inane blather you've suddenly begun spouting."

As they approached the house, Behringer swore. "She's here."

Rebecca glanced at the house, noticing the dainty buggy tethered outside the front gate. "Give her the benefit of the doubt. If the woman's going to be your wife, you'll have to learn to trust her."

He turned the buggy toward the stables. "When I can predict a tornado in May, I'll put my faith in Vivian Fairchild."

Behringer put the leather straps into a young boy's hand when they stopped at the stables. "How's your mother, Amos?"

The boy beamed at Behringer's friendly greeting. "She just fine, Mr. Behringer. She makin' me a new shirt fo' my birthday, sir. It the fines' thing I ever have seen."

Rebecca unwillingly noticed Behringer's gentleness with the boy, but remained silent as she followed him toward the back of the house. As they approached the door, she heard a male voice, soothing a sobbing woman.

"Oh, hell."

Vivian Fairchild stood in the parlor, sobbing softly in the arms of a man who was an older version of Garitson. She knew before they were introduced that this was Jacob Behringer, the man who'd braved a frontier with a young tavern girl from New Orleans and forged a reputation as a leader in the Jefferson community.

Jacob Behringer's face darkened to an undisguised hatred as he glared at Rebecca. "How dare you!" he whispered, his eyes black as they swept Rebecca with open contempt. "How dare you come into my home. You are not welcome here."

Startled at the stranger's pointed, undeserved wrath, Rebecca swallowed. "I . . ." she began weakly. Her chin quivered, and she clamped her mouth shut. She refused to bring herself down to that spoiled child's level.

"Papa!" Behringer exploded. "I will not have Miss Reynolds spoken to in that fashion."

Jacob turned that scorching gaze upon his son, and for a charged moment, each of the two men dared the other to speak. Finally, the elder man's fury gave way to righteous indignation. "You have the gall to take her defense against your betrothed?"

"Miss Reynolds is a close friend of Katy's," Behringer said coolly. "They met in Shreveport last summer, and they have been in correspondence since then. Katy arranged to have Miss Reynolds keep Mama company in her absence. She wanted to surprise Mama, and I promised to keep her secret."

Behringer stalked to the window and jammed his hands inside his trousers pockets. His voice betrayed none of the emotion in his movements. "But if this nonsense continues, I'll simply have to accompany Miss Reynolds back to her home, and Mama will be terribly lonely. Unless Miss Fairchild would care to spend her days with her," he proposed impulsively, glancing at the blonde.

Rebecca watched Behringer closely, a smile twitching at her lips. What a gloriously shameless liar! His skill at fiction approached her own.

Vivian batted her eyelashes helplessly, and Rebecca noticed the vengeful shrew in the restaurant had vanished, leaving this harmless ditz instead.

Jacob Behringer peered at his son, unconvinced. His eyes rested on Vivian before speaking, then he plunged on. "You slept in her arms last night, Garitson. I will not have Vivian insulted."

"It isn't Miss Fairchild who's being slandered," Behringer retorted. "Katy had reserved the suite for Miss Reynolds until she was introduced to the family, but her chaperone was unable to accompany her. She made the entire trip alone, all to do Katy a favor.

"Once she arrived, she was shaken, tired, and alone. And it was too late to arrange another chaperone. I stayed on the other side of a locked door, in a separate bedchamber. And, frankly, I'm bored with this discussion. Miss Fairchild may be accustomed to discussing sleeping arrangements in the company of men, but Miss Reynolds is not. Last night was difficult enough without this." He returned to Rebecca's side.

"Are you all right, my dear?" he asked solicitously.

Rebecca patted his arm, summoning a pale smile. "I'm fine, really I am."

"Where's Mama?" Behringer asked his father.

"The garden," the man responded tersely.

Behringer's words were equally clipped. "Then if you would excuse me, I'll take Miss Reynolds to her room. I'm sure she understands that you'll apologize to her later, Papa."

Without further explanation, Behringer led Rebecca away from a confused Jacob Behringer and an unavenged Vivian.

Inside Katy's room, Rebecca wasn't surprised to find a grin sparkling in Behringer's eyes. He closed the door silently.

"Well," she said dryly, "aren't you worried about soiling my name by being behind closed doors with me?"

He moved inevitably closer to her, and his hands rested on her shoulders. "I was worried that I wouldn't make it inside first," he murmured.

He hesitated, then rested his cheek against the top of her head. She unwisely allowed him to. "And it worries me that after it's all said and done, I don't give a damn about your reputation. I should, you know. My priorities suddenly have a mind of their own."

"I never imagined such a respectable man would be such a smooth liar," Rebecca said, moving away from him to stand by the window. "I'll be sure to remember that."

He was silent as he approached her, and she felt his warmth before she heard the soft huskiness of his voice. "You smell like a spring dawn."

A delicious shiver crept over her as Behringer lightly brushed her shoulder. "Are the garments as lovely on you as I imagined?"

"This is insane."

"No," he said, turning her to him. A disturbing heat kindled in his gaze. "Not touching you is insane. You're the freshest, loveliest woman I've ever known. You make me forget things I shouldn't forget. You remind me . . ." His eyes darkened, and the troubling poignance there disappeared. He abruptly withdrew from her, walking to the door. "I'll let Mama know you're here. Get some rest."

Rebecca watched him leave, and she knew as surely as if a distinct female form had walked into the room, Garitson Behringer was in love with another woman. And it wasn't Vivian Fairchild.

❧ Eleven ❧

Garitson Behringer stood on the bank of the Big Cypress Bayou, watching the steamboats pass. He was late for a meeting with Silas Fairchild, but he didn't much care. The August day was hotter than the tip of a rattle-snake's tongue, and Behringer's state of mind was nearly as venomous.

Dropping down on a grassy patch beside the red clay, Behringer plucked a thin straw and idly·chewed it. He had a whole new set of problems, least of which was the economic recovery Silas Fairchild sought. He thought of his future fa-ther-in-law, the widely respected town leader and financier. Silas was protecting his own scrawny ass, Behringer thought wryly. He was suffering as much as everybody else in Jefferson.

Staring at the other side of the bayou, he wondered about the young girl who'd turned his life upside down within the span of sixteen hours. His father was furious, his fiancée was apoplectic, and if he knew the fair city of Jefferson, three-fourths of his closest friends had already heard of his latest indiscretion. The irony of his innocence of this particular misdeed made it all the more precious.

Vivian wanted this girl on the first train back to Shreve-port. His better judgment agreed, for the first time, with Viv-ian's reasoning. But somehow, sound reasoning paled beside the temptation offered in Katy's friend. Behringer frowned at the memory of his young sister, less than half his age. Rebecca Reynolds, the girl sleeping in his father's home at this very moment, did not behave like a girl Katy's age. She had an unnerving wisdom and self-assurance that made him feel as if he were the eighteen-year-old.

What difference did it really make if he married Vivian? he wondered suddenly, with a schoolboy's peevish reluctance.

Of course, there was nothing to keep him from having them both, he thought, arguing his own point. Doubtless, the girl would be willing enough, given the proper persuading. Within her slumbered yearnings which, given a gentle rousing, would awaken into passions he'd once only imagined knowing in a woman.

The memory of last night came over him without warning, and he closed his eyes. Brief glimpses of her creamy flesh innocently yearning for his touch, scored indelibly on his memory, taunted him. You certainly know how to slice out a piece of hell for yourself, fella, he thought wryly.

Where did she come from?

He thought of Katy, and a smile crossed his face. He hoped to God she'd never grow up, for it was that childlike impishness that gave her a charm the right man would fall in love with daily. If nothing else, that convinced him of the friendship Katy and Rebecca certainly shared, for they were cut from the same warp.

Tossing a pebble into the murky waters, he reminded himself to send a telegram of thanks to Katy for the entertainment. He imagined how horrified she would be to think her trick had backfired, her friend successfully compromised. Assured that this would repay her scheming, he smiled.

Where the hell did she come from?

As though conjured from his fantasies, summoned from an abyss of longing that seemed to have dwelled within him forever, she'd materialized in his life, her soft curves sparkling damply in the candles' light, her eyes shining with something he'd waited nearly forty years to see. Dangling the straw in the water, he considered releasing it, to watch it float downstream, out of his grasp forever.

He swore at the unholy hunger eating at him. He wasn't satisfied with a beautiful, brainless bride whose father would unwittingly give Behringer an ironic authority. Desperately needed authority, if he were to succeed at solving the seven-year-old mystery that had turned his life into a living hell. Now, he desperately desired a simple schoolgirl with the wisdom of a woman much older, to whom he could offer nothing in return. Nothing at all.

Behringer rose and dusted off his trousers, then pulled out his watch and frowned. He'd spent a full forty-five minutes daydreaming like a schoolboy, and no doubt Fairchild had already left his office. Walking over the footbridge, Behringer reached Fairchild's office on Market Street in less than five minutes. As he walked into the gray building, he yanked off his coat.

"In here, Garitson." The voice called from the inner room. "You're late."

Behringer walked into Fairchild's private office and sat in the chair opposite him.

"I'm moving the meeting Friday night back an hour so it doesn't conflict with the party."

"The expert on iron ore I've engaged was planning to be there at eight," Behringer said, irritated that for all practical purposes, Vivian Fairchild ran the town. "I don't know that he can make it any later."

Fairchild jotted unimpressive figures in a ledger, and he spoke without looking up. "He'll make it if he wants his fee."

Behringer sighed. "Nine it is."

"I hear you've distressed my daughter."

"The poor girl would be jealous of her shadow," Behringer said with a scowl, "if not for its unfashionably dark complexion."

"Who is the girl?"

Behringer was not taken in by the amusement twinkling

in Fairchild's silver-blue eyes. Though the man seemingly made light of his daughter, he adored every frivolous fiber of her nature.

"She's a friend of Katy's. She's staying as a companion to my mother while Katy's away at school."

He despised the sound of the excuse given Fairchild, the words of a schoolboy explaining how he'd dropped his books in the bayou. The sentence had rolled smoothly off his tongue each time he'd uttered it, but this time, it stuck. He wanted nothing more than to tell Silas Fairchild that his daughter was an impudent child, deservant of a good spanking. Of course, he didn't. Until he was firmly in control of Fairchild & Sons, Behringer had no intention of proving himself to be anything other than the loving fiancé.

Since he'd had five daughters, Silas had begun searching for the appropriate successor as soon as his eldest daughter, Vivian, was fourteen. And seven years ago, when Garitson Behringer became the most favorable marriage prospect in the area, Fairchild began to cultivate a match with Behringer and Vivian, then seventeen.

Behringer had his own reasons for marrying Vivian, and marry her he would. It was an ironic twist of fate that marriage to another woman would put him in a position to get to the bottom of the fire that had killed his wife and son.

Silas rose and slowly walked to the window of his office, idly rubbing his thumb over the face of his pocket watch. "Garitson, Vivian was still a child when I decided I wanted you to take over Fairchild and Sons. Course, you've always felt more like a brother to me than anything else." He paused thoughtfully as a steamboat whistle blew, its shrillness echoing mournfully.

"You know that sound as well as I do. It's the dying wail of an industry that's kept this town since the days your father settled here. If we don't all keep our wits about us, Jefferson's not going to make it."

Behringer rubbed his eyes. "It's going to take more than wits, Silas."

"Yes. Things haven't gone quite the way we anticipated. Everyone knows how much the water level's dropped since the raft was cleared in '73."

"Forget the raft!" Behringer exploded. "Forget the damned boats. I'm so sick of hearing about the bayou I could scream."

"If it weren't for the bayou, Garitson, there wouldn't be a Jefferson."

"That's a rather fundamental fact which no one seems capable of progressing past. All right. We all made a lot of money in steamboat traffic. Now we're not. It isn't as if there aren't any other possibilities for industry. They're there, just waiting for someone to take advantage of them."

"Well, they'd better present themselves posthaste. Garitson, I have a stack of papers at the bank which would grieve you as much as they do me."

Behringer's head jerked up. "The bank?"

Fairchild nodded, sighing. "Deeds of sale. Even worse, notices of foreclosure. Jefferson is disappearing, a dozen faces a month."

"May I see the papers?"

Fairchild waved his hand impatiently. "See them? You should be worrying about preventing them."

Behringer nodded. "Silas, I believe having access to your bank files might benefit us both."

Fairchild raised an eyebrow, his expression remote. "How?"

Behringer crossed his arms in front of him, leaning against the wall, carefully considering his words. How indeed? It might benefit him immeasurably, but it likely could land Fairchild in prison. Fairchild had no idea why Behringer wanted into his files.

"You have information about the businesses of Jefferson that I don't. I'm sure it would be helpful. Fairchild and Sons' downturn can be arrested immediately if I have all the facts surrounding Jefferson."

Fairchild turned a keen eye on Behringer. "If there's information you need, Garitson, please tell me what it is. You can help keep Jefferson alive. You know that as well as I do. With you in charge of my company, it's a financial institution that'll provide a solid future for my daughter and her family."

Amazing, Behringer thought, as Silas smoothly diverted the discussion away from his private files. Behringer sat impassively as his future father-in-law prepared his speech.

"During the course of your marriage, there will doubtless be other women. That makes no difference to me. What matters to me is Vivian's happiness. You know there are a hundred men who'd give anything to be in your shoes, none of them wanting anything more than to get their hands on my money and my daughter."

Fairchild sat on the edge of the desk. "Garitson, as long as you continue to treat Vivian with the honor she deserves, I can ask no more of you." He paused. "The first time I ever hear that you've hurt her, intentionally or otherwise, I'll make you the most miserable man alive. You can bank on that."

Behringer sat, outwardly unmoved by the impact of Fairchild's pleasant promise. With any other man, the understatement would be meaningless. Silas Fairchild did not waste time on idle threats. Garitson Behringer had learned that painful lesson a long time ago.

Rising from his chair, Behringer took his coat from the rack near the door. "I thank you for your generosity with all this insight," he murmured.

"I'm dead serious, Garitson."

Behringer smiled. "I know the tone well."

As he left Fairchild's office, Behringer frowned at his anger over the man's conventional counsel and his own rebellion against the suggested scenario. It certainly wasn't anything Garitson hadn't already thought of. Everything he'd learned about manhood since he was thirteen told him there was only one solution, one completely acceptable to everyone involved. Unfortunately, that prospect no longer appealed to him.

Once before in his life, he'd been fortunate enough to

reach out and find someone who tried to fill that place between his open arms and his empty heart. It was the closest he'd ever come to satisfying that yearning within him, and he knew it was far closer than many men ever came. He should be grateful for that.

Now, somehow, he wanted more.

❧ Twelve ❧

Rebecca ventured into the hall, noticing a young woman dusting a table.

"Excuse me, Miss . . . ?"

"Caroline, ma'am. You must be Miss Reynolds. I'll take you to meet Mrs. Behringer."

Caroline bobbed her head and led Rebecca through the ballroom onto the porch. Rebecca looked for the mirror over the fireplace. A hundred years later, the mystical Behringer wedding gift would hang in the same place. She glanced toward the piano.

Centered on the wall over the piano was the portrait of a beautiful, sandy-haired woman. The feathery hairs on the back of her neck bristled as she gazed at the portrait, and for a moment she forgot that the other mirror was gone. She would have assumed the woman to be Katy Behringer, but there was a depth of soulfulness there that she doubted she'd find in Katy's spirited face. She was older, too, than the mischievous teenager.

"Miss?" The soft voice prodded her.

Rebecca turned. "That's a lovely painting," she said, lingering.

Usually, that was all it took to coax a story out of people. Caroline only smiled and nodded, then continued out to the porch. Rebecca was obliged to follow.

A stunning, statuesque woman, nearly as tall as her husband, sat erect in a porch swing, darning socks. The hair which once had been quite blonde was now well-diluted with silver. Rebecca was instantly charmed by the inner drive that caused the matriarch of an affluent family to darn socks.

Rebecca savored her first glance at Mrs. Behringer. The woman unconsciously touched her foot to the timber porch to set the swing swaying once more. In only a matter of moments, the stern German woman would tell her in specific terms exactly what she thought of Rebecca, but for the time being, Rebecca felt as though she'd found a friend in this unsympathetic thicket. And she didn't know why, but she wanted this woman to like her. She needed this woman to like her.

The woman noticed Rebecca and abruptly lay aside her sewing. She did the strangest thing then. She smiled, a smile that started deep inside and shone in her clear gray eyes.

"You are Rebecca," she murmured as she rose, the still-vibrant accent softened by the gentleness of her voice. Clasping Rebecca's hand between both of hers, she said, "Welcome to our home. I am Maria Behringer." She returned to the porch swing and patted the cushion beside her own. "Would you care for some lemonade? We have ice, you know. A nice glass of beer, perhaps?"

"Lemonade would be fine," she told Caroline. Rebecca smiled and sat beside Mrs. Behringer.

"Garitson tells me you met Katy while we were in Shreveport."

Rebecca dreaded the impending fabrications, terrified she'd stumble without knowing where Behringer had led her.

"I regret I was not able to meet you then," Mrs. Behringer said simply. "I certainly miss our Katerina. Do you sew?"

"No," Rebecca said quickly. "I . . . can't keep the stitches even, and it frustrates me." She vaguely wished she'd taken an embroidery class somewhere along the line, knowing this was a serious character flaw in a Victorian lady.

"Then I shall teach you how, and while you learn it, you will learn much about patience. Sewing is a balm for the spirit, whether it's a new quilt for the winter, or merely darning socks." She smiled conspiritorially, then put her sewing in the basket beside the swing. "It took years for me to find an interest in it, frankly."

Again touching the swing into motion, Mrs. Behringer patted Rebecca's hand. "You are as lovely as Garitson said," she said. "It seems my son has taken a shine to you. I hear there was quite a scuffle in the restaurant this afternoon." As though this was one step short of a lifelong commitment, the woman raised an eyebrow, and Rebecca smiled to see the expression so characteristic of Behringer. "And I hear my dear husband made a bumbling fool of himself as well."

Rebecca tilted her head. "He was doing what he thought was right."

"And Garitson quickly corrected his misperceptions of right and wrong."

"I don't think your son likes to be told what to do."

The woman looked at her with keen interest, nodding. "Clearly he doesn't. Garitson is a complex man; he was born with a personality to charm and challenge all at once. Jacob, naturally, refuses to recognize the restless side of Garitson's nature. It was once a terrible barrier between them."

It was true; Garitson Behringer was nearly impossible to read. As soon as she was convinced he was a closet comedian, he withdrew into himself. He'd nearly seduced her as soon as he'd drawn her away from his father's character assassination. That much, of course, was easy enough to explain; she'd known it in every other man she'd chanced to meet. It was known as hypocrisy.

"Would you care to go to town with me this afternoon, my dear? I need a pair of gloves for the Fairchild party Friday night."

Smiling at the invitation that made her forget she was an employee of the woman, Rebecca smiled. "Of course."

Mrs. Behringer rose. "Then just let me get my hat."

Rebecca stood, smoothing her skirts. "That's lovely," Mrs. Behringer said. "Is that what Garitson chose for you?"

Amazing. The woman who'd penned over two million words on the topic of romance, who'd drawn somewhere between thirty and forty love scenes, blushed at the curious way Behringer's mother inspected the dress, as though trying to put herself in her son's bestial mind. Rebecca nodded.

Finally, the older woman smiled. "My son has excellent taste," she said meaningfully.

Thomas, the Behringers' driver, escorted Mrs. Behringer and her newly hired companion into town. Just down from the Excelsior, he brought the horses to a halt and helped the women down from the carriage.

"What do you plan on wearing Friday night?" Mrs. Behringer said, leading Rebecca into a shop.

Rebecca found herself surprised at the lurch of her heart, recalling Vivian's fuss over matching outfits. Without pausing to wonder why, she blurted, "I can't go."

Mrs. Behringer was aghast. "Why on earth not?"

Rebecca waved a hand vaguely. "Well, it—wouldn't be proper, would it?"

The woman laughed then, long and loudly. "What a prize you are."

"What do you mean?"

"Let's continue this after we leave," Mrs. Behringer whispered, noticing the nosy woman who lived down the road. The woman inched closer to them, eyeing Rebecca furtively.

"Hello, Mrs. Goodman," murmured Mrs. Behringer. "And how is everything going for you this day?"

The woman smiled. "Just fine. And is this your houseguest? I've heard so much about her!"

Mrs. Behringer patted Rebecca's arm protectively. "I'm sure you have. Yes, this is Miss Rebecca Reynolds, of the Shreveport Reynolds."

"Oh?" The woman raised an eyebrow. "I've heard of them."

Rebecca wanted to giggle. Before it was all over, Rebecca Reynolds would go down in history beside Scarlett O'Hara.

"Rebecca, this is Lettie Goodman."

Shaking the woman's hand, Rebecca smiled. "So good to meet you."

"A good day to you, Mrs. Goodman." Without further explanation, Mrs. Behringer turned to the shopkeeper. "Edna, I need a lovely pair of lace gloves. What might you have?"

Eager to satisfy her favorite customer, Edna brought out several pairs of gloves.

Maria chose a pair, then looked at Rebecca. "Which do you like, dear?"

Rebecca shook her head. "Oh, no. I couldn't."

Mrs. Behringer's eyes were expressionless as she looked at the shopkeeper with an amused grin, then at Rebecca for a long moment. "Nonsense."

The single word was unmistakable in its command, and Rebecca understood she was making a scene. Glancing over the gloves, she chose a pair. The gloves wrapped, the two women left the shop, strolling down the street.

"My dear, dear girl," she said pleasantly, in discreet tones. "You are my daughter's friend. You are a very welcome guest in my house. I shall no doubt offend your sense of what is proper and what is not before it's over with. I beg of you, however, to play a game of make-believe. Pretend you were born to a pair of unconventional German parents, and this will all go off splendidly. We don't want people spreading farfetched gossip about you and Garitson, would we now?"

She felt as though the woman's eyes were peering into her mind, seeing last night's memories, reading this afternoon's dreams.

"Of course not," Mrs. Behringer continued pleasantly. "If you like, I can address you as Fraulein Behringer for a while to more properly condition you. But then, if you were my daughter, who would the fine ladies of Jefferson have to discuss behind their teacups?"

Rebecca smiled. Who indeed?

❧ Thirteen ❧

They strolled along the sidewalk another hundred feet or so, with Mrs. Behringer giggling over the stir Rebecca was causing in the parlors of Jefferson's finest. Rebecca's glance strayed to the office before them. The *Jefferson Jimplecute*. She peered into the front window, noticing a man with bushy brown hair, drooping mustache, and an ink-splattered apron over his generous midsection. He was buried up to his arms in a printing press.

"What a peculiar name for a newspaper," Rebecca commented, more as a lead than an opinion. She knew it was not at all unusual for a small town paper.

"It's a . . . a . . . oh, a word puzzle," Mrs. Behringer tried to explain.

"An acrostic?"

"Yes, that's it. Let me see now. Well, never mind. I can't even think of what the first letter stands for."

"May we go in?" Rebecca searched for a ploy which would explain such unseemly curiosity. "The truth is, I worked on the *Shreveport News* this summer as an apprentice. My father didn't approve, but I'm afraid I couldn't stay away. I'm very interested in writing."

"You do newspaper writing?"

"Well, I like made-up stories best, but newspapers are always so exciting."

"Let's go in. Gustav Frank will be able to answer any questions you have."

The outer room was dominated by the press, and the middle-aged man spared them a glance, returning his attention to the machinery.

"Morning, Mrs. Behringer."

Mrs. Behringer nodded. "Gustav, this is Rebecca Reynolds, who will be staying with us for a while."

Gustav nodded impatiently, waving his hand. "Yes, yes, I've heard all about her. Good to meet you, young lady. You're practically tomorrow's featured story."

Rebecca's lips parted in a startled smile at the man's surly greeting.

"Rebecca worked on the *Shreveport News*," Mrs. Behringer volunteered, and Rebecca felt queasy.

"Don't think I've ever heard of that one," he said, still tinkering with the press. "Is it that new daily?"

Rebecca nodded slowly. "Yes."

"They've got all kinds of newfangled ideas over there. Don't surprise me too much, a little girl doing their reporting."

"I was trying to think of what *Jimplecute* meant, Gustav," Mrs. Behringer went on. "Can you help me?"

"It means sweetheart, Maria. You know that."

Maria clucked impatiently. "No, not that. It stands for something."

"Oh, some industrious businessman came up with a little slogan. Probably your son. Look over on the new masthead there."

Rebecca reached for one of the fresh papers, lying stacked by the door. She read, " 'Join Industry, Manufacturing, Planting, Labor, Energy, Capital, in Unity Together Everlastingly.' Everlastingly?"

Mrs. Behringer shook her head. "That doesn't sound like Garitson. Gustav, how is Heidi?"

Rebecca scanned the headlines as they chatted. Cotton news, a story from New Orleans, a piece on a barn that had

burned down. She opened the page. An editorial about rail.
She skimmed the next page, and one column snagged her
straying gaze. *Society News*, it said, but Rebecca translated
that phrase easily enough. She skimmed the gossip column,
increasingly dismayed at what she read. Gustav Frank hadn't
exaggerated.

> *A certain mischievous young lady of Jefferson headed
> east for finishing school on Friday, leaving trouble as
> usual in her wake. She arranged for a friend of hers to
> keep her mother company. The friend wasted no time in
> stealing a well-known piece of family jewelry when she
> found the family home not to her liking and used it to
> procure lodging at the Excelsior. The heirloom was later
> ransomed by a gentleman in the family, who remained all
> night in the hotel room with the woman. One wonders
> exactly whose companion she's intended to be? Also of
> interest; they claim she's from Shreveport, but last night
> at the hotel she said she was from New Orleans.*

Rebecca felt steam rising from her ears, but her righteous
fury was doused by the very next sentence in the column.

> *Speaking of companions, a well-known Cincinnati
> jeweler was also in town last night, looking for his equally
> infamous paramour (or wife, dependent upon whom one
> chooses to believe). Imagine our surprise when we saw
> the young lady from the previous story conversing with his
> paramour in the hallway at the hotel last night. We don't
> know where the jeweler's companion has gone this time,
> or which unsuspecting dupe she's taken on now, but he
> may not be lonely for long. This very morning, he was
> seen chatting at length with the young woman from New
> Orleans before he left for home. We doubt she was giving
> him tips on his paramour's whereabouts. Our guess is
> that she told him she was previously engaged as a com-*

panion. Perhaps she's simply determined to enhance her
jewelry collection.

As Rebecca raised glittering eyes to Gustav Frank, he
slowly straightened, wiping his greasy hands on his apron. "I
expect you've read it," he said.

She nodded. "There's a word for this, Mr. Frank. It's called
slander. Not a favorable feature for a newspaper."

The man tossed his long hair away from his face. "There's
not a paper in the country who doesn't run a gossip column."

"There are plenty of them. The respectable ones refuse
such trash."

"Oh, like your Shreveport paper?" he asked scornfully.

Rebecca nodded, growing inextricably intertwined with
the fictitious modern newspaper operation. "Exactly."

"Miss Reynolds, I'm sorry. Truth is, I don't care for that
kind of news. But Mr. Taylor, he says it sells papers—"

"Oh, Mr. Taylor that shot Mr. Patillo of the *Evening Re-
flector?*" Mrs. Behringer put in. "A charitable competitor."

"Mr. Taylor was found innocent, Mrs. Behringer, and you
know it was in self-defense."

"Mr. Frank, exactly what role do you have in the paper?"
Rebecca asked him.

"I put the news together. Mr. Taylor's wife does the gossip
column. If you'll look on the second page, you'll see a piece I
did on rail."

"Gustav," Mrs. Behringer put in, ending their bickering, "I
would like to order a typewriting machine. How does one go
about it?"

Rebecca was distracted by this peculiar request.

So was Gustav. "A what?" he asked incredulously.

"A typewriting machine," Mrs. Behringer repeated, with a
serene smile.

Suddenly ill at ease, Gustav walked to the counter. "Well,
all right. What is it Jacob wants?"

"Jacob wants me to remember my place and knit booties
for nonexistent grandchildren. I want a typewriting machine.

The newest one available. I assume you know where to get them."

"Of course I do. What do you know about operating typewriters, Maria? They're very expensive."

Maria smiled. "I know they have keys with letters on them. And I understand you need fingers to push the keys. I'm wonderfully equipped to master the challenge."

Then he paused, as though reluctant to continue, ignoring her sweet sarcasm. "I can order such a machine. You understand I'm going to need Jacob's signature on the order."

"Thomas is able to get whatever he needs from any shop in town by merely walking in. My signature will be on the order."

Rebecca's fingertips fluttered upward to contain her grin at the man's mute bewilderment. It took him several attempts at speech before he finally stammered, "But Jacob will be quite angry . . ."

"That," Maria said pleasantly, "is nothing compared to what you're going to see in five seconds if your deportment doesn't improve drastically. You've allowed one of my dearest friends' feelings to be hurt for no reason. Mr. Frank, I believe I find you in my debt."

Gustav gaped helplessly for another moment before he finally moved away to scribble on a sheet of paper, muttering in German.

"What was that?" Maria asked. "I'm sorry, Gustav. I didn't hear you. Could you please speak up?"

"I said," he emphasized, smiling sweetly, "anything for so lovely a lady as Frau Behringer."

"Oh, Gustav," Maria said with a fetching blush. "You're such a charmer."

When they left the shop, Maria burst out in a girlish titter. " 'Jacob will be quite angry,' " she mocked. "What a buffoon."

Thomas helped them into the carriage, and another shop caught Rebecca's eye. HENDERSON INTERESTS, MALCOLM HENDERSON, PROPRIETOR. The windows of the shop were as dusty as when Rebecca first set foot in Jefferson, and she peered to see beyond that glass.

"What's wrong, Rebecca?"

"That shop there. What is it?"

"Oh, that's the Henderson shop. Mr. Henderson deals in imported glass, mirrors and such, and books. Would you like to go in?"

The sign would not change in the next century, Rebecca marveled, disturbed somehow by the shop. She hesitated only momentarily before slowly shaking her head. "No. I don't think so. But I would like to stop in at the Excelsior, if I might."

"Certainly. It's right here. Shall I ask Thomas to accompany us?"

Rebecca shook her head. "No. There's no need for you to go. I'll only be a moment."

She left Mrs. Behringer waiting at the carriage as she stepped inside the Excelsior House, finding the same Mr. Atkins who'd been on duty the previous night. He observed her with no less hauteur now.

"Ah, Miss Reynolds, I believe?"

"I'm looking for a woman named Bessie Moore."

"Oh, might you mean Mrs. Rothschild? It's sometimes confusing, tracking her aliases."

Rebecca stared silently at him for a blistering moment, and he felt her ire. "Do you work at being supercilious, or does it come naturally?"

It came naturally at that particular moment. "Mrs. Rothschild and her, ah, companion left quite early this morning."

"Do you know where they went?"

He swallowed in supreme boredom. "Indeed, I don't. She left this note for you, however." He reached into a box behind him and produced a small envelope.

"And would you have eventually sent it over to me?" Rebecca asked, jerking the envelope from his hand.

"Eventually."

Rebecca sighed and opened the note.

Rebecca,

Benjamin and I left unexpectedly this morning because I heard Abe was in town. I don't know how you knew he was following us, but I'm grateful to you for warning me. Since I don't know that I'll see you again, I wanted to thank you for befriending me while we were in Jefferson. I wish you well.

Bessie

Rebecca turned away from Atkins without a farewell, tucking the note into the deep pocket of her gown. For a woman like Rebecca, accustomed to accomplishing, this impotence was wrenching. She knew she had one thing to accomplish in the next four months: keeping Bessie Moore out of Jefferson, Texas. She had no idea how to effect that small feat, since for practical purposes the woman had vanished. For the time being, she would have to hope that diverting Rothschild had been enough.

Mrs. Behringer was waiting inside the carriage. She smiled at Rebecca. "Did you get your business taken care of?"

Rebecca nodded.

"Fine. We'll go home, then, unless there's something else you'd like to do while we're here."

"No."

The carriage turned toward the Behringer home. "Rebecca, I didn't know you liked to write."

"I don't tell many people."

"I have always wanted to write a book. Will you help me?"

Rebecca was startled. "Well, certainly. I'll help however I can."

"No, you must be very closely involved in this book, I think. I was given an idea today. Writing seems infinitely more absorbing than teaching you to sew."

"Is that why you ordered the typewriter?"

"Yes. What do you know about them?" Maria asked, genuinely worried now.

Rebecca smiled slyly. "I know they have keys with letters on them. And I know you need fingers to push the keys."

Maria and Rebecca's laughter rang out from the carriage as they left the town behind.

The trip home was short, and Mrs. Behringer's step was lively as they mounted the stairs. At Katy's room, she opened the door. "Now then," she said. "What shall you wear to the party?"

Rebecca shook her head. The thought of it made her miserable, and she explained, "I really prefer not to go."

"Of course you do," she said, opening an armoire. "And you most likely prefer to let that idiotic lint ball marry my son, and I'll be lucky if my grandchildren grow up to be anything but brattish morons, if I have any grandchildren at all." She shook her head and muttered, mostly to herself, "If Garitson has it his way, he'll be working around the clock, too busy to father a child, or even eat, and most of all, feel. That can be the only possible explanation."

She withdrew a stunning white gown, sprigged with yellow roses. "Katy wore this only once. Bless her flighty soul."

Rebecca smiled at the whispery fabric that cascaded over her fingers as Mrs. Behringer put it into her hands. "Do try it on."

"Please, I don't—"

"Enough!" Mrs. Behringer snapped impatiently, holding up a hand. "If I hear one more longsuffering word, I shall scream. Now do put the dress on."

Rebecca stepped behind the screen and changed dresses, amused at the woman's directive. When the dress was in place, Rebecca glanced down at her bosom uncertainly. "Is there something missing? Some lace, maybe?"

Mrs. Behringer laughed, a downright scheming giggle. "Unless I miscalculated, it is not lacking in any way."

Rebecca appeared from behind the screen, sternly shaking a finger at Mrs. Behringer. "You are a naughty lady."

The older woman broke up in giggles, clapping her hands

together. "And you're a delight. Garitson will fall in love with you upon sight," she declared.

Rebecca hugged Maria Behringer, wondering what it was like to trust something so completely unpredictable as love.

❦ Fourteen ❦

The disaster of dinner—or supper, as the Behringers quaintly referred to it—was inevitable, regardless of Rebecca's effort at composure, despite Maria's deft direction. Jacob Behringer was the unknown in the formula, and he worked only haphazardly at veiling his hostility toward Rebecca.

Behringer arrived at the table just moments before his father. Maria smiled and asked Caroline to pour the gentlemen a mug of beer.

Behringer raised his hand. "Wine, if you don't mind," he murmured.

Jacob Behringer drew on his beer before setting it on the table with a thump. Rebecca wondered if it was merely the successor in a long line. "So did you see Silas today, Garitson?" he asked in amusement.

Garitson gave his father a sparing glance as he filled his plate. "I can see that's a rhetorical question."

Jacob giggled, and Rebecca's suspicions were confirmed.

"Why, Jacob Behringer," his wife reprimanded him. "I think you've spent an hour at the tavern before making your way home."

He stuffed a slice of roast beef in his mouth and chewed perfunctorily before swallowing. "I think you're becoming a nosy old woman," he retorted, then glanced at Rebecca. "Must be the company you're keeping."

Behringer's fork clattered against the cherrywood table. When he spoke, however, his words were calm. "Papa, I would like to eat in peace. And Rebecca hasn't had one uninterrupted meal since she arrived."

"I hear you have a new pair of gloves, Miss Reynolds. What sort of occasion are you planning to wear them to?" Jacob's interest seemed casual enough, but Rebecca recognized the ploy instantly. She wasn't alone.

Maria spoke pleasantly. "Why, she will be wearing them to the Fairchilds' party Friday night. Foolish man."

Jacob looked at the chandelier. "Of course, what could I have been thinking? How could I have thought that the girl would have enough sense to stay away from the Fairchilds' party? The Fairchilds," he repeated, staring at Rebecca with eyes as black and deep as the moonless August sky.

"She knows Vivian, Papa," Behringer said, steely anger threaded into his pleasant words. "She's had the distinct pleasure of being introduced to her charming disposition."

"She'll think that no more than a welcome to the neighborhood if she insists on going to this party."

"I prefer not to go at all," Rebecca said. "I'm accompanying Mrs. Behringer, and that's all."

Jacob stared at her, struck speechless, looking for all the world as though a slice of beef were lodged in his trachea. He considered her words and weighed with care the knowledge that she had spoken to him gently, as though to assuage his anger. At last, he cleared his throat. "Of course."

Maria Behringer smiled behind her teacup.

Rebecca's appetite was gone. She divided the food on her plate into tiny, uneaten portions, then combined them again and started over. She looked up to find Behringer watching her.

"Try less rearranging and more swallowing," he suggested. "It better captures the nutrients in the food."

"I'd like to be excused," she said.

Maria frowned. "Of course not, my dear. Garitson is going to play the piano for us in the ballroom. You should see what Rebecca is wearing to the party, Garitson," his mother went on, turning to her son.

"Oh?" Behringer asked, sipping his wine, enjoying every moment of his mother's revenge. He knew she'd like Rebecca. They were too much alike for her not to. "What's it like?"

"Oh, a beautiful gown. Summer white, with yellow roses. I shall help her with her hair, and dress it with roses from the garden."

"A new gown?" Jacob joined the conversation, as though he could remain silent no longer.

"Oh, no. Merely something Katy never liked. She wore it on a picnic with Eustace Lee. I knew Rebecca would look lovely in it."

Behringer nodded, looking at his mother. "I remember the dress now." His eyes softened as he looked at Rebecca, his gaze sliding to rest on her breasts. "It didn't seem to fit Katy properly."

Maria was busy buttering a roll, for all outward appearances oblivious to the exchange between her son and their guest. "It fits Rebecca like a glove."

"It would."

Rebecca felt like the butter on Maria's roll.

"Another beer, Caroline." Jacob's words were clipped. "And I'd like to speak with you later in the study, Garitson."

"Papa, I can't stay long," Behringer said with a sigh, turning away from Rebecca, reluctantly shattering the spell. "I have an engagement."

"Exactly my topic of discussion. We have many things to clear up, Garitson. Points, it would seem, that Silas Fairchild was unsuccessful in driving home to you."

Behringer's annoyance matched his father's. "I am not a fifteen-year-old boy, Papa."

Jacob raised his mug to his mouth and paused, carefully

contemplating his son. "One could not tell it by your behavior."

"Mrs. Behringer," Rebecca pleaded, "if you'll excuse me, I'll wait for you in the ballroom."

Maria smiled gently at Rebecca, and Rebecca walked into the ballroom and collapsed in a loveseat. Less than three minutes later, Behringer arrived in the doorway. He slowly, purposefully crossed the room and sat beside her, his arm trailing along the settee behind her.

"You handled yourself well," he said. "I couldn't have done better myself without punching him."

Lively lights sparkled in the depths of his dark eyes, and Rebecca breathed slowly, savoring his nearness, his fragrance. She didn't speak.

"I'm sorry he's behaving this way. You wouldn't believe it from what you've seen of him, but my father's normally the most gracious host within a hundred miles."

"That's what I've heard."

"I cannot wait to see you in that dress. Katy ordered it this spring with the intention of snagging a particularly eligible bachelor. Eustace announced his engagement to another woman the day after Katy wore the dress on a picnic with him, and she cried about her body for two days. She was certain she'd been passed over for her nondescript bosom."

Behringer's glance rested like a caress on Rebecca's breasts, and he bent to drop a kiss at her temple. "I suspect you'll do that dress as much justice as you do this one. I chose it thoughtfully, planning for a moment such as this."

Rebecca shivered. His finger trailed along the low neckline of her dress, and she felt the faint brush of his fingertip as if it were his mouth.

"You see?" he whispered. "Carefully orchestrated for our moments alone." A tanned finger dropped, sliding along the curve of her breasts. "Do you like the dress?"

She firmly shoved his hand away, laughing softly, and left the settee, finding one of Maria's fans in a chair near the piano. She seated herself there, unfolding the fan and stirring a breeze. "You've got to stop kissing me."

"You have a charming laugh."

Rebecca glanced at him, noticing the sobering in his expression. "Your mother is going to be walking through those doors any moment."

"If she knew I was here with you," he said, "she'd lock those doors."

"Don't you have an appointment?"

"It can wait. And I've thus far kissed you only once."

Rebecca did not remind him who had kissed whom that night. "It escaped me," Rebecca said softly.

"I don't see how. The taste of you springs to memory."

Rebecca helplessly met Behringer's brooding gaze.

Maria appeared in the doorway, followed by her husband, and Garitson rose, seating himself at the piano. Jacob sat opposite Rebecca, and her gaze was drawn to the portrait near her. The unknown woman's serene beauty was soothing.

Behringer began playing, softly. In amazement Rebecca listened to the haunting music, almost childlike in its sense of wonder. She recognized the piece immediately, one of Mozart's piano concertos. She'd loved it as a young girl, and as she had sat in an empty theater with a date, watching the credits at the end of *Amadeus*, she'd wept at its beauty. This eerie moment was much too poignant to credit to chance. Overcome by the intensity that reminded her this was a moment she never should have known, she closed her eyes, her throat tight with tears. And when she opened them again, Behringer was staring at her, his eyes turbulent with emotion.

But he wasn't looking at her. His gaze went over her shoulder, to the portrait of the woman.

He stopped playing and rose. "Excuse me, Mama. Papa."

"Garitson," his mother protested.

He shook his head. "I have to go. I'll see you at church in the morning."

Rebecca's gaze followed Behringer out of the room. He didn't look at her.

Rebecca had a hard time falling asleep that night. There was such a jumble of memories to contend with, she scarcely knew where to start. She rose from the bed, venturing out onto the verandah for the comforting aroma of the roses. She walked down the back stairs to the lower level, carefully plucking several roses from the rambling bush nearest her, and a voice drifted through the window near her. The breeze gently billowed the drapery there.

". . . that little display of yours at supper tonight?" The unmistakable accent quickly identified the speaker.

"I have nothing to prove to you, Papa."

Jacob's voice was light. "I see. And do you recall Silas' words?" Silence was his only reply. "He's a very understanding man, Garitson. You could do a lot worse for a father-in-law. Once you marry Vivian, you'll have complete control of Fairchild and Sons, and a beautiful bride as well."

"Everything a man could want out of life," Behringer said quietly.

"So you do have some brains left, after all. And here I thought you'd begun to reason with your—"

Rebecca's breath caught in her throat at Jacob's words.

"My baser urges are normally infallible." Behringer laughed, and Jacob joined him. "It's an instinct I've learned to trust."

"As long as you separate the vital from the trivial," Jacob answered calmly. "I fear you're losing your objectivity. Your good sense is being clouded by your lusts."

Behringer said nothing in protest. Nothing.

"I won't make light of the fact that the girl is splendid," Jacob conceded, recognizing the control he'd gained in the course of the conversation. "Vivian is a pale nursery doll compared to her. Unfortunately, Vivian is aware of that. She won't bend easily to your having a paramour right here in town. That may be a tangle," he mused.

"Vivian Fairchild is not going to tell me how to run my life," Behringer spat.

Jacob chuckled. "No, but when she becomes Vivian Behringer, she'll be able to make your life pure hell. She'll be the perfect wife for you, an exquisite hostess and an adequate mother, with the help of a nanny, of course. By the way," he said, his voice taking on an earnest seriousness, "I remind you to always . . . take care. You don't want to have to deal with an illegitimate family as well."

Rebecca turned and stomped down the brick path, fury and pain cutting into her as she clutched the sweetness of the roses to her heart.

Later, she lay on the bed in Katy's room, tears of anger streaming down her face. It was anger, she told herself. That was all. She stared at the canopy. For him to imagine she would be satisfied with cautious kisses and discreet embraces whenever he could manage to get away, while another woman shared his name, his life, his children . . .

What had she been thinking, to have trusted him? To have believed his sweetly murmured sentiments? The man's magnetic self-assurance suddenly repelled her. Wasn't it just like a man. Then, she was even more furious with herself.

"Rebecca Reynolds," she said wryly, "you should know better."

❧ Fifteen ❧

Things didn't look much better in the morning. Rebecca and Mrs. Behringer ate breakfast alone, and she fought down her curiosity over where the woman's son was. The morning had already grown warm by the time Jacob joined them to leave for mass. She ached at his warm smile, so like his son's, when he greeted her.

As they arrived at the front door of the church, Maria touched her hand. "Remember that we are here to worship, Rebecca," she said softly. Rebecca recognized the steadying warning in Mrs. Behringer's words. "For many, it's just another place to socialize."

They turned then to the church, and a young man standing in the doorway smiled and greeted them, his voice tinged with an English accent, his blue gaze lingering on Rebecca. "Good morning, Mrs. Behringer. Miss."

Rebecca was startled at the man's prettiness. Eyes a shade of blue so deep and unreal the color belonged somewhere on watered silk. A full lower lip, perfectly curved, with the most faintly dimpled square chin. Cheekbones Fabio would die for; this man, in fact, could drive the famous romance model to waiting tables somewhere.

Mrs. Behringer smiled briefly, all but dismissing the man. "Good morning, Charles. Rebecca, this is Charles Norton.

Charles, this is Rebecca Reynolds, a friend of Katy's who's staying with us awhile."

The man focused that startling gaze on her, and she nodded and accepted the hand he offered in greeting.

Just this side of the long, wooden pews, Behringer stood, Vivian Fairchild at his side, poised before a font. Touching his fingertips against the surface of the water, he crossed himself and then led Vivian into the church. Rebecca thought what a stunning pair they made, his dark head bent to hear her whispering in his ear, her pale, silvery curls brushing his shoulder.

Turning to find Mrs. Behringer, she saw the disdain on the woman's face. She smiled encouragingly at Rebecca, sweeping ahead of her. "Come, my dear. Let us be seated."

Rebecca followed Mrs. Behringer as she led her to one of the front pews, and it was not her imagination that two hundred stares were focused on her. She saw the heads turn as they approached the pew where Behringer and Vivian already sat.

The service began and then it seemed without end. The priest gave a divinely chosen sermon on temptation. He went on for days, it seemed, speaking of what marriages should be. From time to time, he glanced pointedly at Behringer and Vivian, seeking the perfect example.

"The only successful marriage in the trying times of the modern era will find a man strong enough to cherish his wife in the face of whatever brash temptation might befall him."

A wave of nausea washed over Rebecca at the realization that the priest had personally chosen her as a sermon. She tried to drive the noise of his words from her aching brain, and was grateful when the service was at an end. She avoided Behringer's searching gaze as she followed Jacob and Maria to their carriage. Rebecca sank into the carriage, leaning miserably against the wall.

"My dear girl," Jacob Behringer said softly, "are you all right?"

Rebecca didn't trust herself to speak, so she nodded

mutely. Never in her life had she been more miserable, and she fought the explanation that was even more sickening than reality.

She couldn't be in love with the man. She didn't know him. She didn't know what he liked for breakfast, or what it was like to sit in church with him. Things Vivian knew well, things she'd learned while sharing his life so far. Things a wife would understand, she thought bitterly. All she knew, it seemed, was that she had never felt this hopeless dejection with Rick Daniels, the man she had almost married.

The carriage had barely paused in front of the Behringer home when Rebecca wrenched open the door and rushed up the steps, ignoring Maria's startled protest. Her heart was a pit of despair, a reality so dark and cheerless she knew there was only one answer. Embracing the solution, she found her way through the house to the grand ballroom. When she gazed up into the mirror, reading the desperation in her own face, she summoned every detail she could remember of the twentieth century Behringer Inn.

Nothing. No flicker of candlelight.

"Please," she said. "I can't take this." Her hoarse whisper was broken by silent tears streaming down her face. "I want to go home."

She stared at the image reflected in the oval mirror, the portrait Garitson had gazed at last night as if its subject were the Holy Mother. It was a woman from the past, a woman of serene beauty. Her hair, a rich, vibrant brown, was gathered up in curls, and her amber eyes watched Rebecca sympathetically. She was dressed in a russet-colored gown that would have been fashionable during the Civil War.

Her questing mind wrested control over the mass of emotions she had become, and she swallowed her pointless tears as she turned toward the opposite wall. As she moved close to the portrait, she heard a quiet voice behind her. "Difficult footsteps to follow in, Sarah's."

Rebecca looked at Maria, knowing her eyes were swollen

from weeping. "She's beautiful," she whispered. "Who is she?"

A sadness tinged Maria's features as she approached the portrait and gazed thoughtfully. "She was Garitson's wife."

Rebecca looked at the picture with new interest. This was the sort of woman he would choose for love, she thought.

"She died over seven years ago, along with my little grandson, Peter. It was the *Mittie Stephens* tragedy."

Maria sank into a chair and Rebecca sat near her, staring at the portrait. "She had been visiting relatives in Shreveport," Maria said, shaking her head. "They were so close to home, just off Swanson's Landing. It was terrible."

"How . . . did they die?" Rebecca asked.

Maria's face withered in sorrow, and her words were whispered. "They burned to death." She cleared her throat and began again. "Garitson was the one who found them. I often prayed that they had been asleep, that their deaths were painless, but it couldn't have been, I know. They were huddled beneath the bed when Garitson found them. He nearly died with them, trying to pull them from the fire as the boat was sinking just offshore."

Rebecca shuddered, horrified. "What a horrible death for a child."

Maria nodded bleakly. "Peter was such a darling boy, more like Sarah than Garitson. Sandy curls all over his angelic head," she said. "Garitson was destroyed."

As though she could no longer bear to be near the portrait, Maria rose and stood by one of the long windows. "His own injuries, he ignored. At first, the doctor told us Garitson wouldn't survive the terrible burns. As much time passed, his condition slowly improved. The beard he grew disguised the scars he suffered while trying to get through the fire. He spent his days locked up in their house, in their bedroom, and the nursery. He sent all the servants away, and would see no one. This went on for months. He ate little and drank a lot.

"For a while I feared Garitson, too, would be a casualty of

the *Mittie Stephens*. A year passed, a year he spent in self-destruction. It's a miracle he wasn't shot in a barroom brawl. He hated everyone he got near, and he hated himself most of all. When I tried to get through to him, he told me to stay out of his affairs." She frowned, still baffled by her son's peculiar behavior.

"Then, suddenly, as though it had never happened, Garitson became his old self. He began to develop a strange interest in social affairs, and he cultivated a friendship with Silas Fairchild. Last year, he agreed to marry Vivian when she turned twenty-four. Her birthday was last month."

The words pitched Rebecca back into the church service this morning. Maria regarded Rebecca with a watchful eye. She crossed the room to put an arm around her shoulders. "They are not to marry until the winter. Ever the social pioneer, she wants to have an entirely white wedding, complete with snow. It's the talk of the town."

The woman shrugged philosophically. "Of course, there is a long fall before the snow," she mused. "And as you know, here in Texas it often doesn't snow at all in the winter. A pity Vivian's plans should go awry, but the *Farmer's Almanac* calls for a warm winter." Her eyes were wide again with innocent mischief.

"Does Vivian know you're her worst enemy?" Rebecca asked.

Maria shrugged. "Vivian sees me as nothing but a dreary old woman."

"That, I would imagine, was not her first stupid mistake in life."

❧ Sixteen ❧

Rebecca folded the newspaper spread before her and tucked it into a blank ledger Maria had given her for notes. She found Maria in a parlor, composing menus.

"Do you mind if I run into town for an hour or so?"

Maria looked up. "Certainly not. Don't dawdle, now. You don't want to be late for the party."

Rebecca shook her head, excited as she summoned Thomas to escort her to the *Jimplecute*. Arranged before her was a bustling, breathing wealth of living history. Added to the old mysteries of Jefferson's past were new, more immediate ones. Even more intriguing was the news she'd read in the paper last night and tried to analyze this morning.

The front room of the *Jimplecute* was empty.

"We're closed," came a bellow from the back. "Go away and come back next year." Rebecca recognized Gustav Frank's surly greeting, and she circumvented the printing press, carefully stepping over wide stacks of newsprint on her way to the back room.

"Good morning," she greeted him cheerfully.

He didn't look up from his page. "As you can see, Miss Reynolds, I am writing. Although I'm sure you think I can't tell a verb from a noun, they pay me to do just that. Good day."

"I read your paper. It was fascinating. You're quite a writer."

He put down his pen and sighed. "Not because I'm taken in by your flattery, but because I recognize the eager reporter face you're wearing and know I won't get any peace otherwise, I'll give you five minutes. Then I need to get back to work."

"Can you tell me what the Jefferson Railroad Company is?"

"Was, Miss Reynolds. It no longer exists. It was incorporated in 1854 and dissolved over ten years ago. It was organized to bring a railroad to Jefferson."

"Do you know if Jay Gould had anything to do with it?"

"Jay Gould?" He shook his head. "He's involved in rail, to be sure, but farther west. And there was the Erie scandal."

"What's that?"

"He sold unsuspecting Erie Rail shareholders sixty-four million dollars worth of fraudulent stock. That's Gould's biggest claim to infamy. But he couldn't have been much more than a boy back when Jefferson Railroad came to be. He spends most of his time on Wall Street. Jefferson Railroad was comprised entirely of Marion County residents, those of us who would directly benefit from rail."

"You quoted Garitson Behringer in your editorial. Did he really say that?"

Gustav's eyes blazed. "I am not Sadie Taylor, miss. He said, and you'll forgive me if I'm obliged to paraphrase, 'Were Jefferson not so preoccupied with keeping the Big Cypress River under Confederate control, she would see a far more immediate threat to her livelihood looming just over her shoulder: the iron horse.' He was twenty-four years old then, and people listened to him. He said it at a city council meeting, and it gave rail transportation for Jefferson a new urgency. Jefferson had already tried for years to lure rail into town, and it had been bypassed for the upper Red River valley. Boats couldn't get through the raft to those areas. Ironic, isn't it?"

"How so?"

"The raft was providence for Jefferson. If not for that big bottleneck of debris floating downstream in the Red River, the steamboats could've never gotten up and down the bayou."

"So if the raft hadn't been blown up, you believe Jefferson would still prosper?"

He snorted impatiently. "Of course not. Steamboat traffic is just too capricious, too archaic. The government's spent millions of dollars trying to humor the steamboat industry, but the design of the steamboat hasn't changed since the first one sailed. She's still a floating balloon just waiting to pop on one stray branch lurking submerged in the water. Anybody with a brain can see that rail is the thing for the future. Jefferson, I'm afraid, is doomed."

"Doomed?"

Gustav leaned back in his chair, enamored with the topic. "This is the irony. Jefferson as a river port supported the movement of cargo between here and Shreveport. When locations for rail service were being plotted, the need existed above Jefferson, below Jefferson, and all around Jefferson. Jefferson was still very successful in river transportation. So the rail went elsewhere. It wasn't until '73 that Jefferson was finally able to lure the Texas and Pacific down through the south end of town. By then, all the other rail centers were firmly established."

Rebecca stared stupidly at him. "You mean, there's a railroad here?"

He nodded. "Sure."

"Then where, for Pete's sake, is the problem?"

He shrugged. "Jefferson isn't known for rail. Dallas is. And Longview. The list goes on, Jefferson excluded from it. Jefferson, my dear, is the Belle of the Bayou."

"Gould's curse is nothing more than fiction," Rebecca murmured.

"Gould? Oh, no. The curse, as you call it, was real enough, but it wasn't Gould's, and it was more of a threat than a curse. Gould's never been to Jefferson, to my knowledge. A man named Scott was doing the negotiating for the Texas and Pacific. When Jefferson hesitated to cough up four hundred thousand dollars in bonds for the project, he said if they refused, grass would grow in her streets and bats would dwell in her empty houses. They coughed quickly enough after that."

"I thought it was the church belfries."

"What?"

Rebecca sighed. "Never mind. What a mess. Jefferson *wanted* railroad?"

"Since it came into existence. Her timing was just off."

Rebecca laughed hollowly, shaking her head in disbelief. "Timing is so important. Look, I know you're busy. Can I look through your back files?"

He chuckled. "Files? You're welcome to look through the back stacks. They're in the safe house, out back. It's unlocked, if you want to go right in. They should be vaguely organized."

"Some safe house. One last question."

"Shoot."

"What do you know about the *Mittie Stephens?*"

His eyes narrowed in concentration. "Oh, let me see. That happened the year I got married. It would've been 1869, February, I think. It was a terrible tragedy."

"What caused it?"

Gustav shook his head. "That's a mystery for all time. Nobody knows. They guess that somebody was smoking on deck and a stray spark landed in a load of hay they had on board."

"Did you know Garitson Behringer's wife?"

He considered her curiously, then sighed. "Yes. Why?"

Rebecca shrugged. "I was just . . . curious."

"Aren't you, though. Ask Behringer about Sarah. Or look through the old papers. It isn't my place to go spreading gossip."

Rebecca smirked. "I forgot. That's left to Mrs. Taylor."

Gustav grew surly. "I believe your five minutes are up, Fräulein. If you'll go around to the back of the building, you'll see a safe house where we keep the papers. It's open. Those'll be toward the back."

Rebecca nodded. "Thanks for your help."

Rebecca started out the front door, then wanted to step back in. Behringer was just leaving the bank across the street. As she hesitated at the doorway, he noticed her. He waved his hand in brief recognition, then began to cross the street. Rebecca ignored him, turning into the alley.

"Rebecca," Behringer called tersely. She stopped. He was fifteen feet short of her, and she sighed impatiently at the people staring as he reached her.

"I have to talk to you. I wanted to make sure you're coming to the party tonight."

Rebecca was pushed beyond the memory of his wife, to the memory of the conversation she'd overheard between Garitson and his father.

"As I told your father, I'm going to keep your mother company. I'll be there for her."

"I want you there for me," he said, his voice taut.

Her eyes glittered as she stared at him, and her words came out like tiny bullets. "Won't your hands be full without me?"

Behringer spoke, his voice low and strained. "I've stayed away from you for five days, Rebecca, and it's been hell."

"Oh?" she asked, with cool cynicism.

"Your memory comes upon me unexpectedly. And when I see you at home . . ." He shook his head slowly. "I see you in the garden bent over the plants, your dress moist from the heat, and I imagine undressing you there, the sunlight kissing parts of you that have never seen the sun."

Rebecca was silent, fighting the slow fire that curled around her at his erotic confession.

"I stand here now, wanting just to take you in my arms and soothe away your anger, and we both know it's impossible. And what I want more than anything is to say to hell with Vivian and her accursed party, and spend the night in your arms."

"How noble of you," she breathed wonderingly, shaken over his words, "to sacrifice a party with Vivian to realize a haphazardly constructed fantasy."

"Don't be unreasonable."

"You have the nerve to call me unreasonable?" she asked, choking in frustration.

"Rebecca," he began. He lifted a hand toward her then helplessly let it fall, staring broodingly at the dust beneath his feet. "As soon as I think I have you figured out, I know I'm wrong. And I know it's unfair, the thoughts I have of you. There's so much I can't begin to explain. So many things you couldn't know, because I'm not even sure that I know myself anymore. All I know is that—"

He looked up, slowly, and the turbulence in those dark eyes startled Rebecca. He opened and closed his mouth in earnest hesitation, and she waited. "Things are different than they were before you came. I'm d—"

"Oh, there you are!" interrupted that sugary overdone drawl, and Rebecca sighed. "Keeping your little sister's little friend company. Garitson, you're such a darling."

Rebecca noticed Vivian's smile didn't quite make it to her eyes, which were twin blue icicles in her perfect face. "Why, hello, Miss Reynolds. Thank you so much for watching over my fiancé."

The accent on their relationship lacked any attempt at subtlety. It was the simple claim of a child for her toy.

"My pleasure, Miss Fairchild."

Rebecca felt Garitson's gaze on her and she ignored it, continuing down the alley toward the storehouse.

Upon reaching it, Rebecca slipped inside, leaving the door open. The windows were shut, and it had to be 110 degrees inside. She found the papers from 1869 situated toward the back of the building, and she began to go through the stacks. At last she arrived there, and she read the headline reserved for announcements of war.

Mittie Stephens Sinks in Flames; Over Sixty Perish

She scanned the article, vaguely irritated at the writing style popular in the nineteenth century. Preoccupied with emotions and propriety, it took pages of reading before she arrived at any facts, and those were obscure. There was no reference to the Behringers, so sweeping was the tragedy. The hysteria on board the sinking inferno, however, came through with haunting realism. No cause for the fire was listed. Rebecca arrived at the last line of the story, and her pulse seemed to stop.

> *"The boat was financed by a Jefferson institution, Fairchild & Sons."*

❧ Seventeen ❧

The summer sun was sinking behind the cypress trees when the Behringer carriage prepared to leave that evening, a carriage rustling with petticoats and organdy. Rebecca couldn't resist a glance at Behringer as he settled himself in the seat beside her.

She clamped her mouth shut to calm the responsive flutter in the middle of her chest as his hard thigh met hers. Behringer's suit was of a café au lait linen, eye-catching among the dark browns, grays, and blacks which were in vogue, and his shirt a brilliant white lawn. The dark tan of his face contrasted against his shirt. She noticed the lemon yellow tie he wore, matching the rosebud at his collar, and the roses in her hair.

Jacob arrived at the carriage last, and his mood was surly. He spoke to his wife as the carriage went into motion. "Woman, I saw Gustav Frank this afternoon."

Rebecca glanced at him nervously. Uh-oh.

"Yes?" Maria asked nonchalantly.

"What were you thinking, ordering a typewriting machine?"

Maria looked at him. "I was thinking to purchase one. I told you I was going to."

"And I forbade you."

She waved a hand at him. "Silly man."

He thumped his fist against the carriage door, and Thomas brought the carriage to a halt.

"Drive on, Thomas," the elder Behringer roared.

Maria murmured something about pigheaded men.

"I am your husband, Maria. You will obey me."

"I am your wife, Jacob, and you will respect me," she responded, her words icy. She lifted her gaze to meet his.

He fell back against the seat as though he'd been struck.

Rebecca glanced at Behringer and found him watching his parents with interest as they volleyed challenges at each other.

Jacob asked quietly, "Why does this matter so much to you?"

"Because it matters so little to you," she retorted.

Jacob sighed, looking at Garitson with a disbelieving kind of pain.

"What do you think of all this, my son? Quite a disgrace, isn't it?"

Behringer looked from his mother to his father. "I think it's sweet," he said finally, his words light.

A sadness crossed Jacob's face. "Sweet. So. A man is humiliated by his wife, his pride stripped, and his son thinks it to be 'sweet.' It wasn't this way in our country. My mother never raised her voice to my father, and his word was supreme. Women knew the place where God had put them."

"Papa, times change."

"Times change," Jacob spat. "Respect for a man goes, and a woman can do whatever she wants."

Behringer gave an impatient groan. "I'd say women hardly do whatever they want. But they will always respect the men they love, just as Mama respects you. There will come a day, Papa, when women are taken seriously, as they should be. We should embrace the future as something better, rather than cowering in our past." He laughed shortly. "There's going to be a time, not too far in the future, when women are given the right to select a president. Perhaps the day will come when one will become president. Don't worry, Papa," he quickly assured the stricken man. "It probably won't happen in our lifetime."

Jacob recovered slowly. "You talk a lot of things to be, Garitson. Have you become a seer? A stargazer?"

Behringer leaned forward. "I have a fascination with the future, Papa. You know that. It seems to me a wonderful place, with nothing at all to fear."

Rebecca was shaken in the face of his impassioned enthusiasm for the future.

Maria abruptly changed the subject. "Don't they look lovely, Jacob?"

"Yes," Jacob grunted, looking suspiciously from one to the other. "They each look charming," he said carefully, refusing to fall into the trap Maria had set for him. Rebecca gazed out the window.

"You are beautiful, Rebecca," Behringer murmured into her ear. "And you smell like the summertime."

"It's just all the roses," she said, still not recovered from his words to his father.

"Oh, yes," he said, thunderstruck. "You're wearing roses, too! What a funny coincidence. I guess we'll be the best-smelling couple at the party."

At times, he lapsed into an absolute denial of Vivian's existence. "We won't be a couple at all, Garitson. You can be a cruel man with very little effort." She stared out the window.

The impressive Fairchild house was near downtown, only a few hundred feet from the Excelsior. The carriage paused near the front gate, and Rebecca stepped down first, ignoring Behringer's attempt to help her.

Behringer alighted and curled her hand around his arm, ignoring her reluctance. "Be still, child. You're trying my patience."

The warmth of his hand over hers made it impossible to concentrate as they approached the door. Suddenly distracted from Behringer, she noticed several couples on the Fairchild porch watching their approach together. The chattering crowd grew quiet as their hostess emerged from their midst, gaping in disbelief at the couple before her.

And then a quiet sort of hell unfurled itself.

"What is she doing here, Garitson?" Every guest within ten feet of the door heard the venomous hiss of Vivian's question. She eyed her fiancé's attire with glittering blue eyes.

Maria stepped forward, gently taking Vivian's arm. "Why, Vivian. I don't think you've been properly introduced to Rebecca."

Neither of them said anything as Maria made introductions. Rebecca grimaced at the process of actually having to shake the girl's hand.

As soon as the contact of hands was broken, Vivian rushed to Behringer's other side, possessively breaking him away from Rebecca.

"You look like a couple on top of a wedding cake," Vivian groused with childish petulance.

Rebecca turned to Maria, masking with a smile the feeling that consumed her. "Well," she said lightly. "I'm glad that's over with."

"Such a charming girl," Maria murmured, smiling, leading her toward the ballroom. "A copperhead could take lessons."

Once Rebecca mastered the art of not looking for Behringer, she began to enjoy herself. A young man appeared at her side, and she recognized him from church. Old Chiseled Cheekbones himself. "Hello," he said, smiling. "Charles Norton, from church?"

"Of course, Mr. Norton." She extended her hand to him, and he held it gently in his. "It's good to see you again."

"I'm charmed. You're with the Behringers tonight?" She noticed the delicately refined British inflection in his speech.

"Mrs. Behringer," she clarified. "And you seem to be a long way from home."

He laughed, delighted at her not-so-brilliant observation. "No, this is my home now. Would you care to dance?"

Putting her hand in his, she nodded. "I'd love to, Mr. Norton."

"Please, do call me Charles."

He spun amusing anecdotes as they danced, and she decided she liked Charles Norton. If for no other virtue than his ability to momentarily push Behringer to the edge of her mind. She was disappointed when he relinquished her to a blond man who tapped his shoulder.

"I'd like to have another dance later, if possible." Norton smiled, and Rebecca pitied whatever poor woman tried to compete with that face in the mirror each morning.

Smiling and nodding, Rebecca turned to greet her new partner. The next hour passed quickly and rather painlessly, shared with numerous dance partners who seemed quite content to overlook the scandal surrounding her. Later, Charles approached her. "Hello, Miss Reynolds. Would you—"

From over his shoulder, a smooth voice sounded suitably pained. "How dreadful, old chap," he mocked gently. "I believe this dance is mine."

"I don't think so, Mr. Behringer," Rebecca said, smiling coquettishly at him.

"Sweet child," he murmured comfortingly. "You promised me the ninth dance, and I'm quite certain this is the ninth. Now I must insist, Charles, for I'll have to leave quite soon for our meeting. Do run along. You'll be late."

Norton regarded Behringer's dismissal with cool amusement. "Behringer, I concede. Perhaps I'll skip the meeting and get the tenth."

Rebecca's breath left her as Behringer swept her onto the floor. "That was rude," she said, her eyes glittering.

"The man is a shark," Behringer said, his jaw tightening petulantly.

She rolled her eyes. "The man is a gentleman, Behringer."

His eyebrows went up. "Behringer? Shall I call you Reynolds?"

"I doubt it. You seem stuck on *witch*."

"You are one."

Rebecca forced her gaze away from Behringer's. Vivian Fairchild came into view, standing with a man Rebecca didn't recognize. Both were staring at Rebecca in Behringer's arms. Vivian's gaze held no affectation of graciousness; her hatred was palpable.

"Miss Fairchild is not pleased at this particular moment," Rebecca remarked.

"Miss Fairchild is giving Mr. Behringer a headache."

Rebecca grew bored with the topic. "Garitson, I read an article Gustav Frank wrote about rail. He quoted you."

"Yes?"

She nodded. "What are your plans for Jefferson?"

He chuckled. "I see the newspaper reporter in you coming out. My plans for Jefferson are not my own. I can't lift one finger to accomplish any of the suggestions I give these hard-headed townsmen. I merely offer advice."

"What sort of advice?"

"The area is a geological fantasy," he remarked. "There's iron ore for the picking. There's plenty of oil, though God knows what a body could do with it all. There's a timber industry yearning for birth. And there's still rail."

"Your meeting tonight—what are you planning to tell them?"

Behringer shrugged. "Tonight's meeting is the first step in setting up a major iron works. I have a hundred men to reckon with, men whose livelihood is still the bayou, and that total is dropping by the day."

"Do you think you can convince them of the value of the iron?"

"The value lies not in the iron, but in the trade, and in the reputation built around something besides that swamp out there. These are the most pigheaded men I've ever known. They seem paralyzed with fear, knowing rail managed to slip by us, and yet denying that painfully obvious fact. Rebecca, please don't make me talk about business tonight. I can scarcely count to ten with you in my arms."

Startled into silence at his soft confession, Rebecca

glanced up at him. Presently his long, slender fingers went sliding down the curve of her spine. "The dress is beautiful," he said. "We make a lovely couple, as Mama said."

"You have no room in your couple for me. There's already a tight fit, it seems. Miss Fairchild certainly wants no one else there."

He leaned close to brush his lips against her ear, in the guise of whispering. And then he did whisper, a few horribly familiar words. "Miss Fairchild does not run my life."

She instantly remembered the conversation she'd overheard between Behringer and his father. "You're rather proud of pointing that out, aren't you? If you'll excuse me."

Rebecca left her dance partner standing in the midst of swirling couples and joined Maria, unhappy to find that she'd watched the entire humiliating episode. Maria merely smiled and patted her hand comfortingly. When Rebecca looked at the dance floor, she noticed Garitson was gone. And as her gaze swept past the entryway, she saw a late-arriving guest.

Bessie Moore.

❧ Eighteen ❧

"Bessie!" Rebecca exclaimed as she arrived at the woman's side. "I thought you'd already left town."

Rebecca knew Bessie had a distinct point to her visit, for she was in the midst of Jefferson's finest society. An entertainer wouldn't welcome such an intimate audience. Bessie glanced around uneasily at the party guests who stared at her. Rebecca noticed the discreet whisper which was circling the room, and she ignored it.

"We're leaving tonight," Bessie said finally.

"Where are you going?"

Bessie shook her head. "I'm not sure. We'd planned to go to New Orleans. I wanted the chance to sing one last time. But we've spent the last week with some friends of Benjamin's in Marshall, and now, New Orleans doesn't hold the same lure. Benjamin wants us to go on to Dallas."

"I saw Abe last Saturday, Bessie. He thought I was you, and he was rather rough with me at first. I made up a story for him. It was a terribly stupid one, but I think he believed me. I told him you were on your way to Cincinnati. He seemed strange."

"In what way?"

Rebecca hesitated. "He says he's changed."

Bessie's face displayed regret and confusion. "Oh, Rebecca, I don't know what to do."

"Stay away from Abe. He's a violent man."

"He always said he wanted to change. I never thought he was capable of it. But perhaps . . ."

"Go to Dallas, Bessie. Forget New Orleans. And forget Abe."

Bessie's face went hopeful with the promise of Benjamin's quiet lifestyle. "I should, shouldn't I?"

Rebecca laughed softly. "Yes. You should. Dallas is a fine city."

"How would you know, supposedly being from *Shreveport?*"

The catty voice just over Rebecca's shoulder made her skin creep. Vivian Fairchild's eyes were frosty as they went from Rebecca to her companion.

"This is a private party, Mrs. Rothschild. Or what name might you be using tonight?"

Bessie's face went white at Vivian's words, spoken in a voice she didn't bother to lower.

"Did your husband introduce you to your new beau?" Vivian went on innocently. "Perhaps originally he was a customer?"

"Rebecca, I only wanted to say good-bye," Bessie began.

"Good-bye," Vivian said, with a sweet smile.

"You're a real credit to your town, Vivian," Rebecca spat, taking Bessie's arm and walking outside with her. "I'm sorry," she said, when they stood in the Fairchilds' front yard.

Bessie shook her head. "It isn't anything I don't deserve," she said. "Rebecca, thank you for your friendship. I shall never forget you."

Rebecca noticed the carriage waiting at the gate, and she hugged Bessie. "Always take care. And never come back to Jefferson."

Bessie frowned thoughtfully. "Why do you say that? I'll never see you again."

Rebecca shook her head. "Trust me, Bessie. You'll be better off without Jefferson."

Rebecca watched the carriage drive away, and she saw Bessie's small hand waving at her from the window.

As Rebecca started inside, a maid approached her in the yard.

"Please, miss," she whispered urgently. "Mr. Behringer has been hurt. He told me to tell no one but you."

Rebecca's alarm constricted her face. "Oh, my God. Where is he?"

"In the woods just behind Mr. Fairchild's office. . . . If you would just go to him until I can find the surgeon."

Rebecca followed the path toward the woods behind Fairchild's office. Then, she noticed the light in Fairchild's office, heard a voice speaking in a casual, businesslike tone. Upset that this meeting was taking place while Garit lay hurt in the woods, she paused just below the window at the back of the office.

A quiet murmur was in the room, signaling the meeting in progress. "Gentlemen," Fairchild was saying calmly, "I'd like to get the meeting under way. We'll begin by having tonight's speaker introduced."

Immediately confused, wondering how he could go on as if nothing were amiss, she hesitated. Another voice spoke. "I say it's a waste of time. We ain't exactly Pennsylvania."

"Brower, you're a fool. If you have it your way, it'll be just like that railroad guy said. Jefferson'll see grass growin' in 'er streets and bats hangin' in th' church belfries."

Raucous chuckles were followed by a familiar voice. Gustav Frank's. "I heard an interesting twist on that. Someone told me Jay Gould said it. Can you imagine the Wizard of Wall Street cursing Jefferson?"

More laughter, and an odd awareness crept over Rebecca. She knew, in that moment, that she was witnessing the birth of a legend. Even more unbelievable—she had fertilized the seed of that legend.

Another voice spoke, shocking her. It was one she loved. "Gentlemen, please. Mr. Robert Graves is with us tonight, and as most of you know, he's a highly respected leader in the field of iron ore mining."

And the rest of Garitson's words were lost, for someone grabbed her from behind in a motion which startled and disarmed her. A hand slapped over her mouth, silencing her startled cries, and another strapped around her chest in a grip which drove away her breath. As her unseen attacker dragged her away from the window, she prayed that someone inside had heard something. In the same moment, she knew there had been nothing to hear.

Mutely screaming, Rebecca kicked wildly, scraping her nails over the forearm banded across her breasts. Though she fought him, her abductor made steady progress toward the woods. Finally, she succeeded in dislodging her arm from his grasp, and she tore at the hand that covered her mouth, sinking her teeth into his palm. Startled, he moved his hand from her mouth. Not pausing to catch a breath, Rebecca began screaming Behringer's name.

Only a few moments passed before the back door of the building swung open, and Garit leapt from the steps there and toward her. Already her abductor had released her, but he had time to go no more than two steps into the shadows before Behringer snatched him by the collar.

A chilling fury seized Behringer, and he strove to contain it. "Murphy, you bastard. I should have known when you weren't there that you were out somewhere digging up trouble."

Harry Murphy raised his hands in front of himself in surrender. "I was late, Behringer. I saw her there peeking in the window, and I thought . . . I didn't know what she was up to."

"If she was at the window, how'd you end up over here?" Behringer demanded sardonically.

"Release him, Behringer." The coolly spoken command shocked Rebecca, and she swung around to see a man a few years older than Garit standing there.

Appalled, Behringer glared at the man. "Are you out of your mind, Fairchild?"

"I said release him." Then he turned those arctic eyes on Rebecca, eyes the same color as his daughter's. "And I'm curious to know why you were listening to our meeting."

"Someone said . . ." she began, then fell silent.

Fairchild continued to stare at her. "Do go on."

As Rebecca glanced around the group of men, she noticed the suspicion in their eyes. "It doesn't matter."

Behringer released Murphy. "Fairchild, you owe Miss Reynolds an apology." His voice shook with anger.

"An apology?" Fairchild repeated softly, turning his head and raising eyebrows above a blank blue gaze. "She's spying on our meeting, Garitson, and you're covering for her. Of course, it wouldn't be the first time you've thrown Shreveport's trash in our face."

Behringer pounced on Fairchild, and he was instantly restrained by Harry Murphy and another man. He stood still, gathering slow, deep breaths, until he contained his anger.

"Are you all right, Rebecca?"

She nodded mutely, staring at her feet. One of her shoes was missing.

"Excuse me, gentlemen," Behringer muttered. "But I'm going to see my guest safely home, if you don't mind. I'm sure you'll do fine without me," he said, his voice carefully controlled. He turned to a man who observed the conflict in disbelief. "Mr. Graves, I apologize. You see before you a shining example of the South and her archaic attitudes. Good night."

Behringer grabbed Rebecca's hand and yanked her after him as he walked across the street to the livery stable and borrowed a horse. Swinging himself into the saddle, he reached down a strong arm and lifted Rebecca in front of him. He settled her across his lap, and they started off at a gallop toward home.

❧ Nineteen ❧

When they arrived at the house, Behringer gave the horse to Thomas. He grasped Rebecca's elbow and propelled her forward to the house, forcing her to hurry after him. He didn't release her all the way up the stairs, and when she would've stopped at the landing and explained her version of the events, he ignored her. He took her arm in his strong grip and jerked her forward. At his room, he shoved open the door and crossed the threshold, slamming it behind him. With purposeful motions, he struck a match and lit the lamp by the bed.

Furious at his mistreatment, she raised a defiant gaze to his, startled at what she saw there.

He stared at her, his face confessing a half dozen conflicting passions. She waited, trying to discern them. Anger. Fear. Arousal. Frustration. Others whose very anguish were displayed plainly in the violent intensity of his gaze. Her breath came in shallow gasps as she battled the emotion, hers and his, which overwhelmed her.

Behringer watched her with a jagged-edged tenderness, and he slowly raised a hand to rest against her face with the fleeting lightness of a butterfly. The touch slipped away as his hand fell to his side. She unraveled at his gentle hesitation and tears slipped quietly from her eyes. He exhaled impatiently. And he took her in his arms.

Her tears fell silently onto his shirt, and he stroked her hair, soothing her as he might have once soothed Katy. Slowly he withdrew, drawing her forward to sit on the bed. He smiled wryly and gently slipped off the remaining shoe.

"You're shivering," he said quietly.

"I'm cold."

"It must be ninety degrees outside."

Behringer crossed his room to a cabinet. Opening the wide glass doors, he chose a crystal decanter from the bottles displayed and splashed a dark liquid into a brandy snifter. Then he returned to the bed. "Drink. Slowly."

"What is it?" Rebecca asked softly, touching the bowl of the glass as he held it up to her lips.

"Cognac." His voice was soft, and she followed his instructions, sipping slowly of the liquid warmth until it was gone. He replaced it with another and leaned against the bedpost, unhurriedly watching her finish it.

Warmed by the cognac and the lazy scrutiny in Behringer's eyes, Rebecca relaxed against his pillow, enclosed in a warm web of tranquillity, sapped of strength, almost floating. For a moment, she considered what kind of girl Garitson Behringer must think she was. Her heroines behaved much more suitably.

He sat on the bed beside her, one leg resting against her hand. "Now tell me what happened, honey."

The gently spoken endearment was her undoing, and all the emotion of the past half hour came rushing back at her.

"I thought you were hurt. And then, I thought all those men were going on with that stupid meeting without you. Even though it was so important to you to be there, they didn't care that you were out in the woods, maybe half beaten to death. And then I thought, maybe they knew."

Rebecca saw his crooked smile as he took her hand. He drew his thumb back and forth across her palm and rested her hand against the strong, muscular heat of his thigh. Not so many minutes before, she had feared for his life. Now, she wanted only to cherish his vitality. She opened her hand and stretched her fingertips over that hardness, kneading the flexed muscle.

"I was afraid. A girl told me you'd been hurt. I thought I'd never see you . . . laughing at me again."

He chuckled softly, and she noticed the uneasy glimmer in his eyes as he glanced at her hand on his thigh. "Rest assured," he murmured. "I'll be laughing at you for a long time."

"What's wrong?"

His smile faded. "Who told you I was hurt?"

"I don't know. A chambermaid," Rebecca said. "She told me she was going for the surgeon." Her fingers slowly memorized the length of his thigh. He was a beautifully made man.

His body went rigid, and her hand fell to the cool coverlet as he left the bed, moving to the window. After a quick, deliberate glance at the deserted road below, he drew the drapes.

"Murphy, of all people."

Not hearing his words, Rebecca forced herself to ask, "Is it Vivian you're worried about?"

He was at her side in a moment. "What?"

"Vivian must be furious by now." Her words were whispered as she awaited his reaction.

Behringer's thigh rested full length against her hips. He leaned close to her, gently resting his fingers on the soft curve of her cheekbone. "You may be a good witch, but you aren't a very smart one," he whispered. "You'd risk your life for an idiot who dared to offer you no more than a country home and stolen weekends, when you deserve the world."

Tilting her chin up, he lowered his mouth to hers, gently drinking the sweetness of her desire for him. Only a kiss, he told himself. Anything more would be criminal. But he couldn't walk away from her without tasting her sweetness just once.

Rebecca ran her palms lightly over his hair, then slid her fingers through its silky richness. Her lips coaxed his apart, tenderly tracing his parted lips with her tongue, and she tasted his surprise.

Behringer caught his breath at the bold enticement in her touch and his hunger deepened. Thrusting his fingers into the hair that fell over her shoulders, the roses gone, Behringer tried to find a way to draw her even closer.

Jesus! He must be losing his mind. He abruptly drew away from her, rising and grasping the bedpost, staring down at the floor. He shoved his fingers through his hair, exhaling heavily.

"What is it?" she asked.

"I should get you out of here. Right now. Back to Shreveport, away from this hell."

"Is that what you want?"

Behringer looked up at her, considering her somberly. His eyes raked her with ravenous, desperate restraint. When he spoke, his voice was softly ironic, his gaze troubled. "What I want? A number of desires come to mind, none of which is that. Life doesn't often ask my opinion, sweetheart."

"I am."

His gaze drifted over her helplessly. "Jesus. You even have to ask?"

"Why are you still here with me?"

Behringer's eyes were half closed as he considered her. His hair was tousled, his expression grim. "You're making this very hard for me."

"Oh?" Her voice was a shallow whisper.

"The chivalrous thing to do would be . . . well, anything except what I'm entertaining. You've had too much cognac."

Rebecca sat up in the bed, her hair falling forward over the full display of her breasts. "Is that it, then? You think I'm too drunk to know what I want?"

He raised an eyebrow. "I've never seduced a child before."

She rose from the bed, moving closer to him until they stood only a hairsbreadth apart. "A child?"

He tilted his head, his gaze dipping to her mouth. Her

tongue slipped out there, invitingly wetting her lower lip. His breath escaped him in a hiss. "Hardly."

"You should go to bed," he said, his voice a narcotic murmur. "You've had a fright."

"I should. I will. In a minute."

She lightly touched the front of his shirt. Her fingertips brushed the rose on his coat, its soft petals unfurling helplessly, then she deftly unpinned it and placed it on the table beside the bed.

"I'll walk you to your room," he said, standing stiffly against the gentle seduction of her movements.

She nodded. "I know the way."

"Rebecca." His voice was deep, and rough, and desperate.

She quietly removed his jacket, then began separating the buttons of his shirt.

He took her hands in his, stopping her. "You're my sister's friend," he said. "She's mixed you up with me, and—"

Rising up on her toes, Rebecca lay her open mouth against his throat, smiling. "And you're a dangerous guy."

Behringer pushed her away with a raw power. His eyes were nearly black in frustration and fury. "Do you think this is all a game Katy made up?" he whispered. Strong fingers closed angrily about her wrist. He pried open her trembling fingers and placed her palm just below his belt. "It's not a game," he said hoarsely.

The potent, violently aroused hardness jutting against her hand enflamed her, and a soft sigh escaped her lips. She stretched her fingertips down along the length of him, learning the shape of that arrogant male thrust.

"Rebecca," he groaned.

He had not expected this. He arched into her touch.

"You are a beautiful man," she said.

Unable to do otherwise, she reached for him, her arms sliding up over his chest and curling around his neck. She drew his vital warmth near. "You're hard . . . all over."

His lips found hers, and his hands slipped down her spine until they cupped her smooth roundness in his palms. He pulled her upward into the juncture of his thighs, and her breath caught against his mouth. A moment later, she was lifted in his arms, and then they were together in his bed.

Behringer heard once more the warnings of his conscience. How differently would she feel about this in morning's harsh light? He knew the honorable thing was to leave her to recover from her trauma. He further knew that honor was the last thing on his mind. He would doubtless hate himself tomorrow, but tonight . . . ah, sweet heavens. Tonight.

Her eyes fluttered shut as she relaxed against the bed's softness, and Behringer studied the flush on her lovely face. She opened her eyes, gazing at him provocatively. Her pupils were dilated, darkening her eyes to a soft amber, and her breath was shallow.

He considered the gentle girl lying beneath him, and his heart tripped in a way he didn't expect. Remembering the terror that had gripped him when he heard her incoherent scream and saw Murphy dragging her fighting body toward the woods, knowing the fate that had awaited her there, he shuddered. It was a horror he had known only once in his forty years. His conscience assaulted him once more.

"Sweet angel. I want more than anything to bury myself in your lovely, hungry body. And if I do, neither of us will ever forgive me."

"Leave my conscience to me," she murmured with a lazy smile, kissing his earlobe. Her tongue toyed with the smooth line of his ear, then dipped inside.

"Ah," Behringer said softly, surrendering to that barely leashed animal of passion that lurked within, the beast that Rebecca was maddeningly enticing. "Let me taste you, love."

Rebecca's mouth traveled over the softness of his beard to that perfectly formed mouth, and she teasingly nipped his full lower lip. Then, her tongue slipped over his lip, soothing the wound.

"Where on earth have you been all these years?" He leaned back, shrewdly watching her.

She looked at him wistfully, remembering the last ten years, then laughed at the thought of explaining.

He laughed, too. "In grammar school," he said bitterly. "Fending off boys young enough to be my son." He frowned. "This isn't a productive line of reasoning."

"I'm a lot older than I said, Garitson."

"Are you? How much?"

"What difference does it make?"

"At this point," he said, his hand trembling as it drifted down the line of her throat, "none."

He carefully drew her hair away from her breast, then he trailed his fingertips backward across the full upper curve. His hand slipped with tantalizing slowness downward, and he watched her breathless reaction. Memorizing her shape, his fingers closed around the firm thrust, and he felt the expectant rise of its peak through the thin layers of fabric.

Rebecca's eyes closed with the onslaught of his touch as she whispered his name.

She looked up at him, finding his dark gaze on her. The emotion blazing in his eyes brought a singularly feminine smile to her lips. Staring at her with an equally lazy smile, he touched his tongue to the corner of his mouth. Watching him curiously, Rebecca drew him down to her, and she kissed him fully, her tongue questing and finding his. She sighed against his lips, vaguely aware of his hands loosening hooks. He lightly touched the dress at her shoulder, drawing it down until it fell away from her.

Never taking his mouth from hers, Behringer caught the strap of her chemise with his fingertip and drew it down as well. Then he moved away slightly, savoring her beauty in the lamp's glow. Gently pulling the dress and chemise down to her waist, his gaze kindled. Full, pale softness, untouched by the summer sun that had kissed her face and arms to a healthy glow, crowned by nipples the same color as her mouth, all of it completely kissable.

Rising up on the bed beside her, Behringer found an intensely male pleasure in removing the layers of dainty muslin and organdy from the fragile silk of her flesh. When she lay naked on his bed, he could only stare, amazed that one woman could be so perfect. Equally amazed she was his. His gaze was harsh and tender as it traveled over her body.

At last, Rebecca could no longer endure his sensual scrutiny, and she softly whispered his name. "I want to touch you," she whispered. "To see you." She rose, standing naked in the lamp's glow, and rested her hands on his shoulders.

She was *his*. Raising his eyes to her face, he thought she was by far the most beautiful woman he'd ever known. Far more beautiful than he deserved.

He leaned over long enough to lower the lamp to a forgiving haze, then stood beside her. Though his instincts warned him, he could not turn off the lamp entirely; just gazing at her was a more achingly sweet pleasure than the most intense sexual act.

Her fingers anxiously released the remaining buttons of his shirt. Behringer watched her impatience with intoxicated delight; she inspired more feelings in his dead heart than he'd known in years. Perhaps ever.

Pushing his shirt off broad, tanned shoulders, Rebecca paused to gaze at the indistinct shadow of his chest in the dim light, moistening her lips, wishing it were daylight. Wanting to inspect every inch of that magnificent chest. She contented herself with brushing her fingertips through the soft, crisp black curls instead.

Behringer watched in fascination as she knelt to remove his shoes. And when her hands paused at his belt, and she looked up into his eyes, he gently touched her cheek, encouraging her.

He was hers. Rebecca's fingers trembled over the buttons of his trousers. His hands stroked her hair, reassuring her. As she slowly stripped him, she paused, considering her next actions, wondering what he would think of this gently bred young lady of Shreveport. It didn't matter, in the end. Her own desire couldn't be dissuaded.

Behringer watched her breathlessly, afraid to speak for fear of breaking the mystical spell she'd woven around him. Her breasts brushed his thighs, and when she touched him, it was with a caress as the whisper of leaves outside his window, cool and hot in the same instant, simple and profound. Then she parted her beautiful lips, and the startled sigh that escaped him was her name.

She heard his whisper of disbelief, and her low murmur of contentment answered him, intensifying her assault on his senses. He couldn't have moved if he'd been foolish enough to want to. He had never known a more giving woman. Where had she learned such exquisite pleasuring of a man?

The thought jarred him instantly, and his jaw tightened as his mind fought the images that invaded, bearing logic and insanity. Rebecca in another man's arms, a man who had tutored her in the art of pleasure. A sadness, and a jealousy he'd never thought himself capable of, ripped through him.

He tilted her head away from him, looking down into her eyes, finding there a mixture of pleasure and hopefulness. Her expression pierced his heart and drove the jealousy away. Only one thing eclipsed her own pleasure at that moment, and it was the knowledge of his.

He lifted her in his arms, one arm underneath the soft smoothness of her thighs. Tossing back the covers, he nestled her once more in his bed. She'd incited his passion until he could barely speak, and that was something to say of the glib Garitson Behringer. He watched her, overcome with a tenderness alien to him.

"You're magnificent," she whispered, touching his shoulders.

A humility went through him. "Rebecca," he whispered, "I doubt that I deserve you."

She smiled. "Perhaps it's repayment for a good deed in a past life," she suggested.

"If there's more than one life, my darling, it's my intention to spend the next one with you. Only you."

A shudder went over Rebecca's slender body, and she

pulled Garit down to her, kissing his ear. "Promise me," she urged him.

"I promise." He chuckled. "If it takes me all of eternity to find you."

Garit lowered his mouth to hers, his thumbs brushing the peaks of her breasts until she arched against him. Slowly, he trailed warm, moist kisses down the line of her shoulder. Fascinated with the texture of her, he took a taut nipple into the shelter of his mouth. As she clutched his head close to her, he trailed his fingers down the smoothness of her body.

Parting her thighs in a movement that Rebecca didn't feel at all, he lightly ran his fingers upward on her inner thigh until he reached her damp warmth.

She reached between their bodies to find him, smooth and hard against her fingers. She raised an imploring gaze to his. "Please."

Probing gently where she led him, he slid within her. His breath caught at the snugness that welcomed him.

It was with a sense of wonder that Behringer felt the barrier separating him from the full velvet sleeve of her desire. It was impossible. He had unhappily reasoned that the selfless lovemaking she lavished upon him couldn't have been gained otherwise than through experience. With the last raveling shred of his reason, he sought to withdraw from her.

She encouraged him with a flex of her thighs, arching up to that part of him that could ease the incredible, ceaseless torment raging within her. A sheen of sweat glistened on his forehead with the sudden force of restraint.

"Jesus, Rebecca, you're a virgin."

"Please don't stop," she said, her voice husky with desire.

"Damn," he breathed.

Behringer sank into her in one thrust, breaching the fine barrier. Rebecca's face, in shadowed profile, intensified his arousal, and he savored the feeling of her heart's beat within her, knowing she felt his as well. He withdrew at last and began passion's slow, steady dance.

A flush of passion suffused Rebecca's face. Soft, blush-rose lips were parted slightly, and long, sweeping lashes fluttered upward as he stared. She caught her lower lip between her teeth, and Behringer lowered his head to capture that tormented mouth with his.

A luscious tension stole over her, into that warm, female place Behringer ruthlessly charmed.

"I . . ." Rebecca's voice came from an inferno Behringer incited with an intense maleness that drove the breath from her. She circled his hips with her thighs, heightening their pleasure, sharpening the tantalizing pressure within her.

He buried his face in the fragrant softness of her hair, nipping her earlobe, soothing it with his tongue. "So sweet," he murmured.

His voice seduced her senses, and Rebecca cried out his name as she was flung over the pinnacle of the fire which was Garitson Behringer. His kisses upon her throat mingled with gentle nips of his teeth and tongue until the tremors passed. He paused, only slightly surprised to feel the stream of her laughter trickling over him.

He smiled grimly, and the moist warmth of his lips brushed against her ear, his voice softly threatening. "You dare to giggle, madam?"

"I dare to be ecstatic, sir," she grinned.

Behringer's movements were determined, purposeful, as he unleashed the tumult of emotions warring within him. He softly murmured dark words of love, and Rebecca's hands moved anxiously over his body, glistening with the sheen of their lovemaking.

She said his name, softly, over and over in a lyric of love. The rippling muscles of his body were tightly drawn, and she urged him toward his climax, meeting his movements with a fervor that finally inflamed him past a point from which he never wanted to return.

As she stroked his shoulders, Behringer shifted to lie beside her, watching with a numb bewilderment. She put her fingertips on his lips, in the way an eight-month-old babe explores her father's mouth. He lazily traced her sweeping curves, pleased at the satiated pliability of her flesh, content to know it was a result of his lovemaking.

He whispered her name, and it was a breath of wonder. He drew her into the circle of his arms, watching her sleepy eyes close.

Safe in the reality of the dreams that existed within his arms, Rebecca's last thought was a distant memory of the legend of Garitson's room. And with that, she drifted to sleep.

❧ Twenty ❧

Behringer was mightily tempted by the prospect of sleeping in her arms, but it was impossible. Too many people had seen him leave Fairchild's office with her, too many would be examining their watches until he returned. He rose from the bed and examined his own. It was after eleven.

He swore silently and dressed. After a quick glance into the empty hallway, he lifted Rebecca in his arms and carried her into Katy's room. He found a nightgown in the bureau and slipped it over her head, thankful for her brandy oblivion. He tucked a sheet over her, then hesitated, gazing down at her instead of leaving.

He didn't like the direction his heart had taken, but he seemed powerless to control it. Making love to her was bad enough; an entire list of immoral traits was attached to it. Her reputation had already been ruined; he had made no halfhearted attempt to prevent a pregnancy; she already had an unhappy relationship with her family; and she was his little sister's friend, an innocent. There, of course, lay the blackest deed of them all. He had seduced a girl half his age. A virgin, one who trusted him, one whose glance stirred in him a host of life's finest emotions. Making love to her was undoubtedly a mistake, one he would repeat in a heartbeat. Falling in love with her would be suicidal for both of them.

He left the room, returning to his own, where he penned a quick note at the desk, then tucked it in his pocket. He yanked a bag from underneath his bed and threw a change of clothes into it. Against his better judgment he stopped once more to check on Rebecca before he left. He opened her door and moved soundlessly into the room.

The moonlight spilled across her lips, which still blushed from his kiss, and he bent, brushing his lips there before he left.

When he closed the door to Katy's room, he noticed his mother standing at the landing, watching him with narrowed eyes. Mothers were peculiar, he thought as he observed her piercing gaze. With one glance, they knew.

"Garitson," she said with disbelieving disapproval.

"Mama, please—" he began, looking at the rug.

"Tell me you didn't."

He raised his gaze to hers. "I would like nothing more than to be able to."

She closed her eyes and exhaled slowly, her lips tightening into a thin line. "How do you feel about the young lady, Garitson?"

Behringer raked his hand through his hair. "How should I feel, or how do I feel?"

"Stop your puzzles and tell me the truth."

He searched for it. "She makes me feel the way I always dreamed a woman could."

"Sarah? Do you love her as you loved Sarah?"

The name conjured within Behringer, as it always did, a trio of spectres: the memory of the laughing little boy she'd given him, the sickening horror over the death she and their son had been forced to suffer, and the last, worst of the three. Guilt.

"I'm going back to the party." He walked past his mother.

Maria gave a sound of frustrated fury. "*Party?* You're going back to rejoin your fiancée's party after seducing a girl who's clearly in love with you?"

Behringer's head snapped around. "I have no choice. The

fine citizens of Jefferson already know she's been with me for over an hour. The least I can do is try to come up with an excuse for my absence that doesn't involve her."

Maria shook her head slowly. "I do not believe what I am hearing."

"I'll be gone for a couple of days, Mama. I'm going to Shreveport."

"I trust you'll be visiting her father?"

"I'll be visiting several people while I'm there, and stop trying to run my life. Marrying Vivian Fairchild is the only way I have of—" He stopped, and the rage flowing between the mother and son held the power and peril of a lightning bolt. "I have to go."

Behringer saddled a horse in the stable and returned to the Fairchild house. Though the party ended some time before, he couldn't drag himself away from Vivian, who was in a fine snit, until after one. When he left her, he turned the horse to the east.

It was late the next morning when he checked into a hotel in Shreveport. As he signed his name on the register, he said, "I'd like to send a telegram."

"We can take care of that for you, sir. What would you like it to say?"

Behringer quickly penned the note.

Katy. Found a very beautiful friend of yours in my bath last Friday. Tasteless prank. Send me her father's name by return message at the Grand Hotel in Shreveport. Need to see him soon. All my love, Garitson. P.S. Grow up. Immediately.

Behringer handed the sheet to the clerk, then reached into his pocket. "I'd also like to send this note to Nels Janssen, at the Janssen Company. And I'd like a hot bath in my room now."

"Certainly, Mr. Behringer. You'll be in room twelve, at the

top of the stairs. We'll send word up as soon as we receive it from Mr. Janssen."

Behringer took the key and climbed the staircase, arriving just before a young boy who tugged a copper tub after him. Minutes later, Behringer sank into the tub, grateful for the heat. As he closed his eyes, he was plagued by the memory of Rebecca, tormented with his imagination which placed her beside his sister and her mischief. He groaned in exhaustion. He was going to give Katy a sound spanking as soon as she got home.

His sister seemed perpetually seven years old, but perhaps he saw her that way because the year Katy turned seven was the year his life began to grow peaceful once more. Katy had started life as an afterthought in his parents' marriage, and she became a bright blessing in their middle age. He'd been twenty-eight years old. The war had ended ten months before, and he'd returned to his beautiful Sarah. Peter had been born that year, and Jacob Behringer found in his grandson a reason to try to reconcile the relationship with his son that had been torn asunder years before.

When Behringer was a boy, his father had doted on him. He smiled grimly at the memory, savoring it. For only ten years later, his father would find cause to hate him. That moment came on the day that Behringer announced he would wed Sarah Stein. First disbelieving, Jacob asked his son to repeat himself. When he still heard the same Jewish name, the elder Behringer was enraged.

Behringer had made it into manhood thinking his father only played at prejudice. He learned that day that Jacob Behringer hated Saul Stein as much as the other man hated him. He couldn't believe that his only son would dare to marry a Jew. And, only slightly lesser in its shame, the daughter of one of Jacob's chief competitors, heiress to a Shreveport steamer line.

Behringer ignored his father's bigotry, married Sarah, and joined the Union army the next month, completing a circle of betrayal. There were still many in Jefferson who remembered Behringer's allegiances, and who hated him for his rejection of everything the South embraced. The merciless killing machine that had raped and humiliated the South counted Behringer among its supporters. Each night on the battlefield, he lay staring into a sky that taunted him with the knowledge that he'd broken his father's heart. That he'd married a woman whose father hated him, then left her to bear that man's cold, simmering rage. He'd married her knowing he might never return from battle, knowing that if they'd made a child, the child would be an orphan whose grandfathers hated him.

Luckily, Sarah hadn't conceived. A mere two months after his return, however, she'd happily announced that she was expecting a child. The child was Peter, and he was a smaller, male version of his mother.

From the day Behringer had announced his wedding plans, Maria had coaxed Jacob to accept Sarah. She never succeeded. When Peter had been born, however, Jacob had visited Behringer's new home on the other side of the bayou, bringing a wagon that the boy wouldn't be able to play with for years. The man had doted on his grandson as though the boy's mother was from the finest Catholic family in Munich.

Peter had only recently discovered the toy by his third birthday, and his mother took him to visit her grandparents in Shreveport. The visit was only to last a few days. Their passage home was booked on the *Mittie Stephens*.

If only he'd been there!

He'd never forgiven his father for the hatred that had tainted his marriage to Sarah, and he'd never forgiven himself for his own feelings of shame. Despite it all, his was a cowardly, contemptible soul. Rather than forsaking his father and remaining faithful to his wife, he'd found himself unable to sleep at nights, watching Sarah sleep, praying for a way to span a chasm as old as Jacob and Esau. Quite simply, Behringer resented Sarah for the rift she caused between his father and himself.

The day Behringer secured passage for Sarah, Peter, and

Sarah's maid, he could have easily included himself. He was so busy with those profiting from the flourishing river trade, he told himself, that he couldn't afford to take off. That was a lie. Behringer had never been so foolish a businessman as to be without a competent associate. So when his best friend and business partner, Harry Murphy, saw Behringer's dilemma, and suggested that he go along on the trip to assure Sarah's safety, Behringer had agreed. He'd assuaged his guilt with the knowledge that he'd sent his most trusted friend in his place. He wouldn't be forced to deal with the unpleasantness of his father-in-law.

The night Sarah was to arrive home, he hadn't been able to sleep. He drove the buggy down toward Caddo Lake, impervious to the chill of the February night. Just after midnight, he passed Swanson's Landing. A half hour later began the hell that would destroy his family and cripple his life.

Just offshore, a once-beautiful, once-sleek stern-wheeler lay fatally wounded, her bow a smoking hulk, her stern engulfed in blazes, already lurching into the murky grave of Caddo Lake. Two stern-wheelers couldn't be approaching Jefferson this hour of the night. Confirming his fears, he saw the name of the boat illuminated and partially obliterated by the flames. Behringer flinched as he remembered the anguished shout that had rent the air. His own shout.

As his heart constricted inside his chest, Behringer stripped off his heavy overcoat and slipped into the icy waters of the lake, swimming toward the wreck. The pandemonium that surrounded the boat was a terror that would never fade from his heart. Women, children, and men were in the water, clinging to debris from the boat. A young woman stood poised at the edge of the stern, only a few feet from him, clutching a child in her arms. The glare from the fire rendered his vision nearly useless, unable to make out the woman's face. For a moment, joy filled his breast, until he realized the boy was too old to be Peter.

Driven by the flames, the woman jumped into the water, hugging her son. Instantly he knew she couldn't swim, and for a hellish split-second he would regret the rest of his life, he deliberated his decision. Then, he imagined his own Sarah emerging from those flames, reaching for him, unable to find him, and he turned away from the woman. A moment later, the unknown woman slipped beneath the surface of the lake, holding her son protectively into eternity.

Later, Behringer understood it was only the water and muck of the lake saturating his clothes that would save him from no worse damage than a few disguisable scars. As he raced the length of the steamer to the cabin where Sarah and Peter were supposed to have been, he felt as though he were gripped in some strange nightmare from which he was convinced he would never awaken. Smoke surrounded him, choking him, blinding him. It continued when he reached the door, the tentacles of fire snaking about him in a hellish embrace until he was gripped in a searing pain that stretched across the breadth of his chest and down his torso.

Only vaguely aware of the pain, he saw that the blackened door he pressed against was locked, for the key remained in the doorknob. He retreated from the smoldering door, from the tongues of flame that wreaked an evil caress across his chest, and kicked the charred door into blackened splinters. Smoke poured out of the room, and he saw them there, huddled underneath the bunk.

He might've screamed. He didn't remember. He remembered only stumbling to his knees, oblivious to the insidious kiss of the flames, the suffocating thickness of the smoke as he groped for the charred, disfigured mass of humanity that once had been his wife. As he drew her to his breast, the agony inside eclipsed the lacerations on the outside. And then he found Peter, no less harmed for the pathetic protection Sarah had endeavored to offer their son.

Behringer scooped their charred bodies into his arms and left the room, glancing back for a brief moment. Later, he would understand why. Countless times after that, he would imagine the last scene Sarah saw before she died.

A dull, grisly nonreality took over in that moment he'd

jumped over the side of the *Stephens*, wishing to God he'd drown. Praying that the fathomless depths of the lake would quench the fire that had separated him from Peter and Sarah. Peter, the son he'd adored. Sarah, the wife he'd never fully accepted, much less loved.

Later, he knew that it was shock which had enabled him to make it through what followed with his sanity intact. His mind wouldn't accept the horrible reality as it was happening, and he couldn't remember it now. He'd lain the pitiful remains of his wife and son on the frozen ground, huddling close to them as though to warm them against February's cruel night. He had been so terrified that they were cold. And he'd lost consciousness. He'd blessed the sensation, certain that he was following Sarah and Peter to his own death.

The only memory which remained of his time spent on the banks of Caddo Lake with Sarah and Peter was of awakening briefly to find a hysterical, wildly babbling Harry Murphy bending over Sarah. He could remember nothing else about his last moments with his wife and son. He knew only that Murphy was beside himself with consternation over his dismal failure. Nor would he ever forget the overpowering smell of whiskey on Murphy. The son of a bitch had been drunk.

When Behringer at last awakened at home, the doctor was at his side and he was swathed in bandages from his chin to his ankles. It was a miracle, the doctor told him, that he was alive. Harry Murphy was credited with saving Behringer's life, quickly rushing him to town so the doctor could treat his terrible burns. Townspeople talked for months about Harry's devotion to Behringer during his fever. The man had been sick with worry that Behringer might die.

Weeks later, when Behringer was able to leave his bed, the doctor pleaded with him to talk to their priest, to find his peace with God. Behringer never sought his priest's counsel, nor any man's. No discussion could ease the guilt which ate at him, the anger at a God who would allow such a fiendish death for two of His innocent creations.

The unnatural sense of sleeping without waking followed Behringer for a year. Much of his time was spent in the Kahan saloon. His frequent drinking companion was Harry Murphy, similarly plagued with the nightmares which were Behringer's nocturnal companions. Some days he spent locked in the nursery, where Peter had played with the wagon his grandfather had brought him the last night Behringer saw his son alive. Six months passed before he was able to admit the servants into the room, and a year before he allowed his mother to change the nursery into a sitting room. Both Sarah's and Peter's clothes were still in his home, packed in the attic. He had ignored his mother's suggestion to donate them to the church. It had been a weekly ritual for him to visit their graves in Oakwood Cemetery, and often he would return to his home and visit the attic and reminisce. His priest would say it was penance.

Behringer always thought of Sarah when he was obliged to travel to Shreveport on business. Never more so than today, when he intended to visit not her grandparents, but the parents of a young girl who now stood between him and the bitter goal which was within his grasp.

❧ Twenty-One ❧

Behringer awakened the next morning and dressed quickly. In the lobby, he found the boy who'd arranged the meeting with Nels Janssen.

"Morning, mister," the boy chimed.

"While I'm meeting with Mr. Janssen, I'd like you to find out about any Reynolds families living in town who might be missing a daughter."

The boy frowned. "Missing a daughter?"

"Find out if there are any families named Reynolds in Shreveport who have a young daughter, about eighteen years old. Her name is Rebecca." Behringer reached into his pocket and withdrew a gold piece. "I need the information as soon as possible."

"Yes, sir."

Behringer first visited the ironworks on the outskirts of town. Here, stoves rather than pots were made. Plows and other farm implements were forged and sold to residents of Jefferson, major products which could be manufactured in Jefferson if they had their own iron operation. Behringer considered inviting the owner to Jefferson for consultation, knowing what a rich laugh that would inspire. Since the first steamboat had traveled Big Cypress Bayou, Jefferson and Shreveport had held no great love for one another.

He arrived back at his hotel hungry for information. He found the boy in the hotel lobby. "What did you find out?"

"There's three Reynoldses in Shreveport, Mr. Behringer. One's a spinster schoolteacher from Birmingham. She don't have any relatives here at all. One's a rich family, but they don't have no missing daughter."

"And the third family?"

The boy shrugged. "They're a Negro family. Is she a Negro?"

Behringer exhaled impatiently. "I don't think so. Thank you for your help."

He left the hotel muttering about sending boys to do men's work. It was almost eleven, time for his scheduled meeting with Janssen. He arrived at their rendezvous, a saloon named the Glass Slipper. He wandered from the porch to the street, growing surly as the minutes passed. He walked into the saloon and had a beer while he waited. Some time later he returned to the street, giving the man just five more minutes before he went after him.

He scowled at the deceptive sign in front of the tavern, kicking at the dusty street and damning the heat. There certainly wasn't a less romantic place in the Western world. Although, he thought, the ladies upstairs would do their level best to fulfill any man's fantasies. As long as they weren't fantasies of romance.

Glancing at his watch, he swore. The man was already an hour late. It would be just his luck for Janssen not to show up.

Behringer paced in front of the saloon, wishing he hadn't decided on a drink while waiting for the man. That beer had turned to several, and had served only to irritate him. His patience was frail as it was, and the beer had shattered it.

He needed nothing more than to assure this man of his composure, and his mind was consumed with the vision of Sarah's arms, fire-ravaged as the rest of her, clutching their dead son to her breast. That image, one of the few surviving that night, held his heart in a death grip.

Another memory, fresher and, oddly, even more shattering; Harry Murphy dragging Rebecca into the woods. He clenched his fists, knowing how vital it was that he discover the truth before it became only pointless revenge. Somehow, the phrase *pointless revenge* disturbed him.

"Mr. Behringer?" A voice a few feet behind him spoke, and he swung round in the street. A small, elderly man, dressed elegantly, stood only a few feet from him. "I'm James Morton. So sorry I had to make you wait. I was delayed. At first, I thought I wasn't going to make it at all."

"Where the hell's Janssen?"

Morton blinked at Behringer's raw anger. "He was diverted at the last minute. I assure you I am able to accommodate any request you may pose, Mr. Behringer. Shall we go inside?"

Behringer forced calm into his voice. A hammer pummeled mercilessly within his head, and he decided that another beer could only help at this point. "I only arrived a little while ago myself," Behringer lied, following Morton into the saloon.

They sat in a quiet corner. A saloon girl, dressed in garish pink and black, brought their drinks.

"I appreciate your meeting me here today, Mr. Morton. What I need is of grave importance to me."

Morton sipped his whiskey, watching Behringer. "As I recall, you're interested in seeing some records of some of the trips made a few years back."

"One, in particular."

Leaning back in his chair, Morton nodded. "I see no problem in furnishing you with such information."

Behringer sighed visibly. "That, I'm happy to say, comes as a great relief."

Morton smiled and withdrew a pen and pad of paper from his satchel. "Always glad to help. Exactly what steamer are you interested in?"

"The *Mittie Stephens*."

Morton blinked. "The *Mittie Stephens*."

"I'm sure you remember her," Behringer said. "She sank in February of '69."

Morton put his pen down. "I'm aware of that. If you've been looking for this information as long as you say, you're certainly aware that the tragedy of the *Mittie Stephens* is an exception to normal regulations."

"I am," growled Behringer, his control slipping away.

The other man paused, as if considering the idea. "Which of her trips would you be interested in learning about?"

"Her last one."

Morton sighed. "Impossible."

"Damn it!" burst Behringer. "There's no such thing as impossible. It's never a question of how, only how much. Of course, I'll make it worth your while."

Morton's face grew hard. "Please don't cast the shadow of impropriety on this meeting, Mr. Behringer. Have the grace to accept my inability to help you."

"You mean your inability to risk your own ass to uncover the truth."

Ignoring Behringer's skyrocketing temper, Morton looked him straight in the eye. "The tragedy was carefully scrutinized and investigated. Whatever caused the blaze will never be known."

Behringer carefully controlled the urge to rip the man's scrawny face apart. "As long as men like you are in control of the answers," he replied coolly.

"You know I have no power to release the papers to you. I have no access to them. That lies solely with Fairchild and Sons, the financier of the *Mittie Stephens*."

Behringer deliberated for a long moment. He'd long ago told himself he'd never risk the connection, for it might put innocent people in peril. The image of Rebecca, helpless as Murphy dragged her toward the woods, flashed through his agonized mind. The image of his mother standing there, despising him, joined it.

For a wild moment, he wondered if he could accomplish his goal with only the shadow of the Fairchild name. Free from his engagement to Vivian, he might . . . his heart gave a wild soar through his chest. He had thought never to entertain the possibility of courting Rebecca as a man should court a woman like her. This vision gave him new purpose, and he spoke with conviction.

"Then you should know that I am to marry Silas Fairchild's oldest daughter very shortly. All I need is a list of names that had full access to the ship's security. In six months, I will have total control over the company, and will be free to do with the records whatever I like."

Morton considered this. "I can see that. And I must wonder why you insist on placing my job in peril by suggesting I part company with confidential company records, rather than merely waiting."

Behringer's eyes flashed. "My wife and son died on that goddamned boat, trapped in a room someone had locked them into!"

Behringer didn't realize his voice was rising until he noticed the sudden quiet of the tables near them. Sighing, he sipped his beer and avoided Morton's stunned gaze. "Why haven't you ever told anyone of that? Mr. Behringer, you're charging that the fire was purposefully set."

Behringer laughed, an unhappy sound. "Mr. Morton, I know the fire was purposefully set. The person that was responsible for it is the same one who's responsible for all this godawful mystery. I trust you're not a gossip. It could be to your regret."

"You aren't insinuating that Mr. Fairchild—"

"Oh, for God's sake, don't be ludicrous. Just because it was his money backing the ship doesn't mean he killed my family. Fairchild stood only to lose when the steamer burned. But it was clearly someone Fairchild trusted."

Morton shook his head, staring into the amber liquid in his glass. "I can only suggest you take Mr. Fairchild into your confidence. He will certainly do all he can to help you."

Behringer drained the rest of his beer. "Then I can only

suggest you go straight to hell. And if you think your job was in peril a few moments ago, wait six months."

With that, he left the saloon, crossing the street to the hotel. He quickly collected his belongings and settled his bill.

"Are there any messages for me?"

"Almost forgot, Mr. Behringer. This came from Richmond. Looks like an answer to the one you sent yesterday."

Behringer took the sheet from the clerk and scanned its contents, strangely unsurprised at what he found there. A grim chuckle escaped him, offering a brief respite from his black mood. That Katy.

Behringer went on to the livery. The sun had begun its slow slide into the horizon, and he had a long, hard ride ahead of him.

❧ Twenty-Two ❧

Rebecca's eyes opened, and she blinked her eyes in protest against the late morning sun. It finally rushed in, with clarity that resounded in her aching head.

At this point, she thought with a grin, she should be wringing her hands in a state of mortification. Any one of her heroines would've. Instead she relished the memories of the night before. Never had she known such passion, such a depth of erotic playfulness as Behringer's.

She looked down at herself with interest, realizing she was fully dressed in a nightie that went from the bottom of her chin to the tips of her toes. And she was in Katy's bed. Alone.

Increasingly curious, she jumped from the bed and paused, holding the bedpost. Nausea gripped her, the cognac's farewell kiss. Swallowing, Rebecca stood still and breathed slow, steadying breaths until the faintness passed. She slipped off the gown, then splashed her face and neck with water. She dressed quickly and ventured into the hall.

Voices came to her from the parlor, and she descended the stairs. At the door to the room, she stopped and looked in. Maria sat there, quietly chatting with Vivian.

As Rebecca approached the door, Maria rose from the settee and rushed to her. "My dear," she whispered, taking Rebecca's hands. "How do you feel this morning? I hope we didn't wake you."

Rebecca hugged the woman, smiling to reassure her. "I'm fine. I'm sorry I slept so late."

"Vivian called to find out how you're doing," Maria said pleasantly. "And to enlist our help in filling out her wedding invitations. We've already finished them."

Rebecca stared stupidly at the list of names on the table between them. Vivian's handwriting was like its creator, beautiful and ostentatious. Mr. and Mrs. W. W. Alley, Mr. and Mrs. T. G. Anderson . . . Each of the flourishing titles taunted her, each M, with its elaborate curlicue, a reminder of the signature Vivian would soon employ. Mrs. Garitson Behringer.

Glancing from Maria's meaningful glance to Vivian, Rebecca was surprised to find only a shy smile on her face. The girl's eyes were now the color of the ocean after a warm summer storm. Hmm.

"And I'm so dreadfully sorry about the way I behaved toward your friend. It was completely uncalled for. I feel awful that you were attacked after leaving my party. Garitson told me all about it," Vivian said softly. "It's all simply horrible. To think Father would be so unsympathetic to your suffering as well."

"Garit?" Rebecca asked. "You've seen him this morning?"

Vivian gazed at Rebecca gently. "No, he told me last night, after he returned to the party."

Rebecca blinked.

Vivian continued. "He said you were badly shaken, and that he'd given you something to help you sleep." She laughed conspiratorially. "If I know Garit, it was probably some of that dreadful brandy he loves."

Two snifters full, Rebecca thought stupidly. Searching her memory desperately, she remembered drifting away in relaxation as the cognac took effect. Surely not so relaxing a place as sleep!

"At any rate, he left town last night. He said he had business to attend to in Shreveport."

Rebecca regained control of her voice, struggling with the memory of Garit's even breathing as he slept in her arms. Or had he slept at all?

"He couldn't have . . ."

Vivian laughed gently. "Oh, dear. I'm sure the whole thing was disturbing for you, Rebecca. Garitson said he escorted you home, stayed long enough to make sure you were comfortably asleep, then returned to the party. By then, his parents had already left for home. He said he feared for my safety, that whoever assaulted you might return."

So, Rebecca thought. Fairchild was protecting Murphy.

"Garitson left for Shreveport sometime after one," Vivian reported.

"How do you know the time?" Maria asked, rising knowingly to Vivian's bait.

"Well," Vivian said, "you see . . ." At this, Vivian had the grace to blush. Rebecca and Maria understood at the same moment.

Maria's expression went cold. "I do see."

Before the words could sink in, Vivian turned to Rebecca and hurried on, "I thought you might not want to dwell on everything that happened last night. I thought that since you don't know anyone yet, I would offer my company today. We might shop, if you like."

Maria was already speaking, staring at Rebecca with that purposeful gaze. "Yes, child, I think you should. You should get to know Vivian." She proceeded to order lemonade for them.

Stifling a gloomy grin at the transparency of the older woman's motive, Rebecca paused. Maria clearly thought it a strategic coup to gain Vivian's confidence. Find out some dark secret she kept to dissuade Garit from marrying the girl.

Rebecca had no use for strategy just now. Her brain was still spinning from the impact of Vivian's revelation, and for the first time in her life she realized the lethal blow cognac dealt. Two doses sipped steadily after a traumatizing ordeal, and she'd slept like a babe, and dreamed the tantalizing dream of the truly tormented woman she was.

No way, Rebecca told herself with stubborn practicality. Obviously Behringer had concocted the alibi. At the thought of the man, her temper steamed. Within the span of three hours, he'd satisfied two women. At another time, she might've admired his stamina.

"I saw you and a certain Englishman dancing together last night. He's in love with you, you know."

"Charles Norton, you mean? He's a nice man."

Vivian tittered delicately behind her hand at Rebecca's words. "Don't let him know you think that. He'd be wounded." Then she sobered. "While I'm thinking of it, I have to apologize for Garitson's thoughtless behavior last night."

Rebecca's guard went up once more at the sound of his name. "What do you mean?"

Vivian frowned. "Oh, he certainly made sure you were comfortable before he left." She hesitated. "It concerns me, though, that he would leave you alone after that."

Rebecca paused, finding her facade of nonchalance slipping. "I'm sure he had more important things to do than watch me sleep."

Like seduce his fiancée.

"But, Rebecca, don't you realize? You were truly in grave danger. He didn't know his parents were on their way home from the party. For all he knew, you were all alone in that house, sleeping innocently, unable to defend yourself."

"Vivian, Mr. Behringer and I arrived before Garitson left. She was completely safe," Maria put in, no longer content with her silence.

Vivian chattered on ceaselessly, content with Rebecca's brief, spare answers. Rebecca's head was starting to throb, and she wished for the ninth time that she hadn't agreed to the madness of this visit.

In an aberration of normal thought process, Rebecca pitied

Vivian. The girl couldn't help it if she was a flake. She had a tough time being the constant target of Behringer's brusque sense of humor. Though he would never dishonor his fiancée in public, Rebecca had learned the first night she met Behringer what sort of regard he held his fiancée in when she eavesdropped on their conversation from the armoire.

"At any rate, Mrs. Wood told the man that if he hadn't brought his cat into the hotel, Jessie never would have attacked the poor thing."

Rebecca became aware of Vivian's words as she mentioned Kate Wood's name. She thought of the newspaper story she'd read yesterday, linking Silas Fairchild's company to the steamboat where Garit's family had died. Surely Vivian, as informed as she was of the goings-on in town, would be privy to any detail to be known. She selected her plot carefully.

"Vivian, have you ever heard of a millionaire named Gould? Jay Gould?"

Vivian screwed up her lovely features in determination, carefully concentrating. "Why, yes. I think he's that man who does the bonnets over in Marshall."

Maria chuckled.

Rebecca pursed her lips. "No. Millionaire, not milliner. I believe he's from New York. I think he finances steamboats."

Vivian dismissed her curiosity. "If I know him, I don't recall."

Rebecca knew this proved nothing. Vivian probably couldn't place Grant as the president.

"But my father might. He keeps that sort of useless information in his office. I could ask him for you if you like," Vivian offered.

"Oh, no. I know how busy he is. But do you think . . ." She hesitated.

"Yes?" Vivian prompted, curious about Rebecca's unusually awkward behavior.

"I shouldn't even ask," she said, laughing nervously. "It's just that . . . last night Charles was talking about the man, and you know how men love to think ladies are interested in their affairs. It would please him so to think that I had taken the effort to learn about it."

"Oh, well then. I think Father is at the blacksmith's this morning. His office is empty, so we could look through his files without ever bothering him."

Rebecca paused. If she could just get inside Fairchild's records, she knew she'd be able to find what she was looking for.

"I'd hate to upset your father, Vivian. Do you think he'll mind?"

"Nonsense!" Vivian giggled, carefully closing the bottle of ink and cleaning her pen.

"Let me get my bag," Rebecca said.

Maria followed Rebecca upstairs. "Who is Jay Gould?"

"He's a railroad tycoon."

"Why did you say he was interested in steamboats?"

"Because," Rebecca answered quietly. "There's one steamboat that sank a few years back that I'm very much interested in."

Maria's gaze was warm, and she spoke softly. "Rebecca, I am grateful for you. I hope my son has the sense to be."

Rebecca smirked. "I seriously doubt that."

❧ Twenty-Three ❧

A few minutes later Rebecca and Vivian were in Vivian's buggy, on their way to Fairchild's office. "Oh, look," Vivian whispered. "There's Daisy Ashe at the Brooks House. She's such a perfectly scandalous woman. Her two children have two different fathers, and now she's marrying a third man."

Rebecca looked at the two-story white house, converted into a hotel, which wouldn't be there a hundred years from now. The Brooks House. The name nagged at the back of her memory, but she couldn't place it. She dismissed the curiosity from her mind, knowing that a thousand old houses lurked there.

A tingle of excitement raced over the surface of Rebecca's skin, and she breathed slowly and deeply to still her agitation. Vivian halted the buggy before the simple frame office building, then led Rebecca inside the cold room. As she'd predicted, Silas Fairchild was absent.

"Those are all his files," Vivian said, gesturing toward the long row of wooden cabinets. "Help yourself. I think he has much of it grouped according to what they do. What did you say he's involved in?"

"Investments. Shipping, I think Charles said, including the railroad. Perhaps steamboats."

Vivian opened one drawer, and Rebecca opened another.

Quickly flipping through the files, looking for any sort of steamer information, she scanned the headings of each file. Nothing. Opening another drawer, Rebecca continued her search.

"Charles mentioned the *Mittie Stephens* last night when he was talking about Mr. Gould," Rebecca ventured distractedly, impatient with her progress, praying for a lead.

Vivian raised her eyebrows. "Why, that's impossible. My father financed the ship. All those records would be in the bank."

A chill draft crossed the room as the door opened, and Rebecca rose to her feet. She smiled carefully as she met the man's gray-blue eyes. "Hello, Mr. Fairchild."

"Miss Reynolds."

"Father, Rebecca is looking for the records for the *Mittie Stephens*. She's trying to find out about a man named Gould. You wouldn't happen to have that file out, would you?"

He stared evenly at Rebecca with a suddenly icy expression. "The *Mittie Stephens?*"

He considered her for a moment longer, then sat at his desk. "Fairchild and Sons financed the *Mittie*, and it's a steamer I'd just as soon not dredge up. Gould's a big man up north, schemes in the market and such, but he wouldn't waste time in Jefferson."

Rebecca regarded his evasion closely. It was preposterous, yet totally believable. Such a genteel-looking man as Silas Fairchild would never dirty his fingernails with the blood of another human being. He would doubtless hire someone to do it, then cover their tracks.

"Why does a little girl like you care about a thing like that?" Fairchild asked.

"I had heard Jay Gould financed the ship, and I'm trying to learn more about him for Charles Norton. I'm sorry to have bothered you, Mr. Fairchild. Thank you for your help." Rebecca crossed the office to the door.

Vivian bent to kiss her father before they left the small building. From there, they strolled down the street and stopped in at the milliner's. Vivian found a piece of frippery that perched jauntily on her blonde curls, then when Rebecca giggled at the concoction, Vivian ordered a similar one for Rebecca.

"Men love them," she confided.

Rebecca knew better. She laughed to herself, knowing the hat matched nothing she had, least of all her character. They walked from the milliner's to Henrique's for lunch, and Rebecca realized that her queasy stomach had vanished, leaving only a ravenous hunger in its wake. "Oh," Vivian whispered. "There's that handsome Charles Norton now. It must be fate."

He noticed them almost immediately, and rose from his table. Vivian smiled at Rebecca.

"Good afternoon, Miss Fairchild. Miss Reynolds," he said softly, grasping her hand and kissing it.

Vivian quickly responded, "Do join us, Mr. Norton. We find ourselves quite bereft of gentlemanly companionship today."

Charles glanced briefly at Vivian. "Oh? And where might that lucky Behringer be hiding?"

Vivian blushed. "He's in Shreveport, on business."

"May I join you?" The dazzling smile he flashed was startling in its effect, complete with a faint dimple in his strong, square chin. Rebecca marveled that a man could look at such a perfect face each morning in the mirror and yet remain unaware of it.

Rebecca smiled. "Please do."

He excused himself from his companions at the other table, two men his age. Vivian grinned knowingly at Rebecca. "What did I tell you?"

"The man's eating with us," Rebecca said, annoyed at Vivian's one-track mind. "That's all."

Charles returned to the table and chose the chair closest to Rebecca. His eyes were kind as he took her hand in his own, gently squeezing it. "I could scarcely believe your dreadful experience last night, Miss Reynolds. Does anyone have any idea who was responsible?"

Vivian answered. "My father is investigating it, Mr. Norton."

"So," Charles said lightly. "I suppose you'll think twice before deserting me at a party again."

Rebecca smiled at his stern expression. "Definitely an error. I was enjoying myself so."

His blue eyes darkened slightly at her comment. "Indeed? Then of course I should like to see that you enjoy yourself again very soon."

Rebecca knew full well that Vivian was scrutinizing Rebecca's flirting.

"Tonight, perhaps?"

The suddenness of his invitation startled Rebecca. She couldn't think of a reason to reject it.

"Of course," Charles said quickly, sensing her mood, "I understand that you may feel out of sorts after last night, so we can certainly make it another time."

"Oh, no," she said, toying with her napkin. "I'm fine. It would be wonderful to see you tonight, Mr. Norton."

"I thought we agreed on Charles."

Vivian began needling him gently. "Where are you going to take her?"

Embarrassed, Rebecca glared at Vivian. Before she could protest, Charles shrugged. "No place special. Supper, I suppose, would be in order."

"I suppose," Vivian said dryly. "I—" Suddenly, she clapped her hands together. "The opening of *A Midsummer Night's Dream!* Of course. What a ninny I am."

Charles rolled his eyes. "Why, thank you, dear girl. Far be it from me to surprise Miss Reynolds." He looked at Rebecca. "Do you like the theater?"

Rebecca smiled, nodding. Vivian once more monopolized the conversation. "Garitson has a box, of course." She frowned. "But he doesn't like to arrive until it starts, and I never have time to speak with anyone. If not for the intermission, I fear no one would even know I was in attendance."

Charles chuckled. "I take it you have no great love for the Bard?"

Vivian frowned.

"Shakespeare," Charles interpreted.

Vivian lifted her nose in distaste. "All his *thees* and *thous* and *forsooths?* I'm sorry, but the English I know is much more understandable."

Rebecca almost laughed out loud at the thought of Vivian's English. Instead, she murmured, "There's something magical about the theater. The echo of the voices, the footlights, the actors . . ."

Vivian was chagrined. "Rebecca," she said softly, "they are horribly scandalous creatures, traveling about like gypsies, with no thought for polite society's opinion of them."

Rebecca didn't further the argument, though it was tempting. She knew Vivian wasn't talking some abstract society protocol. She was talking about Bessie.

It was a reluctant Charles who relinquished Rebecca at Vivian's buggy. He took a daring liberty and kissed her hand. "I shall fetch you at six, Rebecca, so we will have time for a lovely supper beforehand."

When they were out of sight of the town, Vivian drew a deep breath and spoke. "Dear Rebecca, we all know of your friendship with that actress. However, I would suggest that you refrain from speaking so glowingly of the . . . profession . . . during Mr. Norton's courtship. As you know, he is English, and of very fine breeding, as well. It's rumored he's the son of an earl, which of course would make him gentry as well."

Vivian droned on and on about her plans until finally they were in front of the Behringer estate.

"Thank you for the hat," Rebecca said softly, smiling. Perhaps, with enough coolheaded reason, along with Behringer's absence, she would at least be able to tolerate his emptyheaded fiancée.

Somehow, she had managed to disassociate the girl beside her with the childish brat she'd known as Garit's fiancée. Something within her gave an unexpected swell of pain at the thought, and she knew she'd only managed to avoid that reality. Now, it came rushing back at her.

Vivian smiled and leaned over to brush Rebecca's cheek with a kiss. "Of course. I suppose Garitson looks on you as a little sister, and so shall I."

Rebecca was amazed at the quantum leap involved to arrive at that conclusion, but she merely smiled. "You forgot to get your invitations."

"I'll get them next time. There's plenty of time before the first snow."

Rebecca tilted her head teasingly. "It never snows in Texas."

The sudden chill in Vivian's eyes might as well have been snow. "Well, it certainly shall this winter, just for my wedding."

With that command to God in heaven, Vivian obstinately nodded her head once. She softened, then, finding that faux smile of hers and plastering it upon her face. "Good-bye, Rebecca."

Rebecca was disappointed that evening when she couldn't concentrate on the rollicking comedy before her, instead reliving the moments she couldn't have dreamed last night. No more cognac for her, she thought with a smile. It left her too many excuses.

As the show ended, Charles touched her hand. "A fine show," he commented. "The most impishly swaggering Puck I think I've ever seen."

She nodded, sure that it must have been.

"Rebecca," he went on, kissing her hand, oblivious to the glances directed toward his private box, "I'd like to see you again. You must know you're becoming quite dear to me. Last night disturbed me more than I expected. But there's something I must know," he said, then hesitated.

"What is it?"

"Behringer. What are your feelings toward him?"

"Charles," she evaded, "Garitson is engaged to Vivian. How can you even ask?"

He squeezed her hand between both of his. "I was afraid that—I saw you dancing with him last night, and I was jealous. And he took his time coming back to the dance after he escorted you home."

Rebecca looked at him, surprised at the accusation.

"Please forgive me," he said. Twin pink spots shadowed his perfect cheekbones. "I grow rather stupid when I imagine you care for him."

As they started out of the opera house, they encountered Gustav Frank on the steps.

"Hello, Miss Reynolds. Did you enjoy the show?"

"It was wonderful. Are you alone?"

"My wife's been sick," he said slowly. "We lost our third child recently."

"Oh, I'm sorry."

He nodded. "Charles, might I have a word with Miss Reynolds in private?"

Charles tactfully granted his request, and Gustav drew her aside.

"I heard about your attack," he said, his gaze troubled.

She smiled wryly. "News gets around, doesn't it?"

"I was there, after all. By the time I realized there was a crisis and got outside, you were gone. There's something I should've mentioned to you yesterday, Miss Reynolds." He glanced away from her, considering his words. "Did you find the papers on the *Mittie Stephens?*"

She nodded.

"Then you know it was Silas Fairchild's money that financed the boat."

"Yes."

"Don't you think it's curious that Garitson Behringer is engaged to the man's daughter?"

"I don't believe I understand what you're saying."

He sighed and shook his head. "That's because I don't

understand what I'm saying. It's all hearsay, something no self-respecting newspaper man should be repeating. But when I heard about your attack last night, and I knew you were poking around about the *Mittie Stephens* yesterday, I wondered if there was a connection. Garitson Behringer's wife died on the *Mittie*."

"I knew that."

"And now he's marrying the daughter of the man who owned the ship."

"And?" Rebecca prompted, impatient with his innuendo.

"I'm a man who doesn't believe half of what he sees. But when innocent people are threatened, speculation comes into play. I find it extremely curious that you were attacked the very night after trying to discover the truth about the *Mittie*."

"Gustav, no one except you knew I was trying to find out about the boat. Garitson's relationship with Vivian is a coincidence."

"Are you sure? Behringer had no way of knowing?"

It was as if the man grabbed Rebecca's heart and gave it a vicious twist. "What are you saying?"

"A lot of people in Jefferson knew Behringer wasn't happy in his marriage to Sarah. Now, he's engaged to a pretty young lady fourteen years younger than him, and just about ready to take over her papa's company." Gustav hesitated, clearly uncomfortable with the conjecture in his next words. "Miss Reynolds, there are those who say the fire on board the *Mittie Stephens* was no accident."

❧ Twenty-Four ❧

A noise startled Rebecca from her fitful sleep, and she sat up halfway in the bed, glancing around in the darkness. She thought she heard a door down the hall, but she couldn't be sure. The house was silent now except for the patter of summer rain against the windows. She rose and opened the door to the verandah.

Her breath caught as she recognized Behringer in one of the ornamental iron chairs, sipping his beloved brandy. His hair was wet, shoved back from his face, and he wore the wine-colored dressing gown he'd lent her the first night she met him. He spoke without looking up. "Looking for your lover?"

A moment passed as she understood his accusation. "I only wanted to watch the rain." Ignoring his dismissal, she stepped onto the verandah and sat in a chair facing him.

She thought of Gustav Frank's words of warning, his reluctantly offered suspicions. They were obviously wrong. Behringer had nearly died himself trying to save his wife from the fire. And he had rescued Rebecca from Murphy. Yet there was a certain disturbing significance to Gustav's suspicion over Garit's relationship to the man who'd financed the boat where his wife had died.

She risked a glance at him, knowing he'd ridden into town in the eye of the storm. "Hard ride?" she asked.

"Oh, no, not at all. The horse loves dodging lightning."

Her anger more than matched his. "Did you get your business in Shreveport taken care of?"

"It's none of your damn business," Behringer muttered, disturbed at the memory of the crazy fear that had driven him there. He'd returned only to hear talk at the saloon of her rumored engagement to Charles Norton.

Good God, two days! If he hadn't left, Norton never would've gotten near her. He wondered exactly how near the twit had gotten. He reached for the bottle of cognac near his feet and filled the snifter a fourth time.

"Have you discovered yet whether men from across the ocean know how to please a woman?"

"You're disgusting."

"I would imagine he doesn't have the first idea how to even kiss you so that—"

"So that I would plead for him to allow me any moment of his life?"

He looked at her then, at the hair which tumbled about her shoulders, the sheer nightdress. "No," he said, taunting himself with his own folly. "So that he forgets everything he holds dear in life."

It hurt. She should've anticipated it, but his reminder of Vivian came unexpectedly. In the same moment he seemed to deny Vivian. His heated gaze lingered on her, bolder than a caress.

"Charles is a gentleman."

He laughed. "I thought so."

"And I suppose you wrote the book on lovemaking," she muttered, arms folded in disinterest.

His eyes blazed in anger as he rose. "I think you'd be lying to yourself if you thought I didn't do an adequate job of interpreting."

"How sure Vivian's made you of yourself," she muttered. "Her and her rumors."

"Rumors," he said bitterly. "And if I were to trust rumors, I could accept the unthinkable. Your luscious mouth upon

Norton's youthful frame . . ."—the thought gave him a lifetime's torment—"as it was upon mine."

Lightning split the sky, illuminating the agony etched upon his face. Rebecca was too stunned to notice it.

"Me?" she repeated, dumbfounded, rising to face him in righteous fury. "I wasn't the one who poured a pint of cognac down one woman then ran off to another one!"

"Cognac." His word was a numb echo.

"Cognac! You gave me two glasses of it," she reminded him, smacking her fisted hands against his chest for emphasis.

Behringer caught her hands and opened them upon his chest, drawing her close with a menacingly seductive expression, blinded to logic by the blame she lay at his feet, by his own guilt of the crime.

Rebecca's anger transformed itself into something else, and her hands slipped upward to rest on his beard, wanting him to shave it. Wanting to share his pain, wanting to help heal his scars.

He lowered his mouth to hers in a bruising kiss, thrusting his tongue abruptly inside her mouth in a brutal imitation of sex. Suddenly aware of the cold assault in his touch, Rebecca struggled ineffectively against him. Her action brought the firm weight of her breasts against his chest, mellowing his attack into sudden desire, softening his hard kiss into a seductive caress.

Her nipples brushed the front of his robe, and she parted the richness of its material, pressing her breasts against the hard muscles of his chest. His hand slipped inside her nightgown, molding her, grazing a hard peak with deliberate, knowledgeable strokes. Helplessly she arched against his hand, and he obliged her invitation, boldly fondling the pink crest, impatiently brushing aside the crisp muslin, replacing his fingers with his tongue and teeth.

Rebecca sighed his name, and Behringer deftly parted his robe and pressed himself into the hot, damp cradle between her thighs. The contact was searing.

She drew him close to her. "No one's ever made me feel the way you do."

Behringer stiffened.

"Garit?" she asked, confused.

He abruptly released her, tightening the belt around him in awkward, jerky movements. He turned without answering her and walked back toward his room.

Bewildered, Rebecca watched him for another split second, then stubbornly followed him. "You can't leave like this," she said. "I—" Her mouth snapped shut, and she was amazed at the mindless phrase that had nearly gone tumbling out of her lips.

He stepped inside his room and turned, holding the door so she couldn't have entered had she tried. "I'm tired. And I'm sure you're right. It's probably the cognac. Have Norton buy a bottle, and he'll be the best lover you ever had. You won't even notice a difference."

With that, Behringer slammed the door in her face. Rebecca stared, nonplussed, at the door. Finally, she returned to her room. She left the door open, wishing, praying . . . knowing he wouldn't seek her out again, having convinced himself she was involved with Charles Norton. It was fine for him to share his life with another woman and keep her for his occasional pleasure. From her, he would expect nothing but complete fidelity.

A sharp knock on the door brought Rebecca out of her dreamless sleep. "Rebecca, my dear, wake up! You have a visitor."

Rebecca blinked the sleep from her eyes. "Maria?"

The door opened, and the matriarch peeked in. "Did you forget your guest for breakfast?"

"Charles," she said, rising. "I had forgotten."

That clearly pleased Maria. "Well, he just arrived. Come down whenever you're ready. We'll have coffee while you dress."

Quickly, Rebecca dressed and went to the parlor. Charles stood at the fireplace, resting his elbow on the carved mantel. Maria sat in a delicately flowered chair near him. Crossing the room to her, he grasped her hand and kissed it. "You look beautiful this morning, Rebecca," he said. His indigo eyes sparkled, but one of them was distinctly swollen and discolored.

"What happened to your eye?"

He hesitated. "Ah. Well, I ran into Garitson last night at the Kahan saloon. Or more accurately perhaps, I ran into his fist. A rather unfortunate row unfolded between us, I'm afraid, and Garitson emerged the victor."

Rebecca gawked at him.

Charles smiled wryly. "He told me to stay away from you. But the thought of that is far more loathsome to me than facing Garitson's fury."

Rebecca glanced at Maria, noticing the woman's broadening smile. She sighed, taking Charles' arm. "With any luck, he's still asleep."

There was no luck. *Didn't he ever sleep?* Rebecca thought as they arrived in the dining room. Garit and Charles were each annoyed at the sight of the other, and Jacob curiously observed their open animosity. Charles held Rebecca's chair as Garit helped his mother. All three men seated themselves at the same moment, each surveying his companions distrustfully.

Behringer spoke lightly. "So, Norton. How are you this miserable morning?"

Norton smiled coolly. "I consider it a marvelous morning. How could it be otherwise," he murmured, glancing at Rebecca, "given such charming company?"

"And your face," Behringer continued cheerfully. "How does it fare? Not quite as pretty this morning, I see."

Norton touched his chin, testing his jaw. "The eye will recover. The rest seems a bit numb. Perhaps Miss Reynolds will soothe my injuries."

"Perhaps Miss Reynolds inflicts a more lethal blow," Behringer returned with a glittering grimace.

"Rebecca," Charles put in brightly, abruptly changing the subject, "I hear you and Maria are writing a book."

"Yes, we are."

"So you'll be making use of the experience you gained with the newspaper in Shreveport," Behringer said.

"I will," she said simply, focusing her attention on her plate.

"I understand you enjoy writing fictional stories as well," Charles said.

Rebecca nodded.

"Your favorite kind of book . . . would it be a *Jane Eyre* love story, published under the guise of a man's name?" This from Behringer.

She met his eyes, irritated at his flip dismissal. "I believe I've told you before, I enjoy reading anything I can get my hands on."

"Certainly a safe enough answer to save a woman from forming an opinion of her own."

She glared at him.

"Behringer, I believe you're taunting her."

"Oh, Charles, let's not fight," Behringer said, waving his hand. "I asked Miss Reynolds for her opinion as a person. She gave me the answer of a woman."

"I like Mark Twain," Rebecca returned at last, "and Harriet Beecher Stowe. Twain, for his humor. And Stowe, for her conscience."

"Twain," Charles echoed. "I don't believe I've heard of him."

Rebecca blanched, remembering she'd stepped into Twain's era. "He's still rather obscure."

Behringer thoughtfully touched his chin. "Samuel Clemens, old boy. American, you know." Then he looked at Rebecca. "So you would change the world?"

The softly spoken taunt jarred her comatose dreams, and she met Behringer's gaze evenly. "I want to make people think. To touch a life so that it can never be the same."

"You speak as a romantic, Rebecca," Behringer said.

She bristled. "A romantic seeks to persuade the reader that fairy tales exist. The world is not painted in tangerines and turquoises, but in browns, blacks, and many shades of gray. I want only to tell the truth."

Behringer sipped his coffee as he considered her words. "Then I would suggest you learn a greater respect for all forms of writing."

"I admire all great writers, Mr. Behringer."

He laughed. "That would explain the disdain in your eyes when I mentioned Miss Bronte's book, a book about hope, about integrity, about faith. A book you let me deride as a love story. I'm surprised that in the course of your study of writers, you haven't already learned a great book's most fundamental foundation. At the heart of each important piece of literature is a love story. Shakespeare knew it well. As well as Jane Eyre knew the bleak grays of life. And its brilliant sunrises."

Rebecca couldn't speak. The words in her heart couldn't get past the block in her throat. She could only stare at him with a helpless yearning. His words were spoken not in chastisement, but in comfort. As though he knew her overwhelming sense of dismal mediocrity. As she gazed at him, she saw the staunch support in his eyes. For how many years had she longed to find that expression in the face of the man she loved?

Charles spoke. "Integrity indeed. As I recall, the poor girl's employer would've forced her to become his mistress when he couldn't wed her because of his commitment to a prior wife. He brought a rich irony to the vow of 'in sickness and in health.' "

Behringer glanced at Charles. The Englishman had struck a nerve. Behringer excused himself from the table, and Rebecca watched him leave, his black hair contrasting sharply against the snowy white of his shirt. The front door of the house closed quietly behind him.

When Charles left, Rebecca was given time to reflect on

Behringer's quietly supportive speech, and Charles' to-the-point comment about Jane Eyre.

"He cares for you," Maria said abruptly.

Rebecca smiled grimly. "Which one?"

"Garitson, silly girl. He concerns himself with those things you care about."

Rebecca forced the enticing image of Garit's encouragement from her mind. "He's concerned only with Vivian Fairchild and her father's business. And irritating Charles. That, he loves."

"If you tell yourself that many times, perhaps you will begin to believe it," Maria said, smiling.

The woman led Rebecca down the gallery to the library. There, she found a pad of paper and handed it to Rebecca. "So, let us write."

Rebecca laughed at Maria's forthrightness. "Do you know what it is you want to say?"

Maria nodded once, her gray eyes sparkling. "That love can overcome anything."

The familiar theme rang fraudulent in Rebecca's mind. Sometimes love simply can't conquer all.

❧ Twenty-Five ❧

The women remained in the library the entire day, working without pause. Rebecca was inspired by Maria's aptitude for storytelling. She invented characters that would work well opposite each other, although Rebecca had her suspicions little invention was involved. The hero strongly resembled the man Jacob Behringer might have been forty years ago, when Maria met him. Tall, dashing, chivalrous. The sort of man who would rescue a young girl in a New Orleans saloon.

The young, disrespectable heroine, in turn, resembled the girl Maria once had been. Headstrong, confident in the face of contempt, falling in love with the handsome German, a man with whom she had little in common except love.

Those were the starring players, she told Rebecca. From the depths of their hearts would be born a timeless love that would outmaneuver the fates that had brought them together and would try to tear them apart.

At the end of their session Rebecca climbed the stairs to her room, eager to organize Maria's ideas. Crossing the room to the mahogany secretaire between the long windows, Rebecca stopped short.

The Remington. The typewriter she'd seen in Garit's room the day of her arrival in Jefferson. Its black, lustrous surface shone from the center section of the desk.

Some small but unarguably significant bit of Rebecca's soul was impelled forward, and she was plainly terrified of everything the machine represented. Change. Progress. The future; a future where Behringer and all his infuriating, impossible expectations of her didn't exist. She didn't know what day it had happened, but somewhere between the moment she climbed the stairs to bathe in the legendary Garitson's Room and now, this place and this time had become her life. This typewriter was one step closer to that numb chamber of existence that was her old life, and she tried to ignore its reality. She reached out to rest her fingertips on its edge and shut her eyes tightly.

"Hoping a genie'll appear?"

Snatching her fingers away from the machine, Rebecca whirled to find Behringer gazing at her in amusement. "You bought it."

Behringer walked into the room. He brought with him the rich aroma of the pipe he sometimes smoked. "If you're going to write a classic," he said, "you need the tools."

Once more she touched the machine, relieved to know there was nothing magical about it. Except for the mystical quality of Garit's faith in her. "Where did you find it so fast?"

"Malcolm Henderson found it for me. Do you know how to operate one?"

"Oh, yes," she answered in exhilaration.

"Really?"

She nodded, unaware of the oddity of her confession. "My father bought me one when I was ten years old," she told him. "He knew how much I loved to . . ." Then she realized what she was saying. She was talking about a Rebecca Reynolds from Dallas, not one from Shreveport. About a machine that had only recently been made available to the public.

Behringer watched her with open curiosity. "Go on," he said softly.

"I . . ." she began, unable to go on. "Garit, about this morning. I want you to know that I'm sorry."

He nodded, thoughtfully puffing the pipe. "Be specific if you will. Is this regret for the kiss, the cognac remark, or that you ventured out of your room in the first place?"

Rebecca resented the sudden, deliberate distance he placed between them. "I do not regret the kiss, you misunderstood the cognac remark, and I only wish I'd been more . . ."

The implacability in his dark eyes arrested her speech.

"Yes?" he prompted, then supplied, "More seductive? Not possible. More tactful, perhaps, might have been in order. More persistent? If you'd followed me into my room, I assure you I wouldn't have thrown you out."

"I begin to understand why Charles punched you."

He smiled wryly at her. "What is it you see in that English idiot?"

"He is gentle and intelligent."

Behringer considered this. "So's my horse. You're saying I don't have either of those basic traits?"

"I thought we were discussing Charles."

"Answer the question."

"You make me laugh," she admitted.

He frowned. "Laugh? Most women prefer flowers to wit."

Rebecca looked up into the dark, glinting eyes. "Not this one."

"So Norton must have a sense of humor as well."

"He's very funny at times."

The dark brown of Behringer's eyes went black in petulant frustration. Abruptly, he rose, pacing the length of the room. He paused to snuff out his pipe. "I don't like your friendship with the man."

She answered without looking up. "I don't think it's any of your business."

"If I had it my way, every breath you take would be my business."

"If you had it your way," she said lightly, "I'd be a whore."

He spun around, and his gaze was as raw as his voice. "Don't say that."

"Don't deny it," she retorted. "I heard your conversation with your father last weekend."

"You may not remember, but a few things have happened since then."

The memory came to her, along with his remorse this morning. "Yes," she whispered bitterly. "Major strides toward securing a place of honor for me in your life."

His expression was remote. "That isn't fair."

She laughed unhappily. "I'm being unfair? Have I misunderstood your purpose, Garit? Correct me if I'm wrong, but aren't you engaged to another woman?"

He walked slowly toward her, his eyes a quiet blaze of longing, his voice reflecting those unspeakable desires. "When I left for Shreveport, it was with strange new goals living in my heart. In Shreveport, I learned things which further confused the old goals and the new. And when I returned—" He reached her, his gaze tender and pained. His hand slowly rose, and his fingertips lightly stroked her throat. He hesitated only a moment, then lowered his head and brushed his lips against hers with slow, uncertain yearning. When he raised his head, the pain in his eyes was almost tangible.

"I left you sleeping, certain I'd never known a woman with greater passion, a greater capacity for . . . love. I returned from the most intense lovemaking of my life to the news that Charles Norton intends to marry you."

That passion warred within her now, his confession convoluting the truth that he fully intended to marry Vivian Fairchild. She trembled with longing and with fury. "You have no business asking me about Charles."

"No business? Have you considered that you might be carrying my child, even now? Do you think Norton will happily accept that?"

She looked down at the rich softness of the rug beneath her shoes. "There's no child."

Rebecca had discovered she wasn't pregnant only that morning, mercilessly cutting short the fantasies she'd already begun to entertain. If she had been pregnant, she could accept it as proof that this was no surrealistic fantasy. She'd wanted children for more than ten years now. Common sense assured her the worst thing that could happen to her was pregnancy; her heart felt otherwise.

A silence stretched out between them. At last he spoke, quietly. "Well. That's a blessing, I suppose."

She lifted her gaze slowly to his, smiling bitterly at his apparent relief. "And what would you have done, had I been? Would you have kindly broken your engagement to Vivian to marry me?"

Behringer was given pause at the scenario she presented. Before his return from Shreveport, he could've answered it readily enough. Now, he remembered Norton's easy, knowing smile last night at the saloon when one of the men teased him about Rebecca.

He turned away, his mouth set in a bitter line. "I have my reasons for marrying Vivian."

"That's what I thought. As usual, I'd be left on my own." In the end, little had happened to change his heart since that night she'd overheard his conversation with Jacob.

"I'd always honor you."

She stared at him, amazed at his words. "Honor me? You'll marry another woman."

"Only to share my name."

"And your bed." The shadowy vision of Garit making love to Vivian was nauseating, and she turned away, walking to the window.

"For one purpose. Children."

"And what of my children?"

"Our children, Rebecca," he said softly, just behind her. She hadn't heard his approach. "I would care for them as I would hers. You would have my protection for the rest of your life. Except for fathering her children, I will be faithful to you."

A moment passed. Then, suddenly, Rebecca laughed. Loud and long.

Behringer spoke, his confusion masked with irritation. "My comic powers save the day."

She spun to face him, her hair flying. "You're just like every other man!" she raged. "Fidelity is a lot like pregnancy, Garit. Either you are or you aren't. It's kind of an empty gesture to say, 'I'll be faithful to you except for Sunday afternoons.'"

"You're being unreasonable, as usual. You're the one who's accepted Norton's overtures. Don't pretend to know my intentions when your affections are otherwise occupied."

With that he left, slamming the door behind him.

Rebecca turned to the miniature portrait on the dresser. Katy, she had learned, as a small girl of four or five. Dark, unruly curls covered her head, and the same mischievously moody eyes as Behringer's sparkled in a porcelain complexion.

Rebecca lay her hand over the flatness of her abdomen, and felt once more the bereft loneliness she'd known that morning with the arrival of her period. She wondered vainly what the child she and Behringer could have made might have looked like.

She'd never known a more complex man. Somewhere in that sarcastic man lurked a sensitive boy who'd found a successful defense in stinging humor. She thought of Sarah Behringer, the woman whose portrait he treasured. The woman who had borne him a son. The woman he still loved.

Curiosity over his engagement plagued her. Obviously still in love with his wife, he didn't seem the type of man to marry such a mindless girl. Nor would he enter the marriage for financial gain. She remembered Vivian and her impatience with Behringer's lack of social ambition. She recalled, even more vividly, the single line she'd read in the newspaper article about the *Mittie Stephens*. Gustav Frank's suspicions were clearly ludicrous, but it was at least ironic that he would end up marrying a girl whose father was connected to the ship where his wife had died.

She sighed, trying to dismiss the hungry curiosity in her.

Dwelling on Behringer's motives didn't make them any less real; somehow, it only reminded her how little she knew about the man she loved. He liked the theater and was obviously well-read. He loved his parents, loved his sister and her pranks. He was kind to stable boys. And he was a masterful lover.

Sinking to the dainty chair at the desk, she helplessly let the insane memories invade. His mouth and its caustic gentleness, his narcotic voice, his artfully exquisite fingertips, worshipping every detail, every imperfection of her body as though she were the earthly daughter of a goddess.

She straightened willfully, turning to the typewriter, placing her notes to its right. She found a sheet of paper in the desk and rolled it into the typewriter.

It was good to be home.

❧ Twenty-Six ❧

"Rebecca, we've been seeing each other for almost two months."

Rebecca tucked her cloak more snugly around her as she walked along the waterfront with Charles. The rich aroma of clay and cypress and Spanish moss merged with that unmistakably fertile scent of the bayou. Rebecca noticed the steamers docked at the landing. A shiver went over her as she stared at the ships, ghosts of tomorrow.

Charles Norton cleared his throat and went on. "My father will be visiting at Thanksgiving. I'd like you to meet him."

"Then I'll look forward to it."

"I may be returning to England with him for a brief period," he went on. "I'd like you to consider going with us. You'll be well chaperoned, of course. I have only the highest esteem and respect for you, Rebecca. But my family must meet you first."

"Before what?"

He paused, glancing down at his hands. "You must know how much you mean to me."

She patted his hand, touched at his shyness. The man was nearly thirty, but acted like a stammering schoolboy around her. "Charles, I am fond of you, and I enjoy being with you. But if it's marriage we're discussing—"

He laughed. "You don't think I've been courting you to make another woman jealous, do you?"

"Well, of course not. But—"

"I know your feelings are not as strong as mine. I scarcely can tolerate the knowledge that you share a house with Garitson Behringer."

"Garitson?" she asked, dismayed at his words.

He shrugged, clearly uncomfortable. "People talk, you know. And they don't always compose the most intelligent opinions."

"Garitson is marrying Vivian Fairchild." Rebecca heard the bleak emptiness in her voice.

She wasn't the only one. Charles spoke in brittle syllables. "I heartily regret bringing him up. We were discussing us."

"I value your friendship dearly, Charles."

He nodded, softening. "It's a good basis for a marriage. I'll call in the morning, and we can discuss it with Maria."

Charles' carriage stopped in front of the Behringer estate an hour later. At the door, he smiled at her and kissed her hand. When she closed the door behind her, she sighed and leaned against it. She was going to have to end this thing with Charles. She would miss his friendship.

Maria stood just inside the door, in a dressing gown and house slippers. "Jacob brought this for you from town. It arrived this afternoon."

The woman extended to Rebecca a small envelope, and Rebecca took it, examining the small, neat handwriting there. There was no return address. "Who's it from?"

Maria chuckled, leaning forward to kiss Rebecca on the cheek. "I may be nosy, but it doesn't extend to opening others' correspondence. Good night, dear. I'll see you in the morning."

As Maria climbed the stairs to her bedroom, Rebecca broke the seal and withdrew the pages, and a bittersweet smile lit her face as she read. The spelling was atrocious.

My dear Rebecca,

Forgive me for not writing before, but Benjamin and I have been terribly busy for the past month. I hope things are going well for you in Jefferson. As for me, I couldn't be happier. I regret I couldn't resist the lure of the stage, and we're currently in New Orleans. We should be here for another month or so if things go well, and then we'll be on to his home in Dallas.

Much as I would love to, I doubt that I'll be able to see you again before we go on to Dallas. Benjamin is fond of the rail. If ever we have cause to travel to Jefferson again, I expect it'll be on a train coming from the west. I hope that once we're married and settled, you'll consider visiting us there.

Rebecca, since you were so kind to me, I am obliged to try to return your kindness. I usually cause more gossip than I hear, but if I can confess this gently, I heard stories about you while I was in your town. I wanted to tell you the last night we were in town, but our good-bye was cut short. I know how hard it is to be the subject of unfeeling gossip. Especially when you love someone. You deserve happiness and love, so pay no attention to anyone who stands between you and your happiness. I'll write again when I have our new address. Until then, I remain your grateful friend.

Bessie

Rebecca was filled with confusion. She was gratified by Bessie's happiness and touched that the woman encouraged her to find her own contentment. And yet something about the letter disturbed her. A single phrase lingering in its midst. She reread the letter, finding nothing remarkable there aside from the woman's insightful advice. She folded it and tucked it into a pocket in her cloak.

As Rebecca started past the darkened ballroom, a movement inside the room drew her attention. She peered inside.

Behringer sat there in an armchair. He was positioned in the shadow of a giant fern which spilled over a table, his arm slung over the chair's carved back. In that hand, he loosely held an empty brandy snifter. He stared as if hypnotized at the partially obscured portrait of the beautiful woman who once had been his wife.

"She was lovely," Rebecca said softly.

If he heard her, he didn't acknowledge it.

Rebecca walked silently into the room, reluctant to disturb his solitude. Perching quietly on the settee, she spoke again. "Would you rather be alone?"

Silence hung between them. The darkness of the room was unrelieved except for a smattering of moonlight from the verandah, and his expression was in shadow. "I've never been so alone in my whole bloody life," he muttered at last. "No. Don't leave me."

The comforting silence permeated the room, and Rebecca savored their moments alone. Never was she allowed to freely gaze at him as she desired, but he seemed unaware of her. Slowly, her eyes grew accustomed to the dim haze of the room, and at last she could make out his expression. It was a frightening thing.

A loneliness in intensity she'd never seen was etched in Behringer's haggard face. He had loved this woman a great deal. Enough to face the scalding tongues of a killing fire to save her, and their son. Obviously, here was the woman who still held his heart captive.

She thought of her own love for him, tucked neatly away where no one could harm it, and the misery it usually brought her had vanished, ironically, in the face of her stiffest competition. She only felt heavy with the need to give it away to him. To shelter him from this desolation.

She moved to Behringer's chair and sat near his feet. She glanced up at the woman who smiled serenely down upon them as if in approval, then looked at Behringer. She was surprised to find his gaze upon her, the intensity burning brilliantly.

"What was she like?"

"Quiet. Generous. Funny," he said, with a shadow of a smile. "In some ways, very much like you."

Rebecca quietly rested her face against his knee. A moment later, she felt his hand upon her hair. As she pressed her cheek against the smooth fabric of his trousers, she knew that this moment, with time suspended between them, was one she would treasure through eternity. Nothing else mattered except comforting him.

For a minute or two, a gentle silence soothed them as he stroked her hair. "How's the book coming?"

"It's nearly finished."

"I'm impressed. Can you tell me about it?"

"It's a love story," she told him.

He traced her chin. "Destined to be a classic."

"I don't know about classic," she said, smiling at his stubborn optimism. "Your mother's a remarkable storyteller, though."

"I loved the stories she told when I was a child."

Rebecca could easily imagine Maria, thirty years younger, with Garit at her skirts, weaving fairy tales about peasant girls and princes. It took a bit more imagining to envision Garit thirty years ago, as a small, impressionable boy. She softened at the thought. "I think this is an heirloom for your children."

Her words brought fresh, gaudy images of Vivian Fairchild —no, Vivian Behringer—happily pregnant with Garit's child. She shoved the thought away. Yet another pointless one in an endless string of such.

"How can you say that and then predict it won't be a classic?" Behringer asked.

Rebecca shrugged, choosing her words carefully. "There's more to a classic than its binding."

"Yes," he said softly. "I'm sure there is. Its message. Its significance."

"Its endurance."

"As they say, time will tell."

Rebecca found herself wishing a hopeless wish, that she could stay here in this time, with this man, as his wife. It was her every fantasy. If ever the moving hand had written in error, it was the day she was destined to be born in the twentieth century. The same black day, no doubt, it was decreed that Garitson Behringer would ask Vivian Fairchild to share his life.

"Did you have a grand time with Norton?"

She lifted her fingertips to his mouth. The soft tickle of his beard grazed her fingers. "There's no one here except us, Garit."

As though denying her words, he raised his face once more toward the portrait. The unconscious gesture pained her, but she only lay her cheek against his hard thigh. "Do you . . . want to talk about it?"

Behringer's body went rigid at her softly spoken words. Then he sighed. "What is it you'd like to know, Rebecca?"

She regretted her suggestion, and she looked at him. "I'm sorry," she whispered. "I only thought that . . . your mother said—"

"If you've discussed it with my mother, I'm sure you know all you could ever want to know."

Blessed with a sudden, uncommon ineloquence, Rebecca wished for delicate phrases. "I was curious about the portrait, and she told me about it only briefly. That your wife and son died in a fire on board ship, that you loved her very much, and that you nearly died trying to save them."

Behringer grimaced. "Sure didn't try hard enough, did I?"

Rebecca rested her palm against his shirt which lay half-way open, alluding to the shadow of black hair there. "You gave your best. Do you suppose she panicked when the fire broke out?"

"Sarah was an extremely levelheaded woman. Why do you say that?"

"Well . . . well . . ."

"I see my mother informed you." He sighed, then rested his head in his hands. "What Mama doesn't know is that

Sarah and Peter were locked in their room from the outside."
Ignoring Rebecca's gasp, he concluded, "They hid because
they had no alternative."

He was plagued by a memory of old nightmares. His brain
had portrayed countless horrifically accurate images in his
dreams: Sarah's arms tight around their son, attempting to
soothe him, their screams pleading for mercy against the unholy blazes which devoured them, Sarah powerless to answer
her son's pleas. A spasm of nausea gripped him, and he
reached out for Rebecca, clutching her against his breast,
closing his eyes against the fresh fragrance of her hair. "God,
please don't ever leave me."

She stroked his shoulders, murmuring reassurances. "Do
they have any idea who was responsible?"

He sighed, straightening. "The ship's records are completely sealed off from the public by the company that financed it."

"Well," Rebecca said stubbornly, "you have to find a way
to get inside . . ."

And as she spoke the words, she understood. The revelation brought little comfort. In truth, it further distanced him
from her. He cherished this woman's memory so greatly that
he would resign himself to a miserable marriage in order to
solve the puzzle of her death.

Behringer brushed his thumbs against the creamy softness
of her face, gazing at her with grim resolution. His words
were a weary plea, his voice tight with unspoken emotion.
"I've tried every other way there is. Don't you know that if
there was any other way, I'd have found it? Especially now?"

"Now?"

He didn't speak. His hand smoothed a loose strand of hair
away from her face.

"Garit," she said. "You risked your life to save Sarah. Do
you think she would have expected you to give up your happiness to avenge her death? My God, don't you already have
your share of scars to show for that terrible night?" She
touched his hands.

His gaze grew hard and cold. "Are they so distasteful, then?"

She was taken back to that first morning when she'd noticed his fingertips stroking the disfiguring marks. Now, she didn't know whether to apologize or slap him out of his ugly place of retreat. "I never thought you were the sort of man who would be wrapped up in his prettiness," she said softly. "I believed you would recognize your worth based on more important things."

Behringer only stared at her emptily.

"Did I shrink from you the night you made love to me? Don't you remember how I responded to the sight of you?"

His jaw tightened visibly, then he muttered, "I lowered the lamp. You saw nothing."

She gaped at him in disbelief.

Gently, he pushed her away, as though the entire conversation was too much for him. Rising from his chair, he walked away from her. "If you'll excuse me," he said, "I'm tired."

As he climbed the stairs, Rebecca felt the hopelessly inadequate bounds of her love. She had failed to comfort him, had succeeded only in irritating his wounds. Never had she known a more disheartening rejection.

Rebecca glanced up at the portrait. The woman smiled gently, patiently, a Victorian madonna. A smile Garit treasured. The thought pricked her, and she left the ballroom, climbing the stairs to her own room.

❧ Twenty-Seven ❧

Despite the cool breeze of the late October night, sleep eluded Rebecca. Garit's face haunted her, stubbornly convinced that the evidence of his courage, his love, was repulsive to her.

Throwing a wrapper about her thin nightdress, she rose from the bed and silently crept out onto the verandah. At Garitson's room she paused, then turned the knob. The room was dark, and it took a moment before her eyes adjusted to the dimness.

Then she saw Behringer, stretched out in his bed, his bare chest only slightly visible in the pale moonlight. Only then did she realize that she had never seen his chest clearly. He rested against the pillows, his hands locked behind his head, and watched her. For a moment she faltered, then took a steadying breath and slowly crossed the space separating them.

Striking a match beside the lamp, she held it to the wick until a soft glow illuminated the room. She left the bed long enough to close the drapes at the door and the windows. Then she steadily brightened the lamp's shine until they were bathed in its light. She turned to Behringer, moved at the vulnerable tenderness in his expression.

Rebecca rested within the hollow his waist created. Her hands slowly rose to the naked span of his chest. She carefully investigated the scars he'd hidden from her the night of their lovemaking. Bitter lavender splotches and streaks ran erratically over his chest and down the rippling muscles of his shoulders and arms. Disfigurement that someone like Vivian would indeed shrink away from, and she knew her own face held stunned dismay.

"These were serious wounds, Garit," she whispered, moved at the terrible evidence before her. "You must have suffered a great deal of pain."

He didn't speak, watching her with agonized expectancy.

Her fingertips roved over the breadth of his chest, stopping at the brutal marks the fire had left, stroking them. "Someone with divine wisdom once said there is no greater love than that of a man who lays down his life for someone." She paused, unsuccessfully trying to swallow away the emotions he inspired in her.

"Every woman dreams of loving a man who would die for her." She blinked, and the tears fell to her cheeks. "I'm very thankful to God that you're alive. There's no shame in this, for it is no imperfection. If anything, it only makes you more beautiful." She lowered her mouth to the purple streaks, kissing them gently, tears mingling there with her kisses.

Behringer grasped Rebecca's shoulders, pulling her close to him. "Where the hell are you from?"

"It doesn't matter!" Words of desperation.

"It matters," he said. "You're every fantasy I've ever had."

Behringer lowered his mouth to hers in a harsh tenderness. His hands cradled her face, his roughened fingertips cherishing her. She wasn't close enough to him, not nearly enough. His fingers slid into the shimmering thickness of her hair, pressing her even closer. He wanted to hold her so near to him that she became as much a part of him as her memory was. He wanted everything that she was.

The filmy robe slipped from her body, and he paused. Her beauty was displayed with haunting accuracy through the transparency of her gown, the nipples dark, lovely spots against the gauzy fabric. He lowered his head to capture one of those enticing targets in his mouth.

Rebecca shivered at Behringer's candid passion. He gave a sound of contentment when she flickered out her tongue near his ear, and another tremor went over her. "That . . . that is so nice," she laughed nervously, her tears forgotten.

He, too, chuckled, the deep, thrilling rumble that came from somewhere within the depths of his heart. "It gets better."

"Oh?" Her eyes were wide in innocence, and Behringer gave a half smile as he lifted and removed her shift in one fluid movement.

"Oh, yes," he returned, once more capturing her in the warm, wet haven of his mouth. Rebecca helplessly discovered the nuances of this man's body—beyond fantasies, achingly real. His body tightened visibly when Rebecca's restless fingers feathered down to touch him in a delicious, deliberate caress that plumbed the depths of his desire.

He lifted his head slightly to observe her passion washed features. Sleepily, she stared at him, her eyes sparkling with bourbon-colored lights. Her lips parted, and she extended the tip of her tongue upward in an inviting gesture. Behringer lowered his mouth only until his tongue dipped between her open lips, kissing her in a scorching dance.

He began a slow, steady assault upon her senses, the rise of her breasts, the hollow of her waist, her firm, flat abdomen, the long, lean thighs. Those curving, golden limbs with the texture of a September sunset and the flavor of a rich, exotic liqueur. He parted those thighs, and when he glanced up once more, his excitement only grew to find her gazing at him in fascination.

Rebecca sighed at the first touch of Behringer's beard on her inner thigh. "That tickles," she said, with a breathless laugh.

Her laughter caught in a gasp when he covered the vulnerable essence of her with the sanctuary of his lips, and then he, too, sighed. Her eyes closed at the intensity of his intimate kiss, and she thrust her hands into the curling softness of his hair, drawing him closer to her, unafraid to let him know how much he pleased her. His whispered name was a soft plea which he ignored. Or perhaps he knew exactly what she asked, for only a few moments later the fire he stoked within her raged out of control, and she cried out in heavenly anguish.

When Behringer moved upward to look into her bewildered face, a purely male smile shaded his features. "God, you're lovely."

The lulling rhythm of his voice hypnotized Rebecca, and she grasped the firm thrust of his body, guiding him closer. Behringer stared down into her face, into the seductive, searing gleam in her hazel eyes. If he saw that expression every day for the rest of his life, it would never grow old. He felt the sultry invitation between her thighs and probed there, teasing her until, with a sudden thrust of her hips, she captured him within her waiting haven. His breath escaped him in a hiss.

Rebecca murmured indistinct words of love into his ear. He complied with her urging, beginning the long, leisurely journey which would take them both to a place they'd known only once before.

Rebecca opened her eyes. Placing a hand on either side of his face, she stared into the glaze of passion within his half-closed eyes. He met her gaze evenly, and the evident desire in the depths of those dark eyes increased her own pleasure. She clung to him as he quickened the tempo of his knowing, persistent thrusts. Behringer lowered his head to the fragrant softness of her hair, whispering her name in clear possessiveness. At last they saw the crest of their destination, and he wordlessly coaxed her to gaze upon its beauty, to join him in their arrival.

Afterward, while they lay quietly within each other's arms, Behringer gave a small squeak of bewilderment. Rebecca giggled at his amazement, sharing it, stroking his hair. Then, she touched his chin. "Your beard is soft."

He made a wordless sound, then slowly spoke. "One young lady I know would like nothing more than for me to shave it for her."

Rebecca was unwilling to let his fiancée's reality take shape. "That's horrible."

He shrugged his great shoulders as he turned over, propping his head on one hand to observe her. "I think she wants me to prove my affection."

Rebecca nodded wordlessly.

"What do you think about it?"

She smiled. "I think you should do what you like. I already told you I like it."

Behringer nodded, lazily considering this. "Then I think I'll keep it."

Her eyes sparkled as she looked at him. "To prove your affection?"

A corner of his mouth quirked. "To tickle your thighs."

Rebecca shivered and drew him into her arms.

Safe in the room where fantasies came to life, Garitson drifted to sleep.

When he awoke, a smile of supreme satisfaction crawled over his face. A spear of tenderness pricked his heart as his gaze rested on Rebecca's mouth, slightly ajar in the comfort of her slumber. Gently, he touched his fingertip to her chin, closing her mouth. Then, he dropped an echo of a kiss on those sleeping lips.

Reluctantly, he rolled away from her and stood from the bed. With silent movements, he washed and dressed, watching her sleep as he tucked his shirttail within his trousers. He glanced at the clock on the mantel. Too early yet. Even the industrious Charles Norton wouldn't be awake.

How he was going to delight in telling Norton that his services were no longer required. And Vivian? he asked himself.

Vivian. That was another matter entirely. A frown went over his face. Her reaction would no doubt be unpleasant, but that mattered little. What mattered infinitely was making the sight of Rebecca's face against his pillow a legal one. With one last glance at her, Behringer left the room.

Downstairs, he strode through the gallery in an aimless direction that ended at the ballroom. Entering the room as he always did, with a near-reverence, he moved forward hesitantly to stand before Sarah's portrait. His mindlessly happy smile faded as he stared at the woman who'd worshipped him, who had given him a son too angelic for this world.

Behringer struggled with the sudden guilt that sluggishly wound through his heart. He hadn't known this sense of betrayal during his entire engagement to Vivian Fairchild. The answer came to him as easily as the question. He'd never made love to Vivian, either. Nor any other woman, except Rebecca, since Sarah died.

Oh, there had been halfhearted attempts that ended in pathetic frustration either for his partner, himself, or both of them. Most of the time, he simply stayed too busy to think much about it. Until Rebecca arrived, he'd still had occasional dreams of making love to Sarah—tantalizing, eerie experiences that left him shaking with desire when he awoke. A seduction that he was left to fulfill in macabre fantasy, in haunting solitude.

Yet it was more. Rebecca may have been the first woman he'd made love to since Sarah's death, but during his perfunctory attempts otherwise, he'd never felt this intense remorse. And then he knew that this morning's regret was only the culmination of an emotion which had been born the first night he saw her.

Closing his eyes, he remembered her, a full-length fantasy of vitality and summertime come to life in his empty room. The freshness of a warm April breeze thawing the winter of his heart. The moment's intensity had richly distracted him, and he'd been unable to think of anything except her for hours, until he watched her sleep in the suite at the Excelsior. When he was certain that she slept, he had lain on the bed beside her and gazed upon her timeless beauty, and then it had slammed through him for the first time. That terrible guilt which refused to be ignored. Now, it tortured him anew.

Why had Sarah, a woman who loved selflessly, and Peter, a mere babe, been forced to endure such an unthinkably cruel, senseless death? Who had hated him enough to lock them in their room to face such a fate? And, more important still, why hadn't he died with her? Why hadn't he been there to save her? Why hadn't he loved her better? Why hadn't he loved her at all in the way she deserved?

And now, seven years afterward, eons beyond the guilt, what about Rebecca? Why was the simple memory of watching her sleep more profound than any memory of his wife? Why did the thought of losing her terrify him more than any fear he'd ever known? The answer came to him, and it was quite simple.

He was in love with her.

The moment he met Rebecca, his heart had slowly opened its tightly bound doors until his dream in life was no longer death, the pureness of eternity spent with Sarah and Peter, but a dream of advancing to a doddering old age, sharing the rest of his life with Rebecca.

Sarah's gentle smile offered no reproach now, which proved the worst part of it. Just like her, to never fling one word of accusation, to stubbornly believe in him despite what anyone else thought. Just like Rebecca.

You'd like her, Sarah.

The portrait offered only the same smile of serenity. Behringer had often liked to think she smiled that way now, in some other place where the memory of the fire had been obliterated. In that place, she played with Peter, laughing and romping near silver streams that resembled the bayou. The thought gave his heart a mighty jolt, as if he stood poised before a cliff. Once, that place had tempted him, a place where he would be reunited with his family.

His guilt, he knew, stemmed not from making love to Rebecca, but from loving her. From that overwhelming, driving realization that he wanted nothing more than to freely give her the love he'd never quite given the woman he'd married. From the unthinkable idea that Sarah's memory was more dead to him than she was. She had lived her brief life for his happiness. If he let her memory die, what had been the point of her life at all? Inadequacy, his own human frailty, now troubled him as he sought his wife's approval.

Behringer heard the approach of a buggy, and when he strode to the front window, he saw Norton stepping out of the black conveyance. Splendid. As well as being gentle and intelligent, the man was telepathic.

Behringer straightened the cuffs of his shirt in an unconscious gesture as Caroline opened the door. When Norton entered the house, Behringer walked to the entryway. He extended his hand, smiling at the man. "How are you doing this morning, Norton?"

Norton glanced warily at Behringer's hand, then shook it. "Quite famously, thank you."

Indeed. Behringer decided to get right to the point. "I must say, I'm glad to see you this morning. We need to discuss Rebecca."

"Oh? Then I take it you approve of her decision. I assure you, she'll be completely safe on the voyage." Charles smiled. "I can't tell you how pleased I am that this is going smoothly."

Behringer stared at the man without speaking for several awkward moments. At last, he was able to construct a sentence. "Forgive me, Norton. Perhaps I was hasty. A voyage, you say?"

"At Thanksgiving. We shall be sailing to visit my family in London, to gain the approval for our marriage."

The words hit Behringer with the lethal accuracy of a marksman. Every remaining scrap of his fantasy drifted away in the morning sunlight, and a brittle smile plastered itself on his face.

"Then I suppose congratulations are in order, old boy. If you'll wait in the parlor, I'm sure Rebecca will be down shortly."

When Behringer reached for the front door, the open doors of the ballroom beckoned him. He succumbed to the inviting sanctuary of the room, moving woodenly to stand once more before Sarah's portrait. For endless minutes, he numbly gazed at the proof that all of his fantasies had been dead for years. Her smile now was merely sympathetic.

"Garit?"

Rebecca's voice behind him sent a shiver up his spine, and he turned silently. Her face was a mixture of a thousand emotions, none of them discernible, and rage rose up within him. As he passed her on his way out the door, he paused. "If you'll excuse me," he murmured. "I'd forgotten a vital goal I have."

❧ Twenty-Eight ❧

The tradition, love, and romance of a land centuries old were woven into each line of Maria's work. A woman who stubbornly believed that love triumphant was a simple concept, foreign only to the most pathetic of souls, Maria smiled serenely as she delivered her last line.

"And their happiness was before them, as the green of the live oaks, as the curve of the bayou where they settled and raised their children, as the seasons. Timeless, and forevermore."

Rebecca was moved by the woman's obstinately romantic ending. And they lived happily ever after.

Rebecca reread the words she'd copied. "It must go to New York," she said.

"Garitson will publish it," Maria said.

"But, Maria," Rebecca said, "that will be the only way the book will succeed—"

"Garitson will publish it."

"There are publishing houses there. It will remove the pressure from Garit," she said.

"No, Rebecca." Maria sank into the settee. Her words were tired yet passionate. "Garitson will publish the book, and it will belong to the people of Jefferson. People who believe in romance, not in the grappling for a gold coin."

For a moment, Rebecca knew shame. Shame for her treasured childhood dreams of literary success, traded for a gold coin; shame for her disrespect for others' dreams; but oddly enough, and foremost among them all, shame for her scorn of romance.

Jefferson was romance. With all its legends, its folklore, its myths. Those trivial places and events and dates didn't define romance. They were only brought to life by that spirit as old as Adam's staunch support of Eve as they were sent from Paradise. That ageless spirit the majority denied. A majority she was sorry to say she had been proud to belong to.

Maria raised her head and sighed. "I would like to see the complete story when you've finished with it. And ask Caroline to fetch Garitson for me."

Rebecca nodded and rose. At the door, she paused. "Charles has asked me to escort him to the train station. I should be back in another hour."

Maria nodded, and Rebecca left.

Behringer arrived in the library a few minutes later. He noticed his mother's gaze intent upon him.

"Close the door, Garitson."

He obeyed his mother, disturbed at the vulnerability in her mood.

"The book is finished."

He nodded. "Congratulations."

She rose and walked to the desk behind him, and she traced the chair's carved back.

"What are your plans for Rebecca?"

Behringer didn't turn. "You might first ask Rebecca her own plans. They clearly don't include me. You should know her well enough by now to know she won't be ordered about."

"Ordered about? I'm speaking of loving her, son."

"Well," he said softly, "there's a topic of discussion where I'm rather helpless."

"There are steps you must take now to ensure your love will survive what stands between you."

He turned slowly, his eyes a curious blaze. "What are you talking about, Mama?"

"She's finishing the book this afternoon."

"What does the book have to do with Rebecca and me?"
Maria turned to gaze out the window. "Everything."

Behringer tried to contain his temper. His mother was in an enigmatic mood, and he'd learned long ago there was no talking to her when she was like this.

"Do you know Malcolm Henderson, Garitson?"

"Of course. He's that eccentric old elf that collects books. And looking glasses. And nonsense."

"He knows the secret of how Rebecca came to you, and he holds the key to your happiness."

"Mama," Behringer said, his jaw displaying the fury his light tone did not, "what in the name of the Holy Mother are you talking about?"

"Just this. Mr. Henderson will oversee the printing of the book."

"What about Gustav? I thought he was better equipped for such an endeavor."

"When Mr. Henderson has delivered the first book to you, don't let it out of your sight."

"Mother, you've grown dramatic on me."

Maria walked forward, and her eyes glittered with tears. "It's very important, Garitson. Someday you'll understand. Until then, promise me you'll watch over the book as if it were your life, for it is."

Garitson took his mother in his arms, moved at her inexplicable poignance. "I promise, Mama."

"And I have another request. Rebecca is at the train station. Make sure she doesn't get on that train."

"Train station?" he repeated in disbelief.

"Go now, Garitson, or you may miss her."

Behringer drove the buggy a way no sensible man should, and he arrived at the train station fifteen minutes later. His heart gave a great shudder of relief at the sight before him. Rebecca wasn't leaving, she was only telling Charles Norton good-bye.

Rumors abounded regarding Charles' desertion. His father

had arrived at Thanksgiving, wasting no time in expressing, as plainly as a wellborn Englishman could, his distaste for Rebecca. He had quickly let a strategic mouth or two know that he had long ago arranged a marriage between Charles and a woman who was his equal, back in London. Behringer had a hard time keeping his fist out of the man's face. There was something about the prettiness of those Norton men that invited a swift punch.

Behringer's relief was shortlived. Charles was stammering an impassioned declaration of love, and Behringer felt his stomach go queasy. He steeled himself against it, allowing anger to settle in its place.

The train pulled out, and Behringer waited at the door of the station. Rebecca turned, surprised to find him standing there. His anger deepened at the misery etched on her face.

"My mother said you'd need a ride home."

"Thank you, but it's not necessary," she said, waving him away. Clearly, she wasn't up to dealing with him at the moment.

"Nevertheless, I don't renege on promises to my mother." He turned to Charles' driver, dismissing him.

Rebecca's mouth fell open in shock at his arrogance, and at the driver's corresponding obedience. Men. They all assumed they could read your mind, or perhaps they simply assumed you didn't have one.

She walked past him, ignoring him when he would've helped her into the buggy and scrambling up on her own awkward accord.

He tucked a rug about her lap, then seated himself beside her and snapped the reins, turning the horses back toward home. At the sight before him, he groaned. Silas Fairchild and his eldest daughter, crossing the street. Both of them were distinctly displeased at the sight of the approaching couple.

Behringer had reached the point where he wanted to kill Silas far more than he wanted to marry the man's daughter. Silas had to know about the murders of his wife and son, and for the last few weeks Behringer had been taunted with the prospect of his future. He'd been so obsessed with solving the mystery that he'd never lingered over the mess that would unfold when the truth came out. Silas would quite probably be indicted as an accessory to murder if the blame wasn't placed squarely on the man himself. How might his new wife reward him for convicting her father? It had never mattered in the indistinct shadow of reality Behringer had imagined.

Wasn't that precisely what you wanted? he asked himself. Wasn't the goal to punish whoever was responsible, Silas Fairchild included? Fairchild especially? Wasn't revenge, not repercussion, his main concern?

Without question.

All that had mattered for the last seven years was uncovering the truth about the horrible mystery in his past, for he knew he could never find peace without it. The past didn't seem to matter quite so much anymore. With Rebecca nearly married off to Charles Norton, everything that had driven him since Sarah's death was fast paling in importance.

He paused beside the Fairchilds, and Vivian rested both hands on Behringer's knee, leaning up for him to drop a kiss on her cheek. "Hello, darling," she said, her voice dripping possession and her hands lingering without thought for propriety.

He obliged her invitation, landing a kiss in the air somewhere near her nose.

Silas rested his arm on the edge of the buggy. "What are you doing, Garitson?" Fairchild asked lightly.

"I'm escorting Miss Reynolds home," he replied impatiently. "Her would-be fiancé is on his way home."

"Oh," Vivian replied with crestfallen dismay. "How distraught you must be, Rebecca."

Rebecca smiled tightly. "I'm fine, really."

"If you'll excuse us, we must be on our way."

"I assume we'll see you on Christmas Eve for mass?"

Behringer nodded. "Of course. Good day, Vivian. Silas."

The horses were in motion once more, clopping down the

midst of town. Behringer could feel Fairchild's stare burning into his back.

He stole a glance at Rebecca as they turned onto the road which would take them home. Silent tears were rolling down her cheeks.

"Don't," Behringer said tightly.

Wiping her eyes with her fingers, she looked up at him. He withdrew a handkerchief from his pocket, handing it to her. "The man is a fool."

Hazel eyes suddenly took on the fire of burnished gold. "Charles is the dearest friend I have in this place except for your mother."

Her staunch defense irritated him. "You're a bigger fool than he is, to defend him so passionately. Don't you know why he's going home?"

"He's going home because he's in love with Lady Gillian whats-her-name," she said, sniffing her tears away, her back stiffening.

Obviously, the thought of her competition abroad irked her. "The man won't marry you without his mama's approval," he said.

"Charles and I are friends, and that's all."

He recalled the words Norton had spoken as he left, and anger stabbed him now as then. He searched for anything to lighten the heaviness of the ache. As usual, it was a taunt.

"Doesn't it bother you in the least that he must have his family's blessing before marrying you? His father, I've heard, can't stand the sight of you."

"Richard Norton is a pompous idiot."

"He thinks you're a whore from New Orleans."

She swung around to face him.

"How do you know that?"

"That's what the whole town thinks," he said with a shrug. "Except for our friends."

Rebecca peered at Behringer, striving to pierce that veil of reservation carefully draped across his features. Thunderstruck, she gasped, "And so do you!"

Her remark unsettled him. Quiet anger revealed itself in the set of his jaw. "Now you're being ludicrous."

An ache settled over Rebecca at his assumption. Everything seemed to fall into place. She struggled to speak, remembering how she'd taken his affection as something more than sexual. She shook her head in dismay over her stupidity.

"There's one way to prove them wrong," he said blandly.

"I have nothing to prove."

He chuckled. "I'd say if you want to marry Charles Norton, you have quite a few myths to dispel. All it requires is a simple visit from your family."

"You know who I am and where I'm from," she evaded.

"Do I?"

"Please make your accusation clear. One moment you deny rumors, the next you admit you suspect them."

He sighed. "Forget it. It was only in your best interest."

How dare he. How dare he! "This coming from the man who would substantiate the worst rumors there are."

"Then write your parents. Invite them to stay with us for a while. I started to call on them while I was in Shreveport."

Behringer's overly innocent remark deepened Rebecca's rage. "Then why didn't you?"

"And betray your trust?" Again, the epitome of irony.

"I repeat. I have nothing to prove to anyone. You least of all."

❧ Twenty-Nine ❧

Christmas cheer. Behringer was sick to death of it. He sipped buttered rum as he stood on the verandah, one booted heel propped on the rail. Exhaustion wound its way through every vein in his body, yet the merriment inside the house wiped away the possibility for sleep.

Vivian had coyly hinted that it felt like snow this evening, and Behringer glanced up, wryly observing the starry iridescence of the clear Christmas night. The bankrupt state of the girl's intellect amused him anew. How could one human head be stuffed so full of fashions and flirtations and yet be so incredibly bereft of anything else? At least he could spend the rest of his life laughing at her.

On the other side of the window behind his head, he heard conversation. His mother was telling someone about the book she and Rebecca had finished. Behringer sucked in a painful breath, disturbed by his last memory of her, seated in his buggy, ill-equipped to deal with his taunts.

He sighed. She wasn't going to give an inch in this thing about her past. He felt the shiver of powerlessness wrack his serenity. It terrified him to think what might eventually reveal itself if she didn't confront it head-on. It was bound to surface when she was least prepared to deal with it. If only she'd accept his help.

Vivian would be delighted to know of sordid tales from

Rebecca's life before she came to Jefferson, if it didn't mean the alienation of Charles Norton. It was clear to Behringer that his fiancée had cultivated the romance between those two with the goal of keeping Rebecca too busy for him. Well, he thought wryly. She'd done a fine job; Rebecca had ended up in love with a man who wanted to verify her credentials before marrying her. Behringer drained the rest of the mug.

For the hundredth time since September, Behringer thought of Katy's telegram that had awaited him in Shreveport. *"Don't know the girl, Garitson. Guess this time the joke's really on you! Love to you and Mama and Papa."*

He wrestled with a choice of misgivings. He thought of those nights Rebecca was unable to sleep—he knew, for he heard her pacing in the room next to his own—battling God only knew what memories without asking help from anyone. She fought her own private war in solitude. Anyone else would envision her strength as commendable. For Behringer, it was only heartbreaking.

As far as most of the people in Jefferson were concerned, Rebecca's past was revealed the night she was confused with Bessie Rothschild, an entertainer and prostitute who favored New Orleans. A woman who was frequently hired out by her husband, Abe Rothschild. For this reason, he'd heard, Bessie and Abe often maintained separate names.

The name of Rothschild washed a foul taste through Behringer's mouth as he remembered Rebecca's first morning in Jefferson. She had spoken quite comfortably with Bessie's husband, a man that made a buzzard seem humane. That animal, after all, thirsted only after dead carcasses. His type would enjoy feasting on live prey.

All this struggled against that supreme taunt that lay beating at the back of his brain. Rebecca didn't trust him enough to tell him the truth.

"Garitson!"

He swung his head round at his mother's sharp tone.

"You're going to catch your death of cold," she said. "Get inside this house this instant."

He grinned. "I suppose mothers have been saying that since the beginning of time."

"And wasting time doing it," she muttered.

"Where's Rebecca?"

"She's ignoring our party. She's upstairs."

He took the stairs with inevitable purpose, stopping in first at his own room.

Rebecca had retired early in the evening, before the guests arrived, and she'd only just dozed when she felt the sensation of gentle, firm fingertips against her lips.

"Happy Christmas."

Opening her eyes, Rebecca stared silently into Behringer's dark, smiling gaze. "We wouldn't want you announcing to the guests that you're being ravished upstairs, would we?"

Leaning slightly away from her, he reached toward the foot of the bed. "I have something for you."

The package he held out was small, wrapped in brown paper.

"I have nothing for you."

He sighed. Set the gift beside her arm. "Do you think this to be no more than a bribe? A hope for favors?" He tilted his head. "An admirable strategy, now that you mention it."

Her hair tumbled over her shoulders when she sat up, and Behringer watched her. "Open it."

She untied the cord and opened the paper. A book, which she lifted from its wrapper. For a moment, she stared blankly at the book, her stomach somersaulting through her chest. *A Connecticut Yankee in King Arthur's Court.* Mark Twain. She struggled to force breath into her constricted lungs. The book fell from her limp hands.

This book hadn't been published yet.

"Where did you get this?"

"I have my mysterious sources. I thought you liked Twain."

Turning a frantic gaze upon him, she demanded, "Where?"

Behringer arched a dark brow. "The gentleman who's printing Mama's book had it on display. He said it was his only copy."

"Who is he?"

"A book collector. He generally deals in antique glasses and mirrors and rare books. His name is Malcolm Henderson. Why?"

Rebecca's hands trembled uncontrollably as she opened the book to the copyright page.

1889, a novel by Mark Twain.

She recognized it from her first visit to the Henderson shop. She dropped the book, her brain a raging river of anarchy.

"Thank you," she whispered.

Behringer's confusion equaled hers. Watching her carefully, he reached inside his coat. "I almost forgot this."

He took her hand, suddenly cold, and pressed something into her palm.

When he released her hand, she gazed down, still not recovered from the shock of his first gift. Lying on her upturned palm was an exquisite double miniature, framed with mother-of-pearl. She peered at the faces there, faces from fifteen years before. A smoothshaven, unscarred Garitson and his mother in one, Jacob and a toddler she assumed to be Katy in another. "My family," he said. "I'd like you to think of us as your family."

For long seconds, Rebecca couldn't speak.

"Of course, I've never seen any portraits of your family," he said. "What does your mother look like?"

Touched at his poorly disguised ploy, Rebecca softened. "She's gorgeous. Tall, blond, green-eyed, vivacious. I took after my father, the shy bookworm."

Behringer chuckled. "I'd say you were anything but either of those."

"This is sweet of you, Garitson. I wish I had something for you."

"You do."

She raised a suspicious eyebrow at him.

"Oh, let's be sensible," he said impatiently.

She smiled at his modesty.

Just as seriously, he rose from the bed and went to the armoire. Opening it, he withdrew the dress. The amber silk taffeta whispered softly as he brought it to her. "Put it on and come downstairs." As though he knew her next words, he raised his hands. "Please. For me. For Christmas."

"But, Garit," she began, rising from the bed, "it would take forever . . . my hair . . . I—"

"You look beautiful."

Behringer grasped the hairbrush from the dressing table and walked to stand behind her. Carefully spreading the dark tresses over her shoulders, he began to brush her hair.

Behringer's hands rested on Rebecca's shoulders, and he gently kissed her hair. Lingering there, he inhaled her sweet, womanly aroma. He had been too far away from her for far too long.

She stood, paralyzed, as his hands swiftly unbuttoned the simple dress she wore. Tentatively, he touched her bare shoulders with the tips of his fingers. "I've missed you very much," he said softly.

She smiled. Behringer's brashness made his inherently gentle tenderness all the more moving. Turning, she lifted one of his hands to her mouth and kissed the palm. That hand covered her cheek, turning her face up to him.

His face was not wholly peaceful; in fact, a turbulence burned in his eyes more strongly than ever. "Thank you for the portraits," she said. "I know how dear they must be to you."

Moments passed as they gazed at each other, seeking to express those emotions which dwelled within that vulnerable part of themselves. Finally, Behringer stepped back, looking away from her. "I'll see you downstairs."

She watched him go, then dressed quickly. As she descended the stairway, she realized the Christmas ball was well under way. The spirit of the season wafted throughout the house, in the aromas and that intangible something that was as ageless as the holiday.

Reaching the door of the ballroom, she searched for Behringer. He stood at the other end of the room, near Sarah's portrait, talking to a man she recognized as the mayor of Jefferson.

Behringer noticed Rebecca's gaze, and he slowly disengaged himself from the mayor's ceaseless prattle about an advertising venture for Jefferson rail.

"Carolers!" A cry arose near the window.

A woman said, "Why, Charles Norton is with them!"

Reflexively, Behringer searched for Rebecca once more in the crowd. His eyes finally settled unhappily on her. Her face lit up in surprise at the unexpected visitor. Doggedly, Behringer continued to make his way through the throng of people.

The front door burst open, and there he was. Larger than reality, prettier than any man had a right to be. His apeish arms were about Rebecca, clutching at the fragile strength of her. By now, Behringer stood no more than six feet from them. The room suddenly shrank as he heard the man's words, as clearly as fifteen people around them heard. Something about damn England to hell. A lot about how desperately he loved her. And one tragically timely question, beseeching her to spend the rest of her life with him.

❧ Thirty ❧

From his room, Behringer heard the light footsteps on the stairs. He rose from the bed and moved into the hall, not bothering with the shirt he'd removed earlier.

Rebecca arrived at the landing, slowly examining him, and he vaguely knew he looked like hell. She ended her inspection at his bare feet.

"He makes a lovely plea," Behringer said.

She leaned against the railing, her breath shallow. "Doesn't he?"

Her gaze rested on the half-empty tumbler in his hand as he approached, and he laughed. "Yes, I've been drinking. Quite a lot over the last three hours." The tumbler descended slowly to the hall candle stand. "Do you realize you stand beneath the mistletoe?"

She remained unmoved. "Don't be silly."

Stopping mere inches from Rebecca, he pointed his finger at her. "I told you once. I carefully orchestrate our moments alone together."

"And you knew I would be standing in this spot at this moment."

"I did."

"Did you also anticipate that I would be considering a proposal of marriage to another man?"

He raised his eyebrow, conceding her point with a slow

shake of his head. "I must admit, I did not." After a pause, he asked, "Are you?"

"What?"

"Considering it."

"Why shouldn't I?"

He shrugged. "At worst he's a mama's boy, and at best he doesn't know what he's doing from one moment to the next."

"And you plan out . . . carefully orchestrate, as you say . . . each moment of your life."

Behringer nodded.

She laughed. "And what will you be doing twenty years from now?"

"If it's a moment like this one, I'm sure I'll be making love to you."

Rebecca leaned against the rail for support against his whispered words. He stood so near she felt his breath on her temple, tasted brandy and tobacco. "I should like to kiss the bride," he murmured.

"I'm not a bride."

"Imagine the fantasy as I do," he suggested, tracing her face with a gentle fingertip. "You're dressed in white lace, very much a bride. And I kneel with you before the priest, and I lift the veil separating your beautiful face from me—" His hand smoothed back a loose strand of hair from her face.

"You're imagining a distinctly different wedding, Garit," she said, her voice breaking in wonder.

"Hush. It's my fantasy."

With agonizing slowness, he lowered his mouth until his breath mingled with hers. He paused at the first contact of their lips, savoring the rush of emotions that washed over him. She smelled of hollyberry, and she tasted of peppermint. He'd never known a more intoxicating combination. A more maddening woman. Softly pressuring her lips apart, he dipped his tongue within the warmth of her mouth, freely relishing her. The taste of her mouth. The softness of her hair. Now, the slow sweetness of her own tongue against his, her soft hands sliding upward on his bare chest.

Charles Norton had probably kissed her thus less than fifteen minutes ago, and the knowledge terrified him. With a simple word from her, the man would have every right to know the creamy beauty of her body as well. The thought sent chill waves crashing over his mind, drowning his fantasy, and only cold reality remained. He raised his head, overwhelmed by the intensity of his yearning, unable to express the bleakness of a future without her, a future she could very easily spend in Charles Norton's arms. He was seized by the inhuman urge to cut her as deeply as she cut him, and his power existed in an old lie.

"You know," he chuckled breathlessly, "we could go on with our original plans. Norton makes no difference."

She stared up at him in disbelief.

"It would be so much simpler, actually," he went on pleasantly. "I'd be able to sleep better with no worries of how I was robbing you of your respectability."

Shoving ineffectually at his hard shoulders, she muttered fiercely. "You filthy, filthy bastard. You don't know the meaning of the word *remorse*. The plans were yours. Not mine."

"You would make a perfect lovely wife for him, as Vivian will for me. He wants no more than a doll to place on his Chippendale chairs."

She desperately struggled against the slow glide of his lips on her throat. "He gave up everything he had in England for me! He gave up his family for me."

"His father must've revealed the family fortune was in shambles."

"Why is it so hard for you to imagine him wanting to marry me merely because he loves me?" Incensed at his blindly cruel behavior, Rebecca lashed out. "But you know nothing of love. You wouldn't know the first thing about sacrificing anything for a woman, much less your whole family."

Rebecca felt his flinch. As he stared down at her with

dully pained eyes, she knew that she'd unwittingly struck a wound. She suspected even Behringer had his sense of honor. Facing the evidence of her sure injury, she, too, felt his anguish. Slowly, he lifted a hand to touch her cheek.

"I apologize," he said softly. "This should be a happy time for you, Rebecca." Her whispered name sounded like a vow, and he stroked her cheek. "God, you're just so damned lovely. Do you love the man?"

"I'm very fond of Charles."

Another long moment passed, and slowly he drew his hand away from her face. Charles Norton's wife. He tried to put the man beside her in his mind, but the vision enraged him. He thrust his hands inside his trousers pockets. "Run along, dear. Before I forget Charles Norton exists." *Before I do my damnedest to make you forget he exists.*

She obeyed him, and Behringer returned to his room. Somewhere in the night, he exchanged his rum for fresh coffee. He stared at the glowing coals in the fireplace. Errant shards of blazing hickory flicked out at his bare feet. What a hellish holiday. Rising from his chair by the fire, he tossed another heavy chunk of wood on the fire. The flames reached upward toward him, and he flinched, as he always did.

"Garitson, are you awake?" A gentle tap followed his mother's words, then the door parted only slightly and she entered with a tray.

Maria ignored his silence, pouring two cups of steaming, aromatic coffee. She placed one on the table near his chair. "You know of Charles' return."

Nodding slowly, he folded his hands across his waist.

"And you know of his reason."

Behringer straightened in his chair, reaching for the coffee. "I know he's an indecisive worm."

Maria raised her brows as she sipped her coffee. "Yes, well. Even that is better for a girl with nothing in this world."

Rubbing his aching eyes, he said, "Mama, get to your point."

"She's going to marry him, you ninny."

Maria wanted to pour the hot brew into his lap. Perhaps that would awaken him.

He sighed and sipped his coffee. "I don't think you give her enough credit."

"Is that so."

"That's so."

"She told me herself," she invented.

Behringer's head jerked up. "When?"

"Late last night."

Slowly, he exhaled. "She certainly gave it a lot of thought."

Maria set her coffee aside and rose. She began to pace calmly back and forth in front of him, methodically pausing to tap her foot. "She would have to have been as blind as you not to have considered it since the night of the Fairchild party. He fell in love with her, recognizing her for the rarity that she is. Not a sugary bit of meringue like Vivian Fairchild, but a woman of rare wisdom and sensitivity. A woman who would make him a fine wife."

"She deserves better. He would ask his mother's permission before wedding her."

"He would risk all for her love, instead of slapping her in the face by offering her the life of a whore."

Behringer's cup clattered against the saucer. "I see she keeps you well informed on everything I do."

"She tells me little, but what she doesn't say is far more revealing. When Vivian's name enters the conversation, Rebecca grows silent." She sat down once more. "Have you thought of the future, dear son? A year, five years, ten years from now? You will solve your precious mystery, but by then it won't really matter. Charles accepts Rebecca, though everyone he knows is telling him she isn't good enough for him. Eventually she will see that. Though you have her affections now, eventually she will return his love. You'll see Rebecca give birth to his children, children that you will resent, for they should have been yours. With a father you despise, for it should have been you. Of course, Vivian will have your children, but will you ever love the child of a woman you hate?"

"Stop it." Behringer rose from his chair, running a hand through his rumpled hair. For all his certainty that no one suspected why he was marrying Vivian, his mother had known all along. His mother's scenario of the future was identical to the bleak vision which had begun to torment him. "If I marry Vivian Fairchild, it is no one's business but my own."

"True. And it will be no one's misery but your own." With that, an angry Maria turned and left the room, slamming the door behind her.

So, Behringer thought, stripping off his robe and stalking to the armoire. That's that. In less time than a woman needed to select a hat, Rebecca had chosen a husband. A husband who could very well take her back to his homeland, where they would share their lives. Suddenly he felt as though his own life were over.

Jerking trousers and a shirt from the closet, Behringer quickly dressed. He left the house, heading to the stables and saddling his horse. His breath disappeared in small clouds about his face, and he swung into the saddle and turned the horse toward the north. Less than fifteen minutes later, he dismounted and led Satan through the somber, peaceful grounds of the Oakwood Cemetery.

He waited, desperately, for that serenity he'd come to associate with this place. Nearly five months had passed since his last visit. The guilt that had tormented him for the past few weeks was a dynamic thing, transforming itself as he walked past the marble headstones. Serenity was as elusive as the mist about his feet.

He reached the place, enclosed by a shallow marble wall, near the corner of the cemetery. A gust of wind whipped at his coat, but he was oblivious to the cold as he stooped between their headstones. After a long moment, he turned to look at the empty space between Peter's grave and the marble wall. Straightening, he stood at the foot of the space, and he stared down at the lifeless grass. At one time, this place had been his ultimate dream. The only future he had embraced was the day when he, too, would die, to spend the rest of eternity with his wife and son. His most cherished fantasy had been death.

"Sarah," he said softly. "I'm sorry."

God forgive me, I can't do it.

He turned from the grave and led the horse from the cemetery.

🎋 Thirty-One 🎋

🎋 Rebecca arrived at a breakfast table with only one other occupant. Garitson.

He met her eyes with enigmatic interest when he rose, as if she were a new and curious addition to the household. She remembered their last exchange, his crude taunts, his heart-breaking yearning. He held her chair for her, then returned to his seat.

"Charles Norton was here a while ago," he said finally. "He said to tell you that he'll call later this afternoon. And that he loves you."

Behringer lingered over the words, and Rebecca noticed his slow scrutiny.

"I apologize for my behavior on Christmas," he said.

Rebecca nodded. "I understand."

"Do you?" he asked.

It couldn't have been longer than a moment or two, but they seemed suspended for minutes, neither of them desiring to break the gaze that locked them together.

"Would you have dinner with me today?" he said haltingly. "Perhaps a picnic?"

Despite her best defenses she was moved by his romantic suggestion. She sighed helplessly. "Yes. I'd like that very much."

"I have some business in town to take care of," he said,

rising from the table. "I should be finished by early afternoon."

She quietly nodded. "I'll be waiting for you."

The morning swept by as Rebecca quickly prepared for their picnic. She was in the hall when she heard the buggy on the path in front of the house. Grasping the picnic basket, she walked the short distance to the entryway. A smile washed over her face as she saw Behringer's shadow on the stained glass window of the door, and she paused. The door opened.

Surprised to see her waiting there, he frowned sternly. "Shouldn't you be waiting discreetly upstairs until I call for you? You wouldn't want me to think you're bold, you know."

She considered him wonderingly as he closed the door behind him, leaning against it. "You act as if you're courting me, Garitson."

"Do I? Perhaps I am." He scrutinized her with a compelling laziness. "A tribute to a memorable summer's night, perhaps?"

He remembered. She glanced down at the gown sprigged with yellow roses; the dress she'd worn the night they first made love. She was swept away to her youth, agonizing over the right dress for a first date. "I only . . . I thought you might . . ."

"Oh, I do." He moved away from the door and steadily approached her. Reaching her, he relieved her of the heavy basket, placing it on the floor. His hands brushed her shoulders, and he gently lifted the edges of the shawl until it draped off her shoulders, exposing the full swell of her breasts to his gaze. "I very much do." He lifted his face, then, to meet her eyes. "If you'll be patient for a bit longer, I'll only be a moment."

She floated into the parlor and sank into a chair. When Garitson returned, he carried a heavy blanket and a quilt. The grandmother's flower garden quilt! She stared at the quilt, disoriented, unable to speak. Her heart hammered wildly.

"Do you like it? It was a gift from my mother, for Christmas."

She found the courage to remark, "It's beautiful."

Behringer effortlessly lifted the cumbersome basket and opened the door. As they left the house, he walked closely beside her, his free hand lightly resting between her shoulders. Rebecca was surrounded by the faint masculine fragrance of him. He placed the basket behind the seat of the buggy, then helped her up. Opening the quilt, he placed it over her lap. "It may be a bit cool as we drive," he said, tucking the loose ends of the quilt about her legs.

"We're taking a different route today," he explained as he turned the buggy in the opposite direction from town. The road was deserted, and he slowly slipped his arm around her shoulders. "I don't have the patience for any chance meetings with anyone. What do you have tucked inside that basket?"

She lifted a hand and touched his chest, relaxing against him and wondering if she imagined the change that had come over him. She felt the steady thud of his heart, and she rested her head in the hollow of his shoulder. "Oh, just chicken. And some fruit. And a potato salad."

"Shall we drink water from the bayou?" he teased.

"And a bottle of wine."

"Ah."

She said nothing at his quiet sigh, only rubbed her face against the soft wool of his sweater.

"So you think to marry Charles Norton, do you?"

She lifted her hand to touch his mouth, and he pressed his lips there. "I don't want to talk about him today."

"But I do. I intend to talk about nothing except him until you're as bored with the man as I am."

She touched her lips to his throat, and he fell silent, pulling her into his embrace.

As they crossed the bridge spanning the bayou, he spoke. "You've never seen my home, have you?"

"No."

"Well, forgive me my rather painfully consistent stupidity where you're concerned."

The thought of him sharing with her the house where he and Sarah had lived intrigued her. Behringer clicked the horses to a trot, down a smaller, dusty path. The overhanging branches of live oaks extended across the narrow path, and Rebecca closed her eyes and snuggled closer to him, savoring the solitude of their haven. "When will we be there?"

"I know of the most beautiful place, my darling. There will be no one there except you and me and this gorgeous day." Then he took her fingertips and kissed them.

The shelter of the oaks thinned above them, and she followed the direction of his gaze, startled at the house she saw there. It hadn't been included in her first tour of Jefferson, perhaps because of its remoteness. Its grandiose construction equaled Jacob's home; the only difference was in the style of the period. Ornately carved wood trimmed the house, and a widow's walk topped the superb structure.

"I intended for this to be your home. Our home."

"Before Charles Norton set his mind on making an honest woman out of me?" she said wryly.

He gazed at her. "I never intended to dishonor you, Rebecca. Norton complicated everything."

She touched his hand. "I thought the idea of him bored you."

"The idea of him infuriates me. Especially the idea of his hands upon you." He stared at her, and his jealousy was etched in every line of his face.

Once more leaning her head upon his chest, she touched his knee. "We have a picnic waiting for us, Garit. Today's too special for you to be unhappy."

He sighed and turned the buggy down a path that followed behind the house, overshadowed by oaks. They traveled no more than a hundred feet when he stopped the buggy.

"We're not quite there yet."

He helped her down from the buggy, then drew her into the thickness of the woods near his home. He led her down a path overgrown by weeds. After another hundred or so feet, they reached a clearing. A small stream ran through the grassy, mystical place guarded by oak and cypress. The stream's trickle provided an elemental music.

"It's like something out of a fairy tale," she whispered.

He spread the blanket on the ground, and then the quilt above it. There he placed the picnic basket, and then he turned. The tip of his tongue touched his lip, and Rebecca stared at him in fascination. "This was my own private place, back when I lived in the house. No one else has ever been here except you."

Touched at his sharing such a sanctuary with her, she moved forward until she stood near him. He made no effort to touch her, and she slowly sank onto the softness of the quilt, removing her slippers, tucking her feet underneath her. Still, she stared at him. Rising slightly, she leaned forward to unfasten his boots. Behringer sat on the quilt, taking over her task.

"I cooked this myself," she said with a nervous laugh as she arranged their picnic. "I haven't cooked in the longest time, but I love to. Sort of a hobby, I suppose. I can make a wonderful baked chicken, too, and a stuffing made with apples and shallots. Fried chicken seemed best for a picnic, though. I hope you like it. I—"

Behringer kissed her, silencing her agitated rambling. As he leaned across the distance between them, his hand glided up the soft column of her throat. "Relax."

She sighed, soothed by his touch. "Let's skip the plates," he suggested, reaching for the bottle of wine with a grin. "I think we're close enough now to share the same dishes."

"And will we swig the wine right out of the bottle?"

He raised an eyebrow at her saucy taunt as he poured two glasses. He placed one in her hand. "To a memorable summer's night. And an unforgettable December afternoon," he said.

She smiled and touched his glass with hers, then drank to their happiness.

Closing the top of the basket, he sipped his wine again, then placed it atop the smooth wooden surface of the basket. They ate in a comfortable silence for several minutes, until Behringer sliced off a sliver of apple and held it up to her mouth. As she took the small piece of fruit between her lips, her tongue brushed his fingertips. Quietly, she chewed and swallowed the apple, tasting Behringer there. Salty. Smoky. Elementally male.

Behringer reached for his wine, still watching her. He lifted the glass to his lips, then hers.

A breeze danced through the woods, tousling his hair. In the bright light of day, when age was unkindest to the human face, Behringer seemed fifteen years younger. For a desperate moment, Rebecca wished she'd met him before all the scores of scars which had ravaged his heart and hers.

Watching his twinkling gaze, she remembered Bessie's advice. The woman was right. Rebecca knew that neither age, nor time itself, nor anything else which stood between them mattered to her. She loved him. More than she'd ever known it was possible to love a man. And it was plain that he as desperately needed her love. Perhaps, in time, with enough of her love, he could grow to love her as well. That, in the end, was all that mattered. She shivered in the warmth of the afternoon, shaken by the gravity of her decision.

"Are you cold?" Behringer's words were a hushed whisper in the shelter of the trees. He rested on an elbow, watching her.

Rebecca silently shook her head.

His dark eyes scrutinized her face, noticing the solemn expectation there. Her hands were folded demurely in her lap, fiddling with the fringe on the shawl sheltering her from his sight. He reached out with one slender finger, drawing it along her hand, stilling her fidgeting. The same fingertip, moving in a fluid line upward on her arm, slid underneath the shawl and drew it away from her until the offending garment fell to the ground.

Behringer gave a low murmur of approval as his gaze

drifted leisurely over her. His roving finger trailed across the warm, soft curves displayed to him. Then, he met her eyes with somber determination.

"Do you truly intend to marry Charles Norton?" he asked.

She laughed. "Are you joking?"

A triumphant smile curved his mouth before he shrugged. "Mama told me you were."

Rebecca smiled. Behringer joined her. "That scheming mother of mine," he murmured in amusement, savoring the sheer joy of looking at her.

"Has he ever kissed you?"

Rebecca noticed the defenseless expectancy in his gaze, and she silently shook her head.

A gleam lit his eyes. Rebecca waited breathlessly, but Behringer seemed content with his unhurried examination. She was not. Her hand trembled as she rested her palm against his beard, her thumb brushing his lower lip. "I want to kiss you," she said. "Very much."

Behringer's eyebrows rose just briefly, in recognition of her words, and his tongue slowly traced the curve of her thumb before he caught the tip of it inside his mouth, tugging gently.

Rebecca leaned forward, her hands framing his face as she fitted her mouth intimately to his. Slender fingertips slid into his hair as she deepened her kiss, and Behringer leaned back, relaxing against his folded coat as his arms went about her.

Rebecca's mouth traveled to his forehead, his eyes, his cheeks, his ear. "I love kissing you," she whispered.

Behringer sighed and found her mouth once more with his, vaguely aware that her hands were beneath his sweater, methodically releasing the buttons of his shirt. Her motions were purposeful as she allowed the kiss to end only long enough to draw the soft sweater over his head. He heard her murmur of contentment as her fingers slid within his shirt, and she restlessly pulled away from him, pushing the shirt off his shoulders.

Behringer, enflamed by her blatant seduction, spoke quietly, his voice rough with desire. "Undress for me."

Rebecca went still at his provocative request. Her eyes locked with his as she reached over her shoulders. She unhooked the gown and slowly drew it away from her shoulders.

Behringer's fierce arousal grew at her sensual disrobing. It was the first time she'd worn the gown since the night they'd first made love. He had been sure, on that night, that she couldn't be more beautiful. He'd been wrong. She rose as gracefully as the sun and let the gown pool at her feet.

A raw shiver shook him when he saw she wore nothing except the chemise underneath the dress. This garment, too, slipped away like a whisper. Her firm, full breasts were achingly erotic in the bright sunlight, and the rosy nipples which crowned them blushed even darker. His gaze traveled from her long, slender legs to her smooth, flat stomach and gently flaring hips. Her name escaped Behringer in a startled sigh when she knelt astride his legs.

Rebecca's eager hands roamed over his chest, over the gently rounded strength of his shoulders. Her lips followed the path of her fingertips, tasting the urgent virility of him, recognizing the steady thunder of his heart underneath her mouth, knowing the erotic pleasure he knew when she felt his nipples tighten against her tongue. She had never before wanted a man with such desperate need.

"Jesus, Rebecca," he whispered, his fingers sliding into her hair. "Do you have any idea what you're doing to me?"

Behringer's hands slipped down her throat, then lower, cupping her breasts in his hands, catching the erect peaks with thumb and forefinger. His hands slipped to her waist and he lifted her above him, and a groan escaped him when his tongue touched her nipple—first one, and then the other.

The soft cry that arose from her lips encouraged him to take a pouting crest between his teeth, and he methodically drew it in against his tongue, then once more gently nipped it, until her fingers laced within his hair.

"Garit," she whispered. Her hand slipped between their bodies, and she met the full firm thrust that waited for her. Swiftly, she unbuttoned his trousers and touched him with gentle, wondering fingers. Behringer watched her as she tugged off his trousers.

As he witnessed her enticing seduction, he wondered anew how she'd been born with such knowledge of pleasure. Knowledge meant to be enjoyed by him alone. She would never marry Charles Norton, and he would never marry that insipid brat. Before him stood the paradoxical woman with whom he would spend the rest of his life, if he had to kidnap her and hide with her on the other side of the continent.

She trailed her fingertips against his inner thigh, slowly sliding them upward until they curled around the soft, sensitive flesh which lay in vivid contrast to the aching shaft of need just above. Gently, she drew her fingernail upward, inciting sparks of maddening desire from the depths of his longing.

He murmured her name, grasping her hand. He drew her down onto his body, and she braced her hands on either side of his face.

She lowered her lips to his, tasting him. Thrusting his fingers through the thickness of her dark hair, he lifted it away from her neck. He pulled her mouth more closely against his, capturing her tongue and imitating her motion. His hands raced over her body, feverishly wanting to experience all of her in the same heartbeat. He grasped the curve of her hips in both hands, urging the rise of her womanhood into his own hardness, pressing his hips upward. He tasted her moan, felt the arch of her back as she rubbed her breasts against his chest.

With a slight start, he realized he was making love to Rebecca in broad daylight. And when she looked at him, he saw nothing but adoration in her eyes. The thought set his desire ablaze, and his forefinger followed the curve of her thighs until he dipped into her dewy haven, and he made an inarticulate sound of pleasure. She started to withdraw from his kiss, and he caught her lower lip between his teeth, drawing her near to him. As long as she went on kissing him, loving him, this beautiful time would never end.

Behringer clutched the softness of her hips in his palms, kneading their firmness. And then, hardly aware what he was doing, he slid his hands down along the smoothness of her thighs, coaxing them upward until her knees were on either side of his waist. Only then did he allow her to move slightly away from him. She glanced questioningly at him.

"Make love to me," he said.

Her eyes darkened at his suggestion, and he watched her in bewitched captivation as she leaned away from him, arching slightly. The gentle sway of her breasts hypnotized him, and he slid both hands up to capture the softness there, gently rubbing her nipples between his fingers. "Touching you is like the best of dreams."

She grinned at him, her eyes sleepy in arousal. "It only gets better, my love."

He smiled, remembering as she remembered.

Continuing to stare at him, her hazel eyes taking on the hue of whiskey as he met her gaze, she reached to grasp him with her cool, soft hand. The sensation of her fingertips against his rigid flesh sent fire throughout his veins, intensified by the touch of warm, wet flesh which steadily, hungrily welcomed his swollen, waiting need.

Behringer's hands rested on her slender hips, and he thrust upward, savoring the initial ripple of her warm, intimate caress. "Where did you learn that?" His voice was an anguished whisper.

"Learn what?" she whispered. "Everything I know of lovemaking I learned from you, Garit. Each worthwhile moment I've lived was spent concocting the fantasy you are."

She withdrew from him, and his eyes closed at her velvety caress. The intensity of her words. Slowly, with seductive motions, she moved over him, never ending her multileveled seduction. She knew exactly how to wring desire from him until he was no more than a schoolboy, entranced by the rhythmic sway of her hips and thighs. His hands rested on her hips and he thrust upward into her warmth, savoring the vision of her. Her eyes closed as she bit her lip against the exquisite pleasure.

He drew that pouting mouth down to his, taking her tongue between his lips. And then he swung around and he was over her, looking down into the amber eyes that gazed at him in loving desire. He muttered soft, senseless things into her ear, persistently enticing her to a summit she reached not once, but several times. She called to him from the other side of that beautiful place, urging him to join her there. She was there, she knew its wonder, she welcomed the sense of oneness with him he'd known since the first moment he saw her, glistening wet in his room. Then, he heard her bold, descriptive words of the place, and he whispered her name, poised at the crest of the place. Her beguiling movements drew him to the other side.

For several minutes, they silently reminisced over that space where the two of them lived as one. He stroked her hair and the soft, flushed curve of her cheek. She marveled over the strength of his shoulders beneath her fingertips.

Sighing contentedly, he shifted to one side of her and stared up at the leaves of the evergreen oak which shaded them. She turned then, cuddling against his chest. Kissing her hair, he hugged her to him.

"Thank you for sharing your lovely sanctuary with me, Garit."

"It's truly beautiful in the springtime. We'll come back then, when it's warmer. Now I'll never come here without thinking of you."

Her lips curled softly against his chest. "No one else has ever been here?"

He smiled at her curiosity, knowing exactly whom she meant. He shook his head. "Only you."

Satisfied with his answer, she dozed in the afterwarmth of their lovemaking. He, too, thought of the woman to whom he'd once been married. Again that taste of guilt, fainter now, offset by the incredible happiness within his breast, pricked at his heart. For the last time. Yesterday, as the cold December rain drummed against his back, he'd said good-bye to Sarah and Peter forever.

A peacefulness overcame him, and with that serenity, an intense thankfulness for the girl beside him who'd taught him the importance of giving love. Of loving oneself as well. Tonight after supper, he would visit Vivian, would tell her the truth, and let fly the age-old furies beyond hell. He hugged Rebecca to him tightly, then he frowned when she stirred.

"I'm sorry," he whispered. "Go back to sleep."

Rebecca opened her eyes, smiling. Her wonderful dream was real. Behringer was there, holding her in his arms, and sharing the most private place in his life with her. Slowly, she raised herself to her elbows, scrutinizing the man who lay next to her. Certainly the most arrogant and infuriating and flippant man she'd ever known. Certainly the most beautiful. She told him so.

He chuckled, and a tenderness crept over her heart at the pleasure in his expression. He enjoyed her admiration. "I think it's you, my child, who's beautiful."

They lay within each other's arms, drinking the rest of the wine, until the afternoon's warmth faded in the murmur of the soft, vespertine breeze. Dressing quickly, they assembled the remains of their lunch and tucked it away in the picnic basket. As they left the clearing, Rebecca paused.

Turning to look back at their lovely sanctuary, a heaviness gripped her heart, not unlike that eerie precognition which had encompassed her upon her arrival in Jefferson. She was filled with a sudden stark knowledge that this was the last time she was gazing upon its beauty. That never again would they share such splendorous, tender moments together, and she would certainly never see its beauty in the spring. Once more that voice within her breast spoke, the voice which had reminded her that her purpose here was only to prevent a needless death.

The next time you stand in this spot, you will be alone. There will be no gentle Garit standing beside you, and this space will never be the same. Accept it now, and your pain will be easier to bear.

Why hadn't she told him, as she lay within his arms, how much she loved him? It would only have softened his heart that much more, would have made that much more real his ability to love. To love her.

"Rebecca?" Garit's voice, just over her shoulder, roused her from her regret. As she turned to look at him, she contemplated telling him now.

He stared at her, a glint of humor about his eyes and lips, and she laughed softly, taking his arm. Neither said anything as they walked arm in arm to the buggy. He tucked her against his chest, stroking her loose hair.

"Would you like to have supper in town with me tonight?"

In town. He was taking her into town, despite all those who would gawk nosily. A smile went over her lips, and she nodded. "I need to deliver your mother's book to the printer first, but after that, I believe my schedule is free."

She could not have anticipated the direct route he would take returning from the bayou, straight through downtown, with her hair tumbling down her back, her clothes wrinkled from their recent lovemaking, and his silent declaration stunned her. As she shivered from a chill breeze which reminded her that winter still reigned supreme, Behringer silently placed an arm around her shoulders, drawing her nearer to his warmth.

The late afternoon sun was just dipping into the trees as they arrived home. He dropped a kiss near her temple.

"Oh, dear," Behringer said softly, glancing toward the verandah, drawing her gaze away from his face.

Charles Norton sat with Maria on the front porch swing. The two watched the approach of the buggy, and the easy, intimate embrace of a man and a woman who were quite obviously lovers.

❧ Thirty-Two ❧

Garit discreetly removed his arm from Rebecca, allowing her to salvage some dignity for the confrontation ahead. Norton rose from the porch swing and walked to the steps. "Behringer?"

The word was a question, an accusation, and a challenge. Behringer was prepared to answer all three.

"No, Garit. This is between Charles and me."

She stepped down from the carriage, and Maria and her son left Rebecca and Charles alone. Rebecca rested on a step, and Charles leaned against one of the columns. A minute of silence passed as she tried to find a way to explain it all.

"Should I offer congratulations?" Charles asked dryly, with a half smile.

Rebecca raised her gaze to his. "Charles, I'm sorry."

"Are you in love with him?"

"I love him in a way I didn't think possible."

Charles nodded slowly. "I suppose that's what I've needed to hear all this time. Heaven knows I refused any other hint."

"I handled it unforgivably. You didn't deserve it."

"Well. I can catch up with Father if I leave in the morning. Now all that's left is good-bye."

"Good-bye?"

"I'll return to London, of course. My life in America has been exciting, but not fulfilling. Your love would've made my life complete, Rebecca." Then, embarrassed to hear what sounded like an accusation, he went on, "But I'm pleased that you're happy."

"There is no need for you to leave Jefferson, Charles. I value your friendship dearly."

"Friendship, my dear, cannot give a man children."

She closed her eyes.

"We would have made a lovely couple, you know," he said in a halfhearted attempt at humor.

She heard his words, and for a moment she pictured them, dressed in vibrant colors, sprawled across the cover of a cheap paperback, bathed in a magenta sunset. The perfect couple.

"What about your home?"

"My solicitor should be able to tie things up for me."

"Your business—what of that?"

"It shall be dissolved, I'm afraid."

With his words came a realization, and she was filled with sudden desperation for him to stay. To build his life, his future, in Jefferson. "Jefferson needs you, Charles."

He laughed. "And I need you. We can't all have what we want, my love."

"There are many, many eligible young ladies here, Charles."

He smiled at her. "You think to marry me off to Vivian?"

"Well, no, but—"

"If I'm going to resign myself to a loveless marriage, I might as well do it in England. At home."

Crossing the space between them, he took her hands in his. For a moment, he stared down at her, desolation chilling the blue of his eyes. Then, he closed those indigo eyes and crushed her fingers to his lips. "I wish you happiness."

With that, he left. Rebecca. Jefferson. Forever.

Rebecca found Maria in the dining room, setting the table for supper.

The woman paused, looking up at Rebecca, her eyes bright with question. Slowly, Rebecca said, "Garit and I will be eating at Henrique's tonight."

Maria smiled slowly, peacefully. "He loves you, I knew it. And you will marry."

"He said neither. For all I know, he still intends to marry Vivian. But I love him, and that's all that matters. I will love him the best way I know, and someday, I may know his love as well."

Maria lay her hands on Rebecca's arms with chilling gravity. "Be patient, Rebecca. Before you find a time of happiness with Garit, there will be many treacherous bridges for you to cross, and much sorrow. But never give up your love for him, and most of all, never relinquish your belief in that love. Eventually, it will conquer all your obstacles. Someday, you will look at my story and believe in every word I wrote. Remember, when you do, that I loved you very much."

Tears clouded Rebecca's eyes, and she said, "Oh, Maria, I—"

Maria silenced Rebecca with her fingertips. "Be patient," she repeated. "There will first come a time when you think me no more than a lying old woman. A truly foolish romantic."

The sadness in Maria's eyes frightened Rebecca. Then, the woman once more hugged her, and crossed the room to the sideboard. Lifting the heavy stack of papers in her arms, she returned to Rebecca and placed her burden of love in the younger woman's hands.

"Do you remember where Mr. Henderson's shop is?"

Rebecca remembered the curious old shop which would survive into the twentieth century with the same family running it. She nodded.

"He's expecting it. Hurry now, for he may already be closed. And guard it well," she said, sparks of amusement in her eyes. "It's a very important work."

Rebecca left the room, glancing over her shoulder at Maria just one last time. The woman's peacefully supportive expression strengthened her as she fetched a buggy from the stables and headed toward town. In front of Henderson's shop, she stopped the horses and secured the buggy, then went inside. She looked around the shop in eerie wonder. It looked so very similar to the place where she'd met the peculiar old man.

A young man stood behind the counter. "Miss Reynolds?" Rebecca nodded, startled from her reverie.

"I'm Malcolm Henderson's assistant, David. You got Mrs. Behringer's manuscript?"

She returned his smile. "Here it is," she said, placing it in his hands. The dread that had nagged at her the entire time she worked on the book jabbed once more. Now, handing the treasure into his hands, she sighed heavily. "Please take care of it. It's the only copy of the book that exists."

"I'll guard it like gold, Miss Reynolds."

"It's far more valuable."

She paused another moment to gaze at the stack of papers then left the office, a little early yet for her appointment with Behringer. When she perched on the seat of the buggy, she decided against the turn that would have taken her back to Henrique's, then instead turned in the direction of Caddo Lake, the place where Behringer had lost the woman he'd loved, as well as his capacity for love.

She meandered along the path of the bayou until she reached the turn basin, then stopped. It was impossible to fathom the depth of loss Behringer had suffered near this place. Sighing, she decided to turn back for Henrique's. Lifting the straps in her hands, she froze. A now-frigid breeze whipped about her face and neck, bringing with it an eerie sensation of impending disaster.

The awareness passed, and she chuckled. "Step out of your imagination, dearie, and join us in reality."

The sun had long since set, and Behringer was waiting by now. She was surprised to find the turn basin deserted, but it was, after all, still the holidays. She decided to take a short-cut to Henrique's, through the thicket.

She was only a few hundred feet from the path to Henrique's when the thunder of horses' hooves pounded in her brain. Alarmed at the approach of a rider, she glanced around. A small path intersected her line of travel, and a huge black stallion suddenly emerged from that path, stopping just ten feet in front of her buggy. Desperately, she shut her eyes tightly and pulled on the straps until her arms ached. The horses reared, confused at the chaos. A sudden impact threw her from the buggy, tossing her into the brush beside the path. She cried out as she landed, a cry that sprang more from fear than pain.

As she struggled for footing, groping the slippery, moss-covered brambles beneath her, a man loomed over her, wrenching her from the ground. In the darkness of the shadows, she couldn't make out his face. His long fingers were like wet ropes, tightly constricting about her upper arms. Unfazed by her struggles, he dragged her toward the banks of the bayou. As the depths of the water loomed menacingly before her, she screamed. Fresh from the winter's rains, it would be cold, and deep enough to drown a good swimmer.

Desperately fighting her attacker, she shrieked out in terror, silently praying. *Not now, please, God.* Not when she was within a fingertip of reaching the happiness which had tempted her for a lifetime.

To her surprise, he paused just a few feet from the bayou, forcing her to her knees in the mucky clay. For a moment, she was wracked with relief at the respite, until she saw him toss a fresh, neatly coiled loop of rope near her knees. With a muddied boot against her back, he shoved her to her elbows. Then, he grabbed the rope, and she twisted her head to look up at him. The clear December moonlight clearly outlined his features. Harry Murphy stood over her, his face darkened by a stubble of beard, and terror lurched in her heart.

A shrill whisper sliced the night air as Murphy drew a thin, sharp knife from his boot. Fear slammed Rebecca at the silver flash of the knife in the darkness, reflecting the glint in Murphy's eyes. He swiftly sliced off a length of rope.

"Why—why are you doing this? What have I done?"

"I'm finishing what I started last summer." His words were careful, articulate even, as he spoke, belying his appearance. "However," he went on, his leering gaze lingering on the front of her gown, "you've a healthy pair of lungs. And while I doubt that even your shout can reach the town at this point, I'm not going to take chances."

With that, he mockingly waved the handkerchief laced between the fingers of his left hand. Then, through with his taunting, his face darkened into a cruel mask.

"I tell you, it was a lot easier the first time. Jealousy dulls your morals substantially."

Her mind raced, trying to find logic in his words. As she struggled to elude him, scrambling ineffectively in the clay, he snatched one of her hands, then the other, and swiftly bound them together with the rope. Overwhelmed with fear, her screams seemed useless as she uncontrollably sobbed and shouted Behringer's name. This continued for only a moment, then she supposed Murphy struck her. For she felt only a blinding ache at the back of her head, and then the peacefully rippling sounds of the bayou went silent.

For endless moments, she relived the life she'd shared here with Behringer. As far as she was concerned, her life had begun and ended in his arms. Even in those times when she'd hated his arrogance, she'd loved his vulnerability. His smiling face echoed within her memory, teasing and tempting and challenging her to be more than she was. The gleam of his raven black hair in the moonlight, the flex of his golden brown back in the sun's brilliance, the mellow depth of his voice demanding to know her name. All these memories washed over her as she slipped into darkness.

❧ Thirty-Three ❧

Behringer slipped out of Henrique's. Rebecca was ten minutes late. David was just locking up when he arrived at Henderson's.

"David, have you seen Miss Reynolds?"

The man scratched his head in surprise. "Sure. She was here about fifteen minutes ago, I guess. She had your buggy, and headed out toward the turn basin."

"The turn basin?"

David nodded. "Didn't say where she was going."

Behringer turned, forced to waste a few precious minutes fetching a horse from the livery. What the hell was she doing going on a joy ride this time of the evening? Didn't she know how dangerous it was for a woman to go sporting about in a buggy after dark?

He swung onto the animal and nudged him into a gallop. The horse thundered down Austin Street, and Behringer soon reached the hill near the turn basin. Frustrated at the dim light of the half-moon, he peered around at the murky water, and the trees whose branches stretched out over the water. As he scrutinized the deserted area, Behringer heard a scream. It was his name.

As he tried to pinpoint the direction, a dim splash in the water pierced his frustration. He swung in the direction of the sound. A moment later, he saw her, sinking below the surface of the water. A disgustingly familiar figure disappeared into the woods just a dozen feet away.

Pain gripped his chest as he spurred the horse on the distance between them, stripping off his coat as he went. Swiftly splitting the surface of the water, Behringer reached her in less than a minute. Drawing her upward in the deep water, he snatched away the saturated gag. Rebecca's limp body was unresisting as he swam back to shore, and for a timeless moment, fear and memory disoriented him. Once again, numbness overcame him in the wintry water. Once again, he held a woman to his breast. This time, however, the fear that enveloped him was edged by determination; she couldn't die.

His breath came in short, agonized gasps as he stretched her out on the cold ground. Bending on one knee, he tipped her onto her side, supporting her so that the brackish water spilled out. A violent coughing overtook her until her stomach emptied itself.

"Jesus," Behringer rasped, pulling her across his lap, cradling her head against his chest.

She blinked her eyes, and his heart ached at the terror he saw there. With quick, terse movements, he loosened the rope at her wrists. His gaze never left her face. Unable to find his voice, he whispered, "It's all right, honey. You're safe."

Her limp hands lifted to his face. She hoarsely sobbed his name, marveling that she'd conjured him from the dreams of her unconsciousness.

Pressing his lips to her forehead, he lifted a hand to her cold cheek. "My God," he choked. "I thought—" He swallowed, then began again. "Jesus God, Rebecca, when I saw you weren't breathing—"

"It doesn't matter—" she stammered, her teeth chattering.

"Like hell it doesn't!" His voice was tight with emotion, and he lowered his face to her wet hair, desperately trying to warm her in the bitterly frigid December night. "I love you."

Laughter bubbled from her wheezing chest. "You . . . what?"

Behringer smiled grimly at the words which were drawn from him, pulling her against his chest as he rose. "I've got to get you home."

He found his coat and draped it around her, then placed her on the horse. Swinging up behind her, he tucked his arms about her and turned the horse toward home.

The ten-minute ride seemed more like an hour. He held her closely against his body, trying to shield her from the wind that blasted as they thundered down the road toward home.

Maria met them at the door, and she cried out in horror when she saw them. "What in God's name has happened?"

"Rebecca was assaulted at the turn basin," he explained briefly. "I need a hot bath."

As he took the stairs two at a time, Caroline rushed away to heat water. In his room, Behringer paused to light a lamp. Then, he stripped off her clothes and wrapped her in blankets. Only then did he stoke the fire. Minutes later, while the women entered the room and filled the bath, he stepped behind the screen to remove his own clothes. At last, they were alone. When he crossed to the bed, Rebecca gazed up at him, her eyes huge in her pale face. He removed the blankets from her, then drew her into his arms and crossed the room to the tub.

Murmuring quiet love words in her ear, he stepped into the tub. Carefully, he lowered himself into the water until its soothing warmth surrounded them. Rebecca slipped between his thighs, her hips fitted intimately to him. He shifted slightly, bending his knees, until she was comfortable in front of him, the length of her legs gliding against his. A sigh escaped her lips as she relaxed against him. He felt the pliable, smooth warmth of her flesh. "Better?"

She nodded, then touched his hand where it lay across her slim, taut belly. She lifted the tanned fingers to her lips, then turned her head upward to kiss his neck lightly. "I love you," she whispered.

He hugged her against him. He closed his eyes, taking a

deep breath to steady the desire that raced through him even now.

She loved him!

Minutes later they lay curled together in his wide, warm bed. As he stroked her in the fire's glow, he asked with a casualness that concealed his fear, "So what do you think about May?"

"It's a fine month," she murmured.

"Oh, beautiful. The roses generally begin budding again then, you know. They'll look lovely in your hair."

"And in your lapel."

"And on our wedding cake."

Rebecca closed her eyes, savoring the pleasure of his contented words. Our wedding cake. Our wedding.

"Can this be real?"

He hugged her. "God, I hope so."

The glow of the fire flickered over Garitson's room as they slept in each other's arms, wiping away the world outside.

Rebecca awakened and inhaled, thrilled at the masculine scent which greeted her. She rubbed her cheek against his chest, content at the warm, comforting span there. She stroked his beard then, touching the texture which was a compelling blend of sable and finest sandpaper.

To her dismay, he gently disengaged himself from her arms, swinging his long legs over the side of the bed. A tingle went over her as she watched him move, his sleek, naked strength startling in the pale light of the room. He stooped at the fireplace and stirred the embers there, adding a log. A moment later, he returned to the bed, taking her in his arms.

"Sweetheart, tell me about last night. Did Murphy say anything to you?"

She shivered at the memory, closing her eyes. "He said it was easier the first time, that jealousy . . . I can't remember. Something like, jealousy makes you forget what's right and wrong."

Behringer shuddered. "My God," he whispered. "It was Harry."

"Harry?"

"He killed Sarah and Peter."

Behringer was quiet, absently stroking Rebecca's back. She glanced at his face, expecting to find tears. Instead, she found a blank, empty gaze. She rested in his arms, allowing him his silence, soothingly stroking the scars of the fire which Harry Murphy had set. She didn't yet fully understand, but there was time for that.

At last Behringer rose, and she watched him cross the room to gather clothes from the armoire, his face set in taut lines. Desperate to cheer him from his black gloom, she spoke softly. "You are an absolute vision," she murmured appreciatively.

Behringer cocked his head before the dressing mirror. "I suppose."

She laughed. "A legend in your own mind."

He gave a half smile, returning to the bed, tossing the clothes there. "It's this bed," he murmured, brushing his lips over her shoulder.

"Hmm?" she asked distractedly.

"The bed provokes a legend. It's located in a room where you can't fall asleep without falling in love as well."

The smile on Rebecca's face fell away in wonder and in terror. Then, without speaking, she slid her arms around his neck.

Surprised at her fervent, impulsive embrace, Behringer stroked her hair. "Honey?"

She said nothing for a moment, only rested her face in the curve of his throat. "I love you."

He chuckled softly. "I love you. Let's go have breakfast.".

A few minutes later, they entered the dining room with Behringer's arm looped possessively about her waist. Maria and Jacob sat at the table, watching as their son seated the girl and took his own seat.

Silence permeated the room as Jacob stared from his son to Rebecca, then back again. For a moment, even the fireplace hushed itself. Behringer spoke.

"Papa, Rebecca and I are going to be married."

The man's eyes met his for a charged moment. Then, satisfied with what he found there, the older man turned to Rebecca. "This is true, young lady?"

She nodded. "Yes."

Slowly, he sipped the brew in his cup. "Do you love my son as he loves you?"

Behringer watched his father silently, unaware of Rebecca's answer. After all these years, his father still knew every beat of his heart. He couldn't have spoken if anyone had bidden him to.

Then, his father turned his dark eyes upon his son. "Well, I'm very happy for you, Garitson. You will certainly need Rebecca's support to face Miss Fairchild."

The name brought the fire back to life, battling the sudden chill in the room.

"How soon will you tell her?"

Behringer sighed. "I . . . don't know." He toyed with the eggs on his plate. "You know about last night?"

Jacob nodded, looking at Rebecca. "Do you know who attacked you?"

"Harry Murphy," Behringer supplied. "I suspect he's working for Silas Fairchild."

He remembered the morning in Fairchild's office. *Vivian was a child when I decided you would take over Fairchild & Sons.*

"Garitson, don't be ridiculous. Silas has lived here all his life. He's a gentle man."

Behringer reached into his pocket and withdrew a handkerchief. "Murphy used this to gag Rebecca." In the corner was a burgundy monogrammed *F*. "Papa, I know it's Fairchild. He threatened me the first day Rebecca was in town."

Maria gasped. "Why did you never tell anyone?"

"I never believed it myself," he admitted. "I thought it was Murphy himself."

Jacob rose from the table. "Then we shall go get the sheriff."

"Oh, Papa," Behringer groaned. "Please, don't try any heroics. Sheriff Bagby'll laugh you right out of town."

"If the man has attempted murder once, he must be stopped."

"Papa, there's something I've never told you. The fire on the *Mittie Stephens* . . ." He paused, and his mouth straightened into a flat line. "Sarah and Peter were locked in their room. Murphy as much as confessed their murders last night. This won't be his last attempt, and he won't be nearly as sloppy next time, either. If he hears the sheriff's following him around . . ." Behringer shook his head. "I have to protect Rebecca until I have time to talk some sense into Fairchild."

"He killed Sarah?" Jacob asked. "And my little Peter?"

Behringer nodded slowly.

Jacob returned to sit in his chair, leaning heavily on the table. A minute passed as he gazed bleakly at his plate. "Then what do you plan to do?" His voice thundered in the room.

Behringer glanced at Rebecca. "If it's all right with Rebecca, I'll take her to my home tonight. She'll be safe there. Everyone must believe she's still in town. If we keep them busy watching this house, they won't be able to harm her."

"How do you intend to persuade Fairchild to your way of thinking?" Jacob taunted his son.

"All he really wants from me is my judgment. He wants to get his business out of the mess it's in. Apparently enough to kill several people very dear to me. Well, I'll run his damn company for free."

"How do you know he'll agree?"

"He was going to give me the whole thing before. Now he'll have the company, it'll operate in the black again, and he can still sell his little brat to some unsuspecting victim."

Rebecca closed the last trunk, ready to leave. She found Maria in the parlor, and was startled to realize the woman was weeping. She held a crumpled piece of paper in her hand. Rebecca rushed to her side. "Maria?"

Maria's delicate face quivered. "It's my Katerina," she cried.

Drawing her arm around the older woman's shoulders, she hugged her. In the embrace, she tried to give back some of the strength Maria had given her in the past four months. Her own terror grew as the woman's mourning escalated.

"She is with child," she gasped. "She will be home in one month."

Rebecca knew what this would mean to a gentle girl like Katy. A quick, quiet marriage to a man she would loathe. A hundred years from now, if she could make it courageously through the initial trauma, the girl would've been able to bear her child without such stigma. But in the 1800s, she would be known as a whore, and her child a bastard. A mere babe, innocent of his own conception, would be branded the son of a whore.

She hugged Maria to her, absorbing the woman's sobs until they slowly passed. "You have always been strong for me. You stood by me no matter what anyone said. Now, you must do the same for your daughter. You can't turn your back on her."

Maria's back went straight, as if accused of cowardice. "I would never turn my back on Katy," she declared.

Rebecca nodded. "I know that. I know." She continued to stroke the woman. Minutes passed, and from a distance she heard the back door slam.

Garit appeared at the doorway, with Jacob behind him only seconds later. The twinkle in his eyes vanished as he saw the women. He crossed the room and knelt before his mother. "Mama?"

She gazed at him sadly, then thrust the crumpled paper into his hands and rushed to Jacob.

Rebecca looked from the older couple to their son. His eyes were upon her, his consternation poignant. She shook her head, gesturing toward the paper. Swiftly opening the paper, he read the words there. As he did so, Jacob led his wife up the stairs.

Behringer said nothing as he trudged to the fire, staring blankly into it. He let the paper drift into the flames which consumed the words in only a second. Several minutes passed as she watched him, but he seemed unaware of her.

Finally, he sighed. "Well, I suppose there are several men who would love to marry her, even while she's heavy with another man's child."

She frowned, then spoke gently. "Garit, don't jump to conclusions."

He stared down at her, his mouth agape. "What other alternative do you suggest for such a deplorable situation?"

She glared at him. "I could be in her shoes right now."

"It's as different as night and day. You have before you a man who loves you, who'd be thrilled to hear of your child. Our child."

She softened at his words. "Then perhaps there is a man who loves Katy just as much."

He spun on his heel and paced the length of the rug. "She knew no man. The boy denies the child is his. He proposes he was one of many."

"The stinking little shit," she muttered.

He whirled. "I beg your pardon?"

She took a deep breath. "What matters is that she has her family's support in this. That you will all stand beside her."

"I'll find her a good, respectable husband," Behringer assured her.

"How do you know she wants you to find her a husband?" Rebecca asked, rising from the settee, stalking across the space between them.

Behringer snorted. "I'm sure she wants nothing less. She said as much in her letter."

"Then why not listen to her before you go deciding her life for her?"

"I'll do what's right."

She paused, trying to steady her anger. "What if I were pregnant right now?"

"Don't start that again."

"And if I was?"

"If you were, we would merely marry sooner."

"And what if something happened to you first?"

"I would expect you to marry someone else," he said tightly.

"You would," she repeated scornfully.

He turned away. "I would."

"You're lying. You'd never want another man raising your child."

"I'd sure as hell rather know our child had a father, and that you were both taken care of."

"You know I could raise our child myself."

"You aren't Katy."

She sighed. "At one time, you said we were just alike."

"Yes," he thundered, whirling around. "You're both a couple of pigheaded idiots!"

Closing her eyes, she slowly relaxed her clenched fists. Then, she raised her hands to the lapels of his coat. "I'm sorry," she whispered.

He drew her against him in a hard embrace. "It's not you, honey. It's me. God, I'm as bad as anyone in town." He sighed, and his wide shoulders slumped in dejection. "She's just so . . . young."

"She'll need your love now more than ever," Rebecca murmured against his chest.

He nodded slowly. "Sometimes I think you're the only reason I know what it's like to love at all." He raised his head, and his expression was grim. "I'll help her find a husband, if she wants my help," he said, the last phrase emphasized quickly. "Otherwise, I guess she'll just have to settle for my love. I'll see her through to the very end."

❧ Thirty-Four ❧

❧ A smile of anticipation glimmered on Behringer's face as he left the parlor and made his way upstairs with champagne and glasses. The door of their bedroom parted silently as he nudged it open. Stopping short, he gazed at the sight there, his smile laced with tenderness. Rebecca reclined upon the white fur rug, her arms folded across the seat of his rocker, her head pillowed there, her lovely hair feathering over her shoulders like the down of a black swan. As peaceful as sunset, she'd fallen asleep on the unyielding surface of the rocker. Her presence breathed life into his home, the place he'd ignored for years. Her effect on his home rivaled the impact of her love on his heart.

Quietly crossing the room, he placed the glasses and champagne on the gaming table, then lowered himself beside her to the soft rug. Leaning back on his elbows, he scrutinized the girl who sat near his feet and was troubled with an old question. Where did she come from?

He frowned in hopeless frustration at the pointless puzzle. As she said when pressed for an answer, it didn't matter. What mattered was that she was here now. Yet, the oddity of it was too much to bear. He'd arrived home that night, and there she was, bathing in his room as if she thought she belonged, as startled at his appearance as he was by hers. He'd puzzled that over a hundred times since then, but now his curiosity had dwindled to a single mystery. He wanted to know what secret of her past tormented her.

Absently rubbing his foot against the thick softness of the cool fur, he watched the firelight on her lovely face, lingering on her lips, casting her eyes in shadow. Only the crackling of the fire and the lulling tempo of the rain against the windowpanes interrupted the silence of their solitude.

She slept peacefully, oblivious of the cold outside Behringer's house, and the storm within his breast. It scourged him to think of her alone in her fight against whatever memory battered her. She shifted slightly in her sleep, a frown creasing her forehead. As though suddenly aware of his scrutiny, the tranquillity of her dreams drifted away. Expression returned, one of irritation now. Slurred phrases tumbled from her lips. "No, Jackie . . . can't meet the deadline . . . write your own damn book . . ."

Alarmed at her nightmare, reaching to awaken her, his movement was arrested at the next words she spoke. "Going to . . . Jefferson . . . Behringer Inn . . ."

She suddenly gasped in horror, sitting straight up on the rug, her eyes wild in disorientation. Swiftly, he gathered her into his arms. "It's all right, honey. Just a bad dream."

Softly murmuring indistinct reassurances, he stroked her hair, in turmoil over her suffering. Where the hell had she come from?

When at last she'd quietened, he spoke. "Who's Jackie?"

He felt her shudder. "Nobody," she whispered bleakly.

Tenderly, he drew her down on the rug until she lay beside him. He rested on an elbow, gazing down at her. "You said her name in your dreams. Or his name," he added thoughtfully. "Who is it, Rebecca?"

"She's a friend."

"Where does she live?" he pressed.

"In New York," she said, her voice a shallow whisper.

He noticed the stiffness of her body as she spoke, and with gentle fingertips, he smoothed the frown on her forehead. "Is that where you're from?"

She struggled to sit up, then looked away from him. "You know where I'm from."

He recognized her standard evasion, accompanied by averted eyes, and he chose his words carefully. "No, Rebecca. I know where you're not from, and that's Shreveport."

Startled at his words, she faced him. He gazed at her quietly. "While I was in Shreveport last September, I telegraphed Katy to find out the name of your parents, to let them know you're safe."

Behringer watched her as she rose from the rug with agitated, clumsy movements. "Then I suppose you also know I've never met your sister."

He waited without speaking.

She began to move about the room with the hesitant, aware actions of a doe cornered in a snowy meadow. She walked to a window, shivering beside it. "Why did you never tell me? Expose my charade?"

He smiled grimly at the easy answer to that. "It didn't make any difference."

She turned slowly, and her eyes shimmered in the firelight. "It makes a difference," she whispered. Her fingertips impatiently dashed away the tears.

As he rose, the grandfather clock in the corner began to chime. He smiled gently. "It's midnight, Cinderella."

Surprised at the terror etched in her face as she glanced around the room, Behringer crossed the space between them in two strides, and her arms went tightly around his neck. "Sweetheart," he said softly, "it's all right. It's only the new year."

As the clock's chiming finally stopped, he raised his head and touched her chin, lifting it with a gentle fingertip. He met the chameleon eyes which held the pale, clear cast of green. "One of many I plan to spend ringing in with you in my arms."

And soon after, he thought to himself, he would be making a trip to New York, and he'd visit every publishing house there if he had to. She was a writer. A fine one. That much he knew. He'd read her manuscript, and he'd read her notes of what his mother had given her. Rebecca had polished with a delicate hand and had so artfully concealed the art that even his mother wouldn't know the difference. Apparently, she was a much more accomplished writer than he'd imagined. Only employed writers, after all, had deadlines. With or without her help, he was going to get to the bottom of it all. He knew with certainty that only then would they be able to conquer this intangible thing between them.

Taking her small hand in his, he walked to the table and uncorked the champagne, watching her wary expression in great curiosity. How little he really knew about the beat of this girl's agonized heart.

He splashed the bubbly liquid into the glasses, then put one in her hand. Raising his glass, he said, "Happy New Year, Rebecca."

She reluctantly lifted her glass toward his. Behringer sighed and placed his glass on the table without drinking. Setting aside her glass, he gently cupped her face in both hands.

"Honey, I couldn't care less what you did yesterday, or the day before. Except for that day you decided to come to Jefferson, for whatever reason. That matters to me because it brought you into my life. You made it a beautiful place, and I'll be damned if I'm worried about whoever you once were."

He brushed her lips with his. Lightly, then tenderly. Then he drew away from her and handed her the glass of champagne, then took his own.

"To our future," he said firmly, raising his glass once more.

Hypnotically, she gazed at him, then sipped the pale golden liquid. He knew she was drawing from his strength.

"A place," he added, "where time is measured not by our past, but by our love."

As he rubbed his cheek against her shiny, soft hair, Behringer had no way of knowing it wasn't the past—a gentle place she loved, where she belonged—that haunted her. It was that future which he toasted.

❧ Thirty-Five ❧

Restlessly, Rebecca paced the parlor floor. She'd been secluded in Garit's house for five days, and cabin fever was raging. It was all right when he was there, for they took walks in the cool afternoon, and read or talked in quiet companionship in the evening.

But on bright mornings like this, it drove her to distraction to know her every step was being guarded. Poor Jim had to be bored senseless with his vigils. Each day when Behringer went into town, the young man he'd chosen to guard Rebecca trudged up the stairs and took up his watch on the landing. This strategic spot enabled him to keep an eye on the path coming from town, as well as both the front and back doors and the widow's walk.

There he sat now, Rebecca mused. Looking upward, she met his eyes, and he nodded briefly and smiled.

She was going crazy.

Mounting the stairs, she headed for the widow's walk. That place never failed to soothe her agitation. As she reached the door, she heard Jim's heavy steps behind her, and she turned.

"I'm only going out for some air," she explained.

"That's fine, Miz Reynolds. I'll just tag along."

His words deflated her spirit, despite the easygoing companionship in his tone.

"I'm sorry," he said softly. "But Mr. Behringer says—"

"I know," she snapped. "Mr. Behringer thinks the vultures are going to steal me."

Staring at the floor, Jim shifted from one foot to the other.

She sighed. "Never mind, Jim." A door at the end of the narrow hallway caught her eye. "What's that?"

"That's the attic."

Rebecca crossed the small distance toward the door. Then she looked over her shoulder. "You think I might be safe in here?"

He chortled. "Aw, surely. You go on and get you some privacy. I'll go back to m' chair."

She smiled at him, regretting her sharpness with the poor man. He had to be as miserable as she was.

The door opened noiselessly as she turned the knob and stepped into the room. Shut off from the vitality of the rest of the house, the attic air hung cold and dry and stale. Stale most of all.

Closing the door behind her, she made her way through the room to the small window. It took some muscle, but she managed to pry the window open. The fresh, cold breeze slowly stole into the room, overpowering the stagnant atmosphere. She frowned. Not quite stagnant. Peaceful, sort of, in a somber way. And definitely untouched by the present. A sense of wonder stole over her. It felt like a cemetery.

Glancing around, she noticed the rather commonplace items. A spare ladder here, an odd table there. Several dusty trunks stood against one wall of the room, drawing her forward. Carefully opening the latch on one of the trunks, she lifted the heavy lid. Rich, lovely clothes lay there. A woman's clothes. It took little imagination to determine whose they were.

She paused, knowing she should close the trunk and turn away, knowing she should mind her own business. She thought of Behringer, staring at Sarah's portrait in dim moonlight, soothed only by cognac. She slowly lifted the gowns, one at a time, out of the trunk.

At the very bottom of the trunk lay the russet-colored gown Sarah Behringer had worn in the portrait which hung in the Behringers' ballroom. Rebecca lay her palm against the stiffness of the taffeta, knowing Behringer had treasured the clothes. Slowly replacing the garments, she opened another trunk, and her heart turned over. A plethora of tiny gowns lay there, soft woollens and satins and starchy cottons. As well as velvet suits with short pants and frilly shirts. The clothes Behringer's baby son had worn. She lifted the softness of the velvet to her face, treasuring the gentleness there. Behringer's son. That age-old ache of childlessness gripped her, and as she closed her eyes, she imagined the torment inside Behringer. She felt it as her own.

Several minutes passed as she inspected the dainty garments. Finally, she closed the trunk and opened a third, expecting to find more of Sarah's wardrobe. Her curiosity increased as she saw a myriad collection of personal items. A hairbrush, with autumn-tinged hair still clinging to it. She shivered and left the hairbrush where it lay. Bottles of lotions and perfumes, several fans, a selection of combs. And packets of letters, bound together with faded pink ribbons.

Reaching out, she slowly took one of the parcels in her hand and inspected the envelope on the outside. Faded and frayed, the envelope was addressed: "Mrs. Sarah Behringer, in care of Mr. Saul Stein, 164 Houston Street, Jefferson, Texas." The words were written in a bold, masculine handwriting she recognized immediately as Garit's. The letter was dated October 12, 1863. Fourteen years ago, in the midst of the Civil War.

Saul Stein. Her father, apparently. Houston Street—an area of town which, even a hundred years later would be referred to as Jew Town. Prejudice was eternal, it seemed. Rebecca's eyebrow rose in curiosity. Sarah had been Jewish. Interesting.

It took only a moment's deliberation before she put Garit's letters away. What he had once felt for Sarah Behringer didn't matter. And, yet—she hesitated. If it helped her to understand him, to love him better . . .

She looked at the other bundle. The address was written with a girlish hand, to Lieutenant Garitson Behringer. He'd fought with the Union army, she realized with a smile. It would have been a surprise to discover anything different.

This bundle, she untied gently. This letter, she opened carefully. Unfolding the pages, she began to read. Two sentences into the document, Rebecca understood that Sarah had been an intelligent, articulate, and quiet woman. She must have had a sense of humor to have loved Garit, but she seemed somber. Of course, the thought of losing Garit to a war would send any woman into depression.

One line toward the end of the letter caught her eye. "I saw your father in town today. He was with your mother, and he ignored me, as usual. I'll be thankful to God when this war is over, dearest husband, and you are here with me.

"Your mother spoke with me. She said to send you her love, and your father's. She will be writing you soon, she said. And, as she always does, she asks me to tell you Jacob forgives you for our marrying the way we did . . ."

The attic door creaked, and Rebecca turned. Garitson stood there, his dark eyes turbulent with unspoken emotion.

She should have apologized. The desperate unhappiness in Behringer's eyes, however, stopped her. He watched her as though she held his future on her fingertips. "Rebecca . . ."

"I didn't mean to snoop," she said softly, putting away the letter she'd been reading.

"Come downstairs," he said, clearly disturbed by the place. Rebecca remained where she was. "No. Not yet."

The uneasy agony in his eyes nearly made her agree to his plea. At last, he walked inside.

"I should have cleared this out long ago," he said quietly. He sat on a trunk several feet away from Rebecca, facing the window. "It isn't something you should have to reckon with."

"She was a wonderful woman, Garit, and she loved you very much. That is something to treasure always."

Behringer glanced at her over his shoulder. Instantly, she recognized the sliver of remorse in his dark eyes. She waited.

"She deserved a better man than I."

"She couldn't have found one."

Behringer stared, unseeing, out the window. "There was just always so much conflict. I wasn't used to that."

"Did your father ever forgive you for marrying so quickly?"

He glanced at her, puzzled. "Quickly?"

She swallowed, her gaze resting on an open trunk. "Well, you had to get married," she said at last.

He shook his head slowly. "I assume you mean our son. Peter wasn't born until after the war, Rebecca. We'd been married several years by then."

"I thought Peter was six or seven years old at the time of the accident."

Behringer looked away, his face awash with bitter memory. "He'd only just turned three. He was still a baby."

"Then what caused the conflict with your father?"

"There were two, but perhaps he could've forgiven me marrying the granddaughter of the biggest shipping operation in Shreveport. What he couldn't forgive was Sarah's Judaism."

Rebecca's mouth fell open. "Your father?"

Behringer laughed mirthlessly. "Rebecca, you've been the target of his prejudice for five months. Surely you can appreciate it."

She waited for him to go on. After an eternity, it seemed, he did.

"It's so complicated, Rebecca, I can scarcely expect you to understand it. God knows I must love you, for I never expected to tell you this. When I was a boy, my father and I were closer than any man and his son could ever be. I followed him around like a puppy. I used to boast to the other boys that my father was the smartest man on earth. Then I grew up and went away to school and learned to think for myself, and I came back to Jefferson with ideas of my own.

"Oddly enough, the same father that encouraged me to think for myself disliked it when I held my own against him. He was infuriated when I made a business out of advising men how to invest their fortunes, rather than taking over his freight business. My father was perfectly happy with steam transportation. He was irritated by the competition of rail. That's the German in him, of course. In Germany, he would say, they don't usurp another's livelihood. In many a town meeting he screamed how it was illegal in Germany to build a railroad near the path of a river. In one particularly emotional meeting, he said that if God had meant men to travel by rail, He would've placed track instead of rivers across the land."

Rebecca chuckled softly.

Behringer nodded. "I told him that if God hadn't intended us to travel by rail, he wouldn't have given us brains. He retorted that those who foolishly suggested abandoning the lucrative river trade were no more than educated idiots. I, in my sweet way, said that men who could do no more than live in the past were old fools.

"That next night, there was a party in town. I met Sarah there. They had just recently moved from Shreveport. I don't know how she was even there, because her father kept her away from what he saw as impure influences. I think he just wanted her spared from rejection. I was there with Harry Murphy that night," he said, and his jaw went tight at the mention of Murphy's name.

He cleared his throat and went on. "A friendly rivalry arose between us. Both of us competed for her affection, until we learned she was Jewish. Harry Murphy, like any good Christian, conceded."

"And you?" Rebecca prompted.

"I . . . I, from a family whose history goes back to the Crusades, saw a lovely opportunity to separate myself from my father. It worked."

"What?"

He pressed his palms to his face, then raked his fingers through his hair, sighing. "I do choose my precious reasons for marrying, don't I?"

"You can't convince me you married Sarah to spite your father."

"In the end, I don't know. By the time we married, Papa and I were barely talking. I certainly courted her to spite him. It was quite a spectacle. I brought her to church, though she had no intentions of converting. I practically expected Father Michael to kick us both out. The more I saw her, the angrier Papa grew, and the louder his demands that I stop seeing her. When I told him we were marrying, he forbade me, as if I were still seven years old, asking to be spared from piano lessons. I married her almost immediately and joined the Union army. When the war ended, I returned home. Papa and I were no longer talking, and . . ."

Rebecca waited as he groped for words.

"It was killing me. Sarah and I never once talked about the conflict between Papa and me."

"Never?" Rebecca repeated, finding this nearly impossible to believe.

He shook his head. "She was the kind of woman that was always content. It irritated me that this terrible thing stood between me and my father and she seemed oblivious of it. If she'd at least noticed how it was bothering me, maybe . . . I don't know. I began to resent that. I began to resent her." His words were whispered.

Rebecca rose, crossing the room to rest cool fingers between his shoulders. In the winter cold of the room, sweat dampened his back.

"Then Peter was born. My son became my reason for living. He was beautiful, and oh, God, so sweet—" His voice caught in the agony of memory. "Papa might have loved him as much as I did. It took that kind of love to get him to visit us for the first time. I began to think there might be hope for us, after all. And then, we were invited to her family reunion in Shreveport. I didn't go. Sarah did. And I sent Harry Murphy to watch over her."

Rebecca stroked his neck, tears dampening her cheeks at the anguish in his words, the uncertain trembling in his voice.

"After they were gone . . . after I got well, I found her old letters, and I read them in a new light. My God, Rebecca, I was so wrapped up in my father's rejection that I didn't see how much that rejection hurt her. Sarah's entire life revolved around making me happy, and I only resented her. If I had given my heart as freely as Sarah gave hers, she'd be alive today."

A thousand old taunts echoed in her memory. *You know nothing of giving love. You know only how to take it.*

"In all the years we were together," he whispered, "I never once told her I loved her. I gave her not one memory of those words to cherish."

"Garit," Rebecca pleaded, "stop punishing yourself."

She turned his face up to her, and she saw the tears glistening in his dark eyes.

"I never told her, because I never believed it myself."

She unsteadily traced her thumbs underneath his eyes as the tears fell. "Never?" she challenged. "Did you never once look into her eyes as though she was the most beautiful woman on earth? No flowers were brought to her? No gentle trifles such as a fan to cool her, perhaps? A home to warm her, in which to raise your children?"

She rested her face on his shoulder, aware of his deep, shuddering breaths. "Never did you try to make her life better? Did you not tenderly hold her son in your arms and pray for him? And did her name never enter your prayers? Did you not face hell itself for her?"

Rebecca's last question was softly spoken, for tears silently streaked her cheeks, their heat warming the chill flesh. And he turned to her, crushing her against him, burying his face against her hair. She held him tightly, absorbing his pain, feeling the wetness of his face upon the curve of her throat.

"I think you told her many times every day, my darling," she whispered. "We women aren't stupid creatures. And . . . even had you never done for her any of the many kindnesses I know you did . . . her love was still fulfilled. Loving someone isn't sitting around wishing they loved you back. Love is giving the most wonderful gift a person can ever give someone else. Loving you made Sarah Behringer a happy woman. Knowing in her heart, as you can be sure she did, that you loved her also, was just a bonus."

At last, Behringer raised his head. "You're a precious gift in my life, Rebecca. If not for you, I'd have already landed Silas Fairchild in jail and have nothing to look forward to but the bleak remainder of my life without you."

Her lips curved, and she pressed them against his, and she laughed. "Instead of a stunning future with me."

Behringer chuckled softly at her happiness, and the sound soothed her heart. He swept her up in his arms and carried her out of the room, away from his past. And into their future together.

❧ Thirty-Six ❧

The third Saturday morning in 1877 dawned slate gray over Jefferson. Behringer and Rebecca strolled along a sidewalk with carefree steps. All about her, people milled in every direction, men in dapper browns and blacks clustered in groups, ladies laughing gaily, children with runny noses playing with reckless abandon. Rebecca felt as lighthearted as those children, for today she was on a holiday. Silas Fairchild was out of town, and he'd taken his charming daughter with him. In their absence, Behringer had allowed her this outing.

"Doesn't that smell heavenly?" Following the direction of the tempting scent, Rebecca glanced around. "Whoever's cooking is making me awfully hungry."

Behringer chuckled. "It's only the cook here at the Brooks House," he said, gesturing toward the house just in front of them.

Rebecca's heart stopped as she looked toward the house, for the front door opened and a young woman emerged. And she knew why the Brooks House held a terrible significance in her memory. Only twenty feet from them stood Bessie Moore, dressed in a stunning velvet gown of smoke-gray blue, diamonds glittering at her ears and throat.

"What day is today?" Rebecca asked in a choked whisper, her fingers tightening desperately on Behringer's coat.

Disturbed at her terror, he lay his hand over hers. "We're going to have to get you a calendar, darling. It's the twentieth," he added softly.

January 20, 1877. Bessie smoothed her skirts absently, looking in the opposite direction down the street, and Rebecca stared at her in helpless indecision. Her entire purpose in this town, on this date, lay before her. Behringer's hand pressed upon her shoulder, gently questioning, and her heart hammered against her ribs. Bessie had not seen her. Walk away from here, she told herself desperately, and you'll be able to spend the rest of your days with him in happiness.

Bessie Moore is the only reason you were able to spend even some days with him. A voice spoke within her, and she fought its message with every heavy beat of her heart. She knew that were she to choose any other way, her happiness with Garit would never be without guilt, free of the intensity of her failure.

"I have to do it," she whispered.

"Do what, sunshine?"

With a heaviness in her heart, she looked up at Behringer. The pureness of his love was shadowed by his own confusion, and a sudden hope gathered in her breast. Perhaps, if she succeeded . . . just perhaps, a fate softhearted enough to grant her a wish so wild as to change history would allow her own happiness.

Rebecca smiled, her spirit charged with determination, and tiptoed to kiss his cheek. "I'll only be a moment," she whispered. "Wait here for me."

"Believe me," he murmured, "I'm not going anywhere."

She turned and swept up the stone paved path toward Bessie, whose gray gaze settled on her. The pain in those eyes, mirroring the disquieting storminess of the sky, terrified Rebecca.

"Rebecca!" Bessie threw her arms around the other woman.

"How are you? Where's Abe?"

Instantly deflated, Bessie sighed. "He's upstairs. Probably

watching me from the window." Her fingers nervously rested on the heavy diamond necklace at her throat, and she laughed spiritlessly. "How do you like my new necklace?"

"It's lovely," Rebecca remarked hollowly. "Where did you get it?"

"A gift from Abe."

The news startled Rebecca. "He wants to patch things up between us," Bessie went on quietly. "He found Benjamin and me in New Orleans. If we'd only left a day earlier! We wanted to celebrate New Year's Eve there, then move on to our new life in Dallas.

"He says the gift is a symbol of our new life together. The new man he's become. I have to admit," she conceded, "that he's behaving as differently as I could ever have dreamed. He treats me like a woman, rather than a . . ." Suddenly, her voice trembled, and tears slipped out of her eyes. "He wants us to have a family."

Rebecca led her up the steps to the porch swing, an arm supporting her shoulders. "It's all right, Bessie."

"Rebecca, I'm going to have a child, and the baby belongs to Benjamin. If only we'd gone on to Dallas," she sobbed. "Oh, I've made such a terrible mistake. I love him more than anything, but love doesn't buy a child respect. It won't get a little boy into the right schools, and it won't give a little girl the sort of husband and home she dreams of."

Rebecca heard the desperate yearning in Bessie's voice. She'd chosen to return with Rothschild to provide the choices for her child that she herself had never had. Rebecca searched for the wisdom she so badly needed.

Wisdom? She knew that Rothschild intended to kill her, and yet she sat there like the hopelessly eternal romantic she surely would always be, buying into the sweetness of his line. Yet . . . it didn't make sense. Why would the man shower her with jewels if he intended to kill her? She remembered the passion in his voice the morning she'd met him, the threat he'd delivered when he thought she was Bessie. *You'll regret the day you left me.*

"Bessie," she said as calmly as she could manage, "you shouldn't stay with Abe. He's capable of violence. I'm living in Garitson Behringer's home across the bayou. Just go over the bridge, down the path, and you can't miss it. If you want us to help you find Benjamin again, you're welcome to come and live with us. Garit's a powerful man, and I know he'll take you to Benjamin." She paused, then thoughtfully added, "Isn't Benjamin the kind of husband you dreamed of when you were a little girl?"

Bessie stared at her, her dark lashes spiky from the richness of her tears. Rebecca hugged her gently.

Behringer strolled along the sidewalk in front of the Brooks House, pausing from time to time, gazing at the two women who sat on the hotel porch swing. They could pass for twins, he thought absently, glancing from one to the other, noticing the dark hair, the clear complexion, the full, sensuous mouth.

Rebecca's past sorely plagued him as he watched her soothe the prostitute from New Orleans. He recalled her anger the day he'd insisted on finding a husband for Katy. She seemed incensed, assuming he looked on Katy's dilemma as a scandal. She'd stubbornly stood up for her own past, yet she refused to disclose the details surrounding it. Clearly she was a woman impervious to gossip, but she'd despised him when she suspected he wanted her as his mistress. Well, what woman wouldn't?

He glanced again toward the porch. Somehow, it didn't add up. The two were so much alike, yet as different as snow and soot. Vividly, he remembered the shiver of fear that had passed over Rebecca as she stared at Bessie Rothschild. He knew that the secret to Rebecca's past was locked up within this disreputable woman, and when they rose from the swing, he quickly looked away, staring down the street.

Rebecca squared her shoulders as she returned to Behringer. His eyes questioned her as she approached him. "Everything okay?"

She nodded silently and took his arm, keenly aware of his gaze upon her. Later, she would explain it to him.

Their walk to Henderson's shop was brief. The front room was empty, and Garitson walked forward to the counter. Rebecca inspected a piece of glass.

"Morning, Malcolm."

"Good morning, Mr. Behringer."

Rebecca turned slowly at the odd voice, and her gaze rested on the man behind the counter. She might've gasped, except that her breath was lodged in her lungs. The man walked around the display case, shaking Garitson's hand. It had to be a startling coincidence, a case of ancestors strikingly resembling descendants. He turned to face her. And her gaze rested on the jagged scar at the corner of his left eye. The memory of a childhood injury.

She stared blankly at Malcolm Henderson as he approached her.

Garitson followed him. "Rebecca, this is Malcolm Henderson, who'll be overseeing the publishing of Mama's book."

The man's blue eyes smiled merrily. "Well, hello there, young lady. It's good to see you again."

Rebecca opened her mouth slowly, but nothing came out.

"Malcolm gave me the book I gave you for Christmas," Behringer said. "He wouldn't let me buy it from him."

"I thought you'd have a special interest in it," Malcolm went on, looking at Rebecca with eyes which still twinkled. He winked rakishly. "How's that cookbook working out for you?"

Starlights were rotating before Rebecca's gaze, and she sucked in a much-needed breath. "Fine. Just fine."

Malcolm Henderson patted her arm. "I thought so."

She reached for the doorjamb to steady herself, and Behringer was there in a moment, his arms around her.

"I'll go get your package, Garitson," Malcolm said, deserting them.

"Are you all right?" Garitson's voice was soft at her ear.

She nodded slowly.

Malcolm returned. "Here you go. I expect your mama'll be glad to see it at last."

A smile flickered about Behringer's mouth as he untied the package and drew the brown paper aside. Then he paused and glanced up at Rebecca. The smile grew, and he put the tissue wrapped object in her hands.

Silently staring at the small, flat, rectangular-shaped bundle of tissue in her hands, Rebecca made no move to unwrap it. Malcolm excused himself, making his way to the back room of the shop.

In confidential tones, Behringer whispered, "Uh . . . you'll be able to tell a lot more about it if you take the paper off."

Her lip curled, and she slowly unfolded the paper. The smile on her mouth faded as she stared at the soft cloth of mauve and rose, stretched in a wooden frame. The words, embossed in gold script, were centered on the cover. *A Little Girl's Dream*. By Maria Behringer. Just below that, the Behringer brooch had been embossed in gold relief.

Rebecca made no attempt to swallow the emotion that held her throat hostage. In her hands was the first final stage of Maria's dream to publish a book. And yet—she thought of Maria's stubbornness. If ever there was a woman who would do exactly what she wanted, it was Garit's mother. Why had she never tried to write one before? What then, to say of her little girl's dream?

Jacob Behringer. He was Maria's dream. A tad on the chunky side, with more gray in his hair than black, and a constitution that made Old Faithful seem like a capricious hole in the ground. She knew that in him, Maria saw only the handsome young German who had rescued her from New Orleans. In that vision, she knew her dream. In that image, the dream lurking in her little girl's heart would never perish. She thought of Bessie. She thought of herself. Maria's dreams had not, in fact, been exceptional from other little girls'.

"It's beautiful," she murmured finally. She cleared her throat to steady the overwhelming emotions.

"It's a good story. It deserves a grand cover."

She looked up at him in surprise. "Has Maria told you about it, then?"

Behringer's eyes searched her. "No. I told her that I would have no part of distributing the book unless I was allowed to read it."

It had been years since she'd needed to hear praise for her work. Now, she stared up at him expectantly. "What do you think of it?"

He paused, biting his lower lip. "I think I'd rather you tell me what you think of it. It has a rather impossible ending, you know."

"It was the only way it could end."

He took the cover from her hands and lay it aside. Lifting his hands to her cheeks, he tilted her head up to look at him. "And do you believe that love can conquer all, Rebecca? Even the past?"

Tears blurred the vision of his face, gazing beseechingly at her. "Garit, there's so much you don't know. So much you could never understand."

"I love you, Rebecca. Nothing in your past makes any difference to me. Can't you understand that? If only you'll tell me whatever it is, I can help you deal with it."

Her arms encircled his neck, seeking his strength. "It'll take time," she said softly.

He sighed, then chuckled. "If there's one thing I have, it's time. All of eternity."

She clung to him, to the reality that existed in his arms. If only all of eternity didn't stand between them.

Behringer returned the cover to Malcolm, who glanced at Rebecca with his omnipresent twinkle. "I think you'll find it'll work just fine. But only if you believe."

Believe? Believe in what? she wondered, unable to respond. The man spoke as if the book were a talisman.

He chuckled, as if reading her mind. "Now you just relax, young lady. Everything'll turn out in the end."

The carriage awaited them just outside Henderson's shop, and they rode the short way to the Behringer mansion in silence. Maria met them halfway to the door, and she threw her arms around Rebecca in a fierce hug. "How I have missed you!"

Rebecca laughed. "I'm so glad I could come."

The three hurried inside the warm house, to the fire which blazed in fervent greeting. "What in the world is that scrumptious smell, Mama?"

Jacob Behringer joined them at the table, kissing Rebecca soundly on the mouth. A smile went over her at his open gesture of affection, and at last she appreciated the significance of Jacob's acceptance of her. He said a brief, enthusiastic prayer and the family began to eat. Maria spoke.

"Are you excited about the party, Rebecca? The brooch will look so lovely on you."

Several things happened simultaneously in the next moment. Behringer groaned, leaning back in his chair. Maria's eyes widened innocently, her fork pausing halfway to her mouth. Rebecca raised her eyebrow. And Jacob exploded in laughter.

"Once again," Jacob said, wagging his finger at his son, "the speediest form of communication succeeds."

"Many thanks, Mama."

Rebecca smiled. "Garit, is there something you'd like to tell me?"

He turned to her, his face an exaggerated palette of courtesy. "Rebecca, would you care to accompany me to a party of welcome for my sister? It will be here, two weeks from Monday, the day she is to arrive."

"Oh!" Maria gasped. "Then she didn't know about the brooch?"

He glared at his mother, then returned to Rebecca. "I had hoped to surprise you with the announcement of our engagement at the party," he confessed sullenly. "The Behringer brooch will be yours then. Just don't go trading it out for any more hotel rooms."

Startled at the surprise, moved by his humor, she reached out to touch his hand. "How sweet of you."

"Oh, it's Mama's brooch. Mama's gift for the next Behringer bride, as the tradition goes," he continued, still pouting. Again, he scowled at Maria. "All I had to give was the surprise."

"I'm sorry, Rebecca," Maria said softly.

Rebecca laughed. "Please, don't be sorry. You're all so wonderful to plan such a surprise."

"As you can see," Maria chuckled, "I didn't know it was a surprise. I thought only of how happy you and Katy will be to see one another."

Behringer sipped wine. "I can only hope Katy's learned to keep her mouth shut in the five months she's been gone." He chuckled. "You and she are two beans from the same string. It terrifies me to think of you two collaborating."

Rebecca laughed softly. "I'm looking forward to meeting her," she said.

As she reached for her wineglass, Rebecca was aware of the three pairs of eyes focused on her. Slowly realizing her words, she looked from Jacob's inscrutable expression to Maria's gently curious one, finally resting on Garit's smiling twinkle. He leaned his elbow on the table and rested his chin in his hand, idly biting his lower lip.

"If confession's good for the soul," he said lightly, "you two are approaching sainthood."

Looking back at Maria, she began, "I—"

Maria nodded with a smile, her curiosity at last satisfied. "I'm sure she's just as eager to meet you."

In the moment that followed, Rebecca knew neither of them had ever believed she actually knew Katy. A warmth went over her at the generosity of their final acceptance, at their stalwart protection of her when they suspected the worst of her.

They gathered in the parlor after dinner, where they relaxed in the quiet, gray afternoon. After Maria badgered him ceaselessly, Garit treated them to a private concert, choosing sweetly soothing songs from his diverse repertoire. When he lapsed into a soft, haunting melody she'd never heard, his mother rose and stood beside the piano. Her son smiled up at her, and then she sang softly.

Maria's voice, rich and gentle, cherished the German ballad. Rebecca watched them from her chair in the corner of the room, her heart unbelievably full. As the song ended, a faint hiss pervaded the atmosphere of the room, steadily whispering at the window near Rebecca's shoulder. Sleet. She sighed, disappointed to see their visit end.

Jacob walked with his son toward the back of the house, and Maria took Rebecca's hands in hers. "I am so happy for you and Garit. I only wish Katy could find the happiness you know."

"Don't give up on Katy. She's still only a girl. She will no doubt find love in her life before it's over with."

Maria sighed. "I hope you're right. I can't wait for you to meet her. She's so much like you."

"Maria, I'm sorry I never told you the truth."

"Don't worry yourself with the past, Rebecca. And the future is just as meaningless. Past and future are nonexistent. All that matters is this moment. The love you share with Garitson. Everything else will take care of itself, if only you trust his love."

"I love you, Maria. Thank you for your faith in me."

"And I love you, child." The woman raised her head slowly, smiling the same gentle smile Rebecca had seen on her face the first afternoon she met her. The expression Rebecca would always remember on the woman. "Garitson is waiting with the carriage," she said softly.

Inside the carriage, Behringer lifted her onto his lap, then settled the blanket over them both.

She snuggled close to him, resting her head on his shoulder. "They knew all along."

His words were soft. "And they just didn't care."

She touched the comforting width of his chest, thickly layered with wool and fur. "I never knew life could be so incredibly sweet."

His hand smoothed tenderly over her hair, and when he spoke, his voice was a whisper of amazement, sweetened by the brandy's heat. "Holding you is like holding an angel. Looking at you is like a vision of heaven."

She smiled at his gentleness. "I love you."

"I tremble to think what my life would be without you," he went on, then chuckled. "Likely a vision of hell."

Rebecca sighed, touching his beard in wonder, stroking his cheek in amazement, ignoring the dread that began in her heart over something hauntingly familiar in his words. Something of the past, and of the future.

Past and future are nonexistent.

The glassy drum of the sleet faded to silence, driven away by the steady beat of Behringer's heart. The cold in the carriage warmed to a summertime glow, heated by the lingering caress of his kiss. And the fear in her heart was quelled, soothed by the rich reality of his love.

❧ Thirty-Seven ❧

The early morning's fog had vanished by afternoon, and Rebecca walked with Garit to the carriage.

"I'll be back tomorrow afternoon," he said, kissing her on the mouth.

As he turned toward the carriage, Rebecca heard a faint voice calling her name. She glanced toward the sound, and her mouth fell open in amazement.

Delirious joy filled Rebecca at the woman running down the path to her. Bessie Moore. January 21, 1877, and she was alive. Vibrantly, gloriously alive. As alive as every one of Rebecca's dreams.

Her laughter spilled from her as she ran toward Bessie. She crossed the distance between them in moments, it seemed, and embraced Bessie. Rebecca's words were indistinct as she murmured her gladness to see her.

"Did you have your picnic?" Rebecca asked finally.

Bewildered at her words, Bessie stammered, "Why, yes. How did you know?"

Rebecca smiled. Oops. "Never mind. What did he say?"

"He's agreed to let me think about the whole thing," Bessie said softly.

Rebecca smiled, tucking Bessie's arm in hers and leading her up the path toward Behringer. "You have no idea how glad I am to see you. Oh, Bessie, you and Benjamin are going to be so happy."

Bessie lowered her head. "I really must think about it. It's only fair."

Behringer smiled, leaning against the carriage. "Am I ever to meet your mysterious friend, my love?"

Rebecca smiled. "Garit, this is Bessie Moore. Bessie, this is my fiancé, Garitson Behringer."

Behringer looked at the woman, repeating the name in his mind. Her name was Rothschild, that much he knew. Yet the name Bessie Moore was familiar to him in a remote and distressing way. He couldn't place it. Was the woman masquerading as someone else? No. Rebecca had admitted knowing Bessie's husband to be a cruel man.

As he once more prepared to leave, Behringer held Rebecca against the breadth of his chest. "I'm glad for you, darling."

She smiled and lifted her lips to his. "Come back soon."

He nodded. "The weekend, at the latest, for good. Maybe before then."

Rebecca's disappointment over Garit's departure was softened mightily by Bessie's arrival at their house. Bessie was alive! She relished her success.

In the maelstrom of Bessie's arrival, Rebecca hadn't had time to ponder her old dread, occupied instead with the wild exhilaration of her success. Now, staring at Behringer's carriage as it made its way down the lane, faced again with the fear, the hope once more was born within her breast, growing greater than her fears. Her heart was full, her life was full, and if Garitson Behringer dared contract a lethal virus, she'd just have to invent penicillin.

Not quite a week later, Behringer stood outside Silas Fairchild's office, staring up at the forbidding lines of the building. Slowly exhaling, he forced the tension from his body, that fear that manifested itself in his clenched fists, in his tightly knotted neck. If Fairchild knew the extent of

Behringer's own fear, he'd never trust him. At this point, he desperately needed the lifeline of Fairchild's trust. Opening his fingers, he slowly flexed them once, then moved forward to the door.

At least the man was in a good mood, Behringer noticed as he shook his hand in greeting. "Have a seat, Garitson."

Behringer shook his head. "Thanks. Silas, we have an important matter to discuss." Silas watched him, his expression closed. The man never gave an inch of leverage when confronted, and he clearly didn't intend to do so now.

Behringer exhaled, then spoke. "I'll get to the point. I'm not marrying Vivian."

The older man remained seated, his body completely still. If Behringer hadn't been facing him, watching that poker face for any evidence of emotion, he'd have thought the man hadn't heard him.

Only in his eyes was his fury very much apparent. Those normally placid eyes lightened until his pupils were mere pinpoints. Finally, he spoke. "What the hell is the meaning of this?"

Behringer continued to meet his eyes, standing motionless. "I'm marrying Rebecca Reynolds."

If he'd had any doubts about Fairchild's role in Rebecca's attacks, they were resolved in the next moment. The man's face hardened in undisguised rage. "That whore?"

Behringer placed both hands on the desk between them, gazing coolly into Fairchild's eyes. "If you value your life, you'll never say that again."

Then, calmly, Behringer folded his arms over his chest. "It doesn't matter to me whether I marry her here or a thousand miles from here. But marry her I will. I can assure you Vivian is as pure today as when we announced our engagement, appropriate marriage material in every way. And while I regret the scandal that could arise for her, my main concern is for you. Therefore, in exchange for the freedom from my engagement, I'm willing to continue as we planned, until

Fairchild and Sons is back on its feet. I'll run your company and turn it around, as a favor to you."

Behringer's stomach churned at the man's reaction. Fairchild regained his cool, his features tranquil. The son of a bitch would kill Rebecca for no other reason than to save his own ass. It had nothing to do with concern for his daughter.

Fairchild rose then, walking to the window of his office. "Let me make sure I understand this. If I agree to . . . offer no protest, shall we say . . . over your marriage to Miss Reynolds, you'll take over the company, as we had planned?"

Behringer nodded. "Until it's once more in the black."

Turning, Fairchild crossed his arms over his vest. "And until I've appointed an appropriate successor."

Behringer agreed.

"Do you understand how long that may take?"

"I don't care if it takes fifty years."

"It may," Silas said lightly.

"You'll find someone. I'll find someone, if necessary."

Slowly, Fairchild returned to his stance behind his desk. "You have yourself a deal, Garitson."

"Not quite. One thing more."

Fairchild's eyebrow lifted in surprise.

"Stop the attacks."

A veil drew over Fairchild's gaze. "Attacks?"

"The attacks against Rebecca, Fairchild. I have a handkerchief in my possession that matches the one in your pocket. A certain associate of yours used it to try to drown her the other night. I know men in the government who'd be very interested in hearing the reason for the *Mittie Stephens* tragedy. If one more act of violence is even hinted at, they'll be crawling all over this office before you can even blink."

Fairchild's face went white. Behringer turned.

"Garitson."

"What?"

"Have you spoken to Vivian?"

"No."

"Then don't. I'd prefer the opportunity to find another prospect before this version of the story gets out."

Behringer glanced over his shoulder. "You have one week."

Fairchild spoke slowly. "It's fortunate for Miss Reynolds that you're marrying her. Without that, she might be remembered in Jefferson as the woman who destroyed Garitson Behringer."

Behringer didn't try to figure it out. "Don't threaten me, Fairchild."

With that, he left Silas Fairchild to the task of scrambling to find a husband for his oldest daughter.

Rebecca sat in the solarium with Bessie, chatting and sipping coffee. Bessie was past the stage of morning sickness, and the distinct glow of health enhanced her placid happiness.

"You have guts, sewing pink gowns for the baby before it's born."

Bessie smiled. "Before she's born. She's a little girl." She paused. "Poor Abe. He would've loved a boy."

"I'm sure he'll be fine, Bessie."

Bessie's rocking paused. "I don't know. He's a weak man. I always had the strength for both of us. I'm afraid he'll do something . . . desperate."

"What do you mean?"

She shrugged uncomfortably. "He said there was no life for him without me."

"Do you suppose he's still waiting?"

Bessie shook her head slowly. "He's halfway to Cincinnati by now. He said he was leaving by dawn's light on Tuesday, with or without me."

"I still think we ought to get your belongings." Something about Bessie leaving her things at the Brooks House unnerved Rebecca.

"It's all part of the past. My past with Abe. I don't want any of it."

"You kept the diamonds," Rebecca reminded her gently.

She knew she'd stepped over a delicate line when guilt flushed Bessie's face. Bessie lay her embroidery aside, touching the glittering necklace at her throat. The stones were much too glamorous for life in the country, but the woman had yet to remove them. "Rebecca, you know I would treasure a single gardenia from Benjamin far more than all the diamonds in the world. Abe wouldn't take them back. He said he wanted me to remember what I gave up each time I looked at them."

"So you'll punish yourself for the rest of your life for choosing happiness with Benjamin?"

Bessie looked at Rebecca, her face tired. "He thinks that if I don't have the jewels to look at, I'll forget him. There'll be a time when I put them aside. There may come a time when we desperately need them. For now, I'll wear them. For Abe."

Nothing but the silent warmth of the room filled the air as the women returned to their needlework. At last, Bessie spoke.

"I suppose Garitson and you will be having children someday?"

"Someday soon, I hope," Rebecca said softly. Then she grinned. "We'll just have to work harder at it."

"Children are such sweetness," Bessie murmured. "Pure, soft sweetness that love you no matter what you are."

The poignancy of Bessie's words once more drove home the sad truth that the woman had lived her entire life as an object of pointing fingers. Bessie rose. "I'm tired, Rebecca. I think I'll take a nap."

Rebecca watched Bessie leave the room, then put aside her own knitting. As though carried on the wings of her yearning, she heard the wheels of Behringer's carriage. Swiftly Rebecca found her way through the halls of the house to the front door.

The door opened, and the blast of wind paled in effect at the sight of the man who stood there. January's blush was upon his cheeks, its mighty breeze in his hair, and the gleam of happiness sparkled in his dark eyes. Rebecca rushed to the doorway, into the warmth of Behringer's arms. His mouth found hers, his lips cool and warm in the same moment.

Molding her to him, he kissed her deeply, giving and taking of that essence of her. Her presence. Her vitality. Her love.

"What took you so long?" she complained.

"I had to stop at the newspaper," he confessed, sighing heavily. "I had an announcement I needed to make."

Alarmed at his strange behavior, she leaned away from him. "What sort of announcement?"

"Come with me, darling."

Behringer led her to the library, and she watched him expectantly.

"It was one of the most difficult pieces I've ever written. I was putting together this phrase. 'Garitson Behringer, son of Mr. and Mrs. Jacob Behringer, is pleased to announce . . .' and then it hit me. That's not the way to write an engagement announcement."

A smile caught her mouth and held it immobile.

"Of course, it should read from a different viewpoint. For instance, 'The honorable Mr. and Mrs. John Reynolds, of New York State, are delighted to announce the engagement of their beautiful daughter . . .'"

Behringer fell as silent as the woman who turned away from him. Abruptly, he grasped her shoulders. "Rebecca, look at me."

She lifted her chin, gazing coolly at him. "What difference does it make?"

"Not a bit, to me. It might make a world of difference to your parents. And, someday, to you."

"They can't come. Can't you accept that?"

"Why?"

Silence for a brief moment. "They live extremely far away."

"New York is some distance away, but there's plenty of time before May."

She sighed. "Garit, I want you to listen to me. If you love me, please listen. I love my parents, and they love me, but they are very much in my past. If you and I are to be happy, we can never discuss it again." She paused, her words fading to a whisper. "Never. Do you understand? Can you understand?"

Behringer rose. She watched him as he slowly paced the length of the room, her heart echoing the heavy cadence of the grandfather clock. She recognized the angry set of his shoulders. "No," he said. "I can't. I don't understand what you must think of me to continue this deception. It troubles you even more, I know. What am I to believe?"

His pain pierced her own fear, and she crossed the room and lay her hand on his shoulder. "It has nothing to do with you, Garit. If I told you, you'd question my sanity. It's something . . . my God, it's something supernatural. You could never understand it any more than I do. All I do, each day, is thank God we're together."

He turned, and his face blurred before her. The tears pooled hotly in her eyes and when she blinked, they dampened her cheeks. "I'll make you this promise. On the day our first child is born, I'll tell you the whole story."

He gazed at her gently. "Our first child?"

She nodded.

Torn by her words, by her tears, he closed his eyes and held her against him, exhaling with a chuckle. "I'm given new incentive. Care to join me for a walk?"

She nodded, grateful for some air to clear her head.

Behringer hugged her to his side as they left the house. In the other arm, he carried a blanket. They walked down the clay path in comfortable silence, enjoying the crisp aroma of the morning, the faint moisture of the night's gentle rain. Rebecca inhaled the beauty of her life.

Rebecca recognized the path they'd traveled before. He led her carefully through the brambles as they turned down the smaller trail into the thickness of the trees. Only a few minutes later, they stood once more in their sanctuary. The place as out of time as their love. When Behringer would've drawn her forth to the edge of the stream, she paused, relishing the sight before her.

She had thought never to look upon the beauty of this place where the bond of love·had been forged between them. She tilted her face and gazed into his eyes, savoring the love she saw there. Savoring the quiet, cool shelter of the place that surrounded them. Savoring the happiness she'd found. Savoring, at last, her acceptance of it all.

He glanced back, surprised to see moisture shimmering in her eyes. Sighing, shaking his head, he drew her into his arms, tucking her head against his chest. "You never fail to amaze me," he said gently. "Now, about our first child . . ."

Her lips curved in a smile against the warmth of his throat. Together, they celebrated their private sanctuary and went about the serious task of creating their first child.

❦ Thirty-Eight ❦

Winter's brutal breeze ruffled Behringer's raven hair as they stood in the doorway. He tightened the shawl closer about her and kissed her mouth. "Get inside. If that isn't snow in those clouds, I don't know what it is. Don't go outside tonight. Jim!"

The man came forward from his place in the hallway. "Don't let Miss Reynolds out of the house tonight. Understand?"

Jim nodded. "Yes, sir."

"And, Rose, you take good care of Miss Reynolds."

The servant smiled at him. "I always do, Mr. Behringer."

Rebecca stroked Behringer's beard. "How late do you think you'll be?"

Scowling, he shook his head. "Hell, I don't know. Fairchild must be in league with the devil himself to have all these blasted nighttime meetings. Maybe eleven or later, I'm guessing."

"Think of me," she said. "I'll have a hot bath for you when you get home."

His eyes scorched her as he stepped into the carriage. "Be in it."

Her lips curved at his intimate gaze, and she waved silently as he ordered the driver on.

As she entered the house, she met Jim in the living room.

"Miz Reynolds, I'm wondering if it might be all right for me to run out to my house and have Sunday evening supper with my family. I'll be back in about an hour, maybe an hour and a half."

She nodded at the man, touched at his devotion to his family. "Of course, Jim."

"Now you have to promise not to go outside while I'm gone," he reminded her sternly.

She smiled. "I promise."

Rebecca smiled as he left the house, then she skipped up the stairs to her dressing room. Peeking inside the closet, she smiled at the lovely blue velvet gown. Behringer had surprised her with the gown for the party, along with countless other new garments delivered to their doorstep in half a dozen trunks. He'd hired a woman in Marshall to sew her winter wardrobe, with only her rose gown to determine her measurements.

Tomorrow night, she would wear the blue gown to the Behringer house. Katy was to arrive the next day, and both she and Katy would boldly satisfy the curiosity of the many townspeople who would attend, people who had never been invited to a Behringer affair before. It would be the grandest ball of the house's history. Perhaps Jefferson's history. And it would be there that Behringer would announce their upcoming wedding plans. The announcement had been published in the morning paper.

A tap on the bedroom door nudged her out of her dreamy haze.

Bessie opened the door, observing Rebecca, her gray eyes sparkling in mischief. "And what are you fantasizing about?"

Rebecca's dazed grin deepened. "Not fantasizing. There's no need for that."

"Then it must be anticipation you're about," Bessie returned.

Rebecca rose from the bed, chuckling. "Is supper ready?"

Bessie nodded, and they found their way to the dining

room. The kitchen staff had outdone themselves this evening, all of it terrifically unhealthy.

As they served their plates, Bessie rose from her chair, pointing toward the window. She squealed in delight. "Look. It's snowing!"

Rebecca put down her fork in dread, glancing out the window at the large flakes which profusely fell to the cold, hard ground. They quickly began to gather in a thin, gray layer.

Her appetite oddly faded into a thin nothingness as she stared at the snow which methodically floated to the ground. Why did the thought of snow disturb her so tonight? Snow was something she'd always embraced in Dallas, for its pure rarity. Nothing was more comforting than sitting in bed, drinking cocoa and reading during a heavy snow, but outside the panhandle, Texas snowstorms were few and far between. This was the first snow of the year. If she knew Texas, it was probably the last as well. It never snowed in Texas.

A sudden memory pricked her with the familiar phrase.

It shall this winter, just for my wedding.

Rebecca shivered, and for the first time she felt pity for the girl Behringer had rejected to marry her. She imagined the pit of despair Vivian must be in tonight, having read the engagement announcement in the pages of this morning's paper.

Vaguely, she remembered Behringer's assurance. "Fairchild's found someone to marry her. She'll be fine."

She sighed. If anyone could turn a rejection around, it was Vivian Fairchild. Soothed by the thought, understanding her reluctance to enjoy the snow, she sipped her coffee and watched the powder accumulate outside the window.

"Rebecca?"

Glancing up at Bessie's worried expression, Rebecca shook her head reassuringly. "I'm fine. I was just thinking."

"Well, stop it," Bessie ordered. "It makes wrinkles."

Rebecca dismissed her fears. "What are you wearing to the party, Bessie?"

Bessie shrugged. "Oh, I don't know. I thought I might stay home instead."

The hesitation in her features translated clearly to Rebecca. "Don't be stupid." Rebecca scowled. "Let's go find something. Something gorgeous. You wouldn't want to be frumpy if Benjamin happens to show up, would you?"

Bessie giggled.

"Come on. Let's go see what you like."

They skipped up the stairs, laughing over the girlishly mindless task before them. Rebecca was thankful she hadn't yet worn many of the gowns that hung in the armoires.

Rebecca kneeled at her dresser, pulling scarves and fans from the drawers in reckless abandon. "Well, one thing we won't have to supply you with is jewelry," she quipped. The other woman laughed.

A rapid knock on the door brought Rebecca to her feet. When she opened the door, she saw Rose, standing there shaking. "A man brought this," she stammered, her fingers shaking as she thrust an envelope into Rebecca's hands. "I ain't never seen him."

Rebecca glanced down at the face of the fine white stationery, addressed in bold handwriting. "Miss Rebecca Reynolds." Something about the ostentatious writing niggled at her memory. "Who was it?"

Rose shook her head nervously. "He didn't say. Mean lookin' man."

She whispered her thanks, and the door closed behind Rose as she left.

Bessie came to stand near Rebecca as she broke the seal on the envelope. She unfolded the single sheet of paper there, reading its message silently. Terror engulfed her heart at the words printed there, and her own hands began to shiver.

"Bessie . . . my God."

Bessie took the sheet from Rebecca's hands, then quietly read the words aloud.

"My dear Miss Reynolds. Don't you find it tedious when
men have no honor about commitments? I know that if I
were you, I could find no trust for a man who proposed
marriage to a woman then cast her aside for another.
Might this new commitment end just as dishonorably as
the first? The second woman might well wonder. My own
experience is that such a man has no right to make such a
promise, when he hasn't kept his first. My opinion is that
such a man has no right to even live. I certainly hope that
you left your lover with a tender embrace, for I assure
you that you've seen him for the last time."

Bessie looked up at Rebecca with solemn expectation.

Snatching the note from Bessie's hands, Rebecca glanced
at the letter, seeking to confirm her suspicions. My dear Miss
. . . Might this new . . . My own . . . My opinion . . . .

Each of the flourishing Ms taunted her as she placed the
showy handwriting. It had been scrawled across each of the
woman's wedding invitations, the envelopes which were to
have been posted the day of the first snow.

Rebecca moved to the armoire and found her thickest
cloak. She took the stairs two at a time as she raced toward
the front door. Even now, Garit might be lying defenseless,
harmed, bleeding . . . she shoved the confusing thoughts
from her brain.

"Rebecca!" Bessie shouted after her. "You can't do this."

Bessie and Rose caught up with Rebecca at the door. Rebecca fumbled with the catch at her throat, tears streaming
down her face as she pulled the hood up over her hair. "Are
you out of your mind?" Bessie demanded. "I'll go. It isn't far
to Fairchild's office."

"I'll go," Rebecca repeated, grasping the doorknob in a
tenacious grip, clutching her fur hat in her hands.

"Look at you, Rebecca. You don't have any shoes on!"
Bessie said. "Good Lord, you'll probably get lost. Give me
the cloak, honey."

Rebecca angrily brushed the tears from her face, knowing

there was no time to argue. Quickly she struggled to unknot the clasp. Bessie calmly pushed her hands away and removed the cloak. Placing the cloak over her own warm sweater and shawl, Bessie smiled gently at Rebecca. "Don't worry. I'll find him in time."

"Here. Wear the hat. Let me get you a horse."

Bessie opened the door. "It'll take too much time to fetch and saddle one. It's only a short walk."

Rebecca hugged Bessie convulsively. "You are the dearest friend I have."

Gently patting her friend's back, Bessie whispered, "You're an even dearer friend to me, Rebecca. You saw only the good in me when everyone else said there was none."

With a gay wave, Bessie carefully went down the steps, then rushed down the path toward Jefferson. Rebecca stood on the porch, not feeling the bite of the wind that nipped at her cheeks, unaware of the slippery ice beneath her bare feet.

Finally, Rose urged her inside, closing the door behind her. Rebecca moved in a wooden trance as Rose led her inside the warmth of the library and seated her in Garit's armchair. Rose left, returning shortly with hot cider, but Rebecca ignored it.

Her fingers clutched the soft, rich suppleness of the chair, seeking Garit's warmth. He was everywhere in the room. In the aroma of leather and cherry tobacco that pervaded the room, in the silent ivory keys of the piano against the left wall, in the volume of Longfellow which lay where he'd left it earlier. She took the book in her hands and gently stroked its leather cover.

What a magnificent writer to be forced to endure such despair. The poor man's wife burned to death. Rebecca's lips trembled as she remembered his soft words lauding the great poet.

A tragedy from which he never fully recovered. Of course, Longfellow didn't have you.

She held the book against her breast, lowering her head to rest her cheek against the volume. For a haunting moment, a thousand images of a hell without Behringer tormented her, and she lifted her head to gaze emptily at the fireplace. Silently, desperately, she prayed, embracing the richness of his memory. She had so many memories of him. Now, she cherished each of these, reliving them, silently worshiping each of them as a woman might take out old love letters and gently weep over them.

Rose appeared only long enough to stoke the fire. The clock chimed, and Rebecca shivered as she glanced at the clock. That messenger of the time which never paused, which relentlessly marched forward regardless of all else.

Bessie had been gone for over an hour.

Rebecca vaulted from her chair, pacing restlessly across the entire length of the room. She strode to the window and uncertainly pushed back the brocade draperies, staring out into the deep snow which had long since covered Bessie's small footprints. Rebecca stared into the forbidding woods along the path toward Jefferson. And as she gazed blankly into the desolation of winter, a shiver convulsively wracked her body.

"Oh, my God . . ."

The horrible moan that began in the depths of her tormented soul exploded deafeningly in the silent warmth of the room.

They stayed at the Brooks House . . . that was late January 1877 . . . he took her off over the footbridge for a picnic . . . Rothschild came back alone, sayin' Bessie was visiting friends in the country . . . they found her body two weeks later in the snow.

"Rebecca!"

She was unaware that Rose rushed after her as she bolted from the room on her way to the front door. As she wrenched open the door, the cold air assaulted her, and she gasped in shock at the man who stood there.

Stunned at Rebecca's struggle to get past him, Jim wrestled her into his arms. "Good Lord, what's wrong?"

"Damn it, let me go!" She kicked at his legs, scraping at

the arms that were strapped across her stomach, refusing to release her.

"I can't do that, Miss Reynolds. Mr. Behringer, he say—"

Jim dragged her kicking form across the threshold, and Rose closed the door behind him. "She's worried about Mr. Behringer, Jim."

"It's not Garit!" Rebecca shouted shrilly, twisting desperately to be free of the massive arms which held her in place. "They were wrong. Rothschild didn't kill her. Silas did! He thought she was me . . ." She dissolved in helpless tears.

"Oh, my," Rose murmured. "I better get something to calm her."

Rebecca's efforts were useless, yet she continued to struggle against Jim's calm, restraining grip. "You're not going anywhere, Miss Reynolds."

"Let me go!" she shouted, jabbing her elbow into his ribs.

"Ow," he said through clenched teeth. "Please, Miss Rebecca, that hurt."

The stricken household ignored the ceaseless screams that were wrenched from her lungs, yet still the shouting continued, convincing them both that the girl was out of her mind with fear for Behringer.

By the time Rose arrived with a cup of warm milk, Rebecca's voice had dwindled to a raspy grate. Her throat was aflame, and her entire body was drenched in sweat. She collapsed against Jim, limp in his arms. Jim carried her into the parlor and placed her on the couch, and she passively accepted the soothing warmth of the milk that Rose offered her.

"Go find Mr. Behringer," Rose whispered. "And look for Miss Bessie along the way."

Rebecca stared blankly at the maroon rug on the floor of the parlor, unaware of Rose's gentle hands as she stroked her hair, attempting to soothe her. Unaware of the fire which failed to drive her shivers away. Unaware of the heaviness of her eyelids as she succumbed to the sleeping draught Rose had slipped into the warm milk. As she lay silently on the couch, she knew only one memory.

You saw only the good in me when everyone else said there was none.

❧ Thirty-Nine ❧

Rebecca awakened suddenly, and yesterday's memories came rushing back at her. The first sight she saw was Behringer, rising from his chair and crossing the room to her. Silently, he took her in his arms and held her against him.

From his place near the fireplace Behringer had watched her sleep, cursing his own foolishness for leaving her alone, for trusting Fairchild to honor the bargain. He had to hand it to the man, he thought bitterly. Not only did he assure his daughter's happy marriage by needlessly terrorizing Rebecca, he prepared a sound alibi for himself before doing so, in the same action luring her protector away from her. Fairchild could never be accused of threatening Behringer in a note when the two men had sat across from each other the entire night. From what Rose had told him of the note, Fairchild had certainly written it. First thing in the morning, he was sending a telegram to Washington. Behringer now held the proof he needed to build a case against Fairchild.

"We have to go into town, Garit. We have to find Bessie. She may be hurt badly." The hoarseness of her voice, the terror in her words, stabbed Behringer.

"It was a terrible snow last night, honey. I'm sure she sought shelter between here and Fairchild's office. We'll go find her."

Temperatures had begun to rise once more sometime in

the early hours of the morning, and by noon much of the snow had begun to melt. As the carriage made its way down the slushy clay path, Rebecca peered out the window, searching for any sign of Bessie.

"Damn," Behringer muttered. "What's going on?"

She followed his gaze on the other side of the carriage, the side nearest the bayou. Several horses were tied at a tree near the foot of an embankment, and a group of people milled about the place. Behringer ordered the driver to stop, and he opened the door. Rebecca was on the ground in an instant, murmuring half-coherent phrases of prayer. She stumbled slightly, then found her footing and rushed toward the group of people assembled on the small hill. He followed her, his long stride devouring the distance. His heart skipped a beat when her shrill cry shattered the serenity of the winter woods.

He caught up with her only a few moments later. An invisible fist slammed the middle of his chest as Rebecca fell to her knees, silently weeping over the lifeless body sprawled on the ground. Streams of dried blood stained the woman's face, blood which had gathered in a pool and seeped into the melting snow beneath her head. She'd been shot in the temple.

Oblivious to the cold, mucky damp of the clay, Rebecca lifted Bessie's shoulders from the ground, desperately clutching the woman to her breast, unaware of the grisly reality before her, the cold blood of her friend streaming through her fingers. Behringer recognized the cloak and hat which Rebecca had loaned her, and his knees felt weak. Vaguely, he became aware that someone was whispering.

"That's Garitson Behringer's fiancée, isn't it?"

"Yep. She musta loved this one, whoever she is."

"Must be from Shreveport, like the Reynolds girl."

Rebecca's sobs slowly quietened and she removed her cloak, folding it into a pillow and tenderly placing it beneath Bessie's head. Behringer was thankful that among the group of Behringer servants and Bagby and his deputies, all of whom had assembled, none of the town's gossips had made it to the nauseating site.

"Sweet and gentle lookin' girl," someone murmured. "Shame such a tragedy should happen to a fine lady. You'd never find this happening to one of the whores from New Orleans."

Behringer hastily stepped forward as Rebecca scrambled to her feet, turning on the man with the wrath of Jesus in the temple.

"They go through a whole lot worse, mister, but nobody ever gives a damn what happens to them. She isn't from Shreveport any more than I am—"

Behringer gently placed his hand over her mouth, drawing her away. He lowered his mouth to her ear. "Don't, sweetheart. She wouldn't want to be remembered that way."

Only then did she collapse in his arms, weeping softly. "Garit, it would have been me . . . it should have been me . . ."

And from somewhere within his many memories of Rebecca, a spunky answer she'd given him long ago surfaced. *"And I, Mr. Behringer, am Diamond Bessie Moore. I am very tired, very cold, and I want to get a good night's sleep before I go out and have my head blown off . . ."*

His pulse seemed to stop at the memory, at her staggering prescience. She had known. Somehow, Rebecca had known that Bessie Moore would meet this violent end. Everything he'd witnessed between them flashed before him now. Rebecca had desperately, vainly sought to prevent the woman's death.

He shuddered as he gathered her up, slowly walking back to the carriage. As he ordered the driver back to the house, he quietly stroked her hair. Her words were helplessly mumbled over and over. ". . . it should have been me . . ."

Behringer closed his eyes, cupping his palm around the coldness of her cheek, crushing her to his chest as she put into words the horror that had been struck in his heart when he first saw Bessie's lifeless body. His heart swelled with gratitude, and he prayed Bessie would forgive him.

Thank God . . . oh, thank God it wasn't.

❧ Forty ❧

Behringer knew, as he watched her sleep, that she was safe. Bessie Moore had paid dearly for Rebecca's anonymous safety. Fairchild thought Rebecca was already dead. Behringer glanced at the clock over the mantel. Just after one. He leaned down, gently touching her lips with his.

Rebecca wandered in a dream of heaven; she was being kissed. No, she thought. She only dreamed of being kissed. She shoved the reminder away, refusing to face reality. If she opened her eyes, he wouldn't be there. As long as she clung to him, as long as they stayed safely in this dream, she wouldn't be forced to remember that she had failed. She had failed.

"Open your eyes, honey."

Slowly she looked at him, her hazel eyes glinting with slivers of green and russet. He tenderly touched her face. "I'm so sorry, Rebecca."

She cried out softly, her arms encircling his neck with desperate urgency. "I'm still here," she whispered, relishing his nearness, his warmth.

Behringer didn't question the oddity of her words. He only stroked her hair, allowing her to weep against him. At last, she grew calm. Then, softly, almost pragmatically, she said, "I didn't prevent it . . . I caused it. If I hadn't stopped her from going with Rothschild, she'd be alive today."

He rubbed a soft strand of dark hair between his fingers. "If I'd stopped Sarah from going to Shreveport, she'd be alive today."

She turned to look at him. "What are you saying?"

"Nothing." He shrugged. "There are some things you can't change, Rebecca. The past is one of them."

Purpose overcame her, a staggering urge to simply explain to him the entire story. She remembered her first night in Jefferson, struck by the same inspiration. Certainly he would know the solution, the way to get her back to her place in history. Now, the prospect horrified her.

She sat up in the bed and tossed the covers aside. "Aren't you going to get Katy?"

"I'm sending Jim."

"Nonsense." She belted her robe at her waist and stood. "Your sister's going to need your support now more than ever, Mr. Behringer."

"Well, Miss Reynolds . . ." he began, rising with slow, sleek grace. "Speaking of that, I think it's time we solve it."

"Speaking of what?"

"That distracting name. Every time you call me Mr. Behringer, I have the most overwhelming urge to call you Mrs. Behringer."

She smiled quietly. "That's not my name."

"As I said, I suggest we change that. Sunday afternoon, with family and a few friends. People will know the truth tonight, Rebecca. I want you safe."

Rebecca leaned against him, needing his strength, savoring it. "Then until tonight I'll be safe?"

"I'd bet my life on it."

"Then go on to the train station and get Katy."

"Come with me."

She sighed, turning away. "Garit, I need some time alone."

In the end, Behringer reluctantly agreed to allow her privacy. As he prepared to leave, he berated himself for sending the servants off for a holiday. Logic dueled with the fear in his heart. He knew she was safe. He'd purposefully allowed the townspeople to believe Rebecca had been killed. Even now, he was sure they were tearfully discussing the beautiful, dark-haired girl from Shreveport who'd been brutally murdered near the ferry. He imagined the mock astonishment which would flood Fairchild's face when he heard the news.

Courage warred with the pit of despair and fear which churned in Rebecca's heart, and her brave smile wavered as she leaned up to press a kiss against Behringer's cheek as he prepared to leave.

He straightened, watching her closely. After a moment's silence, he touched her cheek. "Wipe that blame off your face," he instructed with a wry smile, rubbing her chin as though to help. "It's a mess."

Failing to cheer her, he tried another tactic. With a gentle hand, he found her left hand and kissed it, toying with her slim, ringless finger. "I have a gift for you," he said softly, enticingly. "Something you can always look at and be reminded of my love."

She watched Behringer wave from the carriage, touched at his boyish attempts to brighten her spirits. Only when he was out of sight did she close the door behind her, walking through the quiet solitude of the house. So, she thought, glancing into the rooms she passed. This was to be her home, after all. The home where she would share the happiness of her life with Garit, would give birth to his children, would grow old and wrinkled, and would know, above all, his love. She was to be rewarded, despite failing in her mission. It was a bittersweet prize.

At the back of the house, she reached the solarium. Its warmth drew her forward, and she lowered herself to the rich red and gold seat of the rocker. Staring out the window, she rocked gently in the late afternoon sunshine. Something brushed her leg as she rocked, and she glanced down. Her rocking halted abruptly.

Underneath the rocker, tucked gently away, innocently expecting to be returned to on another day, sat Bessie's sewing basket, its top still open, where she'd left it.

Rebecca withdrew the basket. Gazing in grim fascination at what lay folded there, she took the gown into her quivering hands. The baby's flowing pink nightdress spilled over her hands, and sewn delicately near the collar of the garment was one small word.

Rebecca.

No sobs wracked Rebecca as she held the soft cotton gown between her fingers. No pointless hysteria, no fruitless remorse. Only one fierce foe burned within her heart, blazing brighter than any October bonfire. Anger.

Anger for a fate that would place happiness within a woman's grasp, then snatch it away with capricious malice. Rage for a destiny that would indiscriminately snuff out innocent lives in the name of greed. Fury for a man who saw nothing beyond indulging his own worthless daughter's whims. Anger, most of all, for a world that would seek no justice for such a needless death.

"Bessie," she whispered. "I'm so sorry."

And then, at last, the tears came, like glittering icicles melting from a heart grown cold with wrath. The baby's gown fell from her fingers, fingers which clenched into twin knots of rage. She had failed Bessie, despite her efforts. She'd been her friend, yet Bessie's own supremely sacrificial friendship had cost her her life. She would not fail Bessie in death. She would indict Silas Fairchild of his crimes, and his daughter would suffer the sort of trauma that was worse than death to a girl of her caliber. The shame of disgrace.

With resolve came hard, grim determination, and an incredible calm as she rose from the chair and walked toward her room. The aging sunshine cast gaunt shadows through the house, but the quiet of the rooms strengthened her, enabling her to think.

She moved past the bed, its covers still in disarray. Carefully opening the doors to the armoire, she removed the velvet gown and spread it over the bed. The reminder of Behringer's steadfast support bolstered her further.

After washing in the basin, she did her own hair in the

simple, upswept style that would become fashionable in another fifteen years or so. She relaxed on the bed, closing her eyes.

The jingle of bells and a rumble of horses' hooves startled her from her dozing, and she calmly rose. That would be Garit's carriage, arriving to take her to the party. She walked to the window, only to find an unfamiliar carriage stopped in front of the house.

She scrutinized the dark vehicle. The door opened and a man emerged, followed by an elegantly dressed woman. Harry Murphy and Vivian Fairchild.

A chill of terror swept up her spine until it arrived at the nape of her neck. Only when she heard the front door open was she spurred into motion. The sharp tapping of heels on the stairs thundered against her brain, echoing the steady drumming of her heart. They must have seen Garit in town, for they thought the house was empty.

She understood with cold realization that they believed her to be dead. Silas Fairchild was truly a brazen bastard.

In quick, silent movements, she gathered her robe, the velvet gown, and the damp towel against her chest and swept quietly into the armoire.

Well, she thought dryly. *Here I am again.*

She was certain she held her breath when they entered the room, and after a moment's silence, their voices carried easily through the pine doors of the closet.

Murphy chuckled. "So this is the lovebirds' nest."

"Shut up, Harry. We came for one reason, and it wasn't to fulfill any of your disgusting fantasies."

Unruffled, he asked, "Is that any way to talk to your intended?"

"It's a temporary state, Harry. You know if it wasn't for that little bitch, I'd already be married to Garitson. And I'll have him before it's over with. You'd better remember that."

"I'm sure you'll never let me forget it."

A lighthearted giggle as she strolled across the room, past the closet. "You're correct, my dearest. Now help me find that brooch. We don't have much time," she said. She stopped at the dresser, where she promptly began jerking drawers open.

Murphy followed her, moving to the chest of drawers. "I just don't understand Behringer. He'll argue over a dime for an hour and a half just for the sport, but he'll let a whole house full of niggers take off for no other reason than to celebrate that brat coming back to town."

Vivian paused in her searching to clap her hands together. "Isn't it rich? That smug little goody two shoes. Her daddy always thought nobody in Jefferson was ever good enough for her, so he sent her off to Richmond to find a husband."

"Well," Murphy said, "sure found something, didn't she?"

"Yes. A round belly."

"That Behringer's a goddamned fool in every way there is. He says it's up to her whether she marries. He'll end up raising her brat."

Vivian resumed her plundering, casually remarking, "You wouldn't understand Garitson Behringer if you thought till your head hurt, Harry. He and you are as alike as a cat and a mop." Then, lightly, "After all, if you'd been Garitson, you wouldn't let a little thing like religion stand between you and the woman you wanted to marry."

The only noise in the room was Rebecca's labored breathing.

"Damn you."

"Oh, it's true and you know it. If you'd married her, life would've been so simple."

"I couldn't, and you know it." His voice was a finely drawn hiss, and he stalked across the room until he stood near the dresser.

"Wouldn't, Harry." Vivian's words fearlessly challenged him.

"Wouldn't, then! How was I supposed to know she was a damned Jew?"

"Harry, Harry, Harry. Does it matter now? I'm sorry I brought it up."

Harry spoke in haunted tones. "When you go thinking you're so smart, just remember what I did for you so you could marry the son of a bitch." ·

"You botched that, too. Garitson nearly died."

"I saved him, Vivian. Did you forget that?"

"Oh, you were an absolute hero, weren't you. If you'd been more careful . . . And did I tell you to kill the boy?"

"No." Murphy's voice was lifeless. A mere echo of years of accusation.

Rebecca's eyes fluttered shut as she heard their words. Oh, God.

"If the boy had been alive, I'd have already been married to Garitson for years, probably. He'd have had a motherless child. I could've learned to put up with him. The business would've been straightened out years before now, and you and I would have had such a lovely time. Now I'm nearly twenty-five—an old maid, almost!—finally getting married."

"You couldn't separate the two," Harry went on quietly, involved in his own private anguish. "I tried to get her to leave him with me a thousand times during the trip, but would she? Hell no, she hung onto him like he was a prize jewel." His words drifted to an envious whisper. "What a hell of a mother she was.

"But then," he said, the hard edge returning to his voice, "we almost made it home, and I had to do something, boy or no boy."

"What a mess," Vivian remarked distastefully. "Couldn't you have done it with a little more finesse? People said you could smell the stench for a mile."

"Sure, I coulda dropped her in the bayou." He laughed then, and Rebecca shivered with the stark absence of remorse in his voice. "Or I coulda shot her in the head."

"Not Sarah, you couldn't have. You had to lock her up, so you wouldn't have to look at her while she died."

"Damn it," he growled. Vivian whimpered suddenly. "If you ever mention anything about that night again, I'll strangle you with that damned necklace, and love every moment of it."

A lengthy pause as Harry's footsteps crossed once more to the chest of drawers, then Vivian slowly spoke. "Th-thank you for the necklace, Harry. And the earrings."

"A dead woman's jewelry," he muttered. "Enjoy it."

"Nothing that wouldn't have been mine if she hadn't shown up in the first place. Just like the brooch. Now let's find it."

Rebecca's fingers curled around the damp towel in sickening, seething frustration. She took soft, steadying breaths to curb the nauseating fury in her heart. He killed Sarah. He killed little Peter. He killed Bessie. And all to please this vicious monster who daintily and consciencelessly searched Rebecca's dresser for something else which wasn't hers. Something which Rebecca felt small satisfaction in knowing she'd never find.

"Hell," Murphy spat. "There's one of the niggers now. Let's get the hell outta here."

The two scurried out of the room, and Rebecca sank in a heap at the bottom of the armoire, tears stinging the back of her eyelids and her throat. For several minutes she huddled there, dully listening as the carriage departed, as the servants approached. At last, her grief spent, she pushed at the door and rose slowly to her feet.

Ultimately she found a faint hint of peace, and with that, the hope that at last Garit would know the same peace. Her movements took on a sudden urgency as she straightened her dress. As Behringer's carriage approached the house, she stepped out near the edge of the path. Glancing at the lovely home, a small smile touched her lips. Not without sadness. But with immense hope for the future. It was a home where she would spend the future with Garit, free from the nightmares of unsolved mysteries from the past.

❧ Forty-One ❧

Retort lamps glowed softly at the corners of the Behringer estate, and the same smile of serenity still wreathed Rebecca's face. The stalwart face of the mansion glimmered faintly in the winter darkness as Rebecca approached in Behringer's carriage. It was the loveliest home she'd ever known, and it never failed to inspire the same sense of gracious peace she'd known the first time she saw it. She knew now that it was a grace Maria Behringer had woven into her husband's life. The same sort of serene love she intended to instill in her relationship with Garit, so that if a romance-starved writer came scoffing a hundred years from now, they wouldn't have merely the legend of a room to disprove. It'd be a whole house.

A servant opened the gates, and the driver delivered her to the front door, where another servant greeted her and helped her down from the carriage. She shivered in the brisk February air. The winter had been vicious, but spring was just around the corner.

Gay laughter spilled from the house as she approached it, enhancing her smile. At the foot of the wide white steps she paused, thinking of this afternoon and everything she'd learned, and a purposefulness overcame her. Garit would be comforted to learn the truth at last, despite its senselessness. It was better for him to know.

Slowly, she climbed the porch steps, a smile of anticipation crossing her features as she recognized the faces of various townspeople through the windows in the parlor. Inside this house, Garit's sister waited to meet her, just as she looked forward to meeting Katy. She knew Katy would be a comfort to her after the loss of Bessie.

She knocked on the door, and Caroline opened it, dressed in a lovely black dress and starchy, frilly apron. The girl's normal reserve vanished, and she rushed forward, throwing her arms about Rebecca. "Miz Reynolds, we missed you so much! We're so glad you're back, safe and sound."

"Rebecca, my love!"

Rebecca turned to see Maria making her way through the crowd, and she turned toward her future mother-in-law. The two women met in the hall, and Maria embraced her jubilantly. "Ah, you look lovely," she murmured with a sly smile. Maria leaned back to scrutinize her face, then glanced down at her flat stomach. "Is there something you'd like to tell me?" she asked.

Understanding her words immediately, Rebecca laughed softly. "There's nothing I'd like more than to tell you that. But I don't think so."

Maria made a face. "I think differently. Katy will be pleased to have someone to share the nursery with."

"Maria, Maria." The thought of carrying Garit's child enhanced the glow on Rebecca's cheeks.

She laughed. "I look forward to a dozen of your children playing throughout this house. Half of them with black eyes, half of them green."

"Hazel."

"In truth, it depends on your mood. Around here, they were green most of the time."

"That's only because of your exasperating son."

Maria gently kissed her cheek. "He loves you so, Rebecca. A love that can conquer anything. Never forget that."

"I think it already has, Maria."

Maria stared at her quietly, then smiled. "If you only believe."

Rebecca gazed at the woman.

As she stared at Maria, she heard Behringer's voice just down the hall. She felt that same somersault she'd known the first night she saw him, lazily watching her from his bed, and she turned to look for him. He sought to disentangle himself from his companion, his eyes glinting in anticipation as they met Rebecca's.

He reached her at last, then drew her into his arms, kissing her full on the mouth. In complete view of a dozen people.

"Garitson," his mother fondly chided him. "Don't embarrass her."

"I thought tonight was the night to satisfy the gossips."

"Tonight, my dear boy, is the night to tell the gossips to go straight to the devil."

He nodded in conviction. "Damn good idea." And he kissed Rebecca again.

Leaning back, he said, "Look at what came in today."

As she looked down at his hands, Maria suddenly snatched away from him the book that lay there. "No," she whispered. "Not yet."

Behringer glanced up at his mother in question. "Aren't you a funny one."

She raised an eyebrow. "And you, my son. Did you not have a much more fascinating gift to give your darling?"

"A couple, as a matter of fact," he said, lifting his nose in the air. "But this is not a matter for prying eyes."

As he took Rebecca's hand, Maria said suddenly, "Rebecca?"

Rebecca turned.

Maria paused, as if unwilling to let Rebecca go. "You haven't met Katy yet."

Rebecca nodded, also strangely reluctant to leave Maria. She smiled quizzically at the woman. "I'll be right back."

Maria nodded placidly. "Don't forget what I've said, Rebecca."

Rebecca puzzled over that as Behringer led her away from the crowd, to the quiet of the library. Not much more time would pass before the room filled with men, puffing on cigars. Now, it lay in quiet solitude.

"Garit," Rebecca began, as soon as the door was closed, "there's something I have to tell you."

"No, honey. Me first."

She touched his chest, her buoyancy dampening as she remembered her news. "Please. I know who . . . killed Sarah. And Peter."

He touched her face gently. "Rebecca."

"And why they were killed."

His silent gaze upon her was like a balm.

"At last," she whispered, stroking his throat, "you can bring her killers to justice."

"Fairchild will never be brought to justice, my darling. But after tonight, he'll give up."

"It wasn't Fairchild, Garit."

"I don't care if it was J. P. Morgan or Jay Gould," he said. "Tonight, it really couldn't matter less."

"Garit! It was—"

Behringer kissed her. When he raised his head, his eyes shone with love. "My sweet Rebecca. We can talk about that later. I've wasted too many years of my life on pointless puzzles. I tormented myself for nearly eight years for one reason. I couldn't face the fact that I'd been too stupid to ever once tell Sarah how I cared for her." He rested his cheek against hers briefly. "If it hadn't been for you, I'd have hated myself for the rest of my life for being such a miserable husband. I don't intend for a moment to make the same mistake with you."

He paused then, kissing her again, lingeringly. "Come with me, sweetheart."

Sighing, she followed him out of the room, hurrying to keep up with his purposeful stride as they made their way down the hall.

"But, Garit," she began. He ignored her.

The ballroom wasn't yet packed, as it would be before long. Most of the guests clustered at one end of the room. Garit drew her toward the other end of the room, and they paused before the piano. "Do you remember the first night we were in this room?"

She smiled. "You sat down beside me on the settee and put your arm around me."

He nodded, his eyes sparkling in the glow of a hundred or more candles. "And you stomped away from me and fanned yourself furiously."

"You made me hot," she confessed.

The grin that began in his eyes, one of anticipation, wandered over his features until it settled on his sensuous mouth. "Did I?"

"You did. Arrogant twerp."

He sobered then. "That night, for the second time in my life, I felt an intensity of guilt I'd never in my life known before I knew you. Do you know why?"

She never took her eyes from that burning gaze. From that beloved face. Silently, she shook her head.

"The same reason I was so torn the first moment I ever saw you. For the first time in over seven years, I was ready to start living again. To give up a dream that began and ended in death. The only peace I would ever know, I was sure, was in finding Sarah and Peter in another life. When I saw you, wet and as full of life as a child on Christmas morning, I wanted nothing more than to live."

"Garit," Rebecca whispered, sliding her arms around his neck, hugging him near to her. Slowly she withdrew, gazing into his eyes. "There is nothing wrong with remembering Sarah fondly. She loved you. She—"

Rebecca lifted her hand in an imploring gesture toward the woman's portrait, then gazed upward. And then she stopped, for it wasn't Sarah's face that gazed at her. The portrait was gone.

In its place was a new, sparkling, rectangular girandole mirror, its gleaming edges somberly, resolutely beckoning her. Hypnotically, she stared into her face on the many mirrors superimposed on each other, each advancing forward further and further into eternity. Finally, she was able to tear her gaze away from the compelling spell of the mirror, and she buried her face in Behringer's shoulder.

"No. No!" Barely a whisper.

A monumental quaking began deep in her soul, and she fought it with every shred of her being. Every beat of her heart. Love can overcome anything, she whispered silently. Anything.

"My first gift, courtesy of Malcolm Henderson," Behringer said softly. "Now, each time you look at this wall, the only thing you'll see is what I fall in love with all over again every day. My every fantasy from when I was fourteen years old."

"I love you, Garit," she sobbed. "You're every dream I've ever had. I'll love you through all eternity." She heard the words come from her lips, and her eyes fluttered shut.

"God, how I must have hurt you," he murmured, stroking her trembling form, attempting to soothe her. With one hand, he reached into his pocket, then held his hand out to her. She stared at the ring nestled there. "The past is over, Rebecca. It's time we start living in the present."

With the grip of a greedy thief clutching the keys to freedom, she grasped his hand, drawing him toward the verandah. "Please, Garitson. Come with me. Now. Out of here. Away from here."

"Rebecca? I don't understand—what's wrong?"

Rebecca reached the door and tried to pull it open. The door resisted her motions, as if rusted shut. Ignoring his confusion, she desperately tugged at his hand.

"I love you, honey. Don't—" His voice echoed oddly, hollowly, in her ears, and he let her hand go to open the door for her.

Rebecca stepped into the night. Trembling, drenched with sweat. She raced forward down the steps toward the stables. And then, a grim terror clutched her heart, nearly stopping it. For on an asphalt driveway, not ten feet from her, sat a gaudy, crimson automobile. Her Mercedes.

"Garit!" Her desperate scream split the still heat of midnight as she swung around toward the ballroom. A silent, empty, desolate place over a hundred and fifty years old.

Staring in horror at the open doorway on the verandah, she started up the steps, then stumbled.

As she crumpled in a heap, tears streamed unheeded down her face, obliterating the reality before her. Destroying her last desperately lingering hope that he had escaped with her, from the vision she'd gazed into. A vision of life without him. A vision of hell.

"I love you, Garit," she sobbed brokenly. "I love you."

❧ Forty-Two ❧

When the first rays of an August sunrise streaked Rebecca's tearstained face, she still lay on the steps of the verandah, her head resting on her arm. A dull ache surrounded her as she watched the sun rise slowly into the sky, and she heard the business of Jefferson resume. Trucks rumbled down the street, but she was unaware of their horns. A car radio blared, but she heard no music. She stared unseeing at the boughs of the oak tree, filtering a glorious sunshine over the morning.

Slowly, her eyes swept in an arc from the branches of the tree down to the ground. And just a few feet away from the roots of the magnificent tree stood a huge rosebush, its thorny limbs heavy with the yellow blooms of late summer. She pulled herself up, staring at the flowers, understanding why she'd loved them all her life. Impervious to the stiffness of every joint and muscle in her body, she rose and went to the bush. Oblivious of the thorns which pricked her forearms, she plucked several roses, then lifted the bouquet and inhaled.

"Maria's roses," she murmured to herself.

"She grieved for you the rest of her life."

The soft Southern voice startled her, and she turned.

Myra Abigail stood there, watching her with joyless kindness. A knife twisted beneath Rebecca's ribs at the woman's compassion.

She knew, Rebecca thought. She'd known all along. She'd known how curious I'd be over the damned mirrors. The beloved mirrors.

The woman took Rebecca in her arms, stroking her hair gently. For several moments, they wordlessly stood there, the older woman absorbing the younger's pain.

Finally, Myra smiled gently. "Let's go inside."

Rebecca shook her head, gasping at the pain which speared her anew. "I can't . . ."

The woman patted her hand. "Come."

Myra led Rebecca up the stairs to Garitson's room. Each step of the way, Rebecca looked at the house with new perspective. She saw the aged scars in the wood around the ballroom doors, marks that spoke of the boards Jacob Behringer had ordered nailed in place there. Perhaps he had loved her a little, after all. Just as she had loved the difficult man.

They reached the landing, and Myra glanced back at her only briefly before opening the heavy door. Rebecca paused just inside the doorway, staring around the room much the same way she had only a day before. The rugged masculinity soothed her, however, in a way it couldn't have the day before. She knew now that it was Behringer's vital presence in this room which calmed her as deftly as his melodies on the piano.

Centered in the room was the bed where she and Behringer had first made love, where she'd slept and fallen in love with him. Over the foot of the bed, where she'd discarded it, lay the grandmother's flower garden quilt. A gift from his mother, for Christmas.

In the claw-footed tub stood several inches of bathwater, now cold. A bath she'd never returned to. And in the corner, covered carefully, as she'd left it, stood the Remington Model One. Once more, she was drawn forward to the instrument. It wasn't, she knew now, its mere oddity in the room which had drawn her before. It was Behringer.

He had taken this which had been so close to her, so much a part of the time they'd shared, and kept it close to him. Had brought it into his own room. She touched the typewriter lovingly, as he once might have.

What ever happened to Garit?

As though hearing her silent, desperate question, Myra spoke. "He . . . left Jefferson a few months after you disappeared, only after his sister's son was born, after he finally accepted that you had vanished. As far as I know, his search for you took the rest of his life."

Rebecca's lip quivered as she turned from the typewriter.

"The legend of Garitson's Room was circulated to draw one jaded romantic in particular," Myra said softly. "No one has ever slept in the room since Garitson left."

With these words, Myra turned and silently left the room. Rebecca stood uncertainly, surrounded by an intensity of hopelessness she'd never imagined. Slowly, she reached for the quilt and hugged it to her breast, sinking to the soft mattress of the bed. An entire night of mourning had dried her tears to a dull ache, and now she curled into a tight ball upon Behringer's bed, drawing one of the pillows to her breast, wishing they were the same ones he'd lain his head upon. Her hand gently stroked the soft down pillow, and she closed her eyes.

She wasn't aware when Myra brought the silver breakfast tray. When she opened her eyes, the shimmering surface of the teapot shone gently in the room's soft light. A finger of sunlight trailed along an object just in front of the silver pot, and she sat up on one elbow to investigate. Reaching forward, she handled the piece of jewelry with wonder. The Behringer brooch. *A gift for the next Behringer bride.* Its ornately carved surface glimmered, and the diamonds glistened with deep blue lights, the emeralds twinkling with the green of a sapling's leaves in spring.

She caressed the lovely piece in overwhelming tenderness, remembering Maria's love and guidance. Cherishing the many lessons she'd taught her. A faint spear of betrayal stabbed at her in the face of the bitter end of Maria's lessons. Rebecca moved woodenly until she sat up in bed. A scrap of paper on the tray caught her eye, and she reached forward to lift the tiny note. Opening the slip of paper, faded and yellowed with age, she saw the gently scrawling handwriting. Just four words were written there.

Only if you believe.

She held the paper to her breast for several moments, then tucked it away in the drawer.

How could a woman believe that in one moment she left the 1990s, traveled to the 1870s and lived a few short months—months more glorious than the thirty-four years she'd spent in this life—only to return in the next moment to the same bleak existence she'd once known? No, not the same bleakness. One much more desolate, for having once known the wonder of love. A glorious love she'd known in Behringer's arms.

Only if you believe.

And then she remembered standing with Garitson in a shop with the baffling old Malcolm Henderson, the man who spoke in riddles. He, too, had spoken the curious phrase.

Only if you believe.

How on earth could she believe, now? And how could she not?

Her hands were surprisingly calm when she pinned the brooch to her blouse. Resolutely, she rose from the bed and walked to the typewriter in the corner. Drawing back the cover, she gazed at the machine. She remembered her determination to write her final love story, the one that would lay to waste her silly notions of romance, on this machine.

The past is over, Rebecca.

Behringer's words rang in her ears with freshness and clarity, and illogical hope filled her heart as she glanced over her shoulder. Nothing more than an empty room. In the opposite corner, her laptop rested against the wall.

It's time to live in the present.

Moving without realizing it, she methodically opened the

case of the laptop and placed the computer atop the desk. She unwound the coil of electrical cord and plugged the computer into the wall, then turned it on. The program retrieved the last document she'd worked on, and she read her own words. *"There is a presence in the house, an undefinable something, peculiar and singularly disturbing, and yet soothing. Consoling. It is as if someone is over my shoulder, watching me type . . ."*

And it was his voice now, filling her. His presence, encompassing her, comforting her. It was Garit's love she had felt upon first entering Jefferson, with the haunting softness and intimacy of an embrace. It no longer frightened her.

I love you, Rebecca.

She relished the intangible embrace, closing her eyes, until finally, it faded. She rested her fingertips on the keyboard, closed her eyes, and remembered Behringer's face staring at her in the candle's light, demanding to know her name. Without her bidding, her fingers began to dance freely over the keys.

An hour passed before the realization came to her, and when it did, she was thunderstruck.

"Of course!" she whispered joyfully. She jumped to her feet and found her purse, her fingers trembling as they searched for the car keys. Malcolm Henderson was the key. Malcolm held the solution, somewhere in his maddening riddles. Malcolm and his bizarre collection of gifts.

Five minutes later, she parked beside the Excelsior House and hurried around the corner. She passed its historic threshold, desperate to get to her destination, to the one man who was her link to Garitson.

She hurried down the street toward the corner where the surrey awaited with another group of tourists eager to learn of Jefferson's fabled past. Just short of the corner, she stopped.

"Oh, God!" Rebecca stifled her soft cry behind her hand.

On the corner was a drugstore. A dozen or so feet farther down was a shop specializing in steamboat memorabilia. Between these two, where Malcolm Henderson's shop should have been, stood a vacant space which had been ravaged by fire. And it clearly wasn't a recent fire. The debris had been cleared away long before, leaving behind only a smoke-stained brick wall at the back of the space between the two remaining shops. She stood, unable to move from the spot for several moments, her mind wildly racing in a circle without answers.

She moved numbly across the street to the tour guide, stopping him before he climbed onto the trolley.

"Yesterday I went on a tour with you," she began.

He nodded with a smile. "I remember. You didn't believe the story about Diamond Bessie Moore."

"What happened to the shop that was there?"

"Over there? Oh, that was Lulie Mae's Shoes, a long time ago. It burned down. Everybody loved Lulie Mae so much, they can't bring themselves to build again."

"No, no! It was Malcolm Henderson's shop. He sold mirrors and books and crystal."

He considered her, slowly shaking his head. "No, ma'am. Nothin' been in that spot for over twenty years."

Rebecca's jaw dropped. It was impossible. The cookbook she'd purchased from him lay next to her laptop.

"Maybe I have the spot wrong. Where would Mr. Henderson's shop be?"

"Now, wait a minute. You say Henderson?"

She nodded.

"That's the spot, all right. A man named Henderson ran some kind of shop there over a hundred years ago. My granddaddy told me about him closing up shop. Didn't nobody know where he went, or how he managed to move all that stuff of his so fast. One morning when my granddaddy came to town, everybody was talking about how he'd cleared everything out in the middle of the night. Didn't leave a thing behind." He shook his head and laughed. "Looked like he'd never been there at all."

❧ Forty-Three ❧

Rebecca shivered in the stillness of the October afternoon. It wasn't the cold, for the day was unseasonably warm. As the wheels of the trolley rumbled past the iron gates of the Oakwood Cemetery, she felt once more the stab of regret that she'd avoided this before, and the piercing fear that she was doing it now.

She hadn't left the Behringer Inn once in the past six weeks until now. Her social life existed in brief strolls in the gardens. The remainder of her day was divided between prolonged hours at her computer and a few hours of sleep. When hunger demanded her attention she left her room long enough for nourishment. She frequently wrote eighteen hours a day, taking small breaks to rest her eyes or wrestle with an ineffective phrase.

Certainly, all this was no sacrifice. Her story burst to life upon the page with a resounding realism she'd never known. Suddenly, writing about love meant something. Describing the hopelessness of separation scourged her soul, and she wept with the intensity of her characters' despondency. Her own despondency.

The book was finished now. She'd reluctantly relinquished the glorious evidence of her labor, that balm which had comforted her in the hopelessness of the last weeks. Only the week before, she had overnighted the final manuscript to

Jackie. The computer files had traveled to New York simultaneously over the telephone line. Garit would smile to know the conveniences available today. He wouldn't be surprised, most likely, she thought with a sad smile.

Straightening on the wooden bench, she steeled herself as the pavement gave way to a dirt path, and a tour guide began speaking. "Jefferson's founders are buried here in the Oakwood Cemetery," he was saying. "As well as its criminals. Over yonder, two convicts are buried, chained together. They hated each other their whole blessed life, and the sheriff they made miserable is buried less than thirty feet away from 'em. Don't seem right now, does it?" He chuckled, then turned the streetcar down another path, one Rebecca had traveled another time, six weeks ago. She trembled.

"Right down here's the Frank family. Lost eight babies, they did."

Rebecca gazed at the stones, and something gave her heart a mighty squeeze. Gustav Frank. Adalheid Frank. Alongside them were eight small headstones. *We lost our third child recently . . .*

She shivered at the memory. Here lay the burly newspaperman who'd tried to help her solve her mystery, who'd feared for her safety. Before Gustav and his wife died, they were forced to watch five more children die. The trolley moved on to its chief destination.

The iron fence surrounding the grave offered pitifully ineffective protection from the grimness of death's far-reaching arms, it seemed. Even now, Bessie was vulnerable. No, she corrected herself. At last, Bessie was impervious. Beyond the careless injury of gossips. If anyone deserved to be a folk hero, Bessie did.

They parked at the fence's gate, and the tourists disembarked, Rebecca trailing reluctantly as the guide began speaking. "Diamond Bessie Moore was killed in Jefferson over a hundred years ago, in early 1877. Her husband, Abe Rothschild, shot her in the head when they went for a picnic one Sunday afternoon. Queer man, that one. By the time the sheriff caught up to him in Cincinnati, he'd already tried to kill himself."

From grief. More than anything, Rebecca was convinced that Abe Rothschild had successfully reformed himself. For one reason: because he desperately loved Bessie Moore.

"That scoundrel was plumb out of his head with guilt when he was finally extradited back to Texas. For the rest of his life, he imagined some guy was following him around. Nothin' as paranoid as a criminal, I reckon."

Rebecca tried to add it up. She should be able to figure it out. She'd known Bessie as no one else had. Hadn't she? For the last two weeks, logic fought with everything she'd learned. It taunted her, mocking from over her shoulder as she penned the triumphant end to her ludicrous story. Love conquers all. A ghost of cynicism pointed its skinny finger at her and scoffed at this story, more outlandish than any of her myths. You just had a bad dream, that's all. She glowered at the foolish solution. *And she woke up.* The ultimate lazy escape from the corner into which a visionless writer had painted herself.

And yet, she thought, how could it have been? Why could it have been? Now, the why and how were important as never before, and both were eclipsed by yet another curiosity. Indeed, could it have been at all?

". . . they say every winter about the time she died, a train stops in the dead of night, and a man gets off and comes to her grave just like he did that afternoon a few years after she died. Always leaves flowers, and cries like a baby each time he comes."

A breeze stirred the branches of the blackjack tree nearby as the tourists strolled, investigating the graves. When Bessie's grave was deserted, Rebecca slowly moved forward to the black fence. Blankly, she stared at the ground, the grass's green faded to a dull brown. One of the blackjack oak leaves fluttered to rest near the headstone, just beside a bouquet of flawless white flowers placed there. Gardenias.

How sweet of you to remember my favorite!

The sweet, musical voice trilled in her memory, like ten nimble fingers trickling over a piano keyboard. She remembered the night she met Bessie, the woman's delight over the flowers.

And I always will remember, my love.

Benjamin Jackson. She knew that when he returned from Dallas to fetch the woman he loved, Benjamin arrived to find only talk of her funeral. The man who had loved Bessie enough to give her up to a better life than he could provide would certainly have sought the death of the man he believed to be responsible. He would've stalked Abe Rothschild, a man grieving just as deeply for the loss. A loss that was a senseless mistake.

"Don't nobody knows who the visitor is, but he comes on a train from the west," the tour guide remarked.

If ever we have cause to travel to Jefferson again, I expect it'll be on a train coming from the west.

Rebecca remembered Bessie's letter, and she knew why it had disturbed her. She had almost identically phrased the tour guide's description of Benjamin's ghostly visits.

Rebecca moved away, aimlessly strolling to a remote corner of the cemetery, the graves of a prominent Jefferson family marked by ornate marble headstones. The cherished names tormented her, along with the names of their descendants.

Maria Elyse Behringer, beloved wife and mother; Jacob Karl Behringer, beloved husband and father; Katerina Behringer, beloved mother; Karl Garitson Behringer, beloved father; Matilda Behringer, beloved daughter.

Rebecca looked at the dates. Maria had died only four years after Rebecca met her, and Jacob had died not quite a month after that. As she had promised, Katy never married, raising her son, whom she named after her father and brother, alone. Rebecca's heart swelled in compassion for the tragedy that Katy Behringer had known, raising a child alone and losing both her parents in the same year. Katy's granddaughter, Matilda, had given the house to the last survivor of their family servants, Myra Abigail.

She stepped aimlessly around the corner from these graves and found another small section of the Behringer family burial place. The high gloss of the marble wall had been eroded by time's elements, and the headstones were bleached white. *Sarah Stein Behringer, Benjamin Peter Behringer,* and . . .

Her heart slammed against her ribs as she stared at the lifeless grass in the empty space between Peter's grave and the wall. Unshed tears pressed against her throat at the image of Behringer finding another life away from Jefferson, an unknown home and happiness and a faraway grave. The thrumming ache intensified as she trudged back to the waiting trolley, recalling yesterday.

In desperate hope, she'd visited the library, searching old newspapers for any bit of information about Garit. About the Behringers. Anything at all. She learned only that she knew details about the Behringers which reporters were never allowed to learn. While searching through the papers, she'd found only one item which brought any sense of reason to her at all. Bittersweet reason, at that.

Newlyweds Perish in Fire, the headline had said.

> *Mr. and Mrs. Harry Murphy, married last month, died in a fire that broke out in their home in the early hours of the morning. Servants said Mr. Murphy was in the habit of smoking just before retiring, and it's believed that he and his wife, the daughter of Mr. Silas Fairchild, never awakened to feel the blaze. Mr. Fairchild, distraught with his grief, attacked an unnamed businessman of the town, accusing him of arson. Mr. Fairchild, who is under a physician's care, insisted the fire was set out of revenge. Mr. Fairchild's business, Fairchild & Sons, operating at a heavy deficit, is expected to close this week.*

Rebecca had felt only a grim satisfaction. Fairchild had known all along of Vivian's deeds, and had gone to great lengths to conceal her guilt. In the end, he'd accused Garit of exacting revenge against his daughter.

Pointless. It had all been pointless. Any brief comfort the article should have brought her was easily obliterated by the stupidity of it all.

What, then, had been gained from her fantastic journey? Certainly history hadn't been improved. It hadn't changed one iota. She'd been there not to prevent, but to facilitate, Bessie's death. She'd been able to do no more than witness the birth of the false curse, not disprove it. It was still believed that Jay Gould had cursed the town, a ludicrous supposition. The man would have been so busy on Wall Street in the sixties and seventies that he'd never have found his way to Jefferson, despite her flourishing gaiety in the years following the Civil War. Rebecca remembered standing beside the black iron around Bessie's grave in August, and with sudden realization, she closed her eyes wearily. She recalled the hopelessness that had filled her even then. She'd known then she couldn't change it. Behringer had told her a half dozen times that you can't change the past. Only now did she accept it. Bessie's daughter was never to have been born. Rebecca's efforts were as futile against the inevitable events as the efforts of townspeople to revive the glory of days gone by. The Jefferson of over a hundred years ago that, in truth, had never died.

The trolley's creaking and groaning swayed to a stop at the busy corner where the Excelsior House stood. She thought of Gould's signature at the Excelsior, proclaiming "End of Jefferson, Texas." Some overblown stories about the town hinted that Jay Gould had built his railroad straight through Dallas because Jefferson had spurned him, blatantly suggesting that Jefferson could have been what Dallas was now, if not for Gould's curse. Rebecca leaned forward to stare down the street, marveling at how little the town had changed in a hundred years.

The golden aura of the town was as heady, as romantic, as picturesque, as the town itself, and her legends. An intangible thing that had been interwoven into the bricks and mortar with the many histories of the people who had lived and died in its past. In the swayed threshold of the Excelsior which they proudly pointed out as evidence of the many travelers who had trod there.

She remembered the last newspaper she'd read from Dallas. One of the few historic buildings remaining in downtown Dallas had been demolished only the previous week, despite the vehement protests of historic groups. Progress burned its indiscriminate brand into every sweeping line of the Dallas skyline, into every crawling highway that spanned the city. Overwhelmed by the sense of rightness she felt, staring at Jefferson's gentle face, she knew that in the end, it was Jefferson, and not Dallas, who had survived intact into the twentieth century. The Dallas of a hundred years ago had vanished in the mists of tomorrow, leaving a city that never quite knew her identity. Treasuring its past, Jefferson was content in its present, whatever that might be. Jefferson celebrated her very existence.

As Rebecca stepped down from the trolley, queasiness nagged at her, as it had every morning for the last week. She knew she'd pushed herself mercilessly for the past few weeks, with great success to show for it. But now that her book had been completed and delivered, her body demanded care. Last month, she'd completely skipped her period, and she easily attributed that to the intensity of everything she'd experienced. Now, she should be having her period any day. She tallied the days in her head, then frowned. She was overdue again.

An irrational hope filled her heart for the most fleeting of moments as she climbed in her car, before that demon, logic, quelled it. The doctor would find a simple explanation for her problem. A vitamin deficiency of some sort.

Pausing at the exit from the parking lot, Rebecca checked for oncoming cars. When she glanced at the street, she faced the bridge which crossed the bayou. A jolt went through her as she remembered the heaven she'd known in her home across the bayou. Garitson's home.

No. She forced herself to turn away from the temptation and toward the Behringer Inn. The last thing she needed was proof that it had never truly happened at all. The house didn't exist, she was convinced, or else it would be a part of the tours. It had been one of the grandest homes in Jefferson. As she stepped over the threshold and into the house, the phone rang, and she reached for it.

Jackie. The woman spoke brightly, buoyantly, as she always did. It's a break from your style, she said. It's breathtaking, she said. It's your best story yet, she said.

The doors of the ballroom stood invitingly open to her, and Jackie's words faded as she noticed the complete difference evident here. When she'd first visited the inn, Myra had been secretive about the mirrors, even about the room, as though afraid to allow Rebecca the adventure contained there. The mirrors called to her even now, and hope filled her heart. Jackie had asked her a question.

"What?" Rebecca asked, irritated.

"That guy. The antique book expert. He still wants to do the interview. It's for *Time*, for Pete's sake. The damn story's been waiting for two months while you got your knots untied."

"I don't care who he is. I'm not going anywhere."

Jackie wasn't happy. She'd get over it, Rebecca thought as she hung up the phone. Stepping forward into the ballroom, she stopped before the mirror. Once again she tried to place it at the same angle as it had been that first day, as she'd tried a hundred times over the last few weeks, but it was impossible to recapture the many images of her face. She saw only a single image reflected there.

Each time you look at this wall, the only thing you'll see is what I fall in love with all over again every day.

She stared openly into the mirror. Hopefully. As she did each night. Many of these nights, as she fell into an exhausted sleep, she dreamed of Garit. Tormenting dreams, soothing dreams. Dreams of the life she might've had with him. Dreams she never could have dreamed had she never known him, at last accurately portrayed in a book she never could've written without knowing his love.

Without knowing his love.

She sank heavily onto the piano seat, resting her hands on her knees. And at last she knew. Yes, it had been a romantic fate indeed which had spirited her away to meet Garitson Behringer, to live long enough with him to learn one thing. Living in the past is a folly equal only to living for the future. Life, she knew now, is a timeless entity that exists only in the present—an entity as tasteless without love as Mozart's symphonies would have been without violins. Had she learned, as well, that love could conquer any of life's obstacles?

She rose slowly. A quiver traced the surface of her skin, and tears welled in her eyes. She turned away from the mirrors, from the despair she saw reflected there.

❧ Forty-Four ❧

"Looks like you're pregnant, Rebecca."

Rebecca cherished the words as Dr. Montgomery turned away from her. A warm haze enveloped her as she rested her hand upon her still flat stomach. It was real.

It was real!

She giggled softly, and the doctor chuckled. "Then I take it congratulations are in order."

"Most definitely. I've wanted this baby forever, it seems." At least a hundred years.

As she left the office, she laughed out loud on the empty sidewalk. "I'm pregnant!"

She'd left the top down on her Mercedes this morning, for which she was thankful. The lingering warmth of the day spilled out across the quiet beauty of Jefferson as she drove through downtown, and she was certain she'd never known a greater satisfaction. She reached a red light, and as she waited for the light to turn, the inviting road toward Caddo Lake beckoned to her. Savoring her happiness, unwilling to return home just yet, knowing finally that every particle of Behringer's love for her was as real as her love for him, she turned down the road. Toward his home.

Another minute later, she turned down a gravel path. Only as the automobile crawled down the path did she understand, in haunting realization, that in some small part of her heart, she'd felt she was on her way to give him the happy news. She frantically tapped the brakes, but it was too late. The house loomed before her, half hidden by the imposing oaks and cypress. Rebecca's elation swiftly plummeted into despair.

What was once one of the grandest homes in Jefferson, its rich splendor haughtily tucked away in the seclusion of the cypress, was a gaunt, emaciated, gray shadow of its former self. She gave an instinctive cry of anguish at the impact of its hopelessness and knew in a moment that Behringer had never again lived in this house. At the moment he'd finally learned to trust life enough to expect its finest, to open his heart to receive its rich gifts, a remorseless fate took over, ruthlessly ravaging the tender place where love had bloomed.

Turning off the key in the ignition, she stepped out of her car and stood there for several minutes before finally hiking through the knee-high weeds that covered the grounds. She walked carefully, guarding her precious cargo, yet fearful no longer, knowing she was safe from any supernatural fate. It had given its all, and it had dealt an even blow. Garitson was gone, and she knew the pain of this loss would never completely leave her. He would not share her life as she had dreamed, but his child would comfort her, enriching her life with purpose and joy.

The ache within her breast intensified as she arrived at the foot of the steps. The windows were broken out, and stray debris had collected around the house's foundation. The paint had long ago chipped and peeled away, leaving nothing more than faded, exposed wood. The scent of the bayou came to her as she inhaled and stepped up onto the porch before she could change her mind. The front door creaked in protest when she turned the doorknob.

She wasn't prepared. The sweeping semicircular staircase dominated the empty entryway, and as her gaze traveled around the room, her heart wept slowly. She wondered what had transpired in this house between the night she left in his.

carriage and today. She knew one thing with certainty. She and Garitson were the last people to live there.

On feet that moved forward involuntarily, she traveled slowly through the house. Each room freshly accused her with memories of the happy weeks she'd spent there. Slowly, she found her way to the library, then pushed open the door. She shivered at the one piece which remained, unbelievably, in the lower level of the house, standing only a few feet from her.

Behringer's piano.

In aching wonder, she touched the dusty surface, and a melody echoed in her memory as if it had been only an hour ago. She closed her eyes, savoring the sound. The memory faded with the distant, overpowering sound of Jefferson. A truck horn. A car's motor. The sound went silent.

She sighed, then walked past the piano, to the window that faced the bayou; the window where she'd stood gazing out when she realized how Bessie Moore would die. She remembered sitting in Behringer's chair where he read poetry to her, where he held her in his arms and shared long, leisurely kisses with her, where he spoke of the children they would have together.

As she stood there in the empty, decaying room where her fantasies had been fulfilled, she tried to tell herself, as she had a thousand times already, that she had been blessed to love him, doubly blessed to have been given his son or daughter. She tried to remind herself that many people go through life never suspecting what rare majesty they were missing by never having known love, and never knowing the eternal hunger the knowledge inspired. Without those months stolen from time, she would've wandered through her zombielike existence and ended up a bitter old woman. She tried to console herself with the knowledge that within her lived a wealth of splendorous memories far more magnificent than any romantic fantasy she could ever craft, and that for the rest of her life, she had only to conjure one of those snapshots in her heart to have him with her once again.

Yet despite her best-intentioned reassurances, only the most selfish, childish, thankless of passions burned within her. For all her many blessings, it was not enough. At times like this, those times when she was forced to confront the truth, she knew she simply hadn't the strength to go on without him.

She wrapped shaking arms around herself, and her heart swelled until she feared she would lose her mind. "I miss you," she whispered bleakly. "I miss you so much."

"What are you doing in here?"

Rebecca closed her eyes, cherishing the sound. The memory of a low, smooth voice that sent tingles up her spine. Still. A voice as rich as coffee laced with the finest whiskey. And the tears spilled.

"Are you a witch? The house is secure."

She opened her eyes at the deep texture of the voice, and she turned.

"Impenetrable."

Impossible. A trembling began in her heart. It can't be. *Behringer.*

No, she told herself. It couldn't be. It was only a stranger who looked like him. After all, this man wore an expensively tailored European suit. And yet, as she gazed into the eyes as dark as midnight, she noticed the rich humor there, humor that quirked at a corner of his unsmiling mouth, in the curve of his brow. The vision began to speak, slowly walking toward her. He stopped near the piano.

"I've been waiting . . . forever, it seems . . . to do a story about you. And that farfetched tale you call your latest work. Jackie was kind enough to lend me a prepublication draft of it."

Her breath caught in her chest, and his gaze traveled over her with expectant languor, lingering everywhere. Her lip quivered, and she caught it in her teeth. His journeying gaze stopped there. She struggled to respond, her throat aching.

"It has a rather impossible ending," he murmured.

Her voice was a shallow whisper. "It was the only way it could end."

"Don't you think," he began softly, piercing her heart with memory, with the intensity of his gaze, "its message is rather conventional?"

Her words were a hoarse whisper. "Love conquers all."

"And do you believe that?"

She nodded slowly, unable to speak. Terrified he was a dream.

He paused, watching her grimly. "I have a certain passion for old books," he said slowly, his deep voice tight with emotion. "I'd like your opinion on this one." Rebecca looked at the fragile old book he held, and she blinked.

A Little Girl's Dream, by Maria Behringer.

In wonder, Rebecca carefully opened the book. Just past the yellowed title page of the book was a page with one line: *"For Rebecca, to make your dream come true."*

"A classic, do you think?"

His face was blurred by the veil of tears that stood in her eyes. She blinked, and as the evidence of her desperate longing slipped down her cheeks, she placed the book on the piano. "The writer, I think, was . . ." She couldn't go on. She was weeping.

He stared down at her, waiting, his eyes burning into hers. Her hand trembled as she lifted it to his beard, and his eyes fluttered closed at her touch. He was motionless as her fingertips touched his collar, loosening the tie. Swiftly, clumsily releasing two buttons of his shirt, she parted the crisp white fabric and trailed her fingertips within, resting them against the first faint streak of mauve. Softly she cried out, then her arms slid around his neck, into the dark hair that softly curled against her fingers. "It's you," she murmured brokenly, her sobs torn from the pit of desolation within her. "It's you."

Behringer helplessly enfolded her in his arms, his hands quaking as they touched her, as if reassuring himself that it was her, and not one of the countless dreams he'd known since losing her. He thrust his fingers into her hair, holding her so near to him that she would never slip away again.

Wild laughter welled up in her along with her sobs, and her laughter mingled with his as his mouth sought hers. He kissed her desperately. Tenderly. Unendingly.

She closed her eyes, certain she was dreaming, knowing it was her best dream yet. She pressed her cheek against his chest, hugging him convulsively. "I can't believe it's you. I can't believe it."

"It wasn't easy. I must have talked to a hundred people between here and New York before I ended up in the right place, and by then it was only . . . fate, maybe."

"Fate, definitely. A nice one."

He laughed, stroking her hair. "I brought the book to New York. I didn't know what difference it made, but Mama did. It's why she wrote the book, you know. She had an old friendship with Malcolm Henderson. He told her the mirror my father had bought her when they were married had magical properties. I always thought old Malcolm was an odd character."

"But how did it happen?"

He shook his head. "You're asking me to logically explain it? The best I can do is just tell you what happened. Malcolm came to me after you were gone. He gave me the first copy of the book. He said you were in another time. Now that took some convincing. I was sure that somehow Fairchild had taken you right from under my nose. Malcolm said that traveling in time isn't as strange as it sounds, that the Twain book he gave me for you was about time travel. Then, when he gave me the copy of Mama's book, he said that it was a part of you that wasn't supposed to exist in the nineteenth century, and that it was a link to you."

"So you went to New York."

"I thought you were from New York. Then Malcolm came to me and told me to look for you there, so out of sheer desperation I did. I was walking up and down these cobblestoned avenues, in and out of publishers, until I arrived at your publisher. Of course, I couldn't have known that at the time. But as soon as I stepped through the doors, I knew there was something very different. It took only one glance at myself to know." He chuckled softly. "This fate of ours took the time to give me an entire identity, with a background in your profession. It took some time to figure out how it all worked. I walked into the building, found the receptionist, and asked if they published you. I didn't need her to tell me, though, because I felt it. I knew I'd finally found you. And I took a long shot, and asked to see Jackie. On my way up to her office, I saw a newsstand. I took the first magazine I saw as a good omen."

"*Time.*"

They laughed together.

Rebecca looked up into his face, into the happiness in his eyes, and she touched his mouth. "You sent me roses that night in Dallas."

He nodded. "I couldn't resist."

"And it was you watching me in the ballroom there at the hotel, wasn't it?"

He sobered at the memory. "I came to hear you speak. I had to see you, just once before you left."

Thunderstruck, she shoved the heel of her hand against his chest. "*Why* did you make me go through all this? I'd waited twenty years for you. And you stood me up!"

He smiled softly. "Would you have had anything to do with me? Or would you have thought I was just another jerk?"

She smiled, her eyes lowering. "Well, actually, that's exactly what I called you after I read your note."

"You weren't ready for me. You had to learn to believe in love, as I did."

"Oh, Garit. It was Vivian. Vivian . . . killed Sarah and Peter."

He nodded. "And Bessie."

"You knew?"

He shook his head. "Not until after you were gone.

Fairchild lost his mind, and he told me the truth, which he didn't know himself until Bessie was killed. I'd known the Fairchilds forever, and I guess Vivian became obsessed with me when she was a child. That was one sick young girl. And she had Harry Murphy wrapped around her finger. A man named Benjamin Jackson arrived on a train from Dallas the day after you disappeared, looking for Bessie. He heard from the townspeople that Bessie had been murdered, and he left for Cincinnati before I could explain to him how she died. He thought her husband killed her, and I think Benjamin tried to kill Abe. It's amazing to me, the way Jefferson remembers her own history."

Rebecca nodded. "They blame it all on Jay Gould. But you know what I think, Garit?"

He traced her cheekbone. "No. I may be able to travel across a century, but I can't read your mind."

She smiled. "I think Jefferson died because you left."

He chuckled. "You always had so much faith in me. Honey, there wasn't any one culprit to blame for Jefferson's demise. It was just one of those towns that progress bypassed. They're everywhere. People notice it in Jefferson because she had such a grand past, and because of the legends that people immortalize."

She nodded. "I thought I'd been sent back to Jefferson to keep Bessie Moore from being murdered."

He smiled grimly. "What did I tell you?"

She nodded. "You were right. You can't change the past."

"So, if it wasn't Bessie, what was the reason?" His voice was soft, knowing.

"To write Maria's story about her and Jacob. To learn that love conquers all."

A silence stretched between them as Behringer fought the emotion that clearly threatened to overcome him. He swallowed, cleared his throat, looked away from her, then looked back, his head tilted in confusion. "My parents? You think the book was about my parents?"

She searched his face, not understanding.

Behringer traced her face with a fingertip, and stroked his thumb against her chin, pressing his trembling lips against hers. When she met his eyes again, his gaze was moist, his voice a hoarse whisper. "The book was about you and me, Rebecca. It was about us."

A heaviness squeezed her heart as she remembered the story, a wealthy German with a troubled past, falling in love with a young girl of questionable origins.

"That was the part of you that was left in my time. The story of our love. If you'd never believed in it, if you and Mama hadn't written it, I wouldn't have been waiting for you when you returned." Behringer whispered the words, stroking her hair.

When Rebecca could speak, she said, "I miss your mother, Garit."

He nodded. "Me, too."

Sighing, she leaned against his strength, stroking his chest. "Oh!" she cried out, looking up at him. "We're going to have a baby!"

He stared down at her, a slow smile warming his features. "Now that is good news."

She met his gaze, savoring the love she saw there. At last, many minutes later, he swallowed and sighed, then shook his head. "These are very strange days," he commented softly, tracing her cheek with one finger. "You can get money out of a machine, Rebecca."

"Strange days," she agreed. "Women have it much easier. And much, much harder."

Tucking her head against his shoulder, he chuckled. "I assure you, I'm never going to open another door for you as long as we live, if it involves letting go of you."

Smiling gently, Rebecca took his hand and walked out of the room with him. "Do you think we could renovate the house?"

"Or mow it down and build a new one right on top of it. It's in a sad shape."

She gasped at him, horrified at his words. "Garit! It's part of the past. You can't just dispense with the past."

He nudged her forward, stroking her hair. "I'm fascinated by the future."

They looked at each other, and words weren't necessary. This moment was all that mattered. That, and the eternity of love mirrored in each other's eyes.

In the end, they closed the Behringer Inn and once more made it a home for Behringer children, a home full of laughter and love. And on warm summer nights, they sat on the verandah, watching their children catching fireflies.

And they saw their happiness before them, as the green of the live oaks, as the curve of the bayou where they settled and raised their children, as the seasons. Timeless, and forevermore.

Author's Note

Bessie Moore died in January of 1877, in Jefferson, Texas. The cause of her death was a gunshot wound to the temple; the person who inflicted that wound will remain forever shrouded in anonymity.

Fred Tarpley, the author of *Jefferson—Riverport of the Southwest*, once said, "History tells you that Bessie Moore was a disease-ridden prostitute, but eventually, everyone falls under her spell, and I did, too. She'll always be a heroine around Jefferson."

Lesser historians than Mr. Tarpley have fallen victim to Bessie Moore's charm. Then there are writers who, in their self-appointed role of setting the world right, are obliged to reinvent history in order to satisfy an insatiable curiosity. Hearing Bessie's tragic story, with too many questions left unanswered, leaves some writers awake at night, atwitter with solutions.

Most of the characters in this book, of course, never existed in history. To draw a dubious line between outright fiction and Jefferson folklore, all the history mentioned before Rebecca's time-travel is gleaned from Jefferson's history, with the notable exception of the Behringer family. For every bit of folklore in Jefferson, there is a poignant account of real individuals who lived and loved in the Belle of the Bayou. There is, for instance, the tragic tale of the young woman who drowned with her little boy while trying to escape the fiery wreck of the *Mittie Stephens* in February of 1869.

Jay Gould may have possessed the villainy that has immortalized him in east Texas. If he cursed the town of Jefferson in 1882, however, he missed the obvious railway already established there. Today Jay Gould and Bessie Moore pay the price of fame—endless subjection to speculation. A cursory study of Gould leads to the conclusion that his curse on Jefferson is a myth; an irresistible myth, however. And as any Texas historian knows, courthouse records can't hold a candle to Texas folklore.

Thus we arrive at an explanation to the premier east Texas whodunit, and although history will forever remember that Bessie Moore was a disease-ridden prostitute, at least one writer can have some peace.

Maybe Bessie can, too.

"My lord, 'tis Marta." The old woman slipped from the darkness. It unnerved him the way she could move with such stealth. "I would speak to you, my lord."

"What is it, old woman? Can you not see I have problems enough with Malvern and his women in the hall?"

"The man is a jackal. The maids are little more than children. Novices from the convent." Her thin lips curved in disgust. "Malvern stole them away."

Ral's hand balled into a fist. "Malvern holds the King's ear. There is naught I can do."

"But, my lord—" Scuffling in the hall drew their attention.

"So, at last you have found her." Stephen's voice, thick with drink, echoed loudly across the hall. "Bring her here."

"She was hiding in the passage, my lord. The bitch was dressed in the garb of a scullery maid, but 'tis hard to mistake those big brown eyes and that thick auburn hair. She's the comeliest of the lot, I'll warrant."

When the tall knight dragged the girl beneath the rushlights, Marta gasped. " 'Tis the lady Caryn," she whispered from her place beside him in the shadows.

Malvern laughed as he gripped the little maid's arm. "So you thought to leave us, did you?"

"She was helping them escape," the knight said, dragging her closer. "Two of the women are missing."

Stephen chuckled. "The little wench has courage, but in this she has outfoxed herself." Standing, he reached below his tunic and pulled the tie on his chausses. "I shall initiate this one myself." He caught the neckline of the young girl's tunic, grabbed hold of the fabric, and ripped it to her waist.

"Let me go!" she screamed, struggling to get away. Stephen slid an arm around her waist and brought her hard against his body, then rent her camise and stripped it off her shoulders.

"I beg you, my lord," Marta pleaded. "Lady Caryn is the old *thegn*'s daughter."

Ral barely heard the old woman's words. Instead his eyes remained fixed on the maid. She was tiny but not fragile, a woman fully grown. He couldn't quite recall what it was, but there was something familiar about her.

"Rest easy," Stephen was saying, forcing her chin up with his hand. "I am not unskilled at bedding an unbroken wench. Give yourself into my care and I will go slowly." He flashed a ruthless smile. "Fight me, and I will tear you in two."

Holding her immobile, he pulled the binding on her thick auburn braid, then sifted his fingers through it, spreading it around her shoulders. The moment he did, the hazy images Ral had been seeing came together with such force he heard a roaring in his ears.

"Sweet Christ," he said, " 'tis her." It was a face he remembered all too well, one of two that had haunted him for the past three years. Stepping from his place in the shadows, he strode forward into the hall. Behind him the heavy oaken door swung wide and in walked a group of his men.

Near a bench in front of the fire, Malvern laughed at the girl's useless struggles, bent her back over his arm, and began to fondle her breasts. They were lush and high, Ral saw, feeling a tightening in his groin; nothing like the tiny plums he had seen that day in the meadow. And her features looked different, her cheeks soft and full, her mouth a rich burnished crimson. She was not the gawky maid he remembered, but nothing could erase the image he carried of her battered face, nor that of her beautiful black-haired sister.

"Hold, Stephen!" Ral strode toward him, his mail and spurs clanking as he moved.

"Well . . . Braxston. Home at last. I could say 'tis good to see you, but we would both know the words for a lie."

"You've been offered the comfort of my hall. 'Tis nothing less than I would expect of you. You've women enough to ease your men's needs. I ask your leave of this one."

Stephen's mauling ceased, but his eyes turned hard. "These women give succor to the enemy." The little maid pulled her coarse brown tunic up over her breasts with trembling hands. "I have claimed them in the name of war. This one will warm my bed 'ere this night is done. She belongs to me and we both know I keep what is mine."

"You have others to amuse you."

"This one has fire." He twisted his fingers in her thick auburn hair and pulled her head back. "I would see her spread beneath me."

"Nay!" said the girl, pulling away. "I belong to no man."

Ral clenched his jaw. He glanced from the girl's pale face to Stephen, whose men had begun to gather around him, their hands resting uneasily on the hilts of their swords. Behind him, his own men fanned out across the hall.

"You are both wrong," he said. "The girl belongs to me."

Malvern's face went dark, his blue eyes flashing with malice. He set her roughly away. "You dare to gainsay me in this?" Feet splayed, he rested his hand on his sword.

"The girl is mine. She is the daughter of the old Saxon *thegn.*" He flashed her a hard look of warning. "Caryn of Ivesham is my betrothed." He smiled at her but it didn't reach his eyes. "Is that not so, my love?"

Caryn reeled as if she had been struck. The Dark Knight her betrothed! Never! She had not forgotten him, would never forget those cool blue-gray eyes, that unforgiving jaw and thick black hair. The shiny strands were longer now, not shorn in the way of most Norman men, but resting softly against his chain mail *hauberk.*

Sweet Mary he must be mad!

She studied him closely, trying to control her fears and read his fierce look of warning. He was handsome, she saw as she hadn't before, in a hard, forbidding way far different from

Lord Stephen. His nose was straight, his lips well-formed, but his jaw was a little too square, his cheekbones a little too prominent. He was a massive man, broad of chest, neck thick, arms corded with heavy muscle, and his legs long.

"Is that not so?" he repeated, the glint of warning more pronounced, a reminder that should she deny him, Lord Stephen and his men would ravish her as they had done the others.

She swallowed hard and stared at the tall dark knight who towered above her. She hadn't forgotten what he and his men had done to her sister. She could still see his face among the others, though the memory was hazy and elusive, mixed with the terror, the anger, and the pain. She did not know the part he had played, but she knew for certain he had been there.

He was just as bad as Malvern.

Still, time was what she needed. She really had no choice. She tried not to tremble beneath his close regard. "Aye, my lord, that is so."

BOLD ANGEL BY KAT MARTIN—AVAILABLE
IN SEPTEMBER FROM ST. MARTIN'S
PAPERBACKS!

Award-winning author of *Creole Fires*

"Kat Martin has a winner. *Gypsy Lord* is a page-turner from beginning to end!"

—Johanna Lindsey